STAY HERE

BY ANNA SAVAS

New England School of Ballet

Hold Me
Stay Here
Shine Bright
Move On

NEW ENGLAND SCHOOL OF BALLET

A NOVEL

ANNA SAVAS

TRANSLATED BY
KATE NORTHROP

LYX

LYX

An imprint of Authors Equity

Authors Equity
1123 Broadway, Suite 1008
New York, New York 10010

First published in Germany in 2023 by LYX, an imprint of Bastei Lübbe AG
First published in the United States in 2026 by LYX, an imprint of Authors Equity

Library of Congress Control Number: 2026931708
Print ISBN 9798893311655
Ebook ISBN 9798893311716

Printed in Canada
First printing

www.lyxbooks.com
www.authorsequity.com

This book contains potentially triggering content. For that reason, you will find a trigger warning on page 437.

Disclaimer: The content warning includes spoilers for the entire book!

We wish you the best possible reading experience.

Love,
Anna & LYX

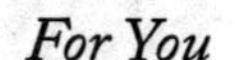
For You

PLAYLIST

Lovely—Billie Eilish, Khalid
Matilda—Harry Styles
Echo (Acoustic)—Alexander Stewart
Good Die Young—Elley Duhé
Love and Hate—Camylio
Sign of the Times—Harry Styles
Me Myself & I—5 Seconds of Summer
Traffic Lights—Sara Kays
House of Cards—Alexander Stewart
Pray—jxdn
Where's My Love (Alternate Version)—SYML
You Don't Go to Parties—5 Seconds of Summer
Feel Something—Bea Miller
Two Ghosts—Harry Styles
Willow—Taylor Swift
Ocean Eyes—Billie Eilish
Bigger Than the Whole Sky—Taylor Swift
Moonlight—Chase Atlantic
Slip Away—UNSECRET, Ruelle
Long Sleeves—Gracie Abrams
Homesick—Lexi Jayde
Just Fucking Let Me Love You—Lowen
Always You—Louis Tomlinson

PART 1

Intro

MOCKINGBIRD

Written and performed by Liam Bellamy

You were always chasing heights
Beautiful and brave
Dancing fearlessly through the nights
Knowing you were safe

Suddenly a voice appears
Rushing through your head
Gives you worries and dark fears
Keeping you awake

Sometimes it's okay to get help
Fighting back the dust
Spread your wings, untie your chains
Let your voice be heard
We'll be dancing in the rain
My lovely mockingbird

Hearts can break from time to time
Fragile little souls
Getting smaller, seem to hide
The things you used to know

When your world just seems too empty
When you lose your way
When you feel like you can't find the
Strength to make you stay
Know that I'll be here to catch you
When you think you fall
Know that I'll be here to guide you
When you lose it all
Promise you'll find your way back to yourself
When you dare to trust

Sometimes it's okay to get help
Fighting back the dust
Spread your wings, untie your chains
Let your voice be heard
We'll be dancing in the rain
My lovely mockingbird

PROLOGUE
Rayne

It begins with a song. My song. Okay, to be precise, it's not *my* song. My father is the one who wrote it, but he wrote it for me: "Mockingbird."

The melody is familiar. So are the lyrics and the sound of the guitar. It's a bit rough, because the instrument is probably old. But that's not a bad thing.

Everything about the song is familiar.

Except the voice. It's also a bit rough around the edges and, at the same time, incredibly gentle. Like silk on sandpaper. I don't know if I've ever heard a voice like that before. Not even Dad has a voice like that, even though it was his voice that made him famous. His is just as rough as this one, but much deeper. It resonates in his chest, and every time I hear him sing, I get goose bumps.

But this voice gets under my skin and makes itself at home in every cell of my body. It goes all the way to my heart, which is dancing excitedly in my chest.

Sometimes it's okay to get help
Fighting back the dust
Spread your wings, untie your chains
Let your voice be heard

We'll be dancing in the rain
My lovely mockingbird

The last notes fade away, and then the song is over. I start the video from the beginning again. For the thirteenth time: It's been on repeat for an hour. I've got to show it to Dad when he comes home. He'd like this version, I know it. It's different from all the others I've found so far. It's more like a mix of pop and rock, closer to pop. It's faster and less melancholy than Dad's acoustic version. Dad's song is dominated by his voice and guitar, nothing else. Most people try to copy the original ballad, but very few succeed. Even if they do, it sounds like an imitation. But these guys have made the song their own.

I've found countless versions of "Mockingbird" because I look for them every day. Maybe I'm a bit obsessed with listening to people sing about me. But none of them have been like this.

I've shown Dad three cover versions so far, one of which he liked. That was two years ago. Casey, the girl who sang it, got a record deal with Dad's label afterward. Now she's singing her own songs, touring the world, and living the life she always dreamed of.

I'm still sitting in the living room of my parents' place in LA, trying to find the perfect cover. Back then, I thought I'd found it.

Now I know it wasn't true. Now I know that this one is better. *He's* better. This guy with a guitar in his hands, standing in a record store singing my song. And he's not just singing it; he's *feeling* it. Every line, every word. *Me.*

He's not alone. There are four guys in We Are No Saints, and they're all good. Very good. There's one with a buzz cut sitting at the drums with a wide grin on his face. He's playing like his life depends on it and he would willingly give everything up just to play. The others seem to feel the same way. The guy with the bass has piercings in his eyebrow and a look of intense concentration on his face. His hands are moving quickly and surely, as though he's played the song a thousand times. There are the two singers, both holding guitars. One blond, the other dark-haired. Rhythm and lead guitar. The blond is singing backing vocals in close harmony. He has a nice voice, soft and clear, that fits perfectly with his bandmate's. The lead singer is the reason I keep repeating the video, though. His voice makes my heart flutter.

He looks to be a few years older than me, probably in his early twenties. Dark, tousled hair that's a little shorter on the sides than at the top, and a face that anyone in Hollywood would kill for. Clearly defined features, full lips, thick brows and lashes. His eyes are half closed so I can't see what color they are, only that they're dark.

He's stunning. But his face isn't the reason that I keep replaying the video. It's because of his voice and hands. I have a weakness for beautiful hands, and his are *extremely* beautiful, with long, slender, dexterous fingers. A shiver goes through me as I start the video from the beginning again. I could listen to him forever.

I feel a tap on my shoulder and whirl around in surprise. Dad's standing behind me. He's saying something, but I can't understand him over the voice that's still singing "Mockingbird" in my headphones. I take them off and hand them to Dad. "You've got to hear this," I say without greeting him or asking what he just said.

His eyebrows go up as he smiles. "That good, huh?"

"Better." I can't hide the sound of excitement in my voice, and my gaze wanders automatically to Dad's Grammy on the mantelpiece, glowing golden in the soft light of the floor lamp, as if the miniature gramophone is trying to tell me something. Dad won the award five years ago for "Mockingbird." For my song. Since then, I've been searching the internet for cover versions.

Dad walks around the sofa and sits down next to me. He's come straight from some gala with Mom and is still wearing his suit, but at least he loosens his tie before putting on the headphones. I press play again and hand him my phone.

My heart is beating way too fast, and I watch every movement of his face, every twitch of his mouth and eyebrows and the flicker of his dark eyes as he listens.

"Liam? Did you—" Mom's voice breaks off at the same time as the click of her high heels on the wooden floor.

I turn to look and see her standing in the doorway, a bemused smile on her face. Her blond hair falls in a cascade of soft waves over her shoulders. She's wearing a gorgeous midnight-blue evening gown, and the grace she exudes, even standing still, fills me with wonder. She's beautiful. A dancer through and through, even though her career was over before I was even born.

I can try as hard as I want; I'll never be like her. The thought flashes through my mind before I can help it. I've never been able to just ignore it, but I push it aside resolutely. This isn't about ballet right now. It's not about Mom. It's not about me, either. It's just about the song.

"I should have known you'd be in here," Mom says, walking over to us. She points to my phone as she sits down next to me and kicks off her killer heels. "What are you listening to?"

"Mockingbird," I reply, glancing at Dad. His eyes are closed, and there's a deep crease between his eyebrows. He's totally focused, and I shift nervously on the sofa cushions because it's been ages since I've seen him like this when he's listening to a cover. Two years, to be precise.

Mom laughs softly, her light-gray eyes gleaming. "Why am I even asking?"

"No clue." I grin at her, and she reaches out to brush a strand of dark hair behind my ear.

"Weren't you going to have Hailey over tonight? I thought you wanted to do a girls' night while you had the place to yourself."

I shrug. Sure, we wanted to take advantage of the fact that my parents weren't home. But sometimes there are more important things. At least for my best friend. "She canceled. The guy she likes finally asked her out, and I didn't want to get in her way."

"That was sweet of you."

I roll my eyes. "That's me."

But that's not the truth. Not the whole truth, anyway. Hailey was the one who decided that nothing would get in her way tonight, not even me. But Mom doesn't have to know that.

She reaches for my hand and squeezes it. "Have you been listening to music all evening, then?"

"More or less." I shrug. "I also started watching a new show."

She stretches. "Sounds like a relaxing evening."

"Yes, I—" I break off as Dad takes off the headphones. "Well?" I demand. "What do you think?"

"You're right. That's good. Really good!" He breaks into a wide smile, and I squeal with excitement.

"Does that mean you're going to show it to Alan?"

"That means I'll see what the guys have to offer, and *then* I'll talk to Alan." He passes back my phone and stands up. "But first, I need to get out of this suit."

Grinning, I press the phone to my chest, my heart beating like crazy. "Thanks, Dad!"

I blow him a kiss and nestle deeper into the sofa cushions as he leaves the living room. He really liked it. And he's going to check out the band. It's silly how happy that makes me.

"Sweetheart, we need to talk about the audition again," Mom says. Her words bring the tingle of happiness in my stomach to an abrupt halt. "Are you sure you don't want to go?"

I turn to face her. "Why should I? I'm not going to get in anyway. I'm not good enough, Mom, and you know that as well as I do."

"That's not true. You've got talent, Rayne." There's an undertone of hope in her voice, and I hate to disappoint her.

"I don't. I may not be a complete disaster, but I'm not good enough for the New England School of Ballet."

She sighs. "What can I do to convince you otherwise? You're good enough. Good enough for anything you want to do."

"Mom, please," I say, feeling awful. We've talked about this so many times, and the result is always the same.

"Okay, I'm sorry. I'll stop." She grabs my hand and squeezes it. "You should do what makes you happy."

I want to say something, anything, but I'm at a loss for words. I don't know what makes me happy. I have no idea what I want to do with my life. But I know perfectly well that I have to make a decision soon. I'll be graduating from high school in a few months, and I haven't applied to any colleges yet. Now it's basically too late, or it would be if I weren't who I am. Or if Mom and Dad weren't who they are. My grades are good, and thanks to their connections, I can probably get into any college I choose. If I only wanted to.

But the truth is, I don't know what I want. My whole life is ahead of me, a road with too many turns and possibilities. I can't make up my mind because I'm afraid I'll make the wrong decision. So I put it off instead, waiting for a sign that will never come. All I know is that my hesitation isn't about the audition. It's not about the school that Mom went to when she was my age.

She sighs again, then picks up the hem of her long dress and stands up. "I'm going to get changed too. Shall we watch a movie together?"

"Sure. I'll pick something out."

She nods and leaves the room. Now that her shoes are off, her footsteps on the stairs are almost silent. Instead of reaching for the remote, I tap my phone and start "Mockingbird" again.

The guy's voice sends a pleasant shiver through me; something inside of me responds. My eyes close, and I let myself be carried away by the sound of his singing.

The familiar words suddenly sound different. They create a different resonance, a different effect. He takes Dad's song and makes it his own. He's singing about a little bird; he's singing about me. But he isn't. Because he's not Dad, just some guy I don't know who's singing about a girl who's both free and lost at the same time.

Something cracks inside of me. It's crazy, because it's just a song, just a guy, just a voice. But it's more than that. He's more than some guy. And it's not just some song; it's *my* song, and that's why I have to know his name.

I close YouTube and open Instagram. My fingers flying, I type in the name of the band. I find them immediately. They don't have many followers, just a few thousand, but I couldn't care less. I scroll through the images until I find one where all four band members are tagged. Two minutes, that's all it took for me to find his name.

Easton Coleman.

I have to smile, and before I can think about whether it's a good idea or completely crazy, I tap the message symbol and begin to write:

APR 17 AT 10:06 PM

mockingbird:

I saw your video of "Mockingbird." You're amazing. I don't think I've ever heard a better version.

I send off the message and immediately wish I hadn't. I couldn't be more of a fangirl. My cheeks are burning with embarrassment. Easton will think I'm completely crazy when he reads it. Maybe if I get lucky, it will end up in his message requests, never to be seen again.

I look up when someone pulls the headphones off my ears, which haven't been playing anything for a few minutes. Dad is standing in front of me. I was so focused on my phone that I didn't even notice him and Mom coming back into the room. They've swapped their formal clothes for sweats.

"Which movie did you choose?" He sits down next to me and pulls Mom onto his lap. The two of them are so in love. They don't act like they've already been married for twenty years. When they're together, sometimes they behave more like teenagers than I do.

I suggest the first movie that pops into my head. *Pride and Prejudice* is one of Mom's favorites; we've watched it so many times together that we can almost recite it by heart. But right now, I'm not really focusing. Not when Mom chooses the movie on Netflix, not as the opening credits flicker across the screen, and not even during the first fifty minutes.

Then after fifty-two minutes, my phone lights up with a notification from Instagram, and the last remnants of my attention fade away.

APR 17 AT 10:58 PM

eastcoleman:

Then you don't know the original very well, do you?

I have to smile, and my heart suddenly starts shifting strangely in my chest. My fingers fly over the display, typing an answer.

That's the moment everything begins. The moment when everything is still fine.

I don't realize yet that I should be enjoying it. This moment, this evening. With my parents on the sofa next to me, laughing quietly, and me holding my phone, looking at Easton's message.

I don't know how much it matters, because moments like this are too easy to take for granted.

Until they're gone.

Easton

Three months later

Rock Star Liam Bellamy Dies in Tragic Car Accident

Los Angeles. Sad news: Rock star Liam Bellamy († 38) died in a tragic car accident on the night of Monday, July 11. His wife, Laura Bellamy († 37), also succumbed to her injuries a few hours after the collision.

The exact cause of the accident is still under investigation.

Lowlight Recording reacted with shock to the tragic death of the star: "Our hearts are broken. Liam has been part of our family for seventeen years. We are devastated by the loss."

Liam and Laura Bellamy are survived by their eighteen-year-old daughter, Rayne Bellamy.

No. No. No.

This can't be true. I stare at my phone in a daze, but there it is, black on white. Liam Bellamy is dead. He's dead, and so is his wife. A car accident. It's all over the internet.

Adrenaline rushes through my veins, the blood pounding so loudly in my ears that I can barely hear the announcer on the TV telling us exactly what we've already read on our phones. Short videos are shown over and over again. A girl leaving a hospital in LA, the hood of her oversized sweatshirt pulled down over her face, her striking purple hair poking out from underneath. Liam and Laura's daughter. Her face is concealed; she keeps her head down. Another video of two completely wrecked cars on the road, debris everywhere. Then one of a visibly shocked representative of Lowlight Recording.

I can't move. I can't speak. I can't do anything. I just sit there and try to understand what the hell just happened. How could Liam, who came to Boston just a week ago to ask us personally to be the opening act for his new tour, be dead?

Liam, who encouraged us to keep going, to keep getting better. He helped me with lyrics. He wrote to us every now and then just to ask how things were going and if we were okay. In the last few months, he was no longer just the singer of one of our favorite bands; he had also somehow become our mentor.

And now he's dead.

It can't be true. But it is. It's not a bad dream that we can wake up from. It's fucking reality.

One moment of carelessness, another driver who wasn't paying attention, and it was over.

Tears threaten to overflow, and I can't breathe. My throat feels tight. I don't remember the last time I cried. It's been so long, I've forgotten what it feels like. Unlike Beck, whom I can hear sniffling quietly next to me, tears already running down his face. He's never had a problem expressing his feelings. Colin is sitting on the floor in front of the TV, silent and pale as a ghost. Jax disappeared into the bathroom earlier. The tap is running, but otherwise there's no sound coming from the room. But I guess that's exactly how he wants it.

I feel sick when I think of Liam's daughter. I don't know Rayne; I only know she's younger than me. Liam told me she just finished high school this year. She found our videos on YouTube and showed them to her father, but we never met her. Liam visited us a few times in Boston, but we never went to LA, and Rayne couldn't travel with him because of her final exams.

She's too young to lose her parents. Shit, you're *always* too young for that.

And then I think of another girl, one whose favorite song is "Mockingbird." I've been calling her "Birdy" because she never told me her name, even though we've been texting for months. She chose her Instagram username after the song that brought us together. She adores that song. She loves all of Liam Bellamy's songs, and I know she's been counting the days until his new album comes out. I know because we both were, together.

My hands are shaking as I open Instagram. I need to know if she's okay, even though I already know the answer. There are people who hear about the death of their favorite musician and they're sad and affected, but it's too far away to really get to them. After a few weeks, they don't think about it anymore.

But Birdy isn't like that. For her, Liam's death isn't far away. It's way too close, because his music means the world to her.

I go to her profile and stare at her photos because I can't bring myself to ask her the question I need to ask. My heart sinks. I'm afraid of her answer. I'm afraid of what this will do to her. Her pictures blur before my eyes. I know every single one of them. The one where she's wearing a faded Liam Bellamy tour T-shirt, her dark hair cascading to her waist. It only shows part of her neck and her upper body. Not her face, which she never shows. We've been writing to each other for three months, and I've never seen her face.

But I know there's a tiny tattoo of a mockingbird over her ribs. I recognize the gold bracelets wrapped around her slender wrist.

Golden stars and a delicate crescent moon dangle from them. A slightly wider silver bracelet with something engraved on it that I can't make out from the photos. I know the rings she wears. Six on her right hand, four on her left. I know she has the grayest eyes I've ever seen, with insanely long lashes, because she once posted a photo where only her eyes are visible. She's looking directly into the camera, deeply and intensely. I know there's a small mole on her right cheekbone from another photo showing her profile, half cut off, only her cheekbones and chin visible. Her hair is tied up in a messy bun, she's wearing very large headphones, and you can see the mole. I know countless tiny fragments of this girl, but I've never seen her whole face.

But I don't need to. I know her, and she knows me. Every thought, every insecurity. Every favorite song. That's why I have to write her this message, ask her this question. Even though I already know the answer.

I tap the message icon, and my fingers find the letters all by themselves, without me even having to look.

JUL 11 AT 6:36 PM

eastcoleman:
You heard, right? How are you?

She doesn't answer. She's not okay.

AFTER

JUL 20 AT 6:05 PM

eastcoleman:
Birdy? Is there anything I can do? Anything at all? No matter what.
Seen

JUL 20 AT 11:58 PM

eastcoleman:
What do you need?
Seen

JUL 21 AT 12:07 AM

eastcoleman:
Talk to me. Or don't. Whatever you feel like. But I'm here, okay?
Seen

JUL 25 AT 3:36 AM

eastcoleman:
Tell me when I should stop texting you. If it's too much, I'll stop.
Seen

JUL 26 AT 2:42 AM

mockingbird:
Don't stop. Please don't stop.

eastcoleman:
Hey, Birdy. There you are. I missed you.

mockingbird:
I can't write to you. It feels like my life has fallen apart, and in a way, it has. I can't talk about it, but please don't stop.

eastcoleman:
Shit, Birdy, I just want to give you a hug right now. You don't have to talk about it if you don't want to. But if you do want to talk, I'm here, okay?

mockingbird:
Don't leave me alone.

eastcoleman:
Never.
Seen

JUL 28 AT 1:13 PM

eastcoleman:
Jax, Colin, and Beck are moving in with me and Willow. I can't

believe she actually said yes. I mean, would you want to live with your brother and his three best friends?
I don't think so.
But okay. It's her decision. She could have said no.
Seen

AUG 1 AT 2:23 PM

eastcoleman:
We're renovating. We have to make room somehow, otherwise there's no way three more guys will fit in this house.
Jax has claimed the basement for himself.
I think I want the attic. I always wanted it when I was a kid, but Dad had his model train set up there, so I couldn't.
Seen

AUG 12 AT 3:56 PM

eastcoleman:
Photo
It's not quite finished yet, but I think I like it in the attic.
Seen

AUG 17 AT 1:19 AM

eastcoleman:
I miss you.
Seen

AUG 25 AT 5:07 PM

eastcoleman:
We're working on new songs, but the guys aren't really helping with the lyrics at the moment.
Seen

AUG 26 AT 6:12 AM

eastcoleman:
I should be sleeping, but I'm stuck on a part of the song. I'm only missing one word, but I can't think of the right one. I'm pretty sure you'd know it.
Do you think you'll ever answer?
Seen

SEP 3 AT 5:34 PM

eastcoleman:
Voice message 0:59
This is part of the new song. I thought you might like it.
Seen

SEP 14 AT 3:54 PM

eastcoleman:
House of Memories—Panic! At The Disco

Seen

SEP 21 AT 4:24 AM

eastcoleman:
Shit, Birdy, I miss you. How can you miss someone so much when you've never even met in real life?
Seen

OCT 4 AT 11:37 PM

eastcoleman:
You could come visit me in Boston sometime. The city isn't that bad. So, if you ever need to get away, wherever you are. I don't know if you're still in California. I know you said you couldn't write, but I'm really worried about you. And I miss you and your messages. The stupid GIFs. The songs you sent me. I miss you.
Seen

OCT 6 AT 10:09 PM

eastcoleman:
Does this really help you? Me constantly writing to you and telling you irrelevant things about my life? I've said it before, but I'll say it again: If you want me to stop, just say so.
Seen

OCT 7 AT 12:03 AM

eastcoleman:
You didn't say anything, so I'll keep going.

You're not alone, Birdy. Don't forget that.

Seen

OCT 23 AT 5:17 PM

eastcoleman:

A Sky Full of Stars—Coldplay

Seen

OCT 31 AT 8:45 PM

eastcoleman:

Jax forced us to dress up for the Halloween party he wanted to throw. I hate dressing up.

Photo

Seen

NOV 28 AT 7:13 PM

eastcoleman:

Sorry I haven't been in touch. The last few weeks have been crazy, I've had to work some extra shifts, the Christmas rush is about to start.

I'm thinking of you.

Every damn day.

Seen

DEC 25 AT 1:57 PM

eastcoleman:
Merry Christmas, Birdy.
Seen

JAN 1 AT 12:01 AM

eastcoleman:
Happy New Year, Birdy.
This year will be better.

mockingbird:
Promise?

eastcoleman:
I promise!
Seen

PART 2
Verse 1

CHAPTER 1
Easton

Miss Missing You—Fall Out Boy

My phone is vibrating in my pocket, and I know it's not her, but I have to check anyway. I can't help it. The message that lights up my screen is from Colin. Of course. It could have been anyone but her.

Disappointment washes over me, and I can't do a thing about it. It still hurts like hell that she doesn't text me or reply to my messages anymore.

"Still nothing?" The sound of Beck's sympathetic voice makes me look up. He's leaning against the other side of the record store checkout counter where I'm working. He blows a strand of hair off his forehead.

I shake my head. *Nope.*

"How long has it been since she stopped writing to you?"

"Six months," I admit reluctantly, which isn't quite true. But the four messages I got in the last six months hardly count. Even though the last one came just five days ago.

"Maybe you should stop." There's a worried expression in his dark eyes, and I understand his concern. In his place, I would probably think the same thing.

But I shake my head anyway. I can't stop. I promised not to leave her alone. So I'm not going to. Even though I've had the feeling for months that there's more behind her silence than the death of her favorite singer. You don't just disappear the way she's doing if someone dies who you basically don't know, do you?

Fuck, I have no idea. Everyone grieves differently, and maybe I don't know her as well as I think I do, regardless of how awful that thought is.

"Have you asked her what's going on? There's more to it, isn't there?" Beck asks, as if he's reading my mind.

Sometimes I think he really can. We're more like brothers than friends; we've known each other practically our whole lives. We grew up together in the same neighborhood, on the same street. There were weeks when he spent more time with my family than with his own. He knows me better than anyone else in the world. *Almost anyone.*

"No," I finally say.

"Why not?"

"Because she wrote and said she can't talk. She said she feels . . ." I stop because I can't tell him how she felt. It's none of his business. Beck knows about Birdy because he knows everything about me, but he has no idea what exactly we talked about. Or what *she* knows about *me*. What I know about her. "I can't ask her because I don't want to push her. I don't want to put pressure on her."

Beck sighs and rolls his eyes. "Sometimes I feel like you're too good for this world."

"One of us has to be," I retort, even though we both know it's bullshit. I'm not that holy.

"I'm definitely not." Grinning, he straightens up and looks around the store. "This place is a ghost town."

"No one forced you to come here and keep me company," I remind him.

I've been working at Repeat Records, a retro vinyl store in Boston's West End, for around seven years. The days after New Year's Day are always slow. Most people are back to work already, and the short breather between the holidays evaporates like it never existed. By the beginning of January, stress levels are already back to where they were before vacation. Most people just don't have time to look for new records or sit in the little café at the back of the store and listen to music.

"I know." Beck shrugs. "I was bored."

"I think you must be the only person who gets bored on their day off."

"Maybe." He picks up one of the pens lying on the counter and twirls it between his fingers. "I need something to do. Something that challenges me. I'm sick of working at my dad's office. How can anyone voluntarily sit in a tiny cubicle with stale air every day and fill out fucking Excel spreadsheets?"

"There are people who like that stuff," I say.

We're definitely not among them. Beck only took the job at his dad's company because it was easy money. Compared to most situations, it's a lot of cash for relatively few hours. I have three jobs and I earn about the same in total. Except I have to work a lot more. But whatever.

I like this job; I feel at home here. I'm surrounded by bands and musicians who have been part of my life for as long as I can remember. People who inspire me. I've learned so much from them. At first glance, the store looks run-down, but that's exactly what gives it charm. Worn leather armchairs, tables with record players and large headphones so you can listen to the LPs. Right now, we have almost a hundred thousand records in the store. I know because I had to catalog most of them in December. There are a few CDs too, still enough that I could work overtime every day. Inventory is really fun . . . not. Beck, Jax, and Colin were here almost every day to help save me from being completely overwhelmed during the Christmas season, but it was still hell.

"I'm going to get coffee, want one?" Beck tosses me the pen he's been playing with and I catch it, sticking it back in the cup where it belongs.

"Yes, please."

"Sure thing. At least then Evie will have something to do," Beck says, strolling between the bins of records to the back of the store, where it opens out into the small café.

Evie, our barista, is sitting at one of the tables, earbuds in her ears, phone in hand. She looks up when Beck stops in front of her. He taps her shoulder and she rolls her eyes in annoyance, probably because now she actually has to do something.

Smiling, I'm just reaching for my own phone when the door opens and the shop bell jingles softly, announcing a new customer. I look up, but the girl who's just coming in doesn't even glance in my direction. She's wearing an oversized coat and has a black knit cap over her hair. A thick scarf is wrapped around her neck, covering half of her face. No wonder; it's freezing outside.

I watch her for a few seconds to see if she needs help or just wants to look around. She doesn't spare me a glance as she walks through the store. She flips through the records but doesn't stop for a second, like she's searching for something very specific and knows exactly where to find it. But I've never seen her here before, and I can remember most people who come here regularly. Then again, I'm not here every day, and certainly not the whole day. The owner, Rudy, is usually here in the morning, manning the shop himself.

The girl turns her back toward me when she finally stops in front of a bin. I know which one it is, and my heart tightens painfully. It's the one with Liam Bellamy's records. All of them. My mind turns immediately to Birdy and the fact that she isn't answering my messages.

I've written to her every day since New Year's. I sent voice messages in which I sang her parts of my new songs. I even sent her pictures from Pinterest. Everything I found that made me think of her. To prove to her that this year really will be better than the last. Even though it's impossible for me to prove that, and I probably shouldn't have promised it.

No answer.

She hasn't even looked at the last messages.

I realize it's stupid. Silly. Completely pointless. I've never even met this girl. I've never heard her voice, because unlike me, she's never sent a voice message. I don't even know her name. We were writing to each other for three months before it all fell apart. And that was that.

Except those three months felt like an eternity. I guess that's how it is when you spend every free moment texting with someone. You get used to each other, get to know each other, and when it's over, it doesn't matter that it was just messages. It still hurts like hell in a very real way.

"Hey." A quiet, strangely unsure voice makes me look up. The girl is standing there, a few steps away from me.

"Did you find something?" I ask, but she's not holding a record or CD. She takes a step closer, biting her lower lip. There's a nervous gleam in her eyes.

Gray eyes. The grayest eyes I've ever seen. Long, dark lashes. A little mole directly on her right cheekbone. A little silver ring in her nose. My gaze drifts automatically to the rings on her fingers. Familiar rings. There are bracelets gleaming on her wrists, peeking out from under her coat. A crescent moon and stars. So familiar.

Adrenaline surges through my body as it realizes who she is before my brain does. My heart beats so hard it hurts as I stare at her and desperately try to understand what's happening.

I know countless tiny pieces of this girl, and now I know her face too.

"Birdy," I say, and my voice doesn't sound like my own. Incredulous and raw, both soft and hard, and completely overwhelmed because she's actually here in Boston. In this record store, right in front of me.

"Rayne," she says, and it takes a few beats for me to realize that after nine months, she's finally told me her name.

Rayne.

The name suits her and her stormy gray eyes. My heart stumbles in my chest, unable to decide what to feel. The skin on the back of my neck starts to prickle as I stare. I'm completely bowled over, and I don't even know if I'm happy to see her. No, that's not true: I am happy.

Joy pulses through me, mixed with relief. It makes my heart race and my stomach flip nervously. I just didn't expect to see her, here, today, ever. How could I? How could I have expected this?

"You're here," I say, because that's all I can say right now. All I can think of. Because somehow, it's all that matters.

CHAPTER 2
Rayne

11 Minutes—YUNGBLUD, Halsey, Travis Barker

A few minutes ago
Oh my God.

Oh. My. God.

What the hell am I doing here?

This is a very, very bad idea.

I turn around and walk back the way I came. The Uber dropped me off two blocks away after I convinced myself that I came to the West End for that thrift shop, not for Repeat Records.

It's raining. It's been raining all day. Not heavily; more like those fine raindrops that sting your skin like needles and soak you through if you stay outside too long. My face is cold, and I'm glad I didn't wear makeup, otherwise my mascara would be a mess by now. But despite the rain, and even though the drops feel like ice on my skin, I'm not cold. I'm warm. It's the excitement, the adrenaline.

My heart is beating much too fast. It's pounding against the bony cage of my ribs, so hard it feels like it could escape if it tried hard enough.

What are you afraid of, Mockingbird?

Dad's voice in my ear, asking me that question over and over again because he wanted to know why I didn't want to go to the meetings with Easton and the others.

You should be there. After all, you found them. Why don't you want to come?

I didn't have an answer for him. Not one that made sense, at least. Maybe I didn't even understand it myself. Because I wanted to meet Easton the whole time.

But after we started writing, it wasn't just a few short messages. It wasn't just small talk that meant nothing, things you write and forget a few days later. It was more, from the very beginning. That's why I couldn't go with Dad. I just couldn't.

Dad was right. I was afraid. I'm *still* afraid.

Last year, I was afraid it wouldn't work in real life. I was afraid that we could be friends online but wouldn't be able to talk the same way in the real world. Things like that happen. You can get along fine when you think you know each other but actually don't, not completely.

If I'd met Easton and the band, I would have had to tell him the truth. I would have had to tell him that the girl he's writing to is Liam Bellamy's daughter. It would have been impossible for me to lie to him. But I was afraid to tell him who I am. Afraid that he would treat me differently if he knew. After all, it wouldn't be the first time. Besides, I wasn't ready for it. Maybe I'm still not ready.

Now I'm scared that he'll hate me because I disappeared for the last six months and didn't answer his texts.

He doesn't hate you. If he did, he'd have stopped writing to you a long time ago. He's your friend. Have some faith.

That's what Mom would have said if she were still alive. A dull pain spreads through my chest, a black hole that threatens to swallow me. It's already swallowed me repeatedly these last few months.

My throat tightens, tears threaten to overflow, and I stop in the middle of the sidewalk. I don't care that the people behind me have to step aside, and they give me dirty looks as they rush past.

Breathe, Rayne, breathe.

But I can't. It's like there are shards of glass in my lungs, tearing me apart. Not for the first time, not for the last. Over and over again.

Breathe, just breathe.

In.

And out.

I gasp for air, and somehow I manage. It's unfair that it still hurts this much even after six months. Whoever said that time heals all wounds was lying. It doesn't. It still hurts just as much, and it hasn't gotten any better. If anything, it's gotten worse, because now the shock has worn off. Now all that's left is the pain, a stab inside of me that takes my breath away.

"You're in the way," a cold voice behind me says, and I flinch. I stumble a couple of steps to the side and freeze in place. I have no idea what to do.

Go to him. He doesn't hate you.

That's Mom's voice again, warm and gentle. I want to cry because I'm not even sure anymore if that's really how she sounded. Was her voice the same as the one I hear now, or have I already started to forget her?

Don't think about it. Just don't. You won't forget her, you can't.

But I can. It's different than it is with Dad. His voice will always be there. As long as I have his records, as long as there are streaming services and the internet, his voice will be there. Mom's won't.

Of course there are videos of Mom and Dad, and of Mom and me. Voice messages. But that's different. I don't know why, but it's different from Dad's songs. They're there, full of his emotions, and that's why a part of him will always be with me.

I can't hold on to Mom like that. She only exists on my phone, only for me. At some point the whole world will forget what she sounded like when she laughed, how bright and soft her voice was when she used to read to me when I was little.

I stop thinking, turn around, and then start walking again. I can't be scared anymore, I need Easton. I need more than just his messages; I need him in the real world. He's my best friend.

Out of breath, I stop in front of Repeat Records. The shop is bigger than I expected it to be. Easton sent me a few photos last year, but it always looked smaller. I see now it actually has two floors, with instruments displayed in the upstairs windows. I remember Easton telling me that he started to work here because he couldn't afford a new guitar. He worked hard for months to save up for one.

I push open the door and hear a soft jingle as I enter, my eyes glued to the ground. I can't bring myself to look around for him, and I don't understand why. Maybe I'm afraid he isn't here. I don't know if I'll be able to make myself come back if I've made the effort for nothing today.

But then I hear the familiar strains of "My Heart Is Lost" by blackbear, and I know immediately that he's here. He sent me the song three days after we started texting.

Nervously, I wander between the bins full of records, my gaze lingering on a few album covers: ABBA, Queen, Taylor Swift, Lana Del Rey. Now I want to look around after all, to make sure Easton is there. But something is still stopping me. It doesn't make any sense. But if I look at him and he looks at me at the same time, then . . . I don't know what will happen. I might go crazy.

Calm down, for heaven's sake.

That's not as easy as it sounds, not with the cramping in my stomach and the racing pulse I can feel in every part of my body. My palms are sweating. What if he hates me? Should I introduce myself? Will he recognize me? But no, how could he? I've never posted photos of my whole face. He has no idea who I am, and I have no clue what I should say to him.

Hi, I know I've ignored you for the last six months, but now I'm here. It would be nice if we could be friends again because I don't know anyone else in this damn city and I feel so lost.

No, probably not.

I had a plan before I came here. I thought long and hard about what I wanted to say to him, and I had my words all picked out. But now, my mind is completely blank. Especially here in my new home that doesn't feel like a home, where I live in a new room that feels strange and wrong.

I had a plan, but now my mind is completely blank. I stop in front of the bin with Dad's records, as if on autopilot. As if my body knows exactly how to find him anytime, anywhere.

The record at the front of the bin is a single, not an album. "Mockingbird." Of course. Coincidence? Maybe. I take a shaky breath as I touch the cover. It's so familiar that I can see it with my eyes closed. After all, it was hanging in my room for years.

There it is again, that stab in my chest. I can't deal with this, not right now. I turn away quickly and then it just happens: I look. The guy standing behind the counter is Easton, there's no doubt about it. I know his face by heart. The dark hair that's a little too long on top is falling over his forehead. I know his tall frame, his broad shoulders. I know his hands. I've probably spent a little too much time watching the band's YouTube videos.

Go on, now, be brave. You're both here in the same room. Go. Talk to him. That's what you've always wanted to do.

Yes, I did. More than anything. I just couldn't, and I'm not sure if I can now. But I don't want to leave, either. I want to hear his voice. Live. Not from speakers, not from my headphones. I want to hear him talk to me.

"Hey," I say, stopping a few steps away from the counter. Breathless. Unsure. Hopeful.

He looks up. I never realized his eyes were so blue.

"Did you find something?" he asks, his voice friendly and warm. A little distant. He doesn't recognize me. Of course not, how could he?

But then his gaze meets mine and his eyes widen, then blink. Now he seems to recognize me, as his expression flicks between confused, incredulous, and hopeful. My heart skips a beat or two.

"Birdy?" That's the name he gave me because I never told him my own. A tingling sensation runs down my spine, and I feel warm. Much too warm.

"Rayne," I say without explanation. Suddenly I want him to know my name. My *real* name. I want to hear him say it.

"You're here," he says instead.

"I live here now." The words taste bitter on my tongue, and I have no idea why that's the first thing that pops out. Why can't I apologize for ghosting him? Explain what happened. Tell him why I couldn't talk to him. Why can't I do that?

His eyebrows go up, and there's a glimmer of hope in his eyes. "Here, in Boston?"

I nod. "Yes."

God, I'm not capable of saying anything meaningful anymore, but all at once everything is uncomfortable and embarrassing. Exactly as it shouldn't be. This is what I was afraid of, that it would be awkward and strange. But that's not really surprising, is it? It's my own fault. I should have written to let him know I was here instead of just showing up like this. What was I thinking?

Apparently not much.

"Why?" He sounds as overwhelmed as I feel.

The question is justified, and the answer is actually quite simple: because I'm studying dance. Ballet. Exactly what I didn't want to do. I wrote to him about it back then, when it was still just an audition, when everything was still fine and I had all the possibilities in the world for my future.

The words are on the tip of my tongue, but I can't get them out. As simple as the answer may seem, it's not that simple. Not at all.

We stare at each other. Why is everything so complicated and difficult?

There's a rushing sound in my ears. This is a mistake. I shouldn't have come here. Not like this, not without telling him first. Now I've ruined everything, and he won't write to me anymore. *Now* he probably hates me.

“I’m sorry, I shouldn’t have come here,” I choke out, backing away. I have to leave. Right now.

“No, Rayne, I—” he breaks off. He said my name, and it sounds different than I imagined. I turn and run, and he calls after me. Part of me wants to stay, hoping that somehow, miraculously, everything will be okay. Another part wishes I had never come.

CHAPTER 3
Easton

Losing You—UNSECRET, Sam Tinnesz

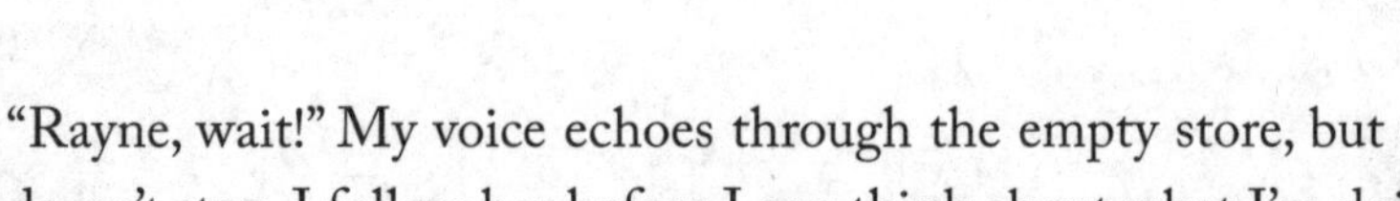

"Rayne, wait!" My voice echoes through the empty store, but she doesn't stop. I follow her before I can think about what I'm doing. Unfortunately, I'm too slow, I started too late. By the time I stumble onto the street, she's long gone.

"Shit! Shit, shit, shit!" Cursing myself for my slow reaction, I tear at my hair. My heart is pounding, I can feel it in my whole body. It's beating way too fast, way too hard. I'm panicked and confused. Completely overwhelmed. She was here. She was really here, and now she's gone again.

Shit, she can't be gone.

But she is, and that feels much worse than her ghosting me. At least then I could convince myself that she might answer again, and it might eventually go back to normal, with questions and answers, songs and memes, with secrets both big and small. Now that's over. I have an awful feeling that she doesn't want to get any more texts from me, either.

She ran away from me. I don't know what that means. I don't even know if I want to know.

"East?" It's Beck, his voice curious and worried. I turn around to see my best friend standing in the entrance to the shop. He's making a face because it's raining, harder than before, and it's icy cold. "Is everything okay?"

I nod and then shake my head. No, it's really not. Nothing is okay.

"Who the hell was that?" Shivering, he crosses his arms over his chest, holding the door open with one foot and obviously waiting for me to come inside. But I don't want to move. I just stay where I am, even though it's cold and raining. Birdy is gone. *Rayne* is gone.

Her name strikes a chord in me, as if I should know it. But I don't. Or do I? Frowning, I stare at the street. Yes, I've heard that name somewhere before, but where?

"East? Hey, get in here already, it's freezing!" Beck complains, sounding annoyed now.

I don't answer. Her name. Damn, where have I heard it before? Or read it? Yes, probably read it. But where?

"East! Move it." Beck comes over to me, grabs my arm, and drags me back into the store. "Colin will wring your neck if you get sick again. And maybe Jax and I will help him this time. We already missed two weeks of rehearsals before Christmas because of your tonsillitis. We really can't afford to take another break right now."

The door closes behind us, the bell jingling softly, and Beck tows me between the record bins to the back of the café. Evie is sitting at one of the round tables again, focused on her phone. She gives us a quick, annoyed glance as Beck disappears behind the counter and grabs a dry dish towel out of the cupboard.

He tosses it to me and points at my wet hair.

"Thanks," I mumble, rubbing my head. The adrenaline is slowly wearing off, and I'm starting to shake.

"That was really stupid," he says, and yeah, he's probably right.

"It's okay," I say, waving him off. But Beck doesn't let me off the hook so easily. I should have known better.

"Do you have another sweater here? The one you're wearing is soaked."

Despite everything, I can't stop the grin from spreading over my face. "Yes, Mom, I'll change it right away."

"Go ahead and make fun of me, but someone has to look out for you." He snorts and reaches for the cup next to the espresso machine.

"It's just a little rain."

"It's freezing rain," he corrects me. "If it gets any colder, it will definitely snow. Go get changed!" He shoos me away, and I do him the favor because I know he won't let up otherwise. I go upstairs, cross over to the spiral staircase to the top floor where Rudy's office is, as well as a small room where we can store our stuff. There's a hoodie in my locker that I left here once as a backup, just in case it got cold unexpectedly. Today is obviously one of those days. I quickly change and go back downstairs, where Beck is standing behind the counter waiting for me.

He pushes a cup toward me. "So are you going to explain what the heck that was?"

"Birdy. That was Birdy." I sigh and shake my head. "Her real name is Rayne."

"Birdy? The girl you've been texting?"

"Yup."

"She was here?"

"Looks like it." I rub my forehead in frustration. I don't understand how our first meeting could have gone so wrong.

"Why?"

"Good question. But it looks like she lives in Boston now."

"What? She *lives* in Boston?" He puts down his cup so suddenly that coffee slops over the edge.

"Apparently."

"Why?"

"No clue." I laugh, even though it's not funny. "We didn't get that far before she ran away."

"Okay, I don't get any of this. I thought she was ghosting you?"

"She was." She just showed up, and I was totally unprepared. Shit, it really shouldn't have happened this way.

"So she just appeared here? Why? I mean, what's the point? She doesn't answer your messages, but suddenly she's living in the same city and turning up in the record store where you work?"

"I told her where I work. It's not a secret."

"It's all a bit strange. You know that, don't you?"

I don't answer. There's nothing strange about it. It's just extremely complicated.

"Why did she run away?"

"I don't know, man," I groan. "If I knew that, I would be able to see the whole thing more clearly."

"So ask her," he retorts, as though it's the easiest thing in the world.

"Sure. This time she'll definitely answer me." I can't disguise the bitterness in my voice. We fall silent, and I take a sip of my coffee and make a face when I discover it's only lukewarm. I hate cold coffee.

"What did you say her name is?" Beck asks a little later.

"Rayne," I say, and in a weird way it feels good to use her real name.

"Rayne? As in *Rayne Bellamy*?"

"No, that's ridiculous, of course not—" I break off, and all at once the world stands still. Rayne. Mockingbird. No photo of her whole face on her account, no mention of her name.

Liam. "Mockingbird," the song. She messaged me just two days before Liam contacted us. He said his daughter had found our video on YouTube and that she would have liked to meet us, but that wasn't an option because she had school. He always visited us in Boston and we never flew to LA, so we never met his family. None of us thought anything of it.

The countless articles about the accident. Her name was mentioned repeatedly, that's why it sounded so familiar. I remember pixelated photos of a petite girl with purple hair and large sunglasses covering half her face. Her hair was hidden by her hat today; she must have tucked it completely underneath.

"Fuck," I whisper. My ears are ringing. How could I have missed this? God, what an idiot I am. She used the name of one of her father's songs as her Instagram handle, and I didn't get it.

But it's her. Birdy is Rayne Bellamy.

CHAPTER 4
Rayne

Better Days—Dermot Kennedy

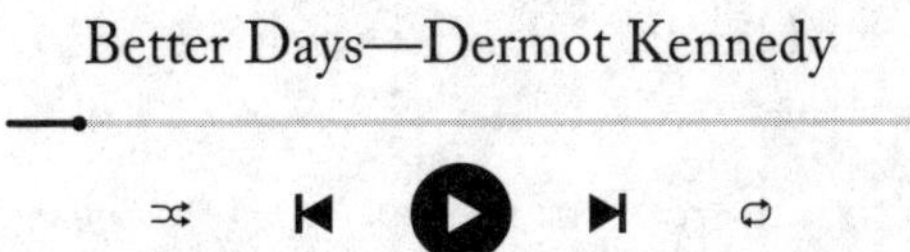

The front door slams behind me with a loud bang. Breathing heavily, I sink down against the door and close my eyes for a moment. Tears burn behind my eyelids, and I have a lump in my throat. Shit. This has gone totally wrong.

My heart aches. I screwed up in the worst possible way, just because I didn't think things through. My hands clench into fists and I bite my lower lip to suppress the sobs that are threatening to break out, even though Grandma isn't here to hear them. The house is completely silent, and I'm glad of it. I wouldn't be able to talk to her, anyway.

Grandma's house in Back Bay is too big for an old woman and a teenager, two people who barely know each other. Everything in this house feels off. The creaky wooden floors, the dark green walls. Dark furniture, dark picture frames. The whole house is dark. The rooms aren't small, but they feel that way because they're so cluttered. Tall bookshelves are stacked with leather-bound volumes that nobody reads. Sideboards are dotted with candles that never burn. Gilded mirrors and lamp bases add a touch of brightness, but that's about it.

Grandma's house is the total opposite of our welcoming villa in LA, where the living room and kitchen were part of the same space. The entire first story was open plan, with floor-to-ceiling windows looking out over the ocean. Here, all you can see out the windows are tiny gardens and backyards. There are wide streets with old-fashioned lanterns and trees that will start to bloom in a few months.

Boston is so different from Los Angeles. Less spread out, less free. The city feels more controlled, more orderly. Just like Grandma. She's exactly like that, and it's one of a thousand reasons I find it difficult to talk to her. Even though she's all that's left of my family.

I swallow hard against the lump in my throat. Drying my eyes, I straighten up and take my shoes and coat off, then pad up the stairs to my room in my socks. Carelessly, I toss my backpack on the floor next to my bed, even though I'm itching to get out my phone and check if Easton has texted me. I don't need to look to know he hasn't. He tried so hard for months, and I still ran away. No, if anyone should get in touch, it's me.

I just don't know what to say to him. Which part of the truth should I share? Or should I tell him all of it? Telling him everything would be only fair, but the whole truth hurts.

With a sigh of frustration, I collapse onto my bed and scream into my pillow again and again, until my throat hurts and my voice is hoarse.

At some point, I've lost track of time. I turn onto my back and try to breathe calmly and not think about Easton. It won't do any good, though. Thinking about nothing is impossible, especially when you're trying so hard not to think. My head is too full and my heart aches. This wasn't the first time I thought about visiting him at the record store. It was just the first day I actually dared to go. I shouldn't have tried.

Sitting up, I pull my knees to my chest and hug myself as I look around the room. It still feels strange, even though I've been living here for almost six months. My new bedroom is as dark as the rest of the house. In a way, it reminds me of my room in LA, except that my old room was cozy and warm in spite of the black walls. There are no pictures hanging above the bed here, no fairy lights creating a soft glow around everything. I haven't plastered every inch of the walls with song lyrics and thoughts with my white pen and messy handwriting. My room told my story. But right now, all my pages are blank.

I couldn't bring myself to settle in here; after all, from the very start, I hadn't planned to stay long. My gaze wanders over to the boxes stacked in a corner. The one on top of the pile teeters dangerously; I've been expecting it to fall for days. Two suitcases lie open in front of my closet. All I have to do is pick up my clothes from the floor and repack them. The closet is empty. I haven't ever used it.

The only thing that I've unpacked properly is Dad's record player and the records that I brought with me from LA. The record player is set up on a tall dresser, right opposite my bed. I can see it every night—every day too, because I usually can't be bothered to get up and leave the room. I found a place for the

LPs on the wide bookshelf next to the window. They couldn't stay in the boxes; that would have broken my heart.

But now it's time to pack them up again. I'll be out of here in two days. I'm not leaving the city, just this room and this house, but it's a start. It's what I need right now.

Living with Grandma is difficult. I think we both feel that way. We just don't know what to do with each other. We haven't played a role in each other's lives for eighteen years, and as much as we've tried to pretend that doesn't matter, it does.

I climb out of bed and pull a record off the shelf. It's Taylor Swift's *Folklore* album, because Taylor is always the right choice and I need her now. Her melodic tunes help keep me from thinking too much.

Then I start packing. I carefully distribute records among several boxes so they don't get too heavy. After all, I have to be able to carry them myself. I just stuff my clothes into the suitcases; they're mostly T-shirts, leggings, and hoodies anyway, so it doesn't matter if anything gets wrinkled.

After a while, everything is packed. Grandma still isn't home, even though it's almost dinner time, and I can't resist the urge to dig my phone out of my backpack to see if Easton has texted me. Which is extremely unlikely, to be honest. But I can't deny that I'm still hoping he will. My hands sweat as I pull out my phone and tap the screen. My stomach sinks in disappointment. No message. Of course. I take a breath and blink, but it still hurts.

My vision blurs as I open Instagram and then our chat. My fingers hover over the letters on the keyboard, but I can't seem to find the right words. Or any words at all, regardless of whether they're the right ones. There's nothing but emptiness. Eventually

I give up and crawl back into bed. I pull the blanket over my head and close my eyes.

* * *

"You really don't have to come with me." I give Grandma a quick glance, my fingers clenched too tightly around the glass of orange juice in my hand. It's Sunday, and we're having breakfast at the table in the formal dining room, which is far too large for the two of us. We're about to set off for my new home—the second in six months.

She shakes her head, giving me a cool smile that doesn't reach her eyes. It never does. I've never seen her smile properly. "I don't mind."

I press my lips together. Maybe she doesn't mind, but I do. I can't protest because I owe her one. My stomach cramps at the thought that I only got accepted to the New England School of Ballet because of her. I didn't even have to audition. Apparently it's enough to be Penelope Bennett's granddaughter. She knows Travis Pearson, the principal, and has been on the school board for years. Basically, all she had to do was snap her fingers to get me in.

It's painful how easy she made it for me, but at the same time, I'm infinitely grateful to her. I couldn't have done it on my own.

"Okay," I say, finally giving in.

"Do you need help packing?"

"No, I can manage. Thanks," I add. I hate that it's so difficult to talk to her. But I can't pretend that nothing ever happened. There's a reason why Grandma never visited us in California. We both know it, but in the six months we've lived together, we've never talked about it once. But then again, we don't talk about Mom or Dad, either.

"All right." She stands up and smooths her tailored wool dress. Grandma still has the figure of the dancer she used to be. Tall and very slim. She's still beautiful, even though her hair has gone gray. The tight bun she wears her hair in is still the same. She looks like an older version of Mom, and sometimes, too often, it hurts me to even look at her. It reminds me that Mom will never become an older version of herself.

I feel it right now. It burns in my chest, but I can't start crying, so I force myself to take a deep breath.

In. And out.

The burning subsides, and when I look at her again, she looks back with the same gray eyes that I have.

"Let's go, then." She leaves the dining room.

I get up and go upstairs, grab my two suitcases, and bring them down. Grandma has called her driver, Francis, even though it's Sunday. She would never just get into an Uber or drive herself.

While Francis stows my suitcases in the back, I run upstairs again to carry down one box after another. My records. The notebooks Dad gave me. The record player. It's too much stuff, but I can't leave anything behind. I just can't.

It takes me fifteen minutes to get all my things into the trunk, and Grandma has already been sitting in the car for a few minutes by the time I finally slide into the back seat. Francis starts the engine, and then we set off for the New England School of Ballet—the ballet academy Mom went to.

She loved the school, I know that. She talked about it often enough. And she wouldn't have tried to convince me to audition last year if she hadn't liked it there. I hope I feel the same way. I hope I fall in love with this place, that I won't feel lost. Also, I hope I'll find a part of her there, the part I always resisted a little because I've loved music more than ballet my entire life. But that was before.

Dad is always with me, somehow.

Mom is the one I have to find again. Myself too.

CHAPTER 5

Rayne

Waking Up (Acoustic)—PVRIS

It's a short drive from Grandma's house to the New England School of Ballet campus.

"Francis, please wait until Rayne and I are back," Grandma says as the car pulls into the school parking lot. I feel briefly guilty, because I'm sure Francis has something better to do on a Sunday morning than wait for me to find out where to put all the stuff that's in the trunk. But it's not like I can take everything with me to my meeting with Mr. Pearson. One suitcase might be okay, everything else . . . probably not. Besides, Grandma still needs to be driven home afterward.

"Of course, Mrs. Bennett," Francis replies politely.

Grandma nods curtly and opens the door. The chilly January wind blows into the car, and I shudder. It's colder than it was a few days ago. The sky is covered with thick gray clouds. It feels like it's going to snow.

"Hurry up, Rayne." Grandma slides her purse over her shoulder and glances at me impatiently.

I repress a sigh and get out of the car. Grandma is already a few steps ahead of me. I follow her over the parking lot, heading to the cast-iron gate set in the sandstone wall that surrounds the campus. The name of the school is emblazoned in unadorned letters above the archway, and I forget to breathe for a moment as we enter and I see my mom's alma mater for the first time.

Of course I've seen photos before, but none of them even come close to reality. The campus is beautiful, built in the Victorian style. Red sandstone, bay windows, high tiled roofs. In the middle of the campus is the New England Theater, the school's own performance venue—and its heart. All the other buildings are positioned around it: the two dormitories, the administration building, and the practice building.

The campus is spacious, with a large lawn and dozens of trees. When everything starts to bloom in spring, it must be breathtaking.

Apart from us, there's hardly anyone outside, but the dorm windows are brightly lit, and lights are also on in the practice studios. Here and there, I can make out the dark shadows of students practicing. It seems like many of them have already returned after the winter break, but I'm too far away to see more.

I only notice that I've slowed down when Grandma gives me an impatient glance over her shoulder.

"Sorry," I murmur, but she doesn't answer, and I'm not even sure if she heard me. I walk faster, but still only catch up with her long after she's reached the administration building.

The entryway is magnificent and totally silent. There's no one here but us; after all, it's Sunday. From the door, we walk straight to the reception desk, past cozy seating areas in front of the tall windows. Pictures of dancers in various poses hang on the walls. My heart skips a beat, and I wonder if there's a picture of Mom here. Instinctively, I move toward the photos, my hands sweating and my chest suddenly feeling much too tight. I saw Mom dance more times than I can count throughout my life. There are many pictures of her dancing. But the pictures hanging on these walls are different. I don't know why I want a photo of her to be here, but I do. So much that it hurts.

"Rayne, please hurry. We're already late." Grandma's voice stops me in my tracks before I can get a good look at the first picture. She disappears into one of the hallways that branch off behind the reception area, her footsteps echoing sharply through the building. I hesitate. I just want to look at these pictures; it won't take long. But of course that's not true: It would take ages to look at them all.

Disappointed, I turn away and follow her again, up two flights of stairs and to the left. She stops in front of a dark wooden door. She's just about to knock when she pauses again. "Are you ready?"

I nod, even though I've never been less ready for anything. My stomach tightens nervously and my hands clench into fists all by themselves. I wish I had something to hold on to, but my suitcase is still in the car.

Grandma knocks, and a moment later the door opens. I see a tall, slender man who smiles warmly at Grandma and then at me.

"Penelope, it's lovely to see you." Mr. Pearson steps aside and ushers us into his office. He's attractive, with a striking face and dark hair streaked with silver and gray. His smile is friendly, and the look in his dark eyes is kind. He's wearing black pants, a white shirt, and a gray jacket. His office is bright and spacious, with a huge desk sitting in front of a tall window. There are three chairs in front of the desk, and apart from a bookshelf and a low sideboard, there's no other furniture in the room. Simple and tasteful.

"Thank you for taking the time to see us, Travis." Grandma puts a hand on my back, and I stiffen. "This is Rayne, my granddaughter."

"Pleased to meet you." His voice is deep and warm. Then his smile fades, and I know what he's going to say. I know because it always comes, but I don't want to hear it. "I'm very sorry about your parents."

When I hear the words, my throat tightens. I have to force myself to answer.

"Thank you." My voice is quiet, almost a murmur.

An uncomfortable silence follows, like it always does when no one knows what to say next.

"Have a seat," Mr. Pearson finally says, his smile back. I'm glad. If he had said anything else about Mom and Dad, I would have started crying.

I sit down on the chair to the right, and Grandma takes the one on the left, while Pearson walks around the desk. The chair between us in the middle is empty.

"Would you like me to tell you a little bit about the school first?" he asks, focusing entirely on me.

"Sure," I reply hoarsely, even though I probably already know everything about it, from either Mom or the school website.

He starts talking, and I like his voice. I like the way he speaks, calmly but with unmistakable pride. You can tell he enjoys being principal here. He tells me about the history of the school, the values we're supposed to learn, and that it's not just about ballet, but about finding our direction. Making friends, getting to know ourselves, and finding out what we really want.

"Do you have any questions?" he finally asks.

I shake my head. "Not at the moment."

"If you do, you can come to me or talk to your teachers any time." He gets up and walks over to a shelf. A moment later, he puts a gray jute bag on the table in front of me. "In this bag, you'll find everything you need for your first few days with us. Your schedule, the school rules, and of course the sweatshirt that everyone gets. You have basically the same schedule as everyone else in your grade, aside from electives. I've already arranged with Miss Chelsea that you won't be dancing in pointe shoes yet. But you'll still attend her class and work on your technique, okay?"

I'm so taken by surprise that I can only nod silently. No pointe work. I'm not sure whether I'm relieved or not. Part of me is glad because I'm not ready after such a long break, and because I found pointe difficult enough before. I don't know how the rest of me feels right now.

Pearson glances briefly at Grandma and then gives me an encouraging smile. "I hope you'll settle in quickly. But please don't put too much pressure on yourself. You're here to learn and grow, and that doesn't happen overnight. You've been through a lot. Take your time, okay?"

I'm not sure why I suddenly feel like crying again. Maybe I just didn't expect him to be so nice.

"Okay."

"Wonderful. Your classes start tomorrow at nine." He turns to my grandmother. "Penelope, do you have a moment? I'd like to discuss something with you."

"Of course."

"Thank you." He glances at his watch and smiles. Then he hands me something that doesn't register with me until a moment later as the key to my new room. "I'm afraid I don't have time to show you around today, but I think I've found someone who can." He walks to the door, and I automatically turn around in my chair as Grandma does the same. The back of my neck prickles nervously. What is he talking about?

The question is answered as two girls enter the office, both with red hair, one more coppery, the other auburn.

"Meet Zoe and Mae," Pearson says, introducing them. "They're also freshmen. You're in the same hallway in the dorm. They'll show you around."

"Hi!" Mae, the girl with auburn hair, grins at me. "Shall we go?"

"Sure." I glance briefly at Grandma, not sure why. I don't need her permission. She nods anyway.

"Go ahead."

I stand up, feeling indecisive for a moment. Hugging Grandma goodbye is out of the question. We don't have that kind of relationship.

"Let's go, then." Mae's smile gets wider.

I nod stiffly to Grandma one last time and give Pearson a grateful smile. Then I take the bag from the desk and follow the two girls who are waiting for me at the door. But before I leave the principal's office, he stops me.

"Oh, Rayne?"

I turn around. Grandma has her back to me already.

Pearson's expression is warm. "Welcome to the New England School of Ballet."

CHAPTER 6
Rayne

Alone—Chandler Leighton

"By the way, I'm Rayne," I say, introducing myself as we walk through the empty hallway back toward the entrance hall.

"We know. Pearson told us about you," Mae replies. Her voice has a gentle, compassionate tone that makes me nervous.

"We're so sorry about your parents," Zoe adds, just as gently and sympathetically.

I blink frantically and take a deep breath. "Thank you." Silence grows between us, the two exchange a quick glance, and it's like when Pearson greeted me before. It feels uncomfortable and weird. They don't know me. They can't say anything to make me feel better, and to be honest, I don't want to hear anything either.

"What's it like here?" I blurt out because I can't stand the silence. I want them to fill it. With anything. It doesn't matter what.

"In three words: exhausting, challenging, awesome," Mae says, counting on her fingers.

Zoe rolls her eyes, but smiles. "You'll definitely like it here.

There are only twenty people in our class. No class has more, either. It's small, but that's the great thing about this school. It means we all get plenty of individual attention."

"Have you been here long?" Mom told me that some students start here even before college. They don't just dance, they get their high school diplomas at the same time.

Mae shakes her head. "Only since September. We're both still pretty new."

We leave the building and I shiver, hunching my shoulders as an icy wind sneaks under my coat.

"Where are your things?" Zoe asks, pulling gloves out of her jacket pockets.

"Still in the car." I point to the parking lot, and the two of them walk purposefully toward it.

"You don't have to help me," I say quickly. I don't want to put them out.

They look at me skeptically. "Of course we'll help," Mae says. "You have more than just one suitcase, don't you?"

"Yeah, I'll have to make a few trips."

"See? Then you definitely need our help." Mae makes a few happy dance steps and looks so pleased that I almost laugh. "Let us help you, you're one of us now. We do these things for each other."

I give in. Something tells me they wouldn't let me talk them out of it anyway.

Mae links arms with Zoe and then reaches for mine like it's the most natural thing in the world. Taken by surprise, I let her. It's been ages since someone treated me like that.

I feel a twinge inside. I can't help thinking about Hailey. She used to be my bestie, but Mom and Dad's death changed not only me but also our friendship. I force myself to put thoughts of Hailey aside before it starts to hurt. Maybe it will always hurt, who knows? There's so much pain inside me that sometimes I don't know if there's any part of me that doesn't feel it.

"Did Pearson give you your schedule?" Zoe asks, with a quick glance at Mae.

"Yeah, it's in here somewhere," I say, holding up the gray bag that the principal just gave me.

"Great, then we can have a look later to see which classes we have together."

"Don't we have them all together?"

She shakes her head. "The whole class has theory in the afternoon together. We also have technique, pointe, and pas de deux together, but the sophomores are in those too. Technique and pointe are every morning, and pas de deux is only twice a week this semester on Tuesdays and Thursdays. On the other days we have practical classes. This semester I'm taking contemporary dance, among other things. In those classes, we're also mixed with students from other years."

"Sounds complicated."

"Not really. You get used to it."

We reach the car, and I tell Francis I want to get my things. A moment later he's opening the trunk, helping us take out the suitcases and boxes.

"Is that a record player?" Zoe asks incredulously, and I feel the blood rush to my cheeks.

"Yes."

"That's so cool! I bought Taylor Swift's *Midnights* on LP even though I don't have anything to play it on. But I just had to own it, I couldn't help myself." She laughs, and I don't know why, but I already like her somehow.

"I have it too," I confess. "And pretty much everything she's ever recorded."

Mae sighs theatrically. "I think you're going to be our new bestie. Just so we can listen to all your records, of course."

"No objections here," I say with a smile. It's a real smile, the first one in ages.

It's strange how easy it is for me to talk to them, and how easy they make it for me. How naturally they accept me. They know who I am and they know what happened. But they don't ask questions, they give me space, and I don't think I've been this grateful for anything in a long time.

There are plenty of people who would have grilled me right away. About LA, about my parents, which musicians and actors I know—all the things I don't want to talk about. I've met people like that. But Mae and Zoe aren't that way at all.

"Even with three of us, I think we'll need to make two trips," Zoe says as she grabs one of my suitcases.

"I'm afraid so." Mae glances briefly in Francis's direction, but there's no way I can ask him for help. If Grandma comes back and he's gone, it would be a problem for him.

"I'm sorry. Honestly, you don't have to help—"

"Don't be silly!" Mae interrupts me. "Of course we'll help you. We don't have anything else to do right now, and Pearson chose us to show you around, so that's what we're going to do."

"Mae can be a bit overdramatic sometimes. Not that you've noticed." Zoe winks at me conspiratorially, and Mae feigns being offended and sighs heavily.

"It's true, I love drama." She stacks two boxes on top of each other. "Now let's go! We've got a lot to do."

* * *

"Hmm, is there anything else we have to show Rayne?" Mae asks Zoe, but she shakes her head. "I don't think so. You'll see the ballet studios early tomorrow morning, and the theory classrooms aren't that exciting."

"What about the gym and the sauna? And the swimming pool?"

"You have a pool and a sauna?" I somehow missed that when I did my research.

"Cool, right? Not that I used either one of them very much last semester, but it's still great to have so many options," Mae says.

Zoe pushes a strand of hair out of her face, her brown eyes glinting happily. "Maybe this semester."

"It's definitely not a bad idea."

Later that day, we're downstairs in the dorm dining room. With its arched windows and green velvet-upholstered armchairs arranged around the tables, it's very cozy. In fact, the whole place is pretty cozy for a school, even if it is a ballet academy.

After putting my things in my room, the two of them showed me around the dorm, our common room, and the roof terrace. We didn't go outside, though, because it started raining again. I guess it's not cold enough for snow yet.

Now we're sitting at one of the tables drinking smoothies, which are freshly made for us every morning.

"That's pretty much everything we wanted to show you for now," Zoe says. "Do you need help unpacking?"

"I think I can manage on my own."

Mae plays with the straw in her glass. "Are you sure we shouldn't—"

"Mae, leave it, okay?" Zoe says, interrupting her friend. "Not everyone needs company when they're unpacking."

"I really enjoyed your company," Mae replies, pouting.

"Yeah, and you're pretty chaotic too." Zoe turns to me. "I totally get it if you want to do this alone."

"Oh, God, please don't tell me you're as much of a perfectionist as Zoe." Mae reaches across the table and takes my hand. Her grip is firm, her skin warm.

I shake my head. "No, I'm part of Team Chaos. But I'd just rather unpack alone."

"All right, I forgive you because you're on my team. See you at dinner?"

I nod. "Sure."

"Super, we'll pick you up." Zoe gets up, and we follow her. Our glasses are empty, and we clear the table before making our way to the fourth floor for the second time today. Our rooms are directly under the roof. In nice weather, the view up there must be breathtaking.

We say goodbye in front of our rooms. Zoe's and Mae's are right next to each other, across from mine. Then I close my door behind me, and I'm finally alone. My shoulders slump in relief. This room is smaller than the one I had in LA and the one I had at Grandma's house, but I already like it better. The floor is dark wood like at Grandma's, but the walls are white and friendly, with pretty plaster moldings. There's a little entry area with a closet and a tiny bathroom. The bed, desk, and dresser complete the furnishings.

My record player has already found a home on the dresser. I'm not quite sure where I'm going to keep all my records, but I'll find a place for them somehow.

I get my earbuds out of my backpack and reach for my phone. I definitely need music to unpack. A couple seconds later, I hear the first notes of "You Don't Go to Parties" by 5 Seconds of Summer. I love this song. I love its vibes, but while I can usually let myself drift away on it, that's not possible at the moment.

I'm still holding my phone, and of course Easton hasn't written to me yet. Somehow I managed to go all morning without thinking about him, but now when I look at the screen and don't see any notifications, I can't help it. It's been two days since I visited Repeat Records. Two days of silence. It can't go on like this. God, I want to talk to him. I want to tell him why I'm here in this city, at this school.

We were friends. He was my only real friend in the past six months, and he doesn't deserve me ghosting him, or running away. I open our chat on Instagram, wanting to tell him everything that's going through my head, every confused thought. I have so many of them. Instead, I only type two words. But I think they're the most important ones.

mockingbird:
I'm sorry.
Seen

BEFORE

APR 28 AT 12:38 PM

mockingbird:
Today is that stupid audition that I haven't wanted to do from the moment my mom first mentioned it. So why am I thinking now that maybe it's a mistake not to do it?

eastcoleman:
I don't know. Why?

mockingbird:
Good question. I don't know. I have no idea what I should do with my life. Maybe a dance education wouldn't be such a bad idea after all.

eastcoleman:
Hmm. Should I be honest?

mockingbird:
No, please, lie to me. Yes, be honest. Always be honest with me.

eastcoleman:
I think you decided not to go to the audition because you might like to dance, but music has always meant more to you. So is

it possible that you feel pressured by your mom? Because she was a dancer and it would make her happy if you went to that school too? And now you have a guilty conscience because you decided against it?

mockingbird:
No, that's not it. Okay, maybe a little. I do feel guilty, and of course Mom would be happy if I did it. For her, ballet was the most important thing in the world. Sometimes I think she's disappointed that I don't love it as much as she does. But I think she's already accepted that. At least I thought so before. I don't know. I'm confused.

eastcoleman:
I can tell. How can I help you, Birdy?

mockingbird:
No clue. If I knew that, I might be better off. I wonder why Mom even wanted me to go there in the first place. The school is in Boston, which is where my grandmother lives.

eastcoleman:
Why does that sound like it's a problem?

mockingbird:
Because it is. My parents don't get along with my grandmother very well. Which is the understatement of the century, by the way. Grandma has never visited us here in LA. I can barely remember her because it's been so long since the last time I saw

her. All I know is that Grandma doesn't like my dad very much. She blames him for Mom dropping out of college.

eastcoleman:
Ugh, sounds complicated.

mockingbird:
You have no idea.

eastcoleman:
Don't feel bad, Birdy. It's your life, and it's up to you to decide. If you don't want to dance, that's okay. If you do want to at some point, you'll do it then. Even though I would be happy if you moved to Boston.

mockingbird:
Why are you so smart?

eastcoleman:
I'm not. I'm just good at giving advice that I probably wouldn't be able to follow myself.

mockingbird:
I like your advice.

eastcoleman:
I'm glad. I just feel like I didn't really help you.

mockingbird:
Yes, you did. You listened to me, that's enough.

CHAPTER 7
Rayne

Face the Music—Louis Tomlinson

My first day at the New England School of Ballet begins with Louis Tomlinson's latest album and a firm knock on the door of my room.

"Just a minute!" I shout as I try to pin my hair into a tidy bun. I didn't think it would be possible to forget how to put my hair up properly, but apparently it is. This is my fourth attempt, and there are still loose strands hanging out in every direction. With a frustrated sigh I throw the brush in the sink and go to the door.

Zoe and Mae are standing in the hallway. Both are wearing the gray school sweatshirt, and have their hair tied back neatly. Very neatly. It feels a little unfair.

"Good morning," Mae says cheerfully. "Are you ready for breakfast?"

I step aside so they can come in. "Not quite. My hair won't behave."

"Do you want help?" Zoe offers, and I sigh with relief.

"Please. I'm a bit out of practice. I haven't danced in months and somehow—" I stop. *Shit.* I shouldn't have said that. No one, absolutely no one, makes it into an elite ballet academy after months of not practicing. Especially if they didn't take the lessons all that seriously even before the time off and only danced halfheartedly. Every break takes its toll, and the longer it lasts, the harder it is to get back into it.

It doesn't matter that Zoe and Mae and everyone else would have noticed sooner or later that I'm not at their level. How am I supposed to dance when I can't even manage to tie back my hair properly?

"No big deal." Zoe smiles gently. "I think all the teachers will understand."

I just nod. Yes, maybe. Still, I feel uneasy. I'm not very good, and everyone will notice right away. And then they'll wonder how I got in. They'll find out who I am, who my parents were, and that I'm only here thanks to my grandmother. Then they'll hate me because I don't deserve to be here.

"Rayne." Zoe puts a hand on my shoulder. "Don't put so much pressure on yourself. You can do this, okay?"

"Exactly. We're going to help you." Mae is standing in front of the dresser with the record player, holding an LP. "First, let's help you with your hair. I'll be right back!" She puts down the record and hurries out of my room, reappearing almost immediately with a brush that has much finer bristles than mine, a whole pile of hairpins, and a can of hairspray. She gives everything to Zoe. "You do it, Little Miss Perfect. You can definitely do it better than I can."

Zoe wrinkles her delicate nose. "You're exaggerating."

"I always do," Mae says.

"I know." Zoe sighs and points to the desk chair. "Do you want to sit down, Rayne?"

"Sure." I do as she asks. Zoe steps behind me and runs the brush through my hair.

"I love your color."

"Thanks," I reply, a pang in my heart as I remember the first time Dad helped me dye my hair, just a few days before the accident.

"It suits you perfectly." Mae sits down on my bed and smiles at us. "It's like it was meant to be. Our colors go well together."

"Actually, they clash a bit," Zoe says dryly. She's right. Copper, auburn, and purple don't harmonize very well.

But Mae waves it off. "Nonsense."

"Do I have to take out my piercings?" I ask, touching the tip of my nose and thinking about all the rings and studs in my ears.

"I don't think so," Zoe replies, tugging at my hair a little too hard. But it's exactly the level of pressure I couldn't manage alone. "Just wait and see if one of the teachers says anything. But I think you can leave them in during class. You'd have to take them off for the stage, but we're not there yet anyway. You should take off the bracelets and rings, though. There, all done. You'd better do the hair-spray yourself." She hands me the can and I stand up.

"Time for breakfast," Mae says when I'm done, hopping off my bed. "It's about time. I need caffeine."

We go down to the dining room together and get our breakfast, sitting down at one of the round tables where a blond boy and a girl with dark hair are sitting. I met a few people at dinner last night, but I couldn't remember most of their names. But I recognize these two as Zoe's boyfriend, Jase, and Skye.

"You're late," Skye says as Zoe bends down to Jase and kisses him lightly on the lips. His green eyes glow.

"We had a little hair problem," Mae explains and sits down next to Skye as I take the chair across from her.

"It looks like you were able to fix it." Skye sizes us up and grins. Her long hair is still hanging loose over her shoulders. I take a sip of coffee while the others chat about their vacations and Christmas.

"How was it with Tristan and his parents?" Skye asks, and Mae blushes.

"Good. Very good, actually."

"Just like I said it would be." A smile of satisfaction spreads across Zoe's face, and Jase shakes his head, laughing.

"Tristan is my boyfriend," Mae explains when she sees my look of confusion. "We haven't been together very long, but he wanted me to spend New Year's with his family and get to know them. It was nice." She sighs happily, and I have to smile even though I barely know her. She looks so happy that I can't help it.

"Griffin and Robyn are just so cute," Mae goes on and tells us about Tristan's much younger brothers. Then the conversation turns to the coming semester. I sit silently next to them and listen, but I'm not uncomfortable. The others make an effort to include me in their conversation without bombarding me with questions that I can't or don't want to answer.

Right before eight thirty, we head to the practice studios so we can warm up before our first class. We say goodbye to Jase and Skye on the stairs. They have to go to a different studio because they're a year ahead of us. Then we go up to the third floor and enter the last studio on the right.

When you enter a ballet studio, no matter which city or country you're in, you can be pretty sure it'll be set up the same. There's a mirrored wall and two walls with ballet barres attached to them, and sometimes freestanding barres. However, large windows with a great view of campus make this room special. The grand piano is to the left of the door in front of the mirror.

Everything feels familiar, even though I've never been in this room before, and my chest tightens painfully as I think of Mom's studio in the attic of our villa. We spent a lot of time up there together when I was a kid and had just started ballet. At some point, I started going upstairs less often and went to Dad instead, listening to him record his songs rather than practicing with Mom. But Mom was always there. She never performed on stage, but she never let go of ballet, either. Dancing was for her what music was for Dad. It was something that belonged to her alone, something she loved and was incomparably good at.

I see images in my mind's eye, memories of Mom standing behind me, correcting my position. Her hands are on my shoulders and waist, gentle but firm. She was always patient with me, even on the days when I behaved badly out of frustration that something wasn't working the way I wanted it to.

Watch your balance, sweetheart. You can do it, I know you can.

My skin prickles in goose bumps, and I feel tears building in my eyes again. I miss Mom. I miss her so much that I don't know how I'm going to get over the fact that she's gone. I can't figure out how that's supposed to work. There are no rules for it.

She should be here with me. I wish she were out there in the hall watching my first class, even if that's silly, because the school doesn't allow parents to watch. Plus, I wouldn't even be here if Mom were still alive.

Tears well up in my eyes, and I can't breathe. For a moment, I forget where I am, that I'm in Boston and not LA. A moment later, a slender hand touches my arm, and I'm pulled back into the here and now, trying to breathe to keep myself from losing it. I can't do that. Not on my first day, in front of all these strangers.

"Rayne?" Zoe sounds worried. "Are you okay?"

I blink frantically to hold back the tears and force a smile. "Yes, everything's fine."

She doesn't seem convinced. She's sensitive enough to realize I'm lying, but she doesn't press the issue. "Are you going to join us?" She nods at the corner where Mae is already sitting on the floor, stretching.

I nod and follow her, feeling empty and numb at the same time. It sucks. It hurts. I determinedly push the memories and images aside. I must, there's no other way. I have to focus on this moment, otherwise I might freak out completely.

I start my warm-up exercises with Zoe, and I quickly realize that I can't even come close to stretching as deeply as she does. My muscles aren't as supple as hers. I feel stiff and awkward and incapable, like I don't belong here. Like I don't deserve it.

"Don't stress," Zoe says so quietly that no one but me can hear her. Can she read minds? Probably not. It must be written all over my face.

"I'll try," I whisper back, but it's hard because as I look around, I can already tell that everyone is better than me, and the class hasn't even started yet.

The movements of the others are fluid, light, and graceful. It looks so easy when they do it. Much easier than it actually is.

I can't keep myself from tensing up, even though it only makes everything more difficult.

"Good morning." I look up when I hear a deep, friendly voice. It's a young man, maybe in his late twenties, who's just come into the studio. He's good-looking and has an infectious smile and bright eyes. "Welcome back, and happy new year."

"That's Mr. Conrad," Zoe whispers to me, and helps me to my feet.

Mr. Conrad looks directly at me. For a brief moment, he sizes me up, and it feels like a test I can't possibly pass. But then he smiles. "I hear we have a new addition. You're Rayne Bellamy, aren't you?"

Curious whispers ripple through the room, and I have to force myself to keep looking at Mr. Conrad and not give in to the instinct to run and hide, because now everyone knows who I am. But I expected that. Dad's name has been in the media for months, as has mine. I was mentioned more often than I can count. I'm trying not to think about the photos that were taken of me. At the funeral. Every time I dared to leave the house. I refused to look at any of the photographers, trying to hide my face and purple hair as well as I could under sunglasses and baseball caps. Too many people know who I am and what I look like.

The fact that I didn't want any of it doesn't change the fact that the articles, photos, and videos that were posted online exist. The paparazzi only left me alone once I moved to Boston and hid out at Grandma's house.

Mr. Conrad clears his throat, snapping me out of my reverie. I realize he's asked me something, and nod belatedly, my mouth so dry I can't answer.

"Welcome, it's nice to have you here," he says, a look of sympathy crossing his face. But he doesn't say how sorry he is that my parents died. Thank God. I don't think I could handle that, not here in front of everyone. It already feels strange enough to be the only new student. The others have had six months to get to know one another and find out how they fit in as part of this class. I feel like an intruder, even though I know it's unlikely anyone sees me that way. Still, I can't help it.

Mr. Conrad gives me a quick, encouraging smile, then turns to the rest of the class. "Unfortunately, Deborah broke her hand during the holidays, so we needed a last-minute replacement to play piano for us."

As if on cue, a tall, slender person enters the room. A very familiar person with dark hair and blue eyes.

"This is Easton Coleman. He'll be taking Deborah's place this semester," Mr. Conrad continues, but his words barely register with me.

I can only stare at Easton. He stares back, his eyes wide, just as stunned as I am. My heart is racing and I feel hot, uncomfortable, and nervous. This is crazy. He can't be here. What kind of weird coincidence is this, him working at my school? It's unbelievable. I don't understand the world anymore. I especially don't understand why he didn't tell me about it.

It's stupid how much that hurts me. It's unjustified and unfair of me, I know. But it still hurts, because he told me everything. Even when I didn't answer, he still told me everything. At least, that's what I thought. Obviously, I was mistaken.

CHAPTER 8

Easton

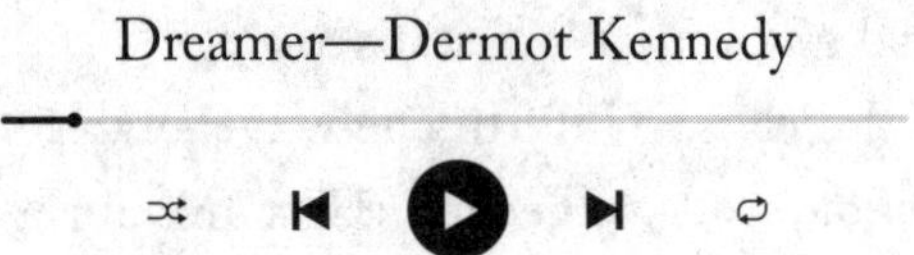

I'm Sorry.

Two words. An apology, but no explanation. I didn't answer Rayne's message yesterday, even though I read it, and now she's standing in front of me, staring at me in horror with those gray eyes. I'm ashamed of myself.

But to answer and tell her that it's okay and she doesn't need to feel bad would have been a complete lie. Asking her why she ran away, and why she didn't tell me she was in Boston, would have been pointless. She probably wouldn't have told me anyway.

Would she really not have told me? the stupid, much-too-persistent voice in my head asks. I've been trying to ignore it for days. First it tried to get me to text Rayne, and then to answer her message. I didn't do either. Now I'm not only ashamed of myself, but I regret not listening to it. Because maybe this time she would have responded, and then we would have started to have a real conversation again. Eventually, we would have both figured out that we'd see each other again this morning. Then we wouldn't be so shocked. Rayne's lips are moving, and I don't have to be a genius to know what she's trying to say.

What are you doing here?

I'm asking myself the same question: What is *she* doing here? She shouldn't be here. Correction: She doesn't *want* to be here.

At least not the Rayne I know. Or knew? I'm not sure. Because I don't really know her, do I? Rayne is Liam Bellamy's daughter, and I didn't notice, didn't know, didn't figure it out. Not even when she was standing right in front of me. Maybe I would have recognized her sooner if she hadn't hidden her hair under her hat. Those long purple locks that are impossible to miss are now pulled back into a tight bun.

"Okay, everyone, to the barres." Mr. Conrad claps his hands and snaps me out of my thoughts. Rayne flinches and turns away abruptly. Only when she turns to the two girls beside her do I notice Zoe and Mae.

Mae waves cheerfully at me, while Zoe smiles warmly. At least they seem happy to see me. Rayne, on the other hand, ignores me completely, and I can see how tense she is. Her shoulders are hunched and her hands are clenched into fists. My instincts urge me to go over and talk to her, but this is not the right time. After all, I'm not here for her; I have a job to do.

I force myself to turn away and sit down at the piano. The instrument is beautiful and probably worth more than all the instruments we have in our living room at home put together—and we have a lot of them.

My heart skips a beat as I place my hands on the keys. I wish I could say that it's no big deal, that this is a job like any other and

I'm only here to earn money. But that's not entirely true. Sure, I'm mainly here for the money, but it's definitely not a typical job. Not like the one at the record store or the one at the Lighthouse.

Working at Repeat Records is chill and not very demanding. And people come to the Lighthouse because of me and my music. They get lost in it and just want to forget their lives and their problems for one night. They want to be free, at least for a few hours. I can help with that.

But this . . . I can't just play anything I want. I'm accompanying the dancers while they practice, and for that, more is necessary than just mastery of the piano and the talent to improvise. For this job you need to understand ballet, and I'm grateful to my sister, Willow, and all the years that I spent accompanying her practice at home for that. I'm also grateful to my friend Jase, of course, who suggested me as a replacement for the usual accompanist when she wasn't able to make it.

I look up and immediately see Rayne in the mirror. She looks different from last time I saw her, which is no surprise. After all, she's wearing a form-fitting black leotard and white tights that cling to her petite body rather than a coat that's too big for her. Her hair is pulled back into a tidy bun. The rings and bracelets are gone, and only the piercings in her nose and ears remain. She's pale, staring stubbornly straight ahead, not even blinking in my direction. But her fingers intertwine nervously with one another, as though she wants to twist the rings that aren't there. Then she looks at me. Only very briefly, but her gaze hits me directly in the heart. I know we have to talk. There's no other way.

I'm going to be here every day, and I'm going to see her. I can't just pretend that nothing happened, that we don't know each other.

We have to talk. I can tell by the way she's watching me with this insecure look in her eyes that she wants to talk as much as I do.

"Let's begin." Mr. Conrad's clear voice brings me back to the task at hand, reminding me to concentrate on why I came here. I begin to play.

CHAPTER 9

Rayne

This Is Me Trying—Taylor Swift

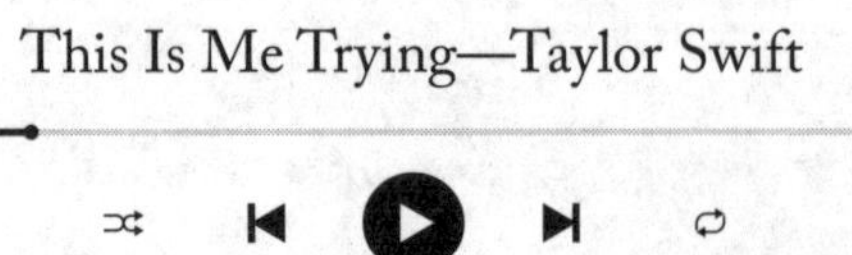

I can't concentrate. Not with Easton in the same room. He's not looking at me, but I'm still too aware of his presence. Much too aware. Especially considering we've only been texting and have just seen each other in person once, which barely counts because we didn't really talk to each other.

I can feel his presence. There's a warm tingling sensation in my stomach, a nervous restlessness that feels like fear but also a little bit like hope. He distracts me, and I know that's not good. I can't keep up with the others at all. The pace set by Mr. Conrad, which Easton has adapted to on the piano, is much too fast for me.

I know all the exercises, I've done them a thousand times in the past: plié, relevé, échappé. I know how to place my feet and move my arms. Unfortunately, my body won't cooperate. My muscle memory isn't working properly. The months of practice that I've missed make themselves painfully clear after just a few moments: Everything hurts, and I'm out of breath far too quickly.

Beads of sweat form on my neck and forehead, my pulse races, and now I remember why dancers don't just dance but also do cross-training and cardio. We need endurance and coordination, and our muscles have to be strong.

Mr. Conrad is watching me. I can feel his gaze on my back. Every now and then he comes over to correct my posture, straighten my hips, and apply light pressure to my shoulders. He doesn't remark on my mistakes, even though he does with everyone else's. Maybe he feels sorry for me. Or maybe he doesn't want to completely demotivate me on my first day. I hope it's the latter, because I'm not here to be pitied. I'm here to learn and improve. I'm here to honor Mom and her talent.

I keep going, tensing the muscles in my stomach and the insides of my thighs a little more, lifting my heels a little higher in half-pointe while struggling to keep my balance. The fact that I also have problems while holding the barre says it all. It's not enough, not like this. I have to try harder.

When we move from the barre to the center of the room, the thin fabric of my leotard is already sticking to my body and my face is red, while everyone else looks exactly like they did at the beginning of the class. A little warm, perhaps, but not as exhausted as I am. Unfortunately, I'm not surprised.

"You're doing great," Zoe whispers to me as we stand in the middle, waiting for Mr. Conrad to tell us what to do next. I grimace and force a smile. She's lying and we both know it, but I'm still grateful to her for trying. Mr. Conrad comes to stand in front of us, and I should be concentrating on him, but from where I'm standing, I only have to turn my head a tiny bit to see Easton. I'd like to say that it's easy for me not to watch him, but that would be a lie.

I'm captivated by the way he sits at the grand piano, with his back straight and his head slightly lowered. Dark hair falls over his forehead. I can only see his profile, but I can still make out the expression of concentration on his face. He's biting his lower lip, and I remember a photo on Instagram where all you can see is his smile. He has a gorgeous smile.

He looks up and his eyes meet mine in the mirror, and for a moment time stands still as he just looks at me. His gaze is clear and uncomplicated; there's no anger in his eyes, not even any disappointment. My heart skips a beat.

I nod at him, a reflex and a response to his silent question. We need to talk.

"Rayne, did you hear me?" Mr. Conrad's voice makes me jump, and my cheeks turn even redder. I'm burning with embarrassment. I hastily take my eyes off Easton and look to Mr. Conrad, who signals for us to begin. After just a few seconds, it becomes alarmingly clear that I can't do what he expects, and I hate that Easton is here to watch me fail. I'm pretty sure I know what he's thinking.

What are you doing here?

I don't know what he would think of my answer.

* * *

When Mr. Conrad ends the lesson, my legs feel so weak that I'm afraid they might collapse at any moment. I'd like to say that it's just because my muscles are overtaxed, that I've overdone it. But there's another reason for it, and I walk straight toward him.

This time I can't run away, and I don't want to. At least I don't think I do. My fingernails dig into my palms, and I'm so tense it hurts.

Calm down. Everything will be fine. He knows you.

Except he doesn't know me, not really. He still doesn't know who I am. I told him my first name, but he has no idea who my father was. Or does he? In any case, I have to tell him now; I have no other choice. Everyone else knows, and I want him to hear it from me, not through some stupid gossip.

But how do you tell your best friend that you've been lying to him for months?

Easton has turned his back to me. He's still sitting at the piano, but now he has his phone in his hand and is texting. Unfortunately, I want to know who he's talking to, even though it's absolutely none of my business.

"Hey," I say, and I can barely speak. My voice is shaking and sounds all choked. I shift uncomfortably from one foot to the other, too aware of the curious glances from my classmates. I don't want to worry about what they think, but I do anyway. They don't know that I already know Easton, so they're probably wondering why I'm talking to him. To be honest, there aren't that many real possibilities. Maybe all my worrying is just an attempt to suppress the fear that he might not even want to talk to me at all. He might just get up and leave . . .

He turns toward me, looking surprised but pleased. There's a gleam in his eyes, and my heart slows down a little. I suddenly feel calmer, and the tension in my shoulders eases.

"Hey."

"I—" I falter, suddenly at a loss for words. My mind has

gone completely blank, and then I blurt out something totally inappropriate. "You didn't answer."

He stands up, and he's so much taller than me that all at once I feel terribly small. Now he's definitely going to leave. I screwed up again. God, what's wrong with me?

But he doesn't. He just puts his phone in his pocket and then fidgets with a bracelet on his wrist that I never noticed before. I haven't seen it in any videos or photos.

"I know. I'm sorry—"

"You don't have to apologize," I say hastily, because he *really* hasn't done anything wrong. I, on the other hand, have messed up a lot. "I'm sorry I didn't answer *you*. I behaved terribly, and I completely understand if you never want to talk to me again. But if you do still want to be friends, it would mean a lot to me," I say, too rushed to censor my words.

He laughs softly. It's a gentle, warm sound, and it sends flashes of heat through my body. Only now do I realize that I've never heard him laugh before. I like his laugh, and I want to hear it again. But he quickly becomes serious, and his gaze is so sad that my throat tightens.

"I need to talk to you, Rayne." He's saying my name, and again, it sounds different than I imagined. Different in a good way. So good that I get a fluttering sensation in my chest. I think it's my heart. "It's not your fault, you don't have to explain," he continues.

"Yes, I do." All at once, it's shockingly easy to talk to him. "I have to explain a lot of things." Above all, I have to tell him who I am and why I've been so distant over the last few months.

"Okay." His hand starts to move toward me, and then he pulls it back. Like he wanted to touch me but stopped himself. I feel a twinge of disappointment. But we're definitely not ready for that yet. We've only just started talking to each other.

"Do you have time later?" I ask him. I'm suddenly aware of where we are again, and that we're not alone. It's neither the right place nor the right time, especially with everything I want to tell him. Not to mention that my next class starts in a few minutes.

"Yes," he says, without hesitation.

I breathe a sigh of relief. "Okay, good."

"Would you like to come over to my place? The guys aren't there, just my sister. I mean, you don't have to if you don't want to. I just thought—" he breaks off, his cheeks turning red. It's kind of cute that he's the one blushing now.

"No, that sounds good. I'd love to."

"Okay, good." He repeats what I just said, and it's clear he realizes it because his blush deepens. "I'll text you the address, okay?"

"Sure. I have to go to another class. See you later."

"Around eight?"

"Sounds good."

"See you." I smile, and it feels almost like it used to. Maybe I haven't completely forgotten how, after all.

He walks past me toward the door, but before he steps into the hallway, I stop him again. I can't help it.

"Easton, are we still friends?"

He turns back to me, a crooked, familiar smile on his face that puts butterflies in my stomach.

"Always, Birdy."

PART 3

Pre-Chorus

BEFORE

MAY 2 AT 8:34 PM

eastcoleman:
Birdy?
Hey, Birdy, come on.
Be online.
Please.

mockingbird:
I'm here. Why the stress?

eastcoleman:
I'm not stressed, I'm freaking out!!

mockingbird:
Why, what happened?
Should I freak out with you or calm you down?

eastcoleman:
Do you remember that Liam Bellamy wrote to us? THE Liam Bellamy?

mockingbird:
Uh-oh. When you use caps like that, it's got to be serious. But yeah, of course I remember. How could I forget?

eastcoleman:
He wants to come to Boston to discuss our future. To see if he can help us. Can you imagine that? Maybe we'll actually get somewhere!

mockingbird:
Omg, Easton!!! That's amazing. I'm so happy for you!
Do you know when?

eastcoleman:
No, not yet. Oh God, fuck. I don't believe it.

mockingbird:
I do. You guys are so good! So, so good! And you know it.

eastcoleman:
Yes, but this is a totally new level. It's all completely insane.

mockingbird:
I get that, but you deserve this. You all do.

eastcoleman:
Yeah, maybe.

mockingbird:
Not maybe. Definitely!
How long has the band been together?

eastcoleman:
We started when we were 15.

mockingbird:
Then think about how much time you've invested in music. You deserve it.

eastcoleman:
Okay, maybe you're right. But there are other bands that invest a lot of time in their music and aren't so lucky.

mockingbird:
That has nothing to do with you. By the way, you still haven't told me how you got started.

eastcoleman:
It's not that exciting.

mockingbird:
Tell me anyway.

eastcoleman:
It's a big cliché.

mockingbird:
I don't care. I love clichés.

eastcoleman:
heavy sigh

mockingbird:
Tell me!

eastcoleman:
Beck and I went to music school when we were kids. Our mothers thought it would be good for us to learn to play instruments, so we'd have less time to get into trouble. I'm not sure if they regretted it in hindsight. In high school we met Colin and Jax. We had music class together, and the four of us were put in a group for a project. Basically that was it. We got along and had fun together. After the project, Beck asked if we wanted to continue, and none of us could imagine stopping. Music connected us, even if that sounds corny (don't laugh)! In the beginning we just played covers, but I was always writing down my thoughts, even as a kid. They were silly diary entries. Eventually they became lyrics, and then we started playing our songs.

mockingbird:
That sounds really nice.

eastcoleman:
It was. We enjoyed writing songs, and we finally found something we were good at. None of us were very good at school, but we could play and write songs well.

mockingbird:
You still can!

eastcoleman:
Now that I think about it, I'm getting a little nostalgic. Back then everything was simple. We felt free when we made music and nothing else mattered. Not school, not our parents, nothing. Just us and our instruments.

mockingbird:
Is it different now?

eastcoleman:
Yes, there's more to it than there used to be. We have higher expectations of ourselves.

mockingbird:
You'll get everything you want, I know it.

eastcoleman:
Do you really think so?

mockingbird:
I'm absolutely sure. You'll achieve everything you want because you're good. Besides, I'm not the only one who thinks so. Liam Bellamy is coming to Boston for you.

eastcoleman:
Yeah, that's really amazing.

mockingbird:
It is, but above all, it's totally deserved. Proud of you.

CHAPTER 10
Rayne

Smile Again—blackbear

Pointe class is a total disaster. Miss Chelsea, our teacher, is nice. Very nice, even. She doesn't make a big deal over the fact that I'm the only one in the class who doesn't dance en pointe. But I suddenly feel like an outsider. It's humiliating to be the only one still wearing soft ballet slippers instead of the hard, uncomfortable pointe shoes. It's also embarrassing to be the only one who can't do the exercises properly, even with soft slippers. The other girls can do it with such ease that I want to cry because I feel so incompetent.

But I grit my teeth to hold back the tears, because I don't want to let anyone see how much it matters to me. Zoe and Mae keep giving me sympathetic looks, which I have to ignore; otherwise I'll really start crying.

Don't overthink it, sweetie. Pay attention to the music, listen to your body, feel the rhythm. You can do this. There's more to ballet than perfect technique.

I can hear Mom's voice in my head, and I want to listen to her, but I can't. She's too quiet, and my self-doubt is too loud.

By the end of class, my feet hurt like hell. Strictly speaking, everything hurts. I'm completely exhausted. Somehow, I imagined that my first day would be different. Less awful.

"Take your time," Zoe says for what feels like the thousandth time as we leave the practice studios after class. Mae stays behind because she has another class. Zoe and I are supposed to have contemporary dance now, but it doesn't start until Wednesday because it's being taught by a guest instructor from New York who isn't here yet. My relief that the first day of training is over almost overshadows my frustration at my utter failure. But only almost.

"I don't know if time will help. I'll never be as good as you," I whimper. I hate the sound of self-pity in my voice.

"You don't know that. Besides, you're really not as bad as you think you are."

"Hmm," I say, and Zoe rolls her eyes.

"Really. You're just a little out of practice."

"I'm not even sure I ever had any practice," I sigh. "I should have taken it more seriously when I had the time."

Zoe stops in the middle of campus. She drops her gym bag on the ground with a thud. "You have time, okay?" she says firmly. "You don't have to get everything perfect right from the start."

"Zoe, I'm not trying to be difficult, but you're incredible. You're so good that I—"

"I can't do everything, either," she says, interrupting me. "At the beginning of my first semester, I had terrible problems with the pas de deux. I couldn't figure it out at all. That's why . . . I know how you feel, believe me. I also know that it can actually start working if you take your time and put a little less pressure on yourself."

She looks at me and I'm immediately overcome with guilt. "I'm sorry, that was stupid. I didn't mean to snap at you."

"You didn't." She smiles. "You're just frustrated. Believe me, no one understands better than I do. Look, if in a few days or weeks you still feel like you can't get the hang of it, we can squeeze in a few extra practice sessions, okay?"

"You'd do that for me?" I ask, surprised.

She grabs her bag and slings it back over her shoulder. "Of course. That's what friends are for."

"Are we friends?" I can't suppress the sound of uncertainty in my voice, and the glimmer of hope.

"If you want," she says kindly.

I almost don't dare to say yes, because I think of Hailey and how badly our friendship ended. I don't know if I can get so deeply involved with someone and end up being disappointed again.

You've already gotten involved, the quiet voice in my head reminds me. It's true. Except with Easton, it's somehow different.

"Can you just decide something like that?"

"Yes. Mae would have loved to adopt you yesterday; she's good at that. She doesn't need a day to know if she wants someone in her life or not. And she wants you in it. Both of us do." She smiles at me again, and I believe her. We slowly start walking again and head toward the dorm.

"I'm not very good at friendship," I say after a while, because I think she should know.

"Neither am I," she replies honestly. "But Mae is, and she'll show us the ropes."

I take a deep breath and exhale slowly. "Okay."

"Of course, that means at some point we're going to grill you about how you know Easton." She grins, and I know, I just know, that they would never pressure me to tell them everything if I didn't want to. She's just trying to lighten things up a little.

"It's a long story."

"Those are the best and the worst."

Apparently, she's speaking from experience.

"How do you know him?"

"Also kind of a long story. Well, no, that's not totally true. Jase and Easton are friends. That's how I know him."

I glance at her, knowing there's more to it. "But there's a long story behind that?"

"There always is. Maybe one day we'll tell each other our stories." She opens the front door of the dorm, and I step into the warm hallway.

"That would be nice," I reply. I guess there are people who it's easy to become friends with and trust. People I can be myself with. Actually, it shouldn't surprise me. After all, it was the same with Easton.

* * *

The sky is clear and dark as I set off for Easton's place that evening. I'm so nervous that I ask the Uber driver to circle the block twice once we've reached the house where the band lives with Willow, Easton's sister. The third time, she gives me a skeptical look, a wordless query whether I really want to be here or if she should take me back to the school after all. But I decide to get out.

I'm late, and I'm sure Easton is wondering where I am.

Take a deep breath. Open the door. Get out. None of this is hard, not at all. It just feels that way. Somehow I manage to walk toward Easton's place. The house has definitely seen better days, but the light shining through the windows onto the street is warm and welcoming.

My pulse races as I stand in front of the door and raise my hand to knock. I finally manage to do it. I don't understand why I'm so nervous. We talked this morning, and he said we're still friends. Everything is fine. Still, I have butterflies in my stomach, and my palms are sweating again. Maybe it's because he still doesn't know who I really am.

The door opens, and Easton is there. He looks at me and smiles, and I have no idea how he does it, but I'm suddenly calm and warm inside.

"There you are," he says.

"Sorry I'm late."

"No big deal. We're not in a rush."

"I know, but I hate being late."

He gives me a knowing grin. "Yes, I remember."

Of course. After all, I told him.

"Come on in."

He steps aside and takes my jacket, and my heart leaps with excitement as I enter the hallway and then the living room. The interior of the house is a little shabby, with wallpaper peeling in places and a wooden floor that's old and scuffed, but it's cozy and filled with music.

I recognize the sound of "Smile Again" by blackbear coming from the large speakers in the living room, and I can't help but smile because I sent Easton that song last June. Just for a second, I imagine he put the song on for me, but I'm sure it's just a coincidence.

Atop a fluffy beige rug sits a huge dark brown sofa with a seat so wide that two people could easily lie down next to each other. To the right of the couch is a small coffee table. One wall is covered by a tall bookcase, which contains hardly any books but mostly records. Easton has already told me which records he has, but I know that at some point I'll stand in front of that bookcase and flip through every single one of them.

The room is dominated by the band's instruments and equipment. Jax's drums, the other guys' guitars, and the piano Jax plays when they're practicing acoustically. On the walls behind the instruments are various band posters, neatly arranged in black frames. I see one of Dad's tour posters in the middle and quickly look away, because my heart immediately starts to ache.

Strings of lights are attached to the shelves and windows, and the tiny bulbs fill the room with a soft glow. The whole room exudes a warm coziness that takes my breath away for a moment. This feels like a real home. Like my old home.

"The fairy lights and candles are Willow's contribution," he says.

"It's nice here."

"We put a lot of effort into renovating this room."

He's standing in the doorway, hands buried in his pockets. "I can see that," I tell him.

We go silent for a moment, but it's not an uncomfortable silence. More . . . thoughtful.

"Will you show me your room?" I ask, not quite sure why. But I really want to see the part of the house that belongs only to Easton. Maybe I also want to avoid meeting his sister and his friends, even though he already said the guys wouldn't be here tonight. Who knows when they'll be back.

"Sure," he says, sounding so surprised that I immediately backtrack when I realize how it might have sounded.

"You don't have to if you don't want to. Sorry, that was a dumb idea." Heat rises to my cheeks. God, what was I thinking? That was totally rude. I'm afraid I've forgotten how to interact with other people normally. With *friends*.

"No, it's not. I'd love to show you my room. Come on."

My face is burning, and part of me wants to run away again, but this time I resist the damn escape reflex and follow him upstairs. One flight up to the second floor and another, much narrower one to the attic. I don't know what his old room looked like, but I've already fallen in love with this new one thanks to a photo he sent me last fall. It was one of those moments when I wanted to answer but couldn't bring myself to do it.

The ceiling is low, just high enough for Easton to stand upright. Under the slope of the roof are his bed and a small table. Opposite those sit a couple of low dressers. There's no closet, but there are two large beanbag chairs. Directly across from the door are an acoustic guitar and an electric keyboard. I can't help thinking about him sitting at the grand piano in the studio this morning, his fingers dancing across the keys. Maybe I'll ask him to play something for me later.

The main reason I wanted to see his room, though, is the walls. His are dark blue, not black like mine used to be, but something about them feels familiar. He's also written all over them in white.

His handwriting is messy. I can't make out the words from a distance, but I'm sure they must be song lyrics and thoughts. Just like mine.

I walk carefully across the room, acutely aware that I'm in his private inner sanctum. It almost feels like I'm inside his head, and he willingly let me in. I stop in front of the keyboard on the low stool and press a key. A low sound rings out, and I'm not at all surprised that it's turned on.

"I like your room," I say quietly.

"I'm glad you're here," he answers.

"I have so many things to tell you." Nervously, I push a strand of hair behind my ear. The time has come; I have to tell him. "My silence . . . It had nothing to do with you. It was just about who I am, and who my parents are—"

"You don't have to say it," he interrupts me gently. His voice is so soft and warm.

"But I want you to know." Still sitting on the stool, I turn to face him. He's sprawled on one of the beanbag chairs, looking at me intently, and I can see how blue his eyes are even from a couple of yards away. Maybe I'm only seeing it because I actually *know* how blue his eyes are.

"I know. I know who you are, Rayne Bellamy."

My breath catches. I have no idea what my heart is doing, whether it's beating too fast or not at all. It's possible that the whole world has stopped for a second.

"How?" I stammer, feeling dizzy,

"Your name is unique. I've read the articles. I've seen pictures of you. Your purple hair is pretty distinctive. And your Insta name is Mockingbird. You told your father about us. He said his daughter showed him our YouTube video. You wrote to me just a few days before he did. Looking back, I wonder how it could have taken me so long to figure it out."

I stare at him in a daze. He's right. There were many clues, and taken together, they paint a pretty clear picture of me.

"I'm sorry, I should have told you sooner." My voice is strained. I'm so overwhelmed I don't know what to do with myself. He knows. "Does that change anything?"

He shakes his head. "It doesn't have to. If I were you, I probably wouldn't have told me either. After all, we hardly knew each other."

"But I didn't even tell you after we got to know each other."

"You're still the same person."

"Am I?" I ask, trembling. How can he make this so easy for me?

A crooked smile appears on his face. "Yes. It doesn't matter if I call you Birdy or Rayne. You're the same. We're friends, and I'm sorry about what happened. I'm so sorry."

Blinking, I avoid his gaze, unable to utter a word. I'm going to start crying, I'm sure of it.

"Rayne?" His eyes are so, so blue. And worried.

My heart tightens, and there it is again, that black hole in my chest. The pain that claws at my insides and takes my breath away.

"How are you?" he asks me.

CHAPTER 11
Easton

Fix You—Coldplay

She laughs nervously, and the sound makes my stomach tense. I don't like how lost she sounds.

"You're going for the hard questions, huh?" She's wearing her bracelets and rings again, now anxiously twisting the two rings on her left hand.

"We never bothered with small talk before," I reply calmly, wondering if I should have just asked her a harmless question instead. But what would have been the right question? There aren't any. We haven't spoken to each other for too long, and we know each other too well to dance around the hard stuff.

"I know." She sighs softly, pushing a strand of her purple hair behind her ear. Her hair is loose and cascading over her shoulders, not like the tight bun it was in this morning. She seems more like herself without the perfect hairstyle and tight leotard. I can tell she seems to feel much more at home in her oversized hoodie and loose jeans. She moves differently. Less uptight. Less controlled. Not as insecure.

"Ask me something else," she pleads, and I agree because I would do anything for her. I can't help it.

"How long have you been in Boston?"

One of her eyebrows goes up, incredulity written all over her face. I shrug. I'm probably just as overwhelmed by the whole situation as she is.

She sighs again and her shoulders slump, then she looks away. "Just under six months." Her voice is barely audible and she holds her breath, as if she doesn't know how I'll react.

But I don't even know myself. Six months. We've been living in the same city for six months, and she didn't say a word.

"You're pissed off, aren't you?"

She sounds so helpless that I want to get up and put my arms around her. But I stay where I am and shake my head. "No, I'm not."

"Disappointed?"

"Maybe a little," I admit, because there's no point in lying. Besides, we promised that we'd always be honest with each other.

"I'm sorry I didn't tell you."

"You don't have to be." That's the truth. She had her reasons for not telling me, and to a certain degree I understand. I can't fully comprehend it, and I never will because I didn't have to go through what she did. She has no reason to feel sorry that I'm disappointed. She didn't do anything wrong. I just wish things had been different, that we'd met under better circumstances.

"I didn't know how to explain. If you had known I was in Boston, and if you had known . . . who I am, you would have wanted to help me. Because you're just that kind of person who has to help everyone."

I remain silent because she's right.

"I didn't want anyone to help me." Her voice breaks and I can feel my nails digging into my palms. "I just wanted to hide and forget everything." She blinks frantically, and a painful laugh escapes from her lips. I hate this. I want to stop her, tell her not to talk about it if she doesn't want to, but I can't get the words out. And who knows, maybe she does want to talk about it. "It didn't work out like I hoped."

"Rayne . . ." She shakes her head, and I stop immediately.

"I know what I did was unfair. I should have answered you, but I couldn't. I sat in front of my phone so many times wanting to respond, but I didn't know what to say because I didn't know who I was anymore, and everything was a mess." She's staring at her hands, at her rings. "If I had answered I would have told you the truth, because it was the only way to explain what was happening to me." She takes a deep breath. "But at some point, maybe after a few weeks or months, I would have had to pretend that I was feeling better. Not because you'd make me feel like I had to; you'd never do that."

It reassures me that she's so sure about that. At the same time, it hurts that she felt she had to lie to me.

"But your life went on. Mine just stopped." Somehow, she manages to pull her knees up and hug herself, even though there's not much space on the small stool she's sitting on. "Everything else was moving so fast that I couldn't keep up anymore. I still can't. That's why I couldn't answer you. I had nothing to say, except that everything hurts." She gasps for breath, and it's like I can literally feel her pain. I want to take it away from her, but I don't know how. "It hurts so much."

Tears roll down her cheeks, and she doesn't even bother to wipe them away. I can't move, even though all I want to do is go to her and hold her tight. I want to do something that might make it not better but maybe a little more bearable.

"I'm sorry. God, I'm sorry, I'm terrible. You really shouldn't have to put up with this." She jumps up and is almost at the door when I finally snap out of my trance and get up too. In three steps, I'm next to her, one hand closing around hers before I can stop myself, before I can ask myself whether she wants this, whether it's okay.

"Don't run away," I beg her. If she leaves again now . . . I don't know what I'll do or how I'll go on.

Rayne's eyes are filled with tears as she looks up at me. She's so small and thin and very sad.

"We're friends, remember? Friends are there for each other. Even when everything sucks. Even when you're sad. It's okay. I wish you didn't have a reason to be sad, but it's okay that you are."

"I hate it," she whispers. "I hate it, and I want it to stop hurting so damn much."

I press my lips together; I can't answer. There's nothing I can say that will make her feel better. I can't tell her that everything will be okay, because it will never truly be okay again. Not the way it was supposed to be. I can't tell her that the pain will go away eventually, because that's not necessarily going to happen.

Her pain won't go away. It won't get any smaller. Her world will just grow around it, maybe. Hopefully.

If she lets me in, and if she wants me to be there, I will be. I've been here the whole time, and I don't plan on going anywhere now.

Gently, I pull her toward me, and she doesn't resist. She lets herself fall against my chest. A rough sob breaks out, and she lets herself go. I hope with all my heart that I'm the right person to catch her.

CHAPTER 12
Rayne

Wildflower Wildfire—Lana Del Rey

I didn't know you could forget what hugs feel like. But after six months without a single one, it seems you can. Maybe this hug just feels so strange because it's Easton who's holding me. Easton, who asked me to stay and not to run away again, even though I'm a wreck. Irreparably broken.

I let myself fall against him. I can't help it; my body goes totally soft in his arms. A desperate sound escapes from my lips. I don't want it to be like this. I don't want to cry, to be out of control, unrestrained. I'm falling into the abyss that I've been avoiding for so long. The last few months, I've stood on the edge many times, looking down. But I never fell. I never let out all the chaos and grief boiling inside of me. I cried more times than I can count, but not like this. Not in a way that makes breathing hurt. Not in a way that makes me break apart.

I sob again and again, and I can't breathe. My chest hurts and everything feels tight. I'm tearing myself apart and I hate that

Easton can see it. At the same time, I feel a strange sense of relief. Because now he really knows everything about me. Especially the side of me that's very sad. The side that feels lost and doesn't know where to go.

I lost my parents, my home, and myself. Easton sees that now, and he sees all that's left of me. But he doesn't leave me alone or push me away. He stays with me and holds me tight. He holds me while I cry hot tears into his soft hoodie until it's completely soaked. He holds me while I dig my fingernails into his arms so hard that it must hurt, but I don't have enough control over myself or my body to stop it. I don't want to hurt him, but there's only pain inside, and it has to come out because I can't stand it anymore.

I can't swallow the pain anymore. I can't hide from him anymore like I've been doing for the last few months. I can't pretend I don't exist anymore. I exist. I'm here. I'm nothing but pain, but I'm here. And he's here. Easton. The only person in the world who still knows me, *really* knows me. The only one who didn't leave me alone during those months when I wanted to collapse into myself. I still want to.

Maybe he can sense that right now, because he pulls me closer to him. So close that I can feel his heart beating under my cheek, fast and hard but steady. His hands on my back are large and warm as he strokes my tense muscles in circular motions, and slowly, very slowly, I start breathing normally again. At least normally enough that I don't feel like I'm suffocating anymore.

He holds me tight and waits until I've cried myself out and gradually calmed down. I feel sick, and my forehead is throbbing painfully. Suddenly I'm tired, so infinitely tired.

Easton gently loosens his embrace, just enough so he can look down at me. But he doesn't let go, and I'm glad of it. My legs feel awfully weak, and I'm not sure they would hold me up if he weren't supporting me. He puts one hand under my chin, lifts it up, and forces me to look up at him. There's sorrow in his eyes and a deep concern that makes me feel comforted inside. Suddenly, I don't feel so alone anymore.

He gently wipes the tears off my cheeks, and I try not to think about the fact that they're not just tears, because my nose is running and so congested that I have to breathe through my mouth to get air. He doesn't seem to mind, though, or at least he's not letting it show if he does.

"What do you need?" he finally asks quietly. His voice is a whisper that sends a shiver up my spine.

"Tissues," I manage to say.

The corners of his mouth twitch, and I almost laugh. I really do. This is totally crazy.

"I'll get you some. Just a sec." Now he lets go of me, and it's also crazy how cold I feel without his hands on my back. I sway slightly without his support but manage to steady myself as he leaves the room. I can hear his footsteps on the stairs; he must not have any tissues up here.

Exhausted, I sit on his bed, even though I know I shouldn't because it's his damn bed and there are enough other places to sit down. But I'm so exhausted I don't care. I don't care what I look like, and I don't even care that I wasn't alone when I broke down. Any other day, at any other moment, I would have been ashamed that someone saw how weak I am. How hurt. But today isn't any other day, and Easton isn't just anyone.

I fall onto my back; the mattress is soft. I sniff, but it doesn't help the congestion. I still have to breathe through my mouth, and my head is pounding just as much as it was before. My eyelids close, and my body feels very, very heavy. My heartbeat slows a little, and then a little more, until it finally finds its normal rhythm again.

I start as I hear a soft squeak on the stairs, but it's only Easton, returning to his room. In one hand he has a pack of tissues and in the other a tub of ice cream.

"I've heard it's supposed to help," he says, holding up the ice cream.

A desperate laugh escapes me. "Yes, I've heard that too."

He hands me the tissues. I sit up and turn away to blow my nose. Easton puts the ice cream down on his bed and goes over to another chest of drawers I didn't notice before. He turns on a Bluetooth speaker sitting atop it, and there's a beep as it connects to his phone. A few seconds later, Lana Del Rey's melancholy voice floats through the room, and I think of the messages I wrote to Easton last year. About how Taylor's music can usually make everything feel better, but Lana is there for the days when everything is unbearable and nothing can make it feel better. Today is one of those days, and he's found the perfect soundtrack for it.

Then he comes back and joins me on the bed, and we lie back down at the same time with the ice cream between us. We stare at the ceiling in silence.

I blink. "There are stars," I say suddenly, stretching an arm toward the sloping ceiling. It's true, his ceiling is dotted with little stars that glow at night when they've gotten enough light during the day. I used to have some like that.

"I like stars," he replies, even though I already know that. There's a reason I wear a bracelet with a star on it.

"Thank you," I whisper to the stars, unable to look at him.

He turns to face me; I can hear the sheets beneath him rustling softly. "What for?"

"For asking me not to run away. And for holding me."

"Anytime."

"And for not making it too weird to be lying here, even though this is the first time we've really talked."

"We were talking for three months. Texting counts."

Now I can't resist; I have to look at him. He returns my gaze unflinchingly, a faint smile playing around his lips. Strands of dark hair fall onto his forehead, and I want to touch them and brush them back, just like he wiped my tears away.

"It really does, doesn't it?" I say.

His fingers brush against mine, a barely perceptible touch, but it sends a warm tingling through my whole body. "Of course."

Our hands are so close together that it would only take a tiny motion for them to intertwine. But neither of us moves. I look up at the ceiling again and count the stars above me. There are twenty-nine of them. The ice cream is melting, but I don't feel like eating anything right now, and Easton isn't making any effort to reach for the spoons lying between us on the bed, either.

Lana is still singing and filling the silence between us, a silence that feels strangely light and uncomplicated.

"I was living with my grandmother for the last six months," I say finally. I don't know why I'm breaking the silence. After being quiet for so long, I feel the urge to talk. "I couldn't stay at my house. Every day the paparazzi were at the door, and everything felt wrong. Mom and Dad . . ." I struggle to get the words past the lump in my throat, and now Easton holds my hand. Our fingers intertwine as though it's the most normal thing in the world, as though we've done it a thousand times. "Without them, it wasn't a home anymore. Do you know what I mean?"

He nods, and I believe him. He really understands. When he looks at me, there's something in his eyes that makes me want to keep talking and let it all out.

"I didn't know where to go. I didn't have anyone left."

"What about Hailey?" he asks, and I grimace as I remember my best friend.

"Her life went on, and she didn't wait for me," I explain briefly. "I can't blame her. It was her last summer before college."

"What does that mean?" He sounds a little angry, which makes me feel better because even though I don't want to admit it, I do resent Hailey for the way she acted.

"She wanted to enjoy it, and I . . . wasn't the best company."

"That's cruel."

"She just couldn't handle it. She couldn't deal with me. I can understand that." I can't, actually. But if I start to think too hard about how my best friend was acting like nothing had happened only two weeks after the accident, I'll probably go crazy. Hailey had slept over almost every weekend and spent movie nights with me until we were fourteen, but that didn't seem to matter to her once I really needed her. I thought I was over it by now, but apparently I was wrong. I should have known better. After all, I haven't dealt with any of it yet: not Hailey's withdrawal or her silence, not the accident or anything that came after it.

"Did she try, at least?" he asks, and it takes me a few seconds to remember what the last thing I said was.

"No," I admit reluctantly.

Easton nods with his lips pressed together. I can see he's struggling to keep from speaking his mind.

"Go ahead," I encourage him.

"Hailey's kind of a selfish bitch."

A hoarse laugh escapes me, but yes, unfortunately he's got it pretty much right.

"So you moved in with your grandmother?" Easton asks.

I nod. "Yes. Looking back, it was probably a stupid idea. But I didn't want to be alone, and she's all that's left of my family." My eyes fill with tears again, and I blink frantically to hold them back, to no avail.

"Why was it stupid?"

"Because I might as well have lived alone and it wouldn't have made any difference. She was never there, and I stayed in my room all day."

"All the time?"

I shrug. "There was no reason to go out." I looked for one, but in the end none of them were good enough to motivate me to leave. Not even the knowledge that Easton was living and working just a few minutes' drive away.

"What was your grandmother doing all that time?"

"No clue," I say with a sigh. "She was out. She stayed with me for three weeks in LA before I came here with her, and she seemed to have missed being here a lot. Or maybe not. I really don't know. She travels a lot, organizes charity events and stuff. She's also on the board of the ballet school."

"Is that why you're there now?"

"No," I say, my voice softer now. "Grandma helped me get in, but that's not the reason I decided to go."

"Because of your mom?" He squeezes my hand, and that warm gesture makes me want to tell him the truth.

"Yes." Now my voice is a barely audible whisper. "I was having a bad day and watched a video of her. One from a long time ago, before she met Dad. When she was still at ballet school. And somehow—" I break off, forcing myself to take a deep breath because my chest is tight again.

"You miss her. That's why you're there."

"Yes." My breath escapes in a sigh. I miss Mom. I miss Dad. I miss home. I miss my old life. I miss the old me. "It feels like I've lost myself, and I don't know how to find myself again," I whisper.

"That's okay. You'll find yourself again. And I'll be with you, okay?" Easton squeezes my hand, and all at once my chest feels a little less tight and my heart hurts a little less, because he's here and I'm not alone anymore.

"You're a good friend, you know that?"

I hear the smile in his voice as he replies. He's definitely thinking the same thing that I am. "I do my best."

BEFORE

MAY 7 AT 5:27 PM

mockingbird:
Guess who canceled again . . .

eastcoleman:
Hailey.

mockingbird:
That was too easy to guess. I'm afraid I don't have enough friends.

eastcoleman:
I'll share mine with you if you want.

mockingbird:
Aww, that's sweet of you.

eastcoleman:
That's just how I am.
Why did she cancel?

mockingbird:
It's Hailey. Why do you think?

eastcoleman:
A guy?

mockingbird:
Ding ding ding! 100 points!

eastcoleman:
You can't be serious. Has she ever canceled for another reason?

mockingbird:
Not lately. I understand it, really. I get that she wants to spend more time with Tony.

eastcoleman:
You're defending her again. I'm not saying this to rub it in, but because you asked me to point it out when you did that again.

mockingbird:
Yes, thank you. I know I should stop doing that. She can't always cancel at the last minute. Even for Tony.

eastcoleman:
No, she really can't.

mockingbird:
Maybe I really do need your friends.

eastcoleman:
I'd be happy to share.

mockingbird:
You're a good friend, do you know that?

eastcoleman:
I do my best.

PART 4

Chorus

CHAPTER 13
Easton

Birds—Imagine Dragons

It's late by the time I drive Rayne back to school in the rattly old van that my dad gave me for my seventeenth birthday. That was right before the guys and I had our first gig and we needed a way to transport our instruments, especially Jax's drum kit. The van wasn't in the best condition even then, and now it's almost falling apart, but somehow it still drives.

Rayne and I didn't talk much more after she told me everything; we just lay next to each other on my bed and listened to music. At some point we ate the ice cream. It was already half melted, but that didn't bother us. The silence between us wasn't uncomfortable, but somehow companionable. It didn't need to be filled with words.

"See you tomorrow morning?" Rayne looks at me questioningly, one hand already on the door, ready to get out, when I stop the van in the parking lot in front of campus.

"If you come to class, I'll see you tomorrow."

She smiles almost imperceptibly, and I can't help but hope that I'll see a real smile on her face soon.

"See you then." She opens the door and a burst of frigid air rushes into the car. Rayne makes a face. "It's too cold in Boston."

I can't disagree with her. It really is much too cold right now. But she probably feels it even more acutely compared to the warm Southern California winters.

"But spring is beautiful here."

"Somehow, that doesn't comfort me at all." She shivers and hunches her shoulders. "That's not for ages."

"About two and a half months."

"Then it'll be March. How warm is it here in March?"

"Hmm. Around forty-five degrees?"

A look of horror crosses her face. "That's still way too cold!"

I have to laugh. "The right clothes help. You'll get used to it."

"Somehow I doubt it. It's nice and warm in LA right now." She sighs wistfully, and suddenly she looks sad. It's clear she's missing more than just the warmer temperatures.

"But it doesn't snow in LA."

She glances meaningfully out the windshield. "It doesn't here, either."

"Yes, but it will soon."

"You sound pretty confident, considering the fact that it's been raining for the last few days. The rain here is horrible, by the way."

"I won't argue with that. But it's going to snow at some point, I promise."

"If you say so." She's about to get out, then changes her mind. Before I can react, she leans over the center console toward me and her lips touch my cheek, just for a moment. It's so brief that

I almost think I imagined it when she quickly pulls back. But the touch is enough to send small, very unexpected shocks through my body. "Thanks for listening. Good night, Easton."

I clear my throat, but my voice is still hoarse when I reply. "Sleep well, Birdy."

This time she actually gets out, closing the door behind her quietly and carefully, not like Beck and Colin, who always slam the door so hard it feels like they're going to tear the van apart every time.

Rayne's shadow blends into the darkness, and I wait until she's walked through the gate before I put the van in gear and drive out of the parking lot.

When I get home, Beck and Colin are in the living room. They're sitting on the sofa watching some Netflix series I don't know.

"Where were you?" Beck doesn't even look up when I enter. He knows it's me, anyway.

"I took Rayne home," I say, and my best friend turns to look at me so abruptly that I hear his back crack.

"*What?* She was *here*?"

"Who's Rayne?" Colin only looks up from his phone briefly before he goes back to texting. He's so clearly distracted that he must be talking to Emma. They've been together since high school, but since Emma started college at Stanford, they only get to see each other every few weeks, and they communicate by text because Colin hates talking on the phone. He was the only one of my friends who didn't make fun of me last year when I spent almost every free minute on my phone texting Birdy.

"Text Girl," Beck explains, and Colin actually puts his phone down. His pierced eyebrow rises in disbelief.

"The girl who's been ignoring you for the last six months?"

"She wasn't ignoring me." Sighing, I collapse onto the sofa next to Beck.

"Um, yes she was?"

I shake my head. "No, she wasn't. She's just been going through a lot," I reply. I haven't told Colin or Jax who Birdy really is. The opportunity didn't come up in the last few days, and it didn't feel right to tell them. I'm not sure why. Beck only knows because he was the one who recognized her at the record store.

"Text Girl is Rayne Bellamy," my best friend says promptly, as if he's reading my mind.

I give him a dirty look, but he just shrugs and grins. *So what? They would have found out sooner or later anyway*, his eyes seem to say. He's probably right, but I would have liked to make that decision for myself.

"Rayne Bellamy? What does that have to do with—" Colin breaks off, blinking frantically. "Wait. Rayne Bellamy? As in Liam Bellamy's daughter?"

"Exactly." Beck sounds way too excited.

"What the hell was Liam Bellamy's daughter doing here? And why didn't I know she was Text Girl?"

I groan. "Because I only found out three days ago."

"How did you find out? Come on, don't make me drag it out of you."

"I didn't know you were so nosy, Colin," I say dryly.

"I'm usually not. But you were texting Liam Bellamy's daughter! I think that deserves some curiosity."

"Her name is Rayne," I say, because it bothers me that he's only talking about her in relation to Liam. She's more than just his daughter.

"Yes, I know. Pretty name." Colin waves it off, and I roll my eyes. "Why was she here? How did you meet?"

"Where's Jax?" I ask, rather than answer his questions.

"Fucking around somewhere. No clue. It doesn't really matter right now."

It does. Since things ended between him and Skye, Jax has hardly been home at all. They weren't even really together—Jax kept saying it was just sex—but now I'm not so sure anymore.

"Just tell the damn story, East."

"I don't want to have to repeat everything two or three times." I try to talk my way out of it, but I should have known that it wouldn't work. Colin can be pretty stubborn when he wants to be.

"Don't worry, I'll tell him," Beck offers. Helpful as usual.

I give in. It's pointless to resist, anyway. My gut tells me that this won't be the last time Rayne comes over, and it would be nice if my friends behaved themselves when they see her.

So I tell Colin about Rayne's visit to the record store—if I didn't, Beck would probably feel compelled to fill him in anyway—and how we ran into each other again at the New England School of Ballet. I give them the short version, without mentioning Rayne's breakdown or anything else she told me. That's none of their business.

Still, Colin looks serious when I finally stop. He's always had a knack for reading between the lines, and since his dad died when he was thirteen, he's probably the only one of us who can truly understand Rayne's pain. "How is she?"

I shrug and sigh. "Not good," I answer honestly. Just because I'm not telling them the whole truth doesn't mean I want to lie to them.

None of us speaks for a few minutes, and the only sound is the voices on the TV.

"She's not Text Girl anymore?" Beck finally asks.

"No, she's not."

"And now you're . . . what, friends?" Colin pushes back his reddish-brown hair and looks at me curiously.

I don't know why I blush. Maybe it's because I have to think about how her lips brushed my cheek and it triggered something in me that I definitely didn't expect.

"Of course, what else?" I make an effort to keep a neutral expression on my face, but when Beck begins to laugh quietly, it's clear that I didn't do such a good job of it.

"Oh boy," he says, and even though it doesn't really mean anything, at the same time it says far too much.

CHAPTER 14
Rayne

Lost Along the Way—All Time Low

I was out like a light as soon as I got home, but I'm still exhausted when my alarm clock rings the next morning and Mae and Zoe come to pick me up for breakfast. Crying at Easton's last night completely wiped me out.

My friends chatter nonstop on the way down to the dining room. Either they don't register how quiet I'm being, or they can tell I'm not feeling well and are respecting my silence. Even though I slept soundly, the night was too short, and yesterday took way too much out of me.

Everything hurts, and when the first class begins, I'm ready to give up right there and then because my muscles are killing me. Of course I don't, though. I grit my teeth and carry on.

It'll get better, sweetheart. You can do it. Every day will be a little easier than the one before.

Mom's words are burned into my memory. I was ten years old; we were practicing in her attic studio, and I had just burst into tears because I couldn't lift my leg as high as all the other girls in my class in an arabesque. She was right. It really did get a little better every day. *I* got better, until I eventually reached my limits. There are reasons that I've only practiced halfheartedly in the last few years.

This is my second day at the New England School of Ballet, and so far it's not getting any better. My muscles are no longer accustomed to the constant tension and strain. It frustrates me even though it shouldn't; I knew this would be difficult. Still, I feel like crying.

The fact that Easton is here stealing glances at me in the mirror doesn't help. It only distracts me. We don't have time to talk today. After our first class together, we both have other things to do. He's in a rush and gives me a quick smile before he disappears. But that smile is enough. It makes me feel a little bit better.

Pointe class is just as much of a disaster as it was yesterday, even without pointe shoes. When we finally join the sophomores for pas de deux, all I want is to crawl back into bed.

Francesca, our teacher, assigns Chester to be my partner. He's a slim, dark-haired boy with a friendly smile and kind brown eyes. He's nice and doesn't let on how awful it must be for him to have me as his partner. Still, I'm infinitely relieved when the day is finally over.

I spend the evening alone in my room with headphones on, reading a book. I'm not used to being around so many people all the time anymore. I need a break from their stares, their conversations, and the unspoken questions that so many of them clearly want to ask but fortunately don't.

At some point I fall asleep, only to wake up in the middle of the night with my headphones still on and music playing. I don't bother getting up and getting ready for bed; I just take off the headphones and go right back to sleep.

When I wake up on Wednesday, I feel better. My muscles still ache, but at least I can move without whimpering in pain.

"It went pretty well today," Mae says cheerfully after pointe class.

"Hmm," I say, and she gives me an encouraging smile.

"Really. You may not see it, but we do."

"Mae, I'm not even wearing pointe shoes." I take off my slippers and toss them carelessly into my bag.

"You'll get there. Just give yourself time. Miss Chelsea probably wouldn't let any of us dance en pointe in our first week back from a six-month break."

I remain silent. I know that's not the only reason. I also can't dance en pointe because my technique is simply not there yet. It doesn't matter that I was able to do it for three years before my world fell apart. Right now, I'm just not good enough.

"She definitely wouldn't," Zoe confirms, but there's a sympathetic undertone in her voice that says she understands exactly how I feel.

I wish it made me feel better, but it doesn't. Instead, I'm drowning in self-pity. It's disgusting.

"You know, I'm a little jealous that you're both taking Melanie's class," Mae says, changing the subject when I don't answer.

I'm grateful to her for that, because I can't deal with this right now.

"It's not every semester you get the chance to work with a choreographer who's worked with One Direction and Lady Gaga."

"Why aren't you in it?" I ask her, forcing myself to shake off thoughts of my failure and my miserable self-pity. I've only been here for three days. I really do need to give myself more time.

"Because Mr. Conrad assigns us to our classes, and he obviously decided that I'm not worthy of working with the fabulous Melanie Duncan."

"Drama, Mae," Zoe says dryly.

"I think drama is very appropriate right now." Mae pouts and stands up. "But it's okay, lyrical jazz is also cool. I have to go now, see you later!" She blows us a kiss and glides out of the room.

Slowly, the studio fills up again. Zoe and I change out of our tights and into black leggings and put on loose shirts over our leotards.

"Oh, shit," she suddenly says softly. I follow her gaze. Two girls are just entering the room, one small and brunette and the other slightly taller, petite and blond and pretty.

"This isn't good," Zoe whispers next to me, but I don't understand what she's talking about.

"Why?"

"That's Lia, Jase's sister."

"So?"

"Jase is in this class too, and the two of them don't get along with each other at all." Zoe's forehead creases with worry. I'm about to ask more when Jase walks in with Skye. His laughter stops abruptly when he sees his sister. She sees him at the same moment and goes pale.

Seeing both of them together, the resemblance is unmistakable. The same blond hair, green eyes, and outrageously attractive features. Hers are softer than his, but now, when Lia sees her brother, her expression hardens. Her smile disappears just as quickly as his.

Jase stiffens, then comes over to us while his sister turns to her friend.

"Hey," Zoe says quietly. He doesn't say anything, just kisses her gently on the temple and looks at her in a way that makes me feel like I should look away. She asks him a question, but I can't hear what it is. I look over at Skye, who just shrugs and then shakes her head with a barely audible sigh.

"Hello, everyone." A bright, cheerful voice gets our attention. A woman with short platinum-blond hair and bright eyes rushes into the studio. She's younger than I expected, maybe in her early thirties. "Nice to see you all here! I'm Melanie Duncan, but please just call me Melanie." Some of the students begin to whisper to each other, but she continues speaking. "I'm very excited to be teaching you this semester. Does anyone here have experience with contemporary dance?"

Most of the students shake their heads, and one boy raises his hand briefly.

"What about modern dance?"

Lia and her friend raise their hands, along with another girl and guy. Five out of thirty-five students.

"Great, then most of you are at the same level. That's good. I'll tell you what my plans are, and then we can get started, okay?"

We nod, and she gestures for us to sit down on the floor. She sits in front of us in one fluid motion and crosses her legs.

"I probably don't have to tell you that contemporary dance is different from ballet; you already know that. But I'm going to say it anyway, because I'm sure that some of you are here even though you don't necessarily want to be."

She sizes us up, her bright eyes wandering from face to face.

Her gaze is open and friendly with no judgment, even though her words make it sound otherwise. "In ballet, you strive for perfection. Cleanly executed moves are very important. You know what you're aiming for and you follow the rules. Contemporary combines elements of ballet with modern and jazz dance. But we don't have any rules. You make up your own. It's all about your interpretation. While ballet strives to defy gravity, we welcome it. We focus on tension and release. We focus on your *emotions*."

Her words send a shiver down my back, and everything inside me freezes up. I don't want to focus on my emotions. Not here. Not with so many people watching.

"Does that sound good?" She smiles at us, but the only answer is a subdued murmur that makes Melanie laugh quietly. "I see that I'll have to convince you that we're going to have fun together. We will, I promise. But of course it isn't just about fun. You're here to learn and grow, and since I only have one semester with you, I'd prefer to make it clear right away what I expect from you. I want you to approach this class with an open mind. Contemporary dance isn't ballet, and I know most of you dream of performing on the world's greatest stages, and that's fine. But don't forget that there's more to life than ballet, and that this could actually help you. That's why you'll all soon be choosing a song and developing your own choreography to it."

"But we already have choreography classes," Lia's friend says.

"I know," Melanie replies. "I'm not asking you to come up with a perfect routine by the end of the semester. I want you to choose a song and let your feelings speak, and then express exactly that through your dance. If you want, and if it's easier for you, you're welcome to work in small groups. But we'll talk about that when the time comes. In these first few weeks, I want you to loosen up a bit and get comfortable with this new territory." She stands up. "Shall we get started?"

We stand up slowly, some with more enthusiasm than others. Contemporary dance is mainly performed without shoes or slippers, and it feels strange to stand on the hard floor in thin socks. The first hour passes quickly, and we hardly dance at all. Melanie mainly shows us some warm-up exercises. We're supposed to familiarize ourselves with gravity, relax our backs and let our shoulders loose. Most of us find it difficult to let go of the tension that's been drummed into us as long as we've been dancing.

I concentrate on my breathing and feeling the floor beneath my feet. My body softens and my muscles work, but it's different from this morning. The tension leaves me as I exhale and my movements become fluid and less cramped.

"Very good, Rayne." Melanie praises me and gives me an appreciative smile, which I automatically return, although not quite as enthusiastically as she does. It feels strange that this is so easy. I've been torturing myself for two and a half days, and now . . . How can it be so easy all of a sudden? It's not supposed to be like this. I came here for ballet, not for . . . whatever this is.

"Zoe, relax. Try to let yourself go. Let gravity work for you."

Melanie walks slowly around the room, correcting the others while soft piano music echoes from the speakers connected to her phone. "Pay attention to your breathing. Breathe deeply into your belly. As you exhale, let everything go."

The hour passes quickly. Faster than all the others, and when Melanie finally ends the lesson and dismisses us for lunch, I actually feel strangely grounded.

"Rayne, do you have a minute?" Melanie stops me as I'm about to leave the studio with Zoe, Jase, and Skye. My stomach cramps, and the calmness that filled me just a moment ago disappears. I hesitate for a second and then nod. "Of course."

"Should we wait?" Zoe asks, but I shake my head.

"Go ahead, I'll catch up with you."

"Okay, see you." She waves, and then the three of them disappear. It's only Melanie and me. I stop a few steps away from her. My fingers search for the rings on my other hand, but they're in my room on top of the dresser.

Something in Melanie's face changes, becoming darker, sadder. *No, please don't.*

"I admired your father very much," she begins. I feel my nails digging into my hands and realize I've clenched them tightly. Why? Why does she have to bring up my dad now?

"Me too," I hear myself say. What the hell am I saying?

"I'm sorry for your loss."

"Thank you." I blink, avoiding her gaze.

"Mr. Pearson told me you just started here."

"Yes." I shift uneasily from one foot to the other. Where is this conversation going?

"I just want you to know that I understand if you have a hard time at first."

"Who says I'm having a hard time?" My voice sounds harsh and cold even to my own ears, and my heart is beating much too hard. Am I so bad that my teachers are already talking about me? Am I doing that poorly?

"No one. But I've been watching you for an hour now. You're less controlled than the others."

"Less perfect, you mean."

"That's in the eye of the beholder." She smiles, and I realize she isn't trying to be mean. Maybe she just wants to help me. "As far as I'm concerned, less perfection is good. You still seem a little inhibited, but you're not as held back as the others. If you give contemporary a chance, you could be very good. You have potential."

"Really?" I stare at her, stunned, not sure what to make of her words. I should be happy. Instead, all at once I feel queasy. I'm new at this school, trying to fit into this world, trying to belong with all the other girls, but I'm not one of them. I'm not here because I have a dream. Not like them.

I don't dream of the big stage. I'm here because of Mom. I'm here to become like her, and even though Melanie is praising me, it feels a bit like a failure at the same time. Because apparently, I have the potential to be imperfect.

"Really. Now off you go. You've got a break now, right?"

I nod.

"See you on Friday, Rayne."

It seems that I'm dismissed. I hesitate for a second and then nod again before leaving the studio. I'm already on the stairs when I hear the soft sounds of a piano coming from the third floor. My feet carry me upstairs of their own accord, even though I don't know for sure it's Easton playing. After all, he's not the only pianist who accompanies classes. Still, I have a feeling it's him.

The music is coming from the middle studio on the right. Sure enough, Easton is sitting at the shiny grand piano. His eyes are closed, completely focused on the music as his fingers dance across the keys. I put my bag on the floor as quietly as possible and stand in the doorway, watching him. Yes, it's rude of me, but I can't just walk away or interrupt him. All I can do is listen and watch.

He has such beautiful hands. And a beautiful smile. With dimples. Oh my God, he has dimples. Why did I never notice that before? I guess I've never seen him smiling like this. His hair is falling into his face. It's longer than it was in the photos that he uploaded to Insta, the last of which is already a few months old. I like this length on him, but I don't know why.

I'm not sure if I made a noise or something, but somehow he senses I'm here and stops playing. He turns around to look at me. I catch my breath as his smile gets wider.

"Birdy," he says, and the way he says my nickname makes my stupid heart skip a beat.

"Hi."

"What are you doing here? Shouldn't you be at lunch?"

"I heard you playing." I feel for my rings again, only to once more find they're not there. I'm not even wearing my bracelets.

"You heard me playing?" He slides over to make space for me on the piano bench.

"Yeah. I thought I'd come and say hello." I swallow and move toward him. As I sit down next to him, there are butterflies in my stomach, and I don't know why. I didn't have them when I lay next to him on his bed, at least not like this. I think. But I was also worn out from all the crying, and it was darker, and I couldn't see his face as well as I can now.

I'm afraid I might just be confused.

"Hi," he says and laughs softly. The sound of his voice makes my skin tingle. I can't help it. Also, he's looking at me so intensely.

I put my right hand on the keys and begin to play a simple melody, one of the first that Dad taught me when I was a kid.

"Why am I surprised that you can play?" Easton asks, sounding amazed.

"I don't know."

His arm brushes my shoulder as he raises his right hand and places it next to mine. He plays the same melody as me, just two octaves lower.

"Do you play any other instruments I don't know about?"

"A little guitar. That's all."

"Why didn't you tell me?"

"You didn't ask."

I don't have to look to know he's rolling his eyes, and I smile a little.

"As if that ever stopped you."

"I'm not good enough to mention it," I reply, my fingers gliding over the keys a little faster now. I haven't played in a long time, and only now that I'm doing it again do I realize how much I've missed it.

"Somehow I don't believe you."

"Then don't." I glance at him for a second, and he really does roll his eyes. But he's grinning. "What are you doing here, anyway?" I ask quickly, before we can talk about me more. Also, I realize I haven't actually asked him yet.

"Right now, or in general?"

"Both." Why does that sound like a question?

"Right now, I'm still here because I fell in love with this grand piano. Honestly, it feels totally different from playing the electric piano at home."

I nod. I can imagine that. I've never played an electric piano. We had pretty much the same kind of piano as this one in our living room.

"Aside from that, I have to go to the record store anyway." He looks at his watch. "In about an hour. It's not really worth going home in the meantime and then leaving again in half an hour. I'd rather stay here and play a little."

My fingers pause mid-motion, and only the notes that Easton is playing ring out for a moment. Then he stops too.

"Sorry. I interrupted you, didn't I? I can leave and let you play." I make a move to get up, but Easton grabs my wrist and gently pulls me back onto the stool.

"You didn't interrupt me, and I don't want you to leave," he says, looking directly into my eyes. So directly that I can feel the blood rising to my cheeks.

"Okay," I say.

"Besides, there's still a lot I have to tell you."

I have to smile, and he stares at my mouth, which suddenly feels terribly dry.

"You have a beautiful smile," he says. He sounds so sincere that my face gets even hotter. His voice sounds a little hoarse too. Help, what's going on here?

"You wanted to tell me some things," I remind both him and myself.

He clears his throat. Is he blushing too? "Right. So basically, I'm here because the school needed a replacement for Deborah, and Jase suggested me."

"How do you and Jase know each other, anyway?"

"He lived with me over the summer. Not last year, but the year before. He was having problems with his parents. He needed a place to sleep, and we had room."

"That was nice of you."

"That's just the way I am," he says, nudging me, and now I roll my eyes. But I can't stop the smile that's sneaking its way onto my face. How does he do that? How can he make me smile so easily?

"I know." I look at him more closely, and now he's definitely blushing. I shouldn't find that cute, but I do.

"Anyway," he continues, "Jase got me the job, and that's why I'm here."

"Isn't that a lot? The job at the record store, here, and also the Lighthouse. You're still working at the Lighthouse, right?"

"Yeah, I am, but it doesn't hurt to have some extra money. We really need a new van."

"But will you have enough time for the band?" I can hear the worry in my voice.

"Yeah. It's no big deal. I'm here in the mornings, at the record store in the afternoons, and I only DJ at the Lighthouse on weekends anyway."

"How's the band going?" I ask, immediately feeling guilty for not asking sooner. I'm a terrible friend.

"Pretty good. We're still waiting for our big break." He laughs, but it sounds hollow.

"So the search for a label is—"

"Slow? Yeah, you could say that."

"Sorry to hear it."

"Don't be. You can't do anything about it."

"Is there any way I can help?" The question slips out before I can stop it.

Easton turns to me in surprise. "No. I really couldn't ask you to do that."

"You didn't, I just offered."

"Still, it wouldn't be fair."

I tilt my head and try to figure out what he's thinking. "Why not?"

"Because . . ." He trails off, takes a deep breath, and shakes his head. "It just doesn't feel right."

My heart skips a beat, because someone else in Easton's situation probably would have taken me up on my offer. But Easton is Easton, and he doesn't do that kind of thing.

"If that ever changes—"

"I'll let you know," he says, finishing my sentence.

"Good. That's what I wanted to hear."

"There's something I want to hear too." He reaches for my hand and puts it on the keys. "Play for me, Rayne."

CHAPTER 15

Easton

I Can Wait Forever—Simple Plan

Rayne has small hands with long, graceful fingers. Her hands are too small for a pianist; she can't spread them wide enough. But she's good anyway. Damn good, even. She plays with such ease, and it's a version of her I've never seen before. Admittedly we haven't spent much time together in the "real world," but I can't help wondering why she never mentioned that she plays piano, and guitar. I wouldn't be surprised if she could sing too.

I'm afraid I might have to ask her soon, and then ask why she's really at this school. She misses her mom, I get that. But I've been watching her every morning for the last three days, because I can't help it when we're in the same room. She's never looked as relaxed dancing as she does now, her fingers gliding confidently over the keys.

Her expression softens and turns introspective, but the sad lines around her mouth have disappeared. She plays and plays, and I try not to think about the fact that I just lied to her. Not a bald-faced lie, but not the whole truth, either. It wasn't just that I couldn't accept her offer to help us because it feels wrong, although that does play a part. But that's not the whole reason. I couldn't accept because she has enough problems of her own. She shouldn't have to worry about ours.

A small, selfish part of me would have liked to say yes, because it would have made everything so much easier. Rayne has all the right connections. She knows the right people, and she knows how the business works. With her help, we might finally find a label. But I couldn't do that to her, or to myself. My guilty conscience would probably kill me, even if putting an end to the endless cycle of sending out demos and getting rejected over and over again does sound appealing.

On the other hand, who knows? Maybe we're just not good enough, even with Rayne's help. There must be some reason why no one wants us.

Liam wanted you, a voice in my head reminds me. It sounds like hope. Only there isn't much of it left now.

Yes, Liam wanted us. But he's dead, and I can't block out the other voice, the one that keeps telling me repeatedly that we're not good enough, that *I'm* not good enough.

What if Liam didn't really think we were that good? What if he only wanted us as the opening act for his tour because his daughter liked our songs? But no, that can't be. You don't take a band you're not completely convinced of on tour just because someone close to you likes them. Or do you? Shit, I hate my mind.

"Easton?" Rayne's voice snaps me out of my thoughts, and now I feel guilty for asking her to play and not even listening properly.

Great, Easton, you really knocked it out of the park this time.

"Is everything okay?"

"Yes, fine. Sorry, I was just thinking."

She smiles a little. "Yeah, I noticed."

"You're good," I say, because at least I heard enough to be able to say that with total confidence.

Her eyes narrow. "Are you only saying that because you like me?"

Now I have to laugh. "No, of course not. You're *really* good."

Now she shrugs, and something about the gesture makes me feel uncomfortable. It's something in her eyes. Something that's very familiar to me. Self-doubt.

I reach for her hand before I can stop myself. "You're good." I look at her intently and her eyes widen. She opens her mouth, and my gaze is drawn to her lips. She has such damn beautiful lips.

Oh, fuck.

Wrong direction, Easton.

I blush. I hate it, but I can't help it. To make matters worse, Rayne blushes too, and it's getting out of control.

"How's the dancing going?" I say, changing the subject awkwardly. We need to talk about something, because silence would kill me right now. Her lips really are beautiful and I'm still holding her hand, which is small and soft in mine.

I quickly let go, but it's too late. Heat is rising in my middle, and that's not good at all.

I feel Rayne tense beside me. "Okay." Her voice sounds different than it did a moment ago, more distant, and the heat inside me is abruptly replaced by an unsettled feeling.

"You don't sound very convinced," I say slowly. My thoughts are racing, and the voice in my head is back, but this time it's telling me very clearly that I should have kept my mouth shut.

"Yeah, well . . . maybe it's because I'm not." She grimaces, reaching for the rings that are usually on her fingers but still aren't there.

Yes, I really should have kept my mouth shut. I know Rayne, and I know ballet isn't an easy subject for her. So why couldn't I have just asked about something else? Unfortunately, the answer is simple: I didn't think before opening my mouth.

"Why are we talking about me right now anyway?" she asks defensively. "A minute ago we were talking about you and the band."

"I know, but—"

"Don't. Don't say it's about me now," she says sharply. I don't understand how everything could have gone so wrong so quickly. "God, why did you have to bring that up?" She jumps up, her hands clenched into fists, her whole body trembling, and I want to take back what I just said, every single damn word of it. "I'm not convinced because I'm not good, okay? I'm really not, and it doesn't help that everyone keeps telling me to take my time and not put pressure on myself. They're telling me it's okay that I'm not keeping up, but it's *not* okay."

Her words are sharp as needles, and I have a sinking feeling that somehow I'm missing something, something I don't know. There must be another part of the puzzle, otherwise she wouldn't react this way when . . . when what? I don't have the slightest clue.

"Rayne." I say her name, and that's all I can say because I'm thrown off balance, and I don't know what else to say. I don't know how to make it better.

"Don't you have to get going?" she asks, and the hard tone in her voice makes it extremely clear that for her, this conversation is over.

I look at my watch, and she's right. I should really go. But I don't want to. Not like this.

"Yes, but—"

"Go ahead. I should leave too."

"Rayne . . ."

She shakes her head, her shoulders slump, and she looks just as lost and hurt as she did the day before yesterday in my room. My heart cramps painfully because this time, it's because of me. This is all a huge mess.

"I'm sorry. I should have kept my mouth shut." Feeling helpless, I run my hands through my hair. We're back at the place we were a few days ago. She wants to leave, and I don't know how to stop her, or even if I should.

No, I definitely shouldn't, because Rayne reaches for her bag, which is lying on the floor next to the door. "It's okay, honestly. I'm sorry. I'll see you tomorrow, okay?"

She doesn't even wait for an answer, just rushes out of the room before I can say a word.

That went well.

* * *

My mind isn't working properly when I'm sitting in the living room with the guys that evening, trying to write a new song. It's totally empty. There are no intelligent thoughts, no words to be set to music. Only emptiness.

And Rayne.

Frustrated, I drop the pen onto the table. Jax, who's sitting at his keyboard trying to fit a melody to my nonexistent lyrics, looks up.

"No joy?"

"Nope."

"Everything okay?" Beck puts down his notebook and takes off his headphones. I need silence when I write, but he needs music. He usually listens to classical music, and I still don't get how that works for him. But in the end it really doesn't matter, as long as it's right for him.

"This isn't my day." I wave dismissively and grab my phone.

"Stress with Text Girl?" Colin asks, and I shoot him a dirty look.

"You could stop calling her that."

He shrugs, grinning. "Maybe if you introduce her to us sometime. What's going on? Are you two having problems?"

"What makes you think so?" I retort, because I don't want to admit he's right.

"Because you look exactly like I do when I'm having trouble with Emma."

I'm about to answer when my phone lights up with a new notification on Insta. Rayne just wrote to me. I breathe a sigh of relief, and Colin laughs.

"And now she's written back. God, you're so lovesick."

"I'm not," I say, rolling my eyes. But I can't stop myself from blushing.

"Yes, you are. What do the rest of you think?" I don't look up from my phone, but I'm sure Colin is winking at Beck and Jax and they're grinning like the idiots they are.

"Pretty much," Beck agrees.

"I'd say so too," says Jax.

"You're so annoying." I get up and give my friends a dirty look.

"Nah, we're awesome." Jax grins broadly. "And you've got a killer crush, dude."

My face burns. Shit, I hate this. "What if you just write that song?" I suggest, because I can't think of a clever comeback right now.

"Sure," Beck says. But he's grinning so much that I wonder what I've done to deserve friends like these. "You could help us, though. Maybe Rayne is your new muse."

"Grow up."

"As your friends, it's our job to be childish. Now go on, answer the girl," Colin replies, pointing to my phone.

"I hate you." I give my friends a charming smile.

"No, you love us," Beck replies, and unfortunately he's right.

"Just a little less right now."

"All the more love for Rayne."

"God, you're terrible." I turn my back to them, because there's no way I'm going to answer Rayne with my friends sitting there and making uncalled-for comments. I ignore their hoots of laughter as I go up to my room and throw myself on the bed before finally opening Instagram.

mockingbird:
We've never argued before.

eastcoleman:
I know, it was awful.

Her reply comes so quickly that I'm sure she was online the whole time waiting for me to read her message. I probably would have done the same thing.

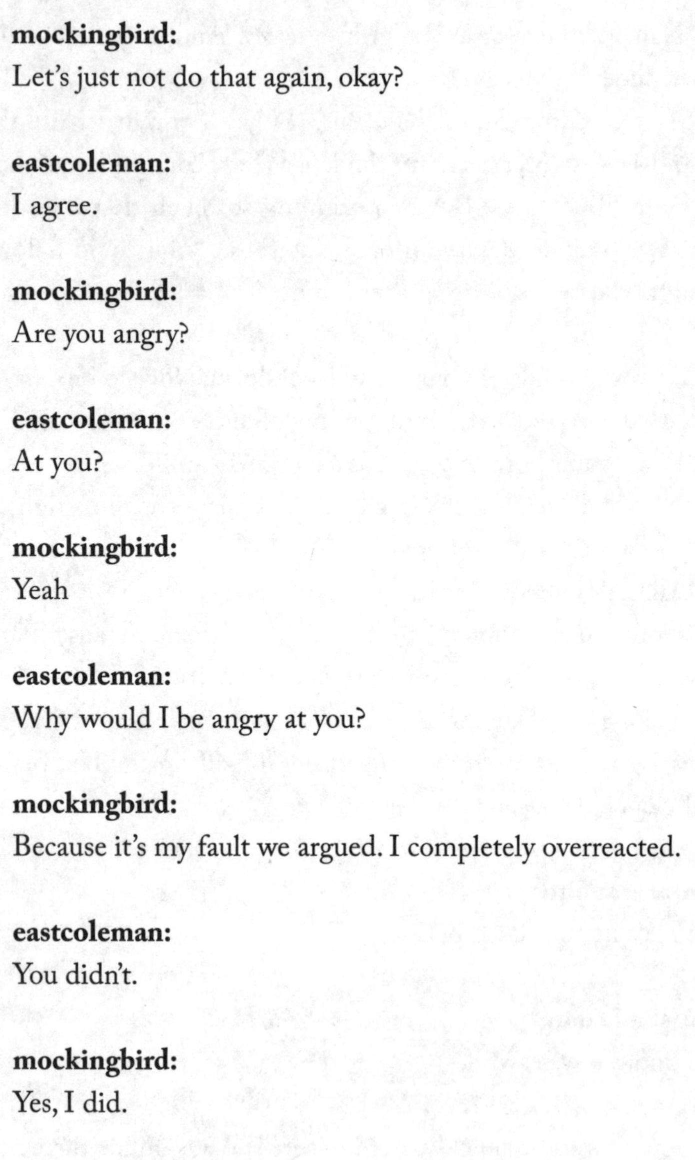

mockingbird:
Let's just not do that again, okay?

eastcoleman:
I agree.

mockingbird:
Are you angry?

eastcoleman:
At you?

mockingbird:
Yeah

eastcoleman:
Why would I be angry at you?

mockingbird:
Because it's my fault we argued. I completely overreacted.

eastcoleman:
You didn't.

mockingbird:
Yes, I did.

eastcoleman:
Maybe a little. But I understand, honestly.

mockingbird:
Really? Because sometimes I feel like I'm completely incompetent.

eastcoleman:
First of all, you're not. And second, yeah, I feel that way sometimes too.

I start when the phone in my hand suddenly begins to ring, announcing an incoming Instagram call.

"Why do you feel incompetent?" Rayne asks without preamble as soon as I've accepted the call. Her voice is soft and gentle, and suddenly I feel much too warm. Shit.

"Because there has to be a reason why we still haven't found a label."

"Yeah, there is. They're all idiots and obviously have no clue what they're doing," she replies so earnestly that I have to laugh.

"Yeah, I doubt that."

"I don't want you to doubt it. You guys are good."

"I don't want you to doubt yourself, either."

"Easton . . ."

"Yeah, okay." I sigh, and then I just say it, the awful truth. The thoughts that so far I've only shared with Beck. "It's just frustrating, you know? We've been giving everything we have for years, and still, nothing seems to be right. I want to write new songs because apparently our old ones aren't good enough, but my head is totally empty. Sometimes I wonder if the whole thing is worth it."

"It is," she says without a second's hesitation. "You're good, and the songs are amazing. Dad believed in you." Her voice cracks as she mentions her dad, and it breaks my heart a little. "Otherwise he wouldn't have wanted to take you on tour with him."

"Are you sure?"

She clears her throat, and I want to see her right now, because I have to know if she's okay. She doesn't sound like it. "Yes, I'm totally sure. He would have never done something like that just because I told him I liked you."

"That would have been okay too," I say softly. It's stupid and it doesn't make sense, but it's totally true, unfortunately.

"That's sweet, but it's also total nonsense. It wouldn't have been okay. But you guys are really good, I'm not just saying that. Have a little faith. You're going to make it, I can tell."

"You believe in us?"

"Of course. Otherwise I wouldn't have offered to help you."

"That's true too." I stare at the ceiling, just like the day before yesterday, and I suddenly wish she was lying right next to me and not a few miles away in her bed in the dorm.

"I have a feeling that the only thing missing is the right song. The one that changes everything. Huge cliché, right?"

"Kind of." I can hear her smiling. "But yeah. Maybe you just need that one song."

"But no pressure, right?" I laugh.

"You don't have to write it alone."

"I know. Beck is a songwriter too."

"But you want to be the one to write it, don't you?"

I sigh. She's seen right through me, which shouldn't surprise me at this point. "Yeah, I do."

"You're going to do it," she says decisively. Just like that.

"Will you help me?"

"Maybe. I'm not very good at it."

I don't like how she keeps saying she's not good enough. Dancing, piano, writing songs. I'm pretty sure she could do all those things very well if she only believed in herself.

"Says who?"

"Me."

"I call bullshit."

"It's not! I just can't."

"Wanna bet?"

"I'd win that one."

"I'm not so sure about that," I say.

"I am."

"Why can't you believe in yourself, Birdy?" My hand wants to reach for her, but she's too far away. I can't touch her or wrap my fingers around hers, even though it's the only thing I want right now.

"I don't know," she replies, sounding lost.

"Believe in yourself. I do."

She's silent for a moment, and so am I, but somehow the silence feels like something more. Like words that need to be said, words that neither of us has enough courage to say.

"Do you know, when you hugged me the other day . . . that was the first time anyone hugged me since the funeral," Rayne says, breaking the silence.

I freeze. I don't know what I expected her to say next, but it wasn't that.

"The first?" I ask. I can't keep the sound of shock out of my voice.

"Sad, huh?"

"What about your grandmother?"

"She's not the hugging kind." A desperate laugh escapes from her. "God, now I'm crying again. I'm sorry, I don't want to cry all the time, it's just—"

"Stop apologizing. You don't need to. Especially not for crying."

"Yes, I do. Otherwise at some point you'll get sick of my whining."

Her words cut me to the heart. "Never," I promise, and I hope she believes me.

CHAPTER 16
Rayne

Shapeshifting—Taylor Acorn

I'm lying in bed staring at the ceiling. It's still too early to go to sleep, but I'm exhausted. Easton hung up twenty minutes ago, and since then my room has been completely silent. Too silent. I can hear my own thoughts.

Why can't you believe in yourself, Birdy?

Yeah, why can't I? It should be a lot easier to believe in yourself than in someone else. After all, no one knows you better than you know yourself.

But I think that's the whole problem. When you know yourself too well, you just set your standards even higher. You want to be perfect and always do your best, but sometimes your best just isn't good enough. I'm decent enough at all kinds of things, but I'm not exceptionally good at any of them. That's why I have so much trouble believing in myself.

I'll never be able to dance as perfectly as Mom. My voice will never be as good as Dad's, or so unique that everyone recognizes it instantly. I can't write songs like he could. I could scribble lyrics all over my walls, but as soon as I sit down in front of a notebook and try to cobble a few lines into a song, something blocks me. I've tried, of course. But every time, my mind goes blank. Nothing. Not a word. I have nothing to say, even though I actually have a lot to say.

It used to be different. I can still remember sitting with Dad in his studio, watching him write songs and then trying to create something of my own. Back then, the stakes were lower. I was a kid, and I just wrote whatever came into my head. It didn't matter if it sounded good or had potential. They were just ideas, but I want that lightheartedness back. Why did it suddenly disappear?

Probably because I grew up. Tears are overflowing from my eyes, not unexpectedly. I cry too much, but I really don't want to anymore. I'm tired of it, but I can't do anything to change it. All at once I hear Dad's voice. He's singing my song, and though I've been resisting it for the past few months, I can't resist it now. I haven't listened to "Mockingbird" . . . since that day. I couldn't. I couldn't bear it. But his voice and words are still in my head.

You were always chasing heights
Beautiful and brave
Dancing fearlessly through the nights
Knowing you were safe

Maybe that's the crux of the problem. I don't feel safe anymore. I'm not brave. I'm scared, and I'm so damn alone that everything hurts.

I'm shaken out of my thoughts when there's a knock at my door. Zoe or Mae, I'm pretty sure. They're out in the hall and want to convince me to come to the common room. Someone got a screen for a movie night, and I should really join in. I need a distraction and to spend time with my new friends. I need to do things teenagers do.

Sighing, I crawl out of bed. Distraction might not be the worst idea. But when I open the door, it's not my friends standing there but Easton. All at once I'm self-conscious in my old sweatpants and school hoodie, my hair tied up in a messy bun. Not to mention the fact that I probably look like I've been crying.

"Hey, Birdy," he says. His voice is so gentle that I almost instantly feel better.

"What are you doing here?" I blink at him. I can hardly believe he's really here. I don't have to ask who let him in or told him which room is mine. It must have been Jase, and the thought of Easton asking his friend about me gives me a warm feeling inside.

"One hug in six months is definitely not enough," he says with that crooked smile that brings out his dimples.

I make a sound that's half laughter, half sob as Easton pulls me close. He kisses my forehead lightly just for a moment before I bury my face in his chest. He holds me tight, and I hope he never lets me go again.

BEFORE

MAY 28 AT 3:58 PM

mockingbird:
Did you always know you wanted to be a musician?

eastcoleman:
No. As a kid I wanted to be a fireman.

mockingbird:
Sweet. Then how did you figure out that music was right for you?

eastcoleman:
I don't know. At some point I just figured it out. I think it was one of those days that I couldn't play because we were on some family outing. Don't ask me where, probably some relative's birthday party. I was at a point when every day that I didn't play or write songs felt wrong, somehow incomplete. It felt like something important was missing.

mockingbird:
Sounds like it was really the right thing for you.

eastcoleman:
I can't imagine it any other way.

mockingbird:
What about your parents? What did they say about you wanting to be a rock star?

eastcoleman:
Mom dealt with it better than Dad. She would have preferred that I study music and become a music teacher instead of performing myself, but she understood. Dad wanted me to teach just so I'd have a secure job to fall back on, but yeah . . . In the end I had to make myself happy, not them.

mockingbird:
So teaching was never an option for you?

eastcoleman:
No, never. I didn't want to watch others living my dream, just because I wasn't brave enough to take the risk that it wouldn't work.

mockingbird:
I get it. That's admirable.

eastcoleman:
What about you, Birdy? What do you want?

mockingbird:
If I only knew. I really don't have the slightest idea. My friends all know what they want to do, and they're all looking forward to college. I just sit here and don't know what to do with my life.

eastcoleman:
You'll figure it out.

mockingbird:
Everyone says that, all the time. But what if I don't? What if I never know what I want?

eastcoleman:
That won't happen.

mockingbird:
How can you be so sure?

eastcoleman:
Because I know you, Birdy.

mockingbird:
Somehow that's not very helpful.

eastcoleman:
Then I'll tell you something that is: Listen to your heart. I think you know what you want, but you just don't dare to admit it.

mockingbird:
I hate you.

eastcoleman:
Liar. Why are you afraid to say it?

mockingbird:
Because I'll never be good enough.

eastcoleman:
Who says?

mockingbird:
Me.

eastcoleman:
Stop standing in your own way. What do you want? Tell me. I won't tell a soul.

mockingbird:
Music. I always wanted to be a musician.

eastcoleman:
Then trust yourself.

mockingbird:
I'll still never be good enough.

eastcoleman:
Yes, you will. I believe it.

CHAPTER 17
Rayne

Older—Shallou, Daya

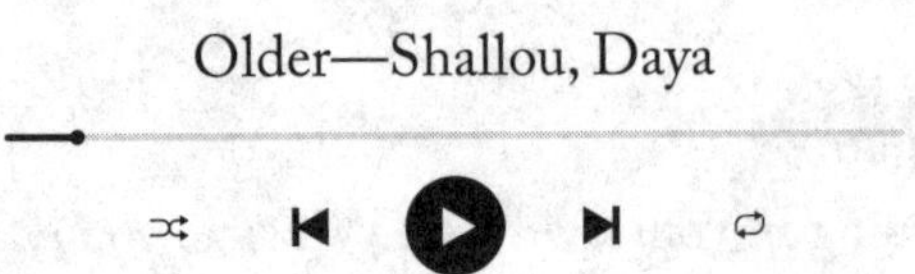

"What's up with you and Easton, anyway?" Mae asks as we pack up our things after class. Fortunately, the most difficult part of our day is already over. It's time for lunch.

"How long have you been wanting to ask Rayne that question?" Zoe asks, giving Mae an amused glance. I, on the other hand, turn red. After all, we're not alone here. Jase and Skye are here too, and Jase is Easton's friend. I can't believe Mae is asking about this when he's standing right next to us.

Jase is putting on his school hoodie, and when he pokes his head through, he's looking straight at me. There's an intense look in his green eyes. He nods at me, in silent reassurance that Easton won't hear anything about the discussion from him. I'm grateful, but I still wish Mae hadn't asked the question in the first place. I also wish she'd drop the subject. But she doesn't, because she's Mae, the most curious person I've ever met.

"Um, since her first day? So just about three weeks," Mae replies.

Three weeks. It's crazy how quickly time has flown. But at the same time, it hasn't. Three weeks at the New England School of Ballet have already challenged me more than two years of lessons combined at my old ballet school. Between dance classes in the morning, theory classes in the afternoons, and sometimes strength training or cardio on top of that, most days leave me so exhausted that I'm usually in bed before ten, falling asleep because my body is totally overwhelmed by what I'm demanding of it.

The soreness in my muscles isn't quite as bad anymore; at least there's been some improvement. Still, I'm nowhere near the level of the others. And it doesn't help to hear at least twice a week that I should take my time and not put so much pressure on myself. First Mr. Conrad and Melanie and now even Francesca have started with it after the lifts with Ches didn't work in class today either.

They don't get that their words just put me under even more pressure. They obviously don't believe I'm up to it. Otherwise, they wouldn't say something like that. They wouldn't try to slow me down. But I'm not giving up. I don't want to. I'm not allowed to.

"We're waiting!" Mae trills, and it takes a moment to remember what she asked me.

"Nothing's going on. We're friends," I reply, reaching for my bag.

"Uh-huh. Sure. I always look at my friends the way you and Easton look at each other every day."

"We don't look at each other like anything," I protest, feeling a telltale flush rising to my cheeks.

"Liar," Mae nudges me, and unfortunately, she's right. We *do* look at each other. Just not the way she thinks we do.

"No. We're really just friends," I say firmly. But then I stupidly think back to that evening two and a half weeks ago when Easton came to my door.

One hug in six months is definitely not enough.

I blush deeply now, because I also remember what he smells like. Like soap and a hint of cinnamon. And I only know that because he hugged me. I buried my face in his chest, and my nose wasn't blocked from crying that time, so I could breathe him in. Then I think about his lips against my forehead, and the heat in my cheeks rushes deeper, through my whole body, gathering in my center. I don't dare look at Mae and Zoe. If I do, I'll blow my cover.

"You're blushing," Mae says. Of course she noticed anyway.

"Mae, leave her alone. If she says they're just friends, they're just friends," Zoe says, but she doesn't sound at all convinced. I think it's unfair that they're so united on this while I refuse to think about it. I certainly can't think about what *might* be going on that I haven't realized yet.

We're friends. Just friends.

Anything else . . . no, I can't deal with that. Not now. I need friends. I need stability. I need security. With Easton, I feel safe.

"Yeah, Mae, leave her alone," Skye says. "You're way too nosy, and someday someone is going to kick your butt."

"Maybe." Mae shrugs nonchalantly. "But not today." She gets up off the floor and puts on her jacket. It's gotten even colder in the last few days. The sky is full of thick gray clouds, and the whole city just seems to be waiting for the snow to start.

I am too. I hope Easton can keep his promise.

"Lunchtime," Mae says, and with that, the subject is dropped. Thank God.

We're the last to leave the practice building because we dawdled so much after pas de deux. Everyone else is probably in the dining room already. We've almost reached the dorm when I spot a familiar slender figure walking quickly toward the parking lot.

"Grandma?" I call, feeling confused. I slow down involuntarily. My friends walk on without me for a bit before they notice I've stopped. Grandma doesn't even notice me. She doesn't look in my direction, and that hurts.

"Rayne?" Zoe sounds worried, but I can't focus on her right now.

"Go on ahead. I'll be there soon," I say, and turn quickly to follow my grandmother. I only catch up with her when she's almost reached her car.

"Grandma!" I call again, and now she finally reacts. She turns slowly to face me. Recognition flashes in her eyes, but the expression on her face is just as distant as it usually is. She doesn't smile. Not even a little.

"Rayne," she says. Just my name, nothing else.

"What are you doing here?" All at once I'm not so sure if I even want to know the answer. She was here at my school, and she was about to leave again without seeing me. Without talking to me.

"I had an appointment with Travis," she replies coolly. No, that's not what I wanted to hear.

"And now?"

"I have to go." She glances at her delicate watch, and my stomach drops.

"Does that mean you didn't even want to say hello?" I sound just as hurt as I feel. I don't understand why I feel this way. We lived together for six months and hardly spoke to each other. Why should she suddenly come and ask how I'm doing? Why is it suddenly important to me that she's interested? When we lived in the same house, I didn't want to talk to her. In the last three weeks . . . I refused to think about the fact that she didn't get in touch. And I didn't reach out to her, either.

But to see her here now, and to know that she just wanted to leave again without even asking me how I'm doing, hurts more than I thought it would. Maybe a part of me hoped that she would reach out to me eventually. Talk to me. After all, she was the one who avoided Mom and Dad and me for years; she's the one who should make the first move.

"Rayne, I'm very busy at the moment." Grandma brushes invisible lint off her black coat, not looking at me.

"So that's it? I moved out, and now we don't even talk to each other anymore?"

"We didn't talk before, either," she retorts, and of course she's right about that. I know that I didn't make any effort. Not recently, and not in the last few months. I'm an adult, I could go to her. But there's a small, childish part of me that resists.

"Why not?" I blurt out. "Why didn't we talk to each other?"

Annoyed, Grandma shifts from one foot to the other. She doesn't want to be here with me; it's all too obvious. "You were holed up in your room for months."

"You didn't come up once to get me out of there." I hate hearing my voice break. Grandma doesn't seem to notice, though.

Why didn't you come?

I want to ask this question that means so much to me right now, but I can't get the words out.

"Rayne, I really don't have time for this right now. Let's talk about it another time." Grandma reaches for the door handle of the car.

"When? When do you want to talk about it?" I snap at her. I have no idea where this anger is coming from. It doesn't make sense. But it's here, and it's making my heart beat way too fast. God, what am I doing? I don't even know if I really want to talk to her. But I do know that it pisses me off that *she* doesn't want to. Shouldn't she want to? She's my grandmother. My parents are dead. We're all that's left of our family. Why doesn't she want to talk to me?

"I'll be in touch," she says curtly, and I know immediately that she won't. I can see it in her face.

I don't say another word. Nothing comes to mind. Instead, I watch her get into the car without even looking at me. The engine starts, and the car drives away. She's gone.

* * *

I skip afternoon classes because I wouldn't be able to concentrate anyway, even if I wanted to. I also ignore Mae's and Zoe's messages asking if everything is okay and where I am. I don't answer because I don't know what to say to them. Instead, I leave campus and walk through the city without the slightest idea where I'm going.

When it starts to get dark, I find myself on a familiar street. I've been to Easton's place a lot in the last few weeks, especially on weekends when Mae was out with Tristan and Zoe was out with Jase, or all four of them were together. Sometimes Zoe's brother, Caleb, and his boyfriend, Parker, were there too. They always invited me to come along, but Skye never wanted to join, and I didn't want to be the third wheel.

Instead, I'd go to Easton's house, and we'd listen to music in his room. I'd watch him playing his electric piano, searching for that one song and not finding it. And now I'm at his door again, unannounced and not really knowing how I got here. The lights are on in the living room, and I can hear music, loud and raw. The guys are practicing, so this is probably the worst time to show up. I could text Easton, but I don't want to disturb him. To be honest, I don't think he'd read my message right now anyway.

Unfortunately, he's the only person I want to talk to at the moment. He's the only one who knows at least a little more than just fragments of my life. He's the only one who knows that my parents and my grandmother have barely spoken since I was born, because I told him. I told him almost everything. Except for the not entirely unimportant fact of who I am. But he knows that now too, so it doesn't count anymore.

"Hey. Need some help?" The friendly voice makes me whirl around in surprise.

Behind me on the sidewalk is a young woman with dark hair and dark eyes. She's a little older than me. I can't tell by exactly how much, maybe a few years. In any case, she looks more grown-up than I do in her fitted beige coat. She's pretty, and something about her seems strangely familiar.

"No. I . . . I was just going to visit a friend," I stammer. "But I don't think this is a good time, so I'd better go."

An indecipherable expression crosses her face, and then unmistakable curiosity. "Who are you here to see?"

"Easton," I say, not knowing why I'm telling her that, since I have no idea who she is.

But then she smiles, and she has the same smile as he does. Even the dimples. Except I find her brother's much cuter.

Oh God, stop it, Rayne. Didn't you say just a few hours ago that you were just friends?

"I'm Willow," she says. Of course I know her name, and now that I know who she is I also know that she's seven years older than me, three years older than Easton. She works as a dancer at the Boston City Ballet. "Come on in. It's always a good time to show up here."

She walks past me into the house, and I feel too shy to follow her right away. On the porch in front of the door, she turns around and looks at me. "Are you coming?"

I nod and hurry after her. "I'm Rayne, by the way," I say after a moment, and a knowing sparkle shines in her eyes.

"Ah, Text Girl."

I blush. "What? I don't get it."

"The guys call you that. Well, Colin does. He's not so good with names." She laughs openly while I briefly consider turning around and running away.

But Willow opens the door and disappears into the house, and somehow I can't help but follow her. Because today, for once, all the guys from We Are No Saints are here, and I'd really like to meet the one who gave me such an unflattering nickname. I don't know if it's just a coincidence or intentional on Easton's part, but I haven't met any of his friends yet, even though I've been here a lot in the last few weeks. Colin has been visiting his girlfriend Emma for a while. She studies at Stanford, but she didn't come home for the holidays, so this was the first time they'd seen each other in weeks. I'm not so sure about Jax and Beck. Beck was out at the gym, and Jax . . . Easton mentioned briefly that he was trying to get over something. I didn't ask what it was about. In any case, none of them were here when I was.

I follow Willow into the house, and as usual, when we enter the hallway, there are jackets hanging over the banister and too many shoes scattered wildly under the coatrack, where even more jackets hang. I get a warm, homey feeling, and the black hole in my chest gets a little smaller, even if it's just a tiny bit.

I can hear Easton singing. His voice fills the house and every cell of my body. It's like silk on sandpaper. That's exactly what it sounds like. That's how it sounded the first time I heard him sing, and that's how it still sounds today, nine months later.

I know the song. "Meet Me at 3 AM." It's one of my favorites, a story about friendship. About always being there when you're needed. Even at three in the morning.

Willow slips out of her coat and shoes. She's so incredibly graceful that you can tell she's a dancer, and I wonder briefly if it's the same for me. Probably not. I take off my jacket while the guys keep playing. Either they didn't notice that someone came in or they're ignoring it. Jax sets the tempo, his sticks thundering on the drums, and the others follow. It's a cheerful pop-rock song with serious lyrics, and I love every second of it. My pulse accelerates to the beat of the music, and when Willow beckons invitingly, I take a step toward the living room. But I still feel like an intruder, because neither Easton nor the others know I'm here, or that I'm watching them. Because there's no way I can't.

I've never seen them play live, only in their videos. But jeez, there's nothing like the real thing. Even here in this small living room, the energy they give off is somehow . . . unreal. Almost magical.

I get goose bumps, and at the same time I break into a wide smile without thinking about it. It just happens, as it always does when I hear this song. Easton's voice gets under my skin, just like it did the first time I heard him, when I found their cover of "Mockingbird" months ago. In another life.

His voice works its way into my heart; but that already happened ages ago. By now, his voice is almost as familiar to me as my own. My stomach flutters just hearing him sing. It's pretty much perfect when his voice blends with Beck's in harmony.

They don't notice me, completely lost in their own world, focused only on the music and the instruments in their hands, until the song fades away. Easton smiles when he stops, and there are those dimples again. They make me smile too.

Silence spreads through the living room until Jax laughs. It's an enthusiastic and oddly relieved laugh. A proud grin spreads across Colin's face.

"That was awesome! I don't think we've been that good in ages," Beck says. I'd agree with him if I could—no matter that I've never heard them play live before—but I can't get a word out.

"No, we really haven't." Easton seems so relieved that it worries me.

"That was fantastic!" Willow agrees. She puts an arm around my shoulders and pulls me all the way into the living room. "By the way, East, you have a visitor." Four pairs of eyes turn to look at me at once.

"Hi," I say, raising my hand in an awkward gesture. Easton's eyes go wide, and then he smiles again. He smiles at me, and damn, my heart starts racing again.

"Rayne," he says, sounding surprised and pleased. "What are you doing here?"

CHAPTER 18
Easton

Not Another Rockstar—Maisie Peters

"I wanted to . . . actually, am I disturbing you? I can leave if it's not a good time." Rayne's gray eyes dart nervously around the room before settling on me. There's something in her gaze that worries me. She wouldn't have just shown up here without telling me unless something was wrong.

I shake my head and put down my guitar. "No, of course you're not disturbing us."

"We're done for today anyway," Beck says, giving me a meaningful look. But I refuse to read anything into his expression.

"That's right. Besides, we're looking forward to finally getting to know Text Girl." There's a slightly cheeky grin on Colin's face. I shoot him a dirty look. Can't he just shut up for once? I know he's only acting this way because for some reason, he feels obliged to look out for all of us, but I don't need anyone to look out for me. Especially not when it comes to Rayne.

"What was your name again?" A crease forms between Rayne's

eyebrows, and I don't do a very good job of disguising the laughter that threatens to break out as a cough. Rayne knows Colin's name. She knows all of us.

"Colin."

"Oh right, I remember." She taps her temple, the corners of her mouth twitching with a suppressed smile. Beck and Jax don't bother trying to hide anything; they burst out laughing. And yes, Colin absolutely deserves it.

"I like her," Beck whispers to me. I'm not sure why my stupid heart skips a beat when he says that.

"You like anyone who stands up to Colin," Jax interjects. He's standing close to us, and I really hope Rayne doesn't hear what my friends are saying.

But when she looks at me with a knowing twinkle in her eyes, it's clear that she heard every word. Willow stands with her arms crossed behind Rayne, watching the whole scene. She looks a little too amused for my comfort.

"What are you doing here, Sunshine?" Beck asks, adding the next silly nickname for Rayne.

Her eyebrows go up. "You two are very creative with nicknames."

Beck shrugs, unconcerned. "And yet they're both so fitting." He winks at her, and that's when I decide it would be a good idea to get out of here.

"I actually quite like my name," Rayne retorts, her chin jutting forward a little.

I push past my friends and stop in front of her. "Everything okay, Birdy?" I ask quietly.

She lifts her head, and there's something in her eyes: a mixture of anger and sadness that makes it pretty clear that nothing is okay.

"He can call her Birdy without her objecting, but we—" Beck stops again abruptly when I give him a warning glance over my shoulder.

"Well, he's her friend. We're just his friends, and let's be honest, Text Girl and Sunshine are really bad nicknames," Jax says. For once, I have to agree with him.

"Thanks," Rayne says, and smiles.

"I'm going to get changed, and then we can go, okay?" I tug at my shirt, which is sticking to my skin from the rehearsal.

"Where to?" Rayne asks, taken aback. I can't blame her. After all, we've spent most of our time together over the last few weeks in my room. But the guys weren't home then. I can't say why, but it's easier to be here with her when they're not around.

"It's a surprise," I say, even though I have no idea where I want to take her. All that matters is that we're not going to stay here. Not with these nosy idiots. "I'll be right back."

I squeeze her hand and hear one of the idiots laughing as I step into the hallway to the stairs. As soon as I'm in my room, I pull my shirt over my head and toss it carelessly next to the bed. I go to the dresser and get a fresh T-shirt, a warm hoodie, and a knit hat. It's cold outside.

Less than five minutes later, I'm back downstairs. Willow and Rayne are sitting on the sofa, my sister with her legs tucked up under her and Rayne perched on the armrest, one of her legs dangling in the air. She's playing with her rings again, but otherwise she seems pretty relaxed, especially considering that my friends are undoubtedly talking crap again.

"Shall we?" I say, and Rayne looks up. She smiles as she gets to her feet.

"I'd say it was great to meet you, but that might be a bit of an exaggeration," she says to the guys. But she's still smiling, and I guess they all know she's kidding. "See you later, Jax, Beck . . . Guitar Boy." She winks at Colin, a gleam in her gray eyes.

He laughs. "Touché, Text Girl."

"Okay, that's it," says Beck. "We're definitely keeping her."

Rayne wrinkles her nose indignantly, but the look of amusement on her face is impossible to miss.

"Jeez, guys, can you please behave yourselves just for once?" Willow rolls her eyes. To her, my friends are like little brothers. Sometimes I think she'd like to teach us all to be a little more mature, but I'm afraid the time for that is long past.

"I have a feeling this is going to be fun." Rayne gets up and comes over to me. I put a hand on her back. It feels like a reflex, though I don't know where it comes from. I seem to have an urgent need to connect with her right now. She glances at me and bites her lower lip, just for a moment, before quickly looking away again. But it's too late. My pulse races to dizzying heights and I feel much too warm.

Beck and Jax are laughing, and honestly, I hate my friends right now because I can't concentrate when they're making fun of me. Especially not when Rayne looks at me like that and bites her lip. Her pink, full lips. Fuck. I think I have a huge problem.

I have to force myself to look away from her, so I put on my shoes while she's slipping into her jacket.

"Did you bring a hat?"

She stops. "No, why? Where are we going?"

"I'll never tell." I take off my hat and put it on her head. It's a little too big for her, but it looks great on her anyway. She blinks up at me as I pull the soft knit hat a little too low on her forehead, my hands touching her face, and that's not good. I let go of her abruptly, but I can see something change in her eyes.

"So it's a surprise?" she asks, her voice a little huskier than a moment ago. But maybe I'm just imagining it.

"Yup," I reply, quickly grabbing Beck's hat, which is lying on the second step. He won't need it anymore tonight.

Rayne looks like she's about to object, then decides against it. We leave the house and walk to the van. It's freezing outside, and the dark clouds are hanging so low that it's bound to start snowing soon. It's about time. The last few weeks have just been cold with no sign of precipitation. I want it to snow soon, otherwise I won't be able to keep my promise to Rayne. Maybe it wasn't such a great idea to promise her something I have absolutely no control over, but now it's too late. I open the passenger door, and Rayne climbs in before I walk around the car and get behind the wheel.

"Are you going to tell me what's going on?" I ask as the engine roars into life with a loud stutter.

She sighs heavily, and out of the corner of my eye, I can see her start playing with her rings again. "Maybe I just wanted to see you."

My heart skips a beat. It's really not good how much I want that to be the truth. Unfortunately, I know it's not. "That sounds like a question."

"But it's not."

My heart falters. No, don't think about why, or what that means—whether it means anything at all. I take a deep breath and smile at her, then force myself to focus on what's important.

"Rayne, I know you. I can see that something's wrong."

She's silent. It's a silence that speaks volumes.

"You don't have to talk about it if you don't want to. That's okay," I say gently, turning to look at her as I stop at a red light.

"It isn't. I just don't know *how* to talk about it." She sounds frustrated.

"Let it out when you're ready. And if you're never ready, that's okay too." It's crazy how much I want to take her hand right now. But the next second, the light turns green, and I hesitate for long enough that someone behind me honks their horn. So my hand stays where it is and the van starts moving again.

"Why are you so understanding, anyway?"

"Willow raised me properly," I reply, and have to laugh when Rayne does.

Hearing her laughter feels like a victory. A victory over what, I don't know, but it still feels that way. My throat feels strangely narrow, and I have to clear it before I point to the cable that's attached to the radio and continue talking. "You can be in charge of the music."

"You trust me with the music?" Rayne sounds almost surprised, but she's already getting out her phone and plugging it in.

"Who could I trust more than you?"

"I don't know. Your friends, maybe? I like them, by the way, even though their nicknames for me are annoying."

"Yeah, seriously. But Rayne, you're my friend too."

Just a friend, Easton. Don't forget that.

"That's different."

"No, it isn't. Besides, I know your taste in music."

"That's true." She taps on her phone screen, and I instantly recognize the song she's chosen.

"Really?"

"So what?" She sounds much too cheerful. Artificially cheerful. "It fits you."

"'Not Another Rockstar' fits me?"

"Yeah. At least a little." She sighs, and I can sense her shoulders slump. "I saw my grandmother," she suddenly says.

I involuntarily clench the steering wheel a little tighter. "It didn't go well?" I guess.

"No. She came to the school. Not to see me, but because she had some meeting with Mr. Pearson. I saw her by chance as she was walking back to the parking lot. I was just on my way to the dorm for lunch."

"Shit, that's not good. Did you talk?"

"Only for a few minutes," she says, and then she tells me about the conversation.

I hate having to concentrate on the road right now. I want to look at her when she's talking. But I also get the feeling me not being able to look at her right now is the only reason she's able to tell me all this.

"You know, in a way I understand where she's coming from. I mean, I didn't try to get in touch with her either. I made no effort when I lived with her, or after I moved out. It was easy not to talk to her. After all, we barely know each other. Maybe it's not fair, and maybe I have no right to be mad at her and blame her. But wasn't it her job to take care of me? And yeah, I know I'm an adult now, at least officially. But I don't feel like one. I really don't." The desperation in her voice pierces my heart. "I don't know why it bothers me so much now. After all, I spent months not caring whether she was there or not. It didn't matter to me if we talked. I didn't even *want* to talk to her, and I still don't. But I want *her* to want it, you know?"

"Yeah, I get it," I say. I really do, but I don't like it. Not any of it. Rayne is an adult, yes, but she lost her parents. Her home. Her friends. And her grandmother doesn't care about her at all. Maybe I'm just biased, and maybe she's partly right that she could have just as easily reached out herself. Still, I'm on her side.

"I'm a terrible person, aren't I?"

"No, definitely not. I think it's very normal to want her to care about you."

"Do you really think so?"

"Yeah. I'd like to give you some wise advice right now, but I don't have any."

"That's okay. You can't have wise advice for every situation." Her voice trembles and I glance at her. Now there's really nothing I can do about it. I put my hand on hers and our fingers intertwine. I squeeze her hand, and the corners of her mouth go up in a faint smile, which quickly fades again.

"It hurt that she came to school and didn't want to see me. I think if she hadn't come and I hadn't seen her, it wouldn't bother me at all. I probably wouldn't even be thinking about her."

"That's not so bad."

"But isn't it a bit hypocritical?"

"Maybe. But I still get it."

She squeezes my hand and then lets go. I wish she wouldn't. My hand feels strangely empty without hers in it.

"That's why I came. Because I knew talking to you would help."

"I always help when I can."

"I know. Okay, enough of my whining," she says. "Where are we going?"

BEFORE

JUNE 2 AT 3:11 AM

eastcoleman:
If you could live anywhere, where would you choose?

mockingbird:
It's three in the morning and that's what you're asking me?

eastcoleman:
Three in the morning for you, six for me. Why are you awake already? Or still?

mockingbird:
I got a message, and I forgot to turn off the sound, so . . .

eastcoleman:
I'd say I was sorry for waking you up, but I'd be lying.

mockingbird:
Are you drunk, Easton?

eastcoleman:
Maybe a little. But answer the question. Where would you want to live?

mockingbird:
In a little house on the ocean. I don't care where. But it's got to be right on the beach. Maybe LA would be nice, at least it's always warm here. I want huge windows and lots of empty walls I can write all over. And a balcony off the bedroom, so I can always watch the sunsets.

eastcoleman:
What is it with you and the ocean?

mockingbird:
I grew up by the ocean.

eastcoleman:
Come on, Birdy, that's not the whole truth, is it?

mockingbird:
No, of course not. But if you noticed that, then you can't be very drunk.

eastcoleman:
Was that a test?

mockingbird:
Just a little one.

eastcoleman:
You're avoiding my question again, right?

mockingbird:
Maybe.

eastcoleman:
Come on, tell me your ocean secret.

mockingbird:
It's not as spectacular as it sounds. It's probably how a lot of people feel about the ocean.

eastcoleman:
I don't mind. Tell me what's up with you and the ocean.

mockingbird:
When I'm by the ocean, everything is quieter. I feel like I can breathe properly and that everything will be okay. Because the ocean is endless and I'm so small in comparison. Then my problems feel a little smaller, and a little less bad. Pretty cliché, huh?

eastcoleman:
No, not really. Just honest.

mockingbird:
Shall I tell you the truth?

eastcoleman:
Always.

mockingbird:
I want to see the stars. It's always dark enough to see them at the beach, no matter where you are. As long as it's not cloudy, at least. My parents gave me a star for my sixteenth birthday, and whenever I'm at the beach I can see it. Okay, I admit it's hard to tell exactly which star is mine, and it's probably just my imagination, but I like to pretend I can see that star from anywhere. Then it always feels a little bit like Dad is with me, even when he's away.

eastcoleman:
You have your own star?

mockingbird:
Crazy, right?

eastcoleman:
Just a little. You'll have to show me sometime.

mockingbird:
Yeah, maybe someday I will.

CHAPTER 19
Rayne

Overflow—Marianne Beaulieu

Easton is taking me to the beach. I've known it since we left the city. As soon as the darkness swallowed us up, broken only by the headlights of oncoming cars, I knew exactly where we were headed. We've left the lights of Boston behind us, and it's dark and quiet now. It gets even darker and quieter when he steers the van into an empty parking lot and turns off the engine. We're in the middle of nowhere, not a soul in sight.

Easton smiles. He gets out but still doesn't say a word. I'm silent too, because there's a lump in my throat and tears in my eyes, which I'm frantically trying to blink away. He brought me to the ocean. He remembered what I wrote to him that night in June, when he messaged me in the middle of the night asking me what my favorite place was. The three-hour time difference between LA and Boston never stopped us from writing to each other.

"Are you coming?"

I look up, realizing only now that I'm still sitting in the passenger seat, staring out the windshield into the darkness, while Easton has been waiting outside for me. I nod and open the door. The cold wind hits me and I shiver, hunching my shoulders. I'm glad Easton gave me his hat.

We set off in silence, leaving the parking lot behind and approaching that quiet, steady sound that's so comforting to me, even though we're in Massachusetts and not California. It's still the same, and it's somewhere right in front of us. My steps quicken of their own accord, and the sound becomes louder. There it is: the ocean, dark and vast. Easton is close behind me; I can hear his footsteps.

"You brought me to the ocean," I say, my voice choked with emotion. I'm about to start crying, I know it. He remembered, and he brought me here because he knew it would help me. The endless sea is spread out in front of us, and the infinite but very cloudy sky is above us. He knows being here makes everything seem a little less bad.

"Yeah. I was hoping you could show me your star, but I don't think that's going to happen tonight." He's right; it's not. Even if the sky were clear, there'd be no guarantee I could find it. I haven't looked for it since I left LA.

"But that's not why we're here," he says before I can remember what I don't want to think about. He caresses my hand, just like he did at the house.

What is it about these fleeting touches that makes them feel like silent questions and answers at the same time? They say things like *I'm here* and *you're not alone*, and they do something to me that they shouldn't.

I feel an ache of longing in my chest. It hurts, but not terribly.

Not like being left alone. It's different this time, because Easton brought me here. Because he's here and isn't leaving me alone, just like he promised.

I don't know what I did to deserve him. I don't know if I even do deserve it, him being here for me. He's somehow helping to hold together whatever is left of me, while I'm not doing anything for him in return. There's nothing I can give. But maybe I don't have to.

Real friendship doesn't work like that, after all. It's not about debts, about somehow repaying each other for help. It's mostly about being there for each other whenever you're needed, isn't it?

"What are you thinking?" Easton whispers, as if he can look into my head and see all the complicated questions in a tangled mess. Now his fingers aren't just brushing against mine; our hands are fully intertwined. I can hardly breathe. Then suddenly I can, as he gently holds my hand. It feels way too right, and that scares me. Part of me wants to let go because I don't know where we stand right now, but letting go is not an option for me. It never was.

I take a deep breath and just tell him the truth. I want him to know what he's doing to me.

"I don't know what I've done to deserve you."

He stops so abruptly that I almost trip over my own feet. "What?"

"You know what I mean." I don't dare look at him, but his grip on my hand tightens, and I almost believe he's afraid I might pull away. But that's just as much an option for him as it is for me.

What's going on here?

"Honestly, I have no idea. You don't have to earn me."

"But you do so much for me, and I—"

"You believe in me," he says, his voice sharp.

Now I have to look at him, because the last thing I want is for him to be angry at me. We promised each other we wouldn't argue anymore. If I've messed things up again, then . . . The voice in my head goes silent as I look into his eyes. I can't see the blue anymore, it's too dark, but I've seen enough of his eyes by now to know how intense it must be.

"You believe in me, Rayne Bellamy," he repeats, a little more gently, but no less emphatically. "You believe in me and the band, in our music and the songs I write. You do more than enough for me. I know that if I ever had a problem, you'd be there for me. You would, wouldn't you?"

"Always," I reply without hesitation.

"So don't tell me you don't deserve me. You do, but even if you didn't, you don't have to. That's not how friendship works. And we're friends, right?"

"Yes," I say, but all at once that quiet voice is there in my head again, shouting *No!* But I can't say it out loud, for way too many reasons that I don't want to think about right now because doing so will only make everything too complicated.

"Then stop worrying about it. It's not necessary. Really." He smiles at me, and a feeling of warmth spreads from my center.

"Okay."

"Good that we talked about it." He gently pulls my hand, and we start walking again in sync, toward the water. The sand gives way underneath our shoes.

"Do you think so? I feel like I'm making a big deal out of nothing."

"I always want to know what you're thinking, Rayne."

"Why?"

"So I can talk you out of the ideas that are bad for you and encourage you to stick with the right ones."

"How do you know which are right?"

"Um . . . I can usually tell by looking at you."

"Is that so?" I raise my eyebrows skeptically.

"Yes. You have a very specific look in your eyes when you're thinking about something you don't like. Like just now." He gives me a mischievous grin.

"What does that look like?" I'm genuinely curious, but he just shakes his head.

"I can't say. It's hard to explain. You'd have to see it for yourself to understand."

I sigh. "Then I guess it's not going to happen. I'm not about to try it in front of a mirror."

He laughs, and I'm overwhelmed by how much I love his laugh. His thumb strokes the back of my hand. Our hands are both chilled, but I'm not cold. How can I not be cold?

"Easton, how can you know me so well?"

"How could it be any other way?"

I don't answer. His question is justified. After all, I know him just as well as he knows me.

"Can I tell you something?" he asks after a while, as we walk side by side along the water. It's low tide, so the waves breaking on the beach are tiny. The air is clear, and although it's cold, much colder than in LA, it smells like home. Easton is still holding my hand, and it doesn't seem like he's going to let go anytime soon. I really don't mind.

"Please do," I manage to say, my voice cracking again. Maybe he can actually read my mind, and maybe he'll answer the questions I don't want to think about because I'm too afraid of the answers.

"I don't believe in fate or anything like that," he begins. I feel butterflies in my stomach, but I can't tell if that's a good thing or not. Strangely enough, it just seems to be a nervous flutter. A curious one. "But I think it was more than just a coincidence that we posted the video of the song your dad wrote for you. And it's not a coincidence that you found it and wrote to me afterward. I think it was meant to be, somehow. You know what I mean? Otherwise, you could have written to Beck or Jax or Colin."

"No, I wouldn't have," I disagree. That wasn't even a remote possibility.

"You wouldn't?" He sounds so surprised that I can't help but smile.

"No, definitely not."

"Why?"

"Because . . ." I hesitate, but it doesn't really matter now. We're alone on a deserted beach, and the world around us is dark and quiet, apart from the soft sound of the waves. I can also hear the much-less-soft pounding of my heart in my ears. "Because the only reason I clicked on that video ninety-seven times in a row was your voice."

For a long moment, Easton says nothing. Long enough that my skin starts to prickle uncomfortably. I've crossed a line, and that's not good. Not good at all.

Somehow, though, the boundaries of the world seem permeable today. I have no idea why, because everything is the same as always.

"Ninety-seven times?" he asks, and there's something in his voice that I can't quite make sense of.

"More or less." An awkward laugh escapes me. *More, actually.*

"That's—"

"A little crazy?" I finish his sentence.

"A little." He grins at me, and I elbow him gently.

"You're not allowed to agree with me."

"Of course I am. After all—" he stops and looks up at the thick, dark clouds. I notice it a moment later too. It's snowing.

CHAPTER 20
Rayne

Snow on the Beach—Taylor Swift, Lana Del Rey

I've never been on the beach when it was snowing before. Not very surprising, because it's usually too warm in LA for snow.

It feels surreal and pretty crazy. And maybe a little cheesy too. But the good kind of cheesy. The kind that makes your heart beat faster and puts a smile on your face.

The sky is still dark. Nothing has changed, but suddenly the night is much brighter because thick white snowflakes are falling on us. They start slowly, only a few at a time, and then more and more follow, falling faster. The snow mixes with grains of sand. Two infinites meeting, because you can't count either one. I want to stay right here in this moment forever.

"So I was able to keep my promise after all," Easton murmurs so softly beside me that I'm not sure if he's talking to me or to himself.

"You keep all your promises," I say.

"I try."

"I know." Two words, an almost-silent whisper because my

throat is tight again, even though everything feels beautiful and right.

All at once, the only thing I can think about is how I won't be able to tell Mom about this tomorrow morning. I won't be able to tell her that I was on the beach with a boy who knows me far too well, watching it snow. I won't be able to tell her about how good it feels when he holds my hand. Or when he looks at me. Or when he's just there.

I want to ask her what it means, or if it means anything at all. Am I just overthinking things that aren't real, like I always do? But Mom isn't here, and I can't talk to her about any of it. I can't ask Dad to distract me like he always did when the voice in my head got too loud. I look up and stare at the sky, my eyes open wide, refusing to blink so I don't cry. It's dark enough that Easton shouldn't notice, but of course he does.

"Hey." He takes my hand and then lets it go, but only to put his arms around me. Now I can't look at the sky and count snowflakes anymore, which is why I start crying. "It's okay," he whispers, his breath warm against my skin. But it really isn't.

"I hate this. I don't want to cry all the time."

"I understand. It's okay anyway."

I bury my face in his shoulder, and he just holds me again until I slowly calm down.

"Is there something I can do?" he asks as I pull away from him and wipe the tears off my cheeks. My skin feels tight, unable to handle the hot, salty tears and the cold, salty sea air at the same time. My chest feels too small for the whirlwind of emotions inside me.

I want to tell him there's nothing he can do, but maybe there is. There used to be one thing I could always do to make myself feel better, but the last few months I've been running away from it because it hurt too much. But obviously, running away didn't help. Who knows, maybe I was wrong to do that. Maybe I need to run toward it instead. Toward the pain, toward the memories. Maybe they'll hurt a little less if I embrace them instead of pushing them away.

Words in my head and a melody in my soul. Suddenly both are there, where they haven't been in so long. Answering Easton's question is suddenly so easy.

"There's nothing you can do for me. I have to . . . write." The word comes out as a sigh.

"Okay," he says, and the tightness in my chest eases a little. He doesn't ask why, even though I told him I couldn't write songs. That was the truth; I really can't. But just because you can't do something doesn't mean you shouldn't do it anyway.

My old room was full of lyrics. I scribbled my thoughts, which I squeezed into poems and lyrics, on every inch of the walls. They were never good enough. Not as good as Dad's. But they were mine. Writing has always helped me, and to be honest, I think that's why I stopped after Mom and Dad died: I didn't want to help myself. Maybe it's time for me to start again.

"Shall we write together?" I ask, because I'm sure I can't do it alone yet. One step at a time.

Easton smiles, his dimples reappearing, and he reaches for my hand again. "If you want."

"I want to," I say with a sigh. But this time it's a different sigh. One of relief.

"Let's do it."

We walk back to the van, but instead of driving back into town, we just stay here. We don't talk about it, but I think we both know that driving back won't help. His room, my room, it doesn't matter. Neither would be right. We'd be alone, but not really. There would be too many people around us, in the rooms above and below us.

Here on the beach, we're completely alone, just us and the snowflakes falling faster and faster, already covering the windshield so we can't see out. Easton gets a few blankets from the back and hands me two while wrapping himself in a third. "Let me know if you get too cold." I shake my head. I really don't want to go back to the city.

"Okay, then . . . may I?" He points to the glove compartment and leans over me when I nod.

All at once he's too close for comfort. So close that my heart doesn't know how to deal with it, which is silly because he just hugged me a few minutes ago. But somehow, this feels different. I can see his profile perfectly, all his features crystal clear, and a small, barely visible scar next to his ear that I didn't notice before. My fingers twitch, and I have to stop myself from touching it. Then he straightens up and pauses. His face is level with mine. He turns to look at me, and that's not okay either. I forget everything around us when he stares at my mouth. My breath catches and he swallows, and I bite my lower lip.

His gaze is burning into mine, and my heart is beating so fast that I can feel it in every cell of my body.

He wants to kiss me, I know it. I can see it in his eyes. They've got a glow in them that I've never seen before but recognize instantly. He wants to kiss me, and I want it too. I don't know why. Why now, of all times? But it comes at exactly the moment when

I want to feel his lips on mine. His gaze burns into mine, and my heart is beating much too fast and so hard that I can feel it in every cell of my body. I want him to kiss me, and he wants it too.

Easton leans forward just a tiny bit, and I want to move toward him, but I can't move at all. I can't look at him anymore. Instead, I close my eyes and lean back.

I can't. I just can't, even though I want to. God, I want to kiss him so badly it hurts.

But what if we do? What then? We're friends. Real friends. He's not the only friend I have anymore, but he's the one I don't want to lose at any price. Losing him . . . I don't think I could survive it. The risk is too great for the fleeting moment of a kiss. And I would lose him; there's no question about it. Sooner or later, it would happen, because that's what always happens.

I feel him pulling away. He clears his throat, and the sound hurts. "What do you want to write about?" he asks, his voice hoarse.

I need a few seconds to pull myself together. It takes a moment to recall why we're sitting in the van in the first place, and why there's a notebook and pen in my lap. But then I remember, and I answer him. We start working and ignore what almost happened. Neither of us mentions it, and after a while I wonder if I just imagined the whole thing. It's possible. It's probably best that way. Yes, I'm sure I just imagined it.

I wish I believed myself.

The first few minutes—or hours?—are a little awkward, a little weird. I can't concentrate, can't turn off my mind, even though that's exactly what I want to do. It's the whole reason we're sitting here, after all. But then Easton starts talking, helping me sort out the chaos in my head, and everything gets easier.

I think of Mom and Dad, and of Easton, and the words flow out of me, unchecked. When I don't know what to say or can't find the right word, he finds it. It's like he knew it all along.

Hours later when we're done, we both know we've just written the song that Easton has been looking for all this time.

DANCE WITH YOU 'TIL MIDNIGHT

Performed by We Are No Saints
Written by Rayne Bellamy and Easton Coleman

Blinking little lights
Seems like a night sky right at my feet
I've been here a while
Wondering if once again we could meet

But when the bell is ringing
The door wide open shut
Hell, everything is changing
And pulls me into the dark

But I won't turn back
I won't give up
I'll make it fucking right
Get lost in music
Lost in you
And dance with you 'til midnight

Forget to breathe
Forget to see
Forget my fucking name
I'm standing here

And hear the words
And I can't run away

There's something inside me
Something dark
That won't fade away
That burns me up
That pulls me down
But I know that I'll stay
I'll keep my head
I'll dry my tears
Set one foot, then the other
Fight for the beat
Run for the song
And fight like it's forever

I won't turn back
I won't give up
I'll make it fucking right
Get lost in music
Lost in you
And dance with you 'til midnight

PART 5

Verse 2

CHAPTER 21

Easton

Meet Me in the Hallway—Harry Styles

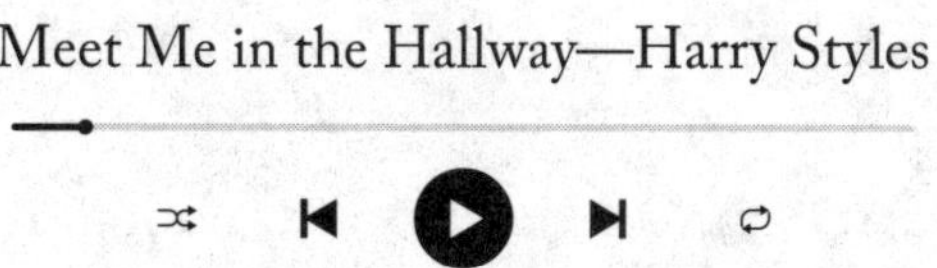

I'm finding it difficult to concentrate. It's Friday, my only short day at the New England School of Ballet. I'm accompanying Rayne's first class, followed by another one with the juniors. After that, I'll be done. It's supposed to be my most chill day of the week. But after getting less than three hours of sleep because I spent most of the night in an unheated van writing a song with a girl I really wanted to kiss, even though we're "just" friends, it's not.

We wrote *the* song.

Rayne and I. We haven't talked about what we're going to do with it, or even if we're going to do *anything* with it. But that's exactly what I want. Damn, I want it so badly that it scares me to death. The song is really, really good. Better than anything the guys and I have come up with lately. But I didn't write it alone, and I can't help but wonder what that says about my abilities. I couldn't get a song like that down on paper on my own. I needed Rayne for it.

I'm probably overthinking it, but I can't help it. It feels unfair, and I can't do a thing about it. I hate how incompetent it makes me feel.

I'm still playing the grand piano I'm sitting at, even though Francesca's last class ended half an hour ago. I haven't been able to bring myself to get up and go home. Part of me is secretly hoping that Rayne will come back later during the break, just like she did almost a month ago now, so she can remind me that writing this song helped her. I need to know that it made her feel better. That's all that matters.

Another part of me isn't sure I actually want to see her because of what happened last night—that one moment that changed everything and nothing at the same time. When her mouth was only inches away from mine. All it would have taken to kiss her was one little motion.

One second, frozen in time. Her hesitating. Backing away. Pretending nothing happened. But it did, and now everything is different and a thousand times more complicated because I can't stop thinking about the way she looked at me. Gray eyes, dark gaze. Full lips.

Just friends, East. You're just friends. That's all she wants. Obviously.

My fingers are moving faster, and my stomach tenses up. I can tell myself we're just friends as many times as I want, but it doesn't feel that way. I wanted to kiss her last night. I've wanted to for weeks. Or to be totally honest, for months. Back when she was still the girl I texted every day. Before I met her in person. I wanted to kiss her when she was still Mockingbird and not Rayne Bellamy, but now I want it so badly it hurts. It really hurts.

It hurts because what I want is so obviously not what she

wants. I don't know where we stand anymore. We're just friends, but somehow, we're not.

And then there's the song. We wrote the best song ever together. I still feel incompetent, just like she does far too often, and I hate that I feel that way about myself. How hypocritical is that? I asked her to help me write a song just a few weeks ago, and now I can't handle the fact that she did.

I groan in frustration. I have to stop all these thoughts from spinning around in my head. But above all, I have to get my feelings about the kiss that didn't happen under control. Because it doesn't matter how much I want to feel her lips on mine. We're friends. Real friends, and I can't be selfish enough to take that away from her just because I'm an idiot and forgot that you can be just friends with a girl.

Unfortunately, Rayne isn't just any girl. She's *the* girl.

And I have a fucking problem.

I close the piano lid harder than necessary and get up. Leaving the ballet studio, I'm about to head to the changing room where I always leave my jacket during class when I spot purple hair in one of the other rooms.

Rayne. I remember that she has contemporary dance class now. I slow down and then stop. She's not alone, of course. There are about thirty dancers in the room. I spot Skye, Zoe, and Jase. Jase turns around at that very moment and flashes a quick grin at me through the glass before turning back to Melanie, the guest instructor from New York Rayne told me about.

Melanie is standing in front of the mirrored wall and seems to be explaining something to them with sweeping gestures. Then she claps her hands and everyone takes their positions. That's my cue to leave; I have no right to be here. Mostly, I shouldn't be standing in the hallway watching Rayne, who's now throwing her long hair back over her shoulder. Most of the girls still have their hair in the strict buns required for ballet class, but they've exchanged their tight leotards for looser shirts.

Rayne is wearing an oversized purple shirt. It falls over the top of her black leggings, which emphasize her long, slender legs. Looking at her, all at once I feel much too warm.

Look away.

I really should stop staring at her and leave, but I'm paralyzed. The music begins, so loud that I recognize the song even through the wall: "Dancing on My Own." It's one of the songs Rayne sent me last year.

I can't move because she starts dancing at the same time as the others, and for the first time that I've seen her dancing, it seems to me that she's totally herself. Over the past few weeks, I've watched her every morning as she's tried day after day to bend the rules of ballet, and I never got the impression she liked what she was doing.

Now it's different. Her movements are more fluid, more relaxed. Less controlled, less perfect. Just the way she is. I watch her, and I think it's possible that she was wrong back then. When she said this wasn't what she wanted, she didn't mean dancing in general. It was about ballet. The rules and the control, the perfection. None of it suits her. She's not controlled or perfect.

She's creative and free. Beautiful. Alive.

I'm just afraid she doesn't know that.

CHAPTER 22
Rayne

Dancing on My Own—Calum Scott

The world around me blurs as I dance. I'm aware of nothing but the music and myself. My heart is pounding, my whole body is working, and for the first time, it all feels right. Being here. Dancing. I have the steps in my head. I know how to place my feet and how to move my arms. I spin, and it feels completely natural.

I can breathe properly. My muscles are tight and burning, and I'm exhausted, but in the best way possible, because I know I'm good. This works. I feel the floor beneath my feet. I feel the music, this song, and I feel *myself*. It's crazy how easy it is when I'm not trying desperately to be perfect. This isn't about perfection. It's about emotion, and I feel so, so much.

Get lost in music
Lost in you
And dance with you 'til midnight.

The words pop into my head so suddenly that I lose my rhythm for a moment and mess up the spin. But I feel the truth in them, and my heart beats in a new rhythm, one that's strange and familiar to me at the same time. Something is happening to me, and it has to do with these words in my head, but I can't quite define what it is. The song ends. The studio falls silent, and I come back to reality, where I'm not alone.

"That was excellent, guys," Melanie says, beaming at us. "Try to let yourselves go a little more. Less control. Try not to focus so much on making every movement perfect. Rayne did that very well just now, for example."

I blush when Melanie says my name. Her praise takes me so much by surprise that I don't know what to do with myself or where to look. I gaze down at the floor, embarrassed. All eyes are on me. My pulse races because I don't like being stared at. It's uncomfortable too, because I don't know what I did that was different from everyone else. Besides, is it really an advantage that I'm good at this class? It's the only one where everyone else is struggling. In all the other classes, I'm the one who struggles. It just doesn't add up.

"You were really great. You can be proud of yourself," Zoe whispers, as if she can read my mind. She squeezes my hand, and her touch makes me feel a little better immediately. Still, I can't bring myself to feel proud, because it feels like I'm even failing at being good.

"Before we're done, I want to get back to the assignment I mentioned a few weeks ago," Melanie continues. "I want each of you to choose a song and choreograph a dance to it using all the elements we've covered so far. One or two minutes is enough. It doesn't have to be a complete song. You can work together, but please, no more than three per group. You have until the end of the semester. We'll go through your work in the last two weeks. It will also count toward your grades for this semester. Of course you can include everything we're going to be doing in the next few weeks. I'm always here to help if you have any questions. And remember, this isn't about perfection. I just want you to learn to listen to your feelings and the music, and to move with both." She smiles, and someone asks a question, but I don't hear it properly. There's a rushing sound in my ears, and those words are here again.

I won't turn back
I won't give up
I'll make it fucking right
Get lost in music
Lost in you
And dance with you 'til midnight

My hands tingle with excitement as a crazy idea starts to form in my head. Totally crazy. Completely absurd. But very, very right.

"Rayne?" Zoe's voice breaks me out of my trance.

"Huh?" I say, and an amused smile spreads over her face.

"Are you coming?"

I look around, blinking. The others are already packing their things, and I didn't even notice that Melanie had ended the lesson.

"Yeah, sure. Sorry, I wasn't paying attention."

"You don't say." Jase grins, putting an arm around Zoe's shoulders. He nods toward the door. "By the way, I think someone's waiting for you."

"Who—" I stop as I turn to look and see Easton. He's standing in the corridor, looking at me. My heart skips a beat. It's totally unfair that it does that whenever he's close. I feel a wave of heat go through me, and I hope I'm not blushing again. Or at least that he doesn't notice if I am.

He doesn't believe in fate. That's what he said, and I've never believed in it either. But I think I'll have to rethink that, because it definitely can't be a coincidence that he's standing in front of this studio just after I had the crazy idea that's stuck in my head now. I want to go tell him about it, but my legs refuse to move.

We saw each other this morning, but we didn't have time to talk. I was glad to see him, but at the same time it felt awful, because I immediately had to think about our almost-kiss and the fact that I was the one who shied away from him.

Last night we were able to ignore it, but it was dark and quiet, and we were writing a song. *The* song. It was easy to block out everything else. But now it's not so simple. We're back in our everyday reality, where everything's the same as it's always been. But not really. After all, we almost kissed. It would be better if I could stop thinking about it. Yes, that would be smart.

I pack my things and follow Zoe, Jase, and Skye out of the studio. Easton is still standing there, hands buried in his jeans pockets. His dark hair is flopping over his forehead.

"Hey," he says when I reach him.

"Hey." I'm much too aware that my friends are here too, watching us curiously. I wish they'd go away; their glances are making me nervous.

"Rayne, we're going over to the dorm, okay?" Zoe reads my mind again, and I nod to her gratefully. "See you later." She gives me a meaningful look, a silent challenge not to skip afternoon classes again.

"Yeah, see you," I say. I'm extremely relieved Mae isn't here, because unlike the others, she wouldn't let me get away so easily.

"What's up? Weren't you finished a while ago?" I ask Easton as soon as they're gone.

He shrugs. "Yeah. I was just playing the piano, and I was about to leave, but then I saw your class . . . so I'm still here."

"Were you watching us?" I ask, trying to keep my tone light, even though everything about this situation feels strange. Unnatural. Not like us.

"Just a little." He gives me a crooked smile. "You were good."

"Do you think so?" I hate how insecure I sound, but I hate how insecure I feel even more. I'm so sick of it; I want it to stop. Why can't I just feel good about myself? Why can't I accept praise without feeling like a total failure at the same time?

"I wouldn't say it if it weren't true," he says gently, and the sound of his voice alone makes something inside me tense with longing.

"Thanks," I murmur, and continue quickly before he says something else I can't handle. "Melanie gave us an assignment. We have to pick a song and come up with choreography for it."

His eyebrows go up. "Sounds complicated."

"Yeah, it probably won't be easy. I've never done it before."

"Do you know which song you want to use?"

"Yes." I take a deep breath, let it out, and can't help but smile. "I want to use our song."

I don't know what I was expecting. Although, no, that's a lie. I do know. I expected joy, that excited sparkle in his eyes that was there all last night while we searched for the right lyrics. It was there as he watched me cross out the wrong words in his notebook and replace them with the right ones as I quietly sang the melody I had in my head. Slower and a little more melancholy than what the guys usually do. A little gentler, a little less rock.

I was expecting the smile that shows his dimples and makes it clear to me that our friendship has changed far too much in a very short time. The fluttering in my stomach and chest, the stumbling of my heart when I see him, and the inevitable compulsion to smile when I think of him are pretty clear signs that we're not just friends, even though that's what we have to be. It's what I need right now.

But Easton doesn't smile. Instead, a shadow I've never seen before crosses his face, causing my stomach to cramp painfully.

"What's wrong?" I ask, suppressing the urge to cross my arms over my chest. "Do you think it's a stupid idea?"

"No. Not at all. It's a good idea. It's just . . ." He shakes his head and breaks off.

"What?"

"Nothing. Just . . . How are you going to do it? We haven't even recorded the song yet."

"So what? We'll just do it. We could go to the studio together and . . ."

"No," he says sharply. A guilty expression appears on his face as I flinch.

"Why not? The song is good, really good, and—"

"And it's your song!" he snaps.

Confused, I blink at him. "No. That's silly. We wrote it together."

"It's still your song. You had the idea. You knew what you wanted to write about, and you wrote it."

"Yes. Together with you," I say firmly. I don't understand what's happening.

"Yes, I helped you. But it's your song."

"No it's not. We wrote it *together*," I repeat. I can't help it; I need him to understand. He has to know. "If anything, it's *our* song. And I want you to play it."

"But what you're asking . . . Fuck, Rayne! It's not as easy as you think." There's unmistakable despair and anger in his voice. Anger at . . . who? Me? Or himself? I don't know, and I don't want to.

"Then explain it to me," I beg and take a step toward him. Everything in me urges me to reach out and touch him, but he steps back as if he knows what I'm about to do. It hurts, right in my heart. I shouldn't get to be hurt by this, I know. I did the same thing to him yesterday when I was the one who backed away. But it still hurts.

"We can't afford to just go into the studio and record a song."

I don't think, I just answer—and promptly say exactly the wrong thing. "I can."

He laughs, and it sounds bitter. "Yeah, I know."

My ears are ringing. Everything is going terribly wrong. I'm missing something. "Easton, I don't get it . . ."

"Of course you don't. How could you? You come from a completely different world than me and . . . Oh, fuck, forget it. This is stupid, and I have to go now." He's lying, and we both know it. He doesn't work at the record store on Fridays, and he doesn't have to be at the Lighthouse for hours. Stunned, I stare after him as he turns away and hurries down the stairs. I want to tell him that we promised not to argue again, but I can't get the words out.

CHAPTER 23
Easton

FUCK ABOUT IT—Waterparks, blackbear

I'm an asshole. That's all there is to it. I screwed up so badly that I have no idea how to fix it. An apology would probably be a good start. An explanation too.

I just don't know what to say to her. How *do* I explain my behavior? Anyone else would have been thrilled. Thrilled that we wrote this song, and that she wants to record it with us and choreograph a dance to it. All of that—going into a real studio and recording the song—would be a step in the right direction. Moving forward.

Still, it feels like a shortcut, like I'd be taking advantage of her. But that's not the reason I'm acting this way. At least, not the only reason. If I'm honest, really honest, it's something else.

In the last few weeks it's been easy to forget who Rayne is and that we come from completely different worlds. She was a dance student at the New England School of Ballet, just like everyone else. She'd go to class, and when she wasn't dancing or studying, we'd spend time together listening to music.

It was easy to forget she inherited millions from her parents. Until today. Until she said she could pay for the studio time and I was immediately reminded of the differences in our financial status. She probably wouldn't even miss the money. The band, on the other hand, would have to save for months to afford it.

It's not fair to blame it on her, I know. It's not her fault. She didn't do anything wrong, it's just my fucking pride getting in the way, and my frustration that I'm not able to write a good song on my own.

Like I said, I'm an asshole.

"What's wrong?" I look up when I hear Beck's voice.

"Huh?"

He points to the knife in my hand and the finely chopped vegetables on the wooden cutting board in front of me. "You've been done for five minutes and you're still staring at the chopped peppers. What's going on?"

"Nothing." I put the knife aside and try to look like I don't care.

"Shit, East, I'm not an idiot. I can see it." He comes over to me, takes the board, and scrapes the vegetables into a pan. He's the only one of us who can cook properly, since his mother's a chef and he spent much of his childhood next to her at the stove. When he wasn't making music, that is. "What's wrong, trouble in paradise?"

I roll my eyes.

"Um, I guess that means yes. If you want to talk about it, I could try to help you," he suggests.

I want to shake my head, but then I give in with a sigh. "I argued with Rayne."

"That's what it looks like." He laughs dryly, and I give him a dirty look, which he answers with a cheeky shrug. "It's true. You were out yesterday for a long time. I heard when you came home, East. I thought it was going well, but ever since you got back from the ballet school, you've been in a horrible mood."

"It's possible there are other reasons," I say, evading the subject. I don't know why I do it, since talking to Beck usually helps me. But usually I also know what's going on in my head. Today I don't understand it.

"Sure, there could be. But there aren't. Why did you argue?"

I slump into one of the chairs around the kitchen table and sigh, frustrated at myself. "It's stupid."

"That doesn't surprise me at all. Start talking already, East."

"We wrote a song together."

Beck stops in the middle of stirring and turns to me in surprise. "You wrote a song together?"

"An extremely good one, actually."

"Then why are you arguing?"

"Because I'm an asshole."

"Hmm. I don't like to disagree with you, but no. You're a lot of things, but not an asshole."

"In this case I am." I groan and then tell my best friend everything. Well, almost everything. I keep the almost-kiss to myself. Beck listens silently while he finishes frying the vegetables. When I'm finally done with my story, he turns around and leans back against the kitchen cabinets with his arms crossed over his chest. He watches me without saying anything for so long and with such an intense stare that at some point I start sliding around on the chair uncomfortably.

"That was totally unnecessary," he finally says.

"Oh, really? Tell me about it." The irony in my voice is unmistakable.

"God, I hate your pride. We could have gone to the studio with Rayne!"

"Don't act like you're better than me. You would have reacted in exactly the same way," I retort. Beck seems to be forgetting how much we have in common. Especially when it comes to our pride and our absolute inability to accept help.

"I know," he says with a grin. "But I didn't. That's why I can give you wise advice that I wouldn't follow myself."

"I hate you."

"I hate you too."

"I always have the feeling I'm a failure." The words taste bitter on my tongue. "I was trying for months to write good songs again, and all that time I couldn't do it. Why does it suddenly work now, with her?"

"I would say it's because you have feelings for her, but I don't think you want to hear that. So I'll say something else. Maybe it's because you two are so similar. Don't argue with me, I know you. I don't know Rayne very well, but I know which songs she likes enough to share with you."

I'm about to ask how he knows that, but he beats me to it.

"Your Spotify account betrayed you. Dude, you made a playlist with all the songs she sent you."

I blush furiously, and I can't deny it because it's the truth. I just didn't think Beck had been aware of it. It's not like I gave the playlist her name. It must be the song choices that gave it away.

"But that's not what this is about," he continues. "She's doing something to you. It's been happening ever since you started writing to each other. Are you really surprised that you could write a good song together?"

I want to say yes, just out of principle, but I would be lying. No, it doesn't surprise me. Not a bit. That's part of the problem.

"Have I ever told you that I hate you?"

"Yeah, just recently. Thanks for repeating it. You like her, don't you?"

I look at him, taken aback. "What does that have to do with this?"

"I mean, you *really* like her," he clarifies.

"That isn't—"

"That means you do. Why is it so hard for you to accept her help?"

"Because . . . I don't know. I don't want to use her."

"You aren't. Not if she's offering her help."

"It's her song."

"You wrote it together. She said so herself. Your dumb excuses don't work anymore, East. What's your damn problem?"

If I only knew.

"Honestly, tell me. Because you must have a problem if you let your false pride get in the way of a chance that affects not only you but the rest of us. We're all in this together, have you forgotten? Sure, you write most of the songs, but we're a band. We're brothers. If you wrote a song with Rayne and she wants us to record it, then it's not only about you."

My guilty conscience hits me like a punch in the gut. "See? I really am an asshole. A totally selfish one, it turns out."

"You're not selfish. I think you're scared. You just have to tell me what you're scared of. Then I can—" Beck stops as the front door slams shut and we hear quiet voices from the hall.

"Easton, where are you? There's someone here to see you," Jax yells so loudly that our neighbors across the street can probably hear him. He must think I'm upstairs in my room.

"Kitchen!" Beck calls back. "And don't yell like that. We can hear you loud and clear."

"How should I know where you are?" Jax grumbles as he comes into the kitchen. I freeze when I spot Rayne behind him. I notice she's wearing my hat again. She didn't give it back to me last night after I drove her to school.

"Hey, Sunshine," Beck says with a grin, then gives me a meaningful look. She gives him a half smile that doesn't quite reach her eyes, then turns to me.

"We need to talk," she says, way too seriously.

I swallow hard, my mouth suddenly dry. My chest tightens and my palms get clammy. I nod. She's right: We need to talk.

BEFORE

JUNE 7 AT 6:37 AM

mockingbird:
Hailey stood me up again. It makes me sick.

eastcoleman:
I can't believe it! Again? Have you told her she's acting like a jerk?

mockingbird:
No. She wouldn't understand what my problem is, and then I'd get mad at her for being so ignorant. Then we'd fight, and it's impossible to fight with Hailey.

eastcoleman:
Why?

mockingbird:
A fight with Hailey wouldn't get me anywhere. At least, it wouldn't get us any closer to a solution. Besides, there are people you can fight with, and some that you can't. Do you know what I mean?

eastcoleman:
I believe that people shouldn't fight at all, so . . .

mockingbird:
Sure, it would be nice if we didn't need conflict and everything was always great. But that's kind of unrealistic. I mean, I can argue with my parents since I know that it won't have any effect on our relationship afterward. Maybe it's different because they're my parents. But I still think it works that way. With some people it's better not to argue, even though they're hurting you, because it doesn't do any good and they just end up being pissed off at you. That's how it is with Hailey, and I'd just be frustrated because I can't tell her that what she's doing is hurting me.

eastcoleman:
Let her be angry. She can't always stand you up and think you'll just let her keep doing it because you're an understanding friend. Which you definitely are, to be clear. But Hailey still shouldn't be able to do whatever she wants to you.

mockingbird:
Yeah, I know. It's really frustrating.

eastcoleman:
I get it. Can you explain again what you mean when you say there are people you can argue with? I don't want you to ever not tell me what you really think because you're afraid of arguing with me.

mockingbird:
It's different with you. It's a bit like with my parents. I don't know if I can explain it properly. Maybe what I'm saying doesn't make any sense to you at all.

eastcoleman:
Fess up, Birdy.

mockingbird:
It's about trust. I think the more you trust someone, the easier it is to argue with them. Because you know they'll still be there after the argument. You know nothing will change, even if you disagree. I think being able to argue has a lot to do with security and respect.

eastcoleman:
That makes a lot of sense. But it also means you don't trust Hailey.

mockingbird:
I don't. Not like that.

eastcoleman:
Do you trust me?

mockingbird:
Yes.

eastcoleman:
That makes me feel better, even though I hope we'll never argue, just because we won't have any reason to.

mockingbird:
Me too. But I don't think it would be a big deal even if we did.

eastcoleman:
I hope not.

CHAPTER 24
Rayne

Kiss Me Kiss Me—5 Seconds of Summer

I spent half the day thinking about Easton's reaction and couldn't figure it out. That's why I'm standing here in the kitchen right now with Easton, Beck, and Jax. Everything is awkward again. This has to stop, otherwise . . . I don't know what will happen, but I'm not very keen to find out. I just want everything to be simple again.

But was it ever? No, not really.

Easton clears his throat and pushes back his hair. "Let's go upstairs."

I nod, and Easton stands up, while Jax shoots Beck a questioning glance, as if he already knows what happened. When Beck shrugs, I'm sure he does.

"Be nice to each other," Beck shouts after us as we leave the kitchen. Yes, he definitely knows. Easton stiffens next to me, I can feel it, but I don't say anything as we're walking up the stairs.

His room is dark until he turns on the lamp on the bedside table. He doesn't like bright lights, which is why there isn't a ceiling light. His room is messier than usual. There are a dozen notebooks on the floor in front of one of the beanbag chairs, along with loose sheets of paper that are full of his handwriting.

They're songs; I can tell without looking closer. It seems like he was searching for something. I stand silently in the middle of the room, unsure about where to start. It seems like he feels the same way, because he doesn't say a word. He's looking at me, and something in his eyes makes me want to put my arms around him and hold on tight, like he's done for me so many times. I want to chase the shadows out of his eyes and make whatever happened today disappear. But it's probably not that easy.

"I think I made a mistake when I asked you never to argue with me again," I finally say.

Easton looks surprised. "Why?" His defensive undertone stings.

"Do you remember when I told you that I can't argue with Hailey because I don't trust her?"

He nods.

"And remember when you asked me if I trusted you?"

Another nod.

"I said yes. I said it's okay if we argue. Because I know you'll always be there for me. When we had our first argument a few weeks ago, I didn't remember that I had said that. Maybe I just forgot because I was overwhelmed. Whatever the reason was, it was a mistake to ask you not to argue with me again. I want us to argue if it means we can tell each other the truth. Because we're friends."

I don't know why I'm saying this. Maybe to convince myself that this is what it's all about?

Easton makes a face, and maybe it wasn't only a few weeks ago that I made a mistake but yesterday too. I can't undo yesterday's mistake, not so easily. The other one, I can.

"So please, tell me the truth," I urge him, straightening my shoulders. There's a faint rushing sound in my ears. "Tell me why you got so angry. What did I do wrong?"

"You didn't do anything wrong." He paces the room, agitated, kneading his hands. "You have nothing to do with this."

"But it felt that way." I can't suppress the hurt undertone in my voice.

"No, I mean it. This is all . . . Fuck, Rayne, you really have nothing to do with it."

"Then what was it?" I instinctively take a step toward him. "Can you just tell me? I want to understand. I've been thinking about it all day, and honestly, all I could think of was . . ." I go quiet as Easton's head goes back with a groan.

"Don't do that. Don't worry about it. I totally overreacted," he says. "It was stupid. Honestly."

"Somehow I don't believe you." I reach out both hands to him. "Just tell me. Tell me what's on your mind."

"I . . . oh, fuck. It's about me, okay?" He looks at me, and a tight knot forms in my stomach. "It's about me and my complete inability to do anything meaningful."

"What?" I don't understand a word he's saying, because if there's one thing he isn't, it's incompetent.

"We've been treading water for months. We can't find a label, and it feels like no one knows we exist! I've been trying for ages to write a song that I really like again. One I can believe in. But I can't do it, and then you show up, and we sit in my van and write a song that's fucking perfect! But it's your song, not mine. Because

I just can't do it on my own. That's why we're going to be stuck in this house in this city forever, and we'll never get to live our fucking dream!"

I stare at him, stunned. He's said before that he feels incompetent, and I thought I understood because I feel the same way about myself, far too often. I guess I was wrong. I had no idea the extent of his feelings, and I'm probably a pretty crappy friend because I've been focusing on my own problems the whole time instead of seeing his. *Really* seeing them.

"Easton, I'm sorry, I—"

"Don't," he interrupts me. "You don't have to apologize. It's not your fault I feel like a total failure because I need you to write a song that wasn't even my idea."

His words cut deep into my heart, and I hate that he feels this way, because it's not true.

"You're not a failure, and you don't need me." My voice has gone quieter and sounds terribly hoarse. Easton grimaces in pain.

"Yes, I do. I need you, but I hate myself for it. I don't want to use you. I want . . ." he goes silent when I flinch. "Shit, that's not the way I meant it. I meant—"

"It's okay." I dismiss his apology, even though what he said hurt somewhere inside. This is all getting completely out of hand, and I'm starting to worry that I made a mistake, that we can't fight after all, because if we do, nothing will be the same as it was before.

"No, it's not okay. I want to record this song, Rayne. I want to go to the studio with you and the guys and record it because it's great. But we can't afford it, and you—"

"I know," I say. I'm starting to comprehend what his problem is.

Even if I don't understand one hundred percent, because I'm not in his financial situation and never have been, I still get it.

"You suggested it like it was some small thing. For you it is, and that's really okay. But right now, it feels to me like we can't do this without you. And that's damn unfair to you and the guys, because it's selfish. I'm selfish and too proud to just get over myself and say yes. I don't want to need you *that* way. I want us to . . ." He trails off, his chest rising and falling heavily, breathing too fast.

What was he about to say? I open my mouth to ask him what he means, but I can't get the words out, because that's not what this is all about. Why is it so damn complicated again?

"We're friends," Easton says, his voice breaking. My heart breaks too, just a little too much. "If we take this song to the recording studio and you help us to record it, then . . . what if something changes? We're not starting in the same place, Rayne. You're . . . who you are, and I'm—"

"So are you!" I interrupt. Tears fill my eyes. He has to stop before he says something else that he doesn't really want to say.

"You know what I mean."

"No, I don't! I can't help who my parents were. I can't help that my father earned a fortune that belongs to me now because he died. I am who I am, that's true. But so are you! God, Easton, do you know what I'd give to have a dream like yours? Or your talent? A family? I would give every damn penny I own to get my parents back. I would give *everything*, but I can't!" My voice breaks, and I lose control. I know I have to get a grip on myself, but I can't. Easton has gone white, and I just hate this. "I'm totally alone in this stupid world, and there's absolutely nothing I can do about it. But yesterday, when we were working on that song together, I had a feeling for the first time that maybe I am good at something. Even if it only works with you. I couldn't have done it without you. I understand everything you just said. I really understand, but it still hurts! And of course it's unfair. Just because it helps me doesn't mean it has to help you. But do you know what hurts the most? That you can't see for yourself how good you are!" I try desperately to find the right words.

"Rayne—"

"No, I'm not done yet!" I shout. It's terrible, but I can't stop now. I have to make him understand. "You're so damn good! I listened to your songs every day for months, because I needed to hear your voice. Because your voice does something to me every damn time I hear it. You're special and you have talent. God, you've got so much talent, and that's not going to change just because songwriting hasn't been working out for a few months. My dad didn't write all his songs by himself, either. I don't think anyone can. And even if they could, who cares? It's not important. That song we wrote yesterday isn't *mine*. It's *our* song, and if you ever say again that you're useless or that you can't do it, I'll have to slap you. Because it's just not true!" Breathing heavily, I fall silent, my heart pounding so hard against my ribs that it hurts.

I only realize I've moved closer to him when I see that my hands are twisted in his shirt, tugging at the soft fabric. His fingers close around my wrists, and at first, I think he wants me to let go, but instead he just holds me tight.

"I'm a bigger asshole than I thought," he says quietly, and I can't help but laugh a little, in spite of it all.

"Are not."

"Am too."

"No. But Easton, I don't want you to think we're on different levels, or that you're in a different league than me. It's not true," I say with difficulty.

"I know." He lets go of me and pulls me into an embrace. I sigh in relief as he puts both arms around me, and I immediately feel calmer.

"Really?" I murmur into his shirt. It smells like him, of course, and even though we just argued, even though there are still a lot of things we need to talk about, my body responds to his scent. I hear his heartbeat under my ear, feel his arms around my waist. Warmth is spreading through me, and it's all wrong.

He should let go of me. I should let go of him. We should let each other go, because I feel horribly weak right now and want to be held by him too much. Far too much.

"Yes." He sighs, and I feel it in my hair. A pleasant tingle goes down my back. I can't let go; I'm just not able to. "I'm just . . . frustrated. And insecure. And annoyed. It was really shitty of me to take that out on you."

"It was. But I understand you."

"Really? Because I don't understand myself." He laughs softly, and I have to smile. Neither one of us moves. We aren't letting go.

"Really. Easton . . . if you don't want to record the song, it's okay. It was wrong of me to assume that you would want to." I look up at him. His hair is in a tangle on his forehead, and I want to smooth it back and find out if it's as soft as I think.

"It was never about not wanting to," he says as I stare at his face without meaning to. His thick eyebrows and lashes, and the bluest eyes in the world. Those lips that wanted to kiss me yesterday, that I wanted to kiss too. I would have if I weren't so scared. He's so beautiful, and I want to run my fingers over his face, touch his lips . . . and that's a real problem.

He takes a deep breath, his chest pressing against mine. We're definitely too close, but neither of us is backing away.

"It was all about me and my stupid self-doubt. I want us to record that song together."

The way he says *us* makes my heart beat faster.

"Okay," I say, wanting to let go of him, because I'm about to do something very, very stupid if he holds me any longer.

"Okay," he says, and swallows. Something dark and longing flickers in his eyes. He has to let me go right now, or we'll go up in flames.

But he doesn't. Instead, his hands caress my face, his fingers warm and a little calloused.

"Rayne," he whispers, and I don't think I've ever liked my name as much as I do at this moment. No one has ever said it like he does. Soft and deep, as if it were infinitely valuable.

He rests his forehead against mine, his breath caresses my skin, and I can't think straight anymore. My mind shuts down. He hesitates, surely because of how I backed away yesterday, and I know I should do it again. Really. But I can't. I forget why I did it yesterday. Instead, I lift my head and pull him closer, just a little, but it's enough. His lips meet mine, hot and hungry. Not gentle, not careful. My body bursts into flames. *We're* burning.

Easton groans, a soft, throaty sound that burrows deep inside me, and I want to hear it again and again. I open my lips and our tongues touch. My knees go soft. I've never been kissed like this before. It's so wild that it almost borders on desperation. It tugs on my heart, and that's exactly what I was afraid of—what I'm still afraid of. But my mind isn't working anymore, and even though I'm afraid, this kiss and him are exactly what I want at this moment.

Everything blurs. There's just Easton and me, one of his hands on my face, the other wandering down my neck, tilting my head back gently and firmly. My body melts into his, my fingers dig into his hair, his groin presses against mine, heat and desire, longing and hunger. Someone is panting, I don't know if it's him or me. It's probably both of us.

I forget my name, forget who we are and what I was afraid of. I forget everything except us.

For one brief moment.

CHAPTER 25
Easton

Fuck Up the Friendship—Leah Kate

Rayne feels very small and slim in my arms. And so perfect. She sighs into my mouth, and I get hard. My blood boils, and I can feel her heart beating against my chest. Her lips are on mine, her tongue is in my mouth. Everything is hot and sensitive. Her fingers stroke the skin on my neck, and I want her to touch me everywhere. I want her to trace every inch of my body with her hands. I want to do the same to her. I need to feel her; I can't help it.

My hands wander under her sweater, and as I stroke her spine, I can feel her breaking into goose bumps, arching her back, getting closer to me. She stands on tiptoes, her hips pressing against mine, and I'm done for. I'm so screwed.

"Easton," she whispers my name, and I love that she's the only one who ever uses my full name, and how her voice sounds when she does. Soft and warm. "Wait."

One word, and I go ice cold. There's something in that word I don't want to hear. Something uncertain and fearful.

"Wait." Breathless, she pulls away, until our mouths are no longer touching. But her hands are still on the back of my neck, her chest is still pressed against me, and her hips are too.

"What is it?" My voice is so hoarse that I have to clear my throat.

"What are we doing?" she asks, and it's clear she's not just talking about the kiss.

I don't know what to say, because I have no fucking clue what we're doing. I just know that nothing has ever felt so right to me as kissing her. Holding her. Breathing her in.

"Easton." She says my name again, but this time it sounds different. Less soft, less warm. Then Rayne sinks back onto her heels and takes a step back. My stomach cramps and my arms fall powerlessly to my sides. She hunches her shoulders, and I can feel her tension. Whatever changed from one moment to the next, whatever made her let go of me, it's not right. It can't be. I don't know what to say.

What are we doing?

I have no idea. All I know is that I want to do it again. Over and over. I never want it to stop.

"You're my best friend, you know that." Her voice trembles, and her eyes glitter with unshed tears.

"Yes, I know, but . . ." *But we could be so much more*, I want to say. But I can't get the words out, and she shakes her head. She's still wearing my hat.

"I can't lose you," she whispers, and I feel a stab in my heart. "I can't . . ." she struggles for breath. It hurts to see her like this.

"You won't." It's a brave, false promise, because I have no control over whether or not I can keep it. But I want it to be true.

"You can't know that."

"Yes, I can." I can't give in. I can't.

"No you can't." She touches her lips, which are pink and a little puffy from our kisses. "If we do this . . . If we let ourselves be more than friends . . . It could easily go wrong. And I can't . . . I can't bear the thought of it falling apart and us ending up with nothing. You're all I have left. I can't lose you too. Not after everything I've already lost." She talks so fast that she swallows some of her words, tears streaming down her cheeks. It hurts because I understand her, even though I don't want to. I don't want any piece of what she's saying to make sense. But it does. At the same time, it doesn't, because this is about *us*. And everything was different with us from the very beginning.

"Hey. Come here." I reach out my hand to her, even though part of me is resisting saying what I know I have to say. Because she's my best friend too, and I can't lose her any more than she can lose me.

She hesitates, and that hesitation hurts like hell. But then she puts her hand in mine. I pull her close, and she leans against my chest again as though that's exactly where she belongs.

"It's okay. We're friends. That's all that matters," I lie, wishing it were the truth.

"I'm sorry, I didn't mean to complicate things." Sniffing, she buries her face in my shirt while I run my hands through her hair, the soft strands that smell like violets and citrus.

"You're not complicating anything."

"Liar." She laughs again, and I can't help but kiss her temple, just for a second, before I remember I shouldn't.

We go silent, and I can hear her quiet breathing and mine. I feel her heartbeat against my chest. I have too many questions, and I can't ask her a single one of them. Not now.

So I just hold her tight and try to convince myself that I'm totally okay with just being her friend.

CHAPTER 26
Rayne

Ceilings—Lizzy McAlpine

"Don't pull with your free leg, Rayne. The turn has to come from your standing leg," Zoe says as she does a perfect pirouette next to me. It looks so easy when she does it. So damn perfect. Every muscle in her body is under tension.

"See?"

"Yes." I groan and lean heavily on my thighs, breathing hard. My heart is beating so fast it feels like it's about to leap out of my chest. "I see what you're doing, but I can't do it."

"No one can do it like Zoe," Mae interjects, getting a reproachful glance from her best friend.

"Not helpful, Mae. Besides, you can do it just as well, and you . . ." She looks at me, a determined expression on her face. "You can do it too."

I grimace but don't reply, because it's not true. Zoe steps behind me and I straighten up.

"May I?" she asks.

"Sure."

She places both hands on my waist. "Try to straighten up a little more. Pull your ribs in, keep the tension, and then start the turn. Your standing leg has to do the work, not your free leg," she repeats.

I press my lips together in frustration. I already know everything she and Mae have explained to me in the last two hours. The problem is putting it into practice.

"Want to try again?" Zoe's eyes meet mine in the mirror. I want to say no, but it's no use. If I give up, I won't get any better.

So I nod, and Zoe lets go of me. I try again, losing my momentum and then my balance. Again and again. It's so frustrating I could cry. I'm still not wearing pointe shoes yet, and even in slippers I can't do it the way it's supposed to be done. The way it *must* be done. I've been dancing long enough that I should be able to do a simple pirouette.

After the fifth miserable turn, I let myself collapse onto the floor with a groan. I'm dizzy because I didn't focus on one point long enough before I moved my head.

"I can't do any more."

"Really? Or have you just had enough of pirouettes?" Mae asks. "We could work on your jetés a little more."

"Please, no," I beg her. If I have to do leaps now, I'll throw up. This week has been hard, and the extra practice today is the last straw.

I hardly slept at all last night because I kept thinking about Easton and that kiss. The expression in his blue eyes as I backed away. The memory of it makes my heart clench.

Don't think about it. Not now.

But I can't stop. I haven't been able to since yesterday evening after I got back to school. It was the first time Easton didn't drive me. I've been trying to convince myself that it was just because he had to go to the Lighthouse, but I know that's not true.

The kiss changed everything, and that can't be denied. It also can't be undone. Do I even want to undo it?

Yes.

No.

I don't know.

God, I really don't know.

"Okay, we'll stop for today," Zoe decides, bringing me back to the present. I resolutely push all thoughts of Easton aside. If I keep thinking about him, I'll go crazy, and I have more than enough problems as it is.

"God, I hate this." Sighing, I bury my face in my hands, not even sure what I'm talking about. My miserable performance, my emotional turmoil, or both. Probably both.

"No, don't do that." Zoe sits down next to me while Mae puts one leg on the barre and stretches in a way that makes me feel bitterly envious.

"I can't. I'm sorry, honestly. I know I whine and annoy you too much, but I can't help it. It's all so incredibly awful."

"You're not annoying," Mae says, smiling at me.

"You're not," Zoe agrees. "And it's understandable that you're complaining. We'd feel the same way. *I* felt the same way myself not long ago. You've only been here for a few weeks, and I'm sure you'll be able to figure it out if that's what you really want." She nudges my foot with hers. "Can I ask you something?"

I just nod.

"Do you enjoy the classes here?"

The question catches me off guard. I open my mouth to say yes, because that's the only acceptable answer here, but no sound comes out.

Zoe raises her eyebrows questioningly, her gaze intent. It feels like she's looking straight inside me and seeing everything that no one else is supposed to see.

"I like it here," I reply, and it's not technically a lie. However, it's only half the truth. I really do like it here at the school. I like living in the dorm with everyone else, and I like that Zoe's and Mae's rooms are right across the hall from mine. I've made friends, which I honestly didn't expect.

"That doesn't answer my question. Is ballet fun for you?"

"Is it about fun?" I'm still evading the question. She definitely notices, but I can't admit that it's not fun for me.

"It should be, at least a little bit," Mae says. "I mean, sure, there's a lot of pressure. We're constantly comparing ourselves, and I bet everyone has had a nervous breakdown at some point because it felt like they were incapable and everyone else was better. But I think most of us know why we put all this pressure on ourselves. Do you?" she asks gently, sliding off the barre and coming over to us.

I don't want to answer; everything in me resists. But maybe it's finally time for the bitter truth. Especially for me to admit it to myself. I exhale sharply. "No."

"It isn't supposed to feel like that," Zoe says quietly. "Why are you here?"

My eyes burn, and I blink frantically. "My mom went here, and I was hoping I could . . . find a part of her here if I did something she loved. But I can't do it. I'm not like her. She was so good, and

I'm just a failure. But I don't know where else to go," I choke out. I guess that's the real truth.

Zoe and Mae are silent, probably not knowing what to say. I get it. I wouldn't know, either. You can't just dismiss it or sugar-coat it. I really don't know where else to go.

"I can't move back in with my grandmother. She's not interested in me, and I . . . I don't know how to deal with her," I blurt out, almost like Zoe's question set something free inside me, and now everything is bursting out all at once. "She's not part of my family. She never visited us; she was never there. She didn't even call on birthdays or holidays. I have no one. My life in LA is over, and there's no one I can talk to, or *want* to talk to. This feels like the only home I have left. Except for Easton's house, but I screwed that up. Now I'm losing him, even though that's the last thing I want. And—" I break off because suddenly I can't breathe.

My chest feels terribly tight, and my heart is beating too fast. Not from exertion, like during ballet practice, but from panic. Only when Zoe reaches for my hand do I realize I'm shaking. I'm shaking and I can't stop. My eyes are burning, my skin feels too tight, and my stomach is rebelling.

I have nowhere to go. I'm losing the only person who matters to me because I'm scared and don't know what I want. I don't know what I want or who I am—and, even less, who I *want* to be.

"Rayne, take a deep breath. Slow down." Zoe's voice sounds distorted and distant. Her hand closes tighter on mine. It's warm. "Breathe deeply, okay? Breathe with me. Look at me. Come on, look, and breathe with me."

She sounds so calm. Why? And why is my heart beating so fast? Why can't I breathe? I have to breathe.

"Hey." A hand under my chin makes me lift my head. Familiar, amber-colored eyes. Her gaze is as calm as her voice. She takes a breath, and somehow I manage to do the same.

Inhale.

Exhale.

Inhale.

Exhale.

"Everything is okay, even if it doesn't feel that way. You're okay. Everything is fine." She keeps talking. I don't understand every word she says, but her voice is my anchor because voices always help me, and gradually I calm down again.

My pulse slows, my lungs expand, and I can breathe again.

"I'm sorry—"

"No," Zoe interrupts me. Her smile is warm. "There's nothing to apologize for."

I want to argue, but I decide not to.

"Shall we go over to the dorm? We could cozy up in bed and eat ice cream," Mae suggests. "And then we can talk about everything, if you want."

I find myself nodding.

"Let's go." Mae grabs my hand, then she and Zoe pull me to my feet. Silently, we gather our things and head over to the dorm.

We each make a quick detour to our own rooms to change and then meet up at Mae's. She's the only one of us who has a mini fridge with a freezer compartment in her room.

"Three cheers for my mom and her constant concern for my feet," Mae says with a grin, bending down to the freezer, where a container of Ben & Jerry's and various ice packs are lying.

"We love your mom," Zoe confirms, nudging me toward Mae's

bed as she walks over to the dresser and connects her phone to the Bluetooth speaker. Then the two of them join me on the bed, one on either side. Mae opens the ice cream and hands us each a spoon.

"So . . ." Mae says. "Do you feel like talking about your mom?"

"No," I blurt out, my pulse racing again. Everything inside me resists the idea of talking about my mother. If I start now, I'll fall apart.

"It's okay. You don't have to talk about her if you don't want to," Zoe says gently. "What about Easton? Do you want to talk about him?"

I close my eyes and sigh a little as my heart returns to its normal rhythm. "Yes. No. I don't know . . . I just feel so stupid."

"You're not," Zoe says, contradicting me immediately. Then she takes a bite of ice cream. "Why do you think you're losing Easton?"

"Because I really, really messed up."

"Rayne, if you tell us everything from the beginning, maybe we can help you." Mae gently nudges me and gives me an encouraging smile. I make a face and give in.

"We went to the beach the other day, and we wrote a song. And then we almost kissed."

"You wrote a song?" Zoe asks.

"You almost kissed?" Mae asks.

They both look at me in utter disbelief.

"Yes."

"What do you mean, you *almost* kissed?" Mae's eyes are wide.

"Well . . . it didn't quite happen. There was a moment when we were a little too close, and we could have . . . but we didn't." I don't know why I don't tell them that we did actually kiss yesterday.

"Why?" Zoe leans toward the foot of the bed and grabs the wool blanket to spread over our legs.

"Because I couldn't." I sigh.

"But you wanted to," Mae says. It's a statement rather than a question. My heart skips a beat as though it wants to agree.

"No," I say. "But somehow also yes. I just don't know. But it doesn't matter what happened then, because yesterday . . . everything went totally wrong."

"What does that mean?" There's an undertone of alarm in Mae's voice.

"We had an argument yesterday, after contemporary dance class."

"I was wondering what happened. You've been so quiet all afternoon," Zoe says sympathetically.

"I kept trying to figure out why he was so angry all of a sudden, but I couldn't understand it. It was strange, and it didn't make any sense at all. So I went over to see him." I take a deep breath.

"Did you argue again?" Mae takes my hand.

"Not exactly. We did, but it wasn't a bad fight, it was just . . ." I go silent. I can't tell them about Easton's self-doubt; it's not my place. "Anyway, it wasn't bad. I mean, it was, but only because it felt bad. Do you know what I mean?"

They both nod, and I think they actually understand me.

"And then . . . we kissed, after all."

Mae squeals enthusiastically. "I knew it! You're too cute together for nothing to happen."

"I'm not done yet." I awkwardly scrape some of the still slightly hard ice cream out of the tub.

"That doesn't sound good." Zoe's brown eyes widen.

"It wasn't," I sigh.

"Wait, quick question: Was it the kiss that wasn't good, or what came after?"

"Really?" Zoe gives Mae a reproachful look, but she just shrugs.

"It's important."

"What came after," I murmur, and suddenly everything comes pouring out. I can't stop myself.

* * *

"Now I think I totally screwed up. We can't just pretend nothing happened, can we?" I finally ask after telling them everything.

"It depends," Zoe says slowly.

"On what?" It's ridiculous how hopeful I sound.

"Whether you kissed in the heat of the moment or because you have feelings for each other."

"Easton is my best friend." My answer comes out too fast, and I can hardly believe it myself.

"Of course he is." Mae smiles. "But this isn't about feelings of friendship."

I swallow and lower my eyes. As if I didn't know that already.

"What are you afraid of?" Zoe asks carefully, and I suspect that's the key to the whole mess.

"What if something goes wrong? What if I lose him because we get carried away by something that might not have a chance of working?"

"Are you letting yourselves get carried away? Easton seems more like the type who overthinks everything. You do too."

"I agree," Mae says. "Maybe that's the problem."

I continue to poke at the ice cream. "No, that's not it. Or maybe it is. I do overthink everything. But it's more than that. I mean, what if this is just a moment of pure attraction, and nothing more?"

There's no point in denying that I'm attracted to Easton. I only have to think about how his lips felt on mine, how his voice sounded when he whispered my name, and I get way too warm.

"Does it feel like nothing but attraction?" Zoe pulls her legs up and rests her chin on her knees.

"I don't know. He's my best friend. I'm not sure if there's more to it than that. I'm completely overwhelmed by the whole thing. I don't know what it feels like to be in love."

"Wait—you've never been in love before?" Mae sounds so shocked that I almost laugh.

"No, it's never happened."

"It doesn't just happen!"

"It's not like I've never had a crush before. I've just never really been in love."

"So how do you feel when you're with Easton, or when you think about him?" Zoe takes the tub and sticks her spoon into the ice cream.

"If I knew that, everything would be so much easier. All I know is that I can't lose him, and that's why we have to stay friends," I say and take a deep breath. "It's always been easy between us. We could talk about anything. That's what I need right now. Security. Easton is my anchor." I shrug helplessly. "I can't risk losing that."

"But what if he has feelings for you?" Mae asks quietly, and I hate that she's asking me the very question I've been trying to avoid since yesterday. I feel cold, and I don't answer. But the words are there.

Then I wouldn't know what to do.

CHAPTER 27

Easton

Hold On—Chord Overstreet

Lost in thought, I strum my guitar. I've had the melody of "Dance with You 'Til Midnight" stuck in my head all weekend, and I know it's time to sit down with the guys so we can work on it together.

But I still haven't had the courage to show them the lyrics, even though they've been giving me curious glances for the last two hours we've spent sitting in our living room, trying to be productive. Beck is working on another song, while Jax and Colin are taking care of our social media accounts. Jax just had the brilliant idea that our search for a label could take care of itself if we went viral on TikTok.

They know I wrote a song with Rayne, and they know she wants to go with us to the studio and record it. I just feel stupid that I don't know if that's still on anymore, since a single kiss plunged us into total chaos. It's not that I think she'd change her mind, but I also didn't think that we would kiss, and now it's totally strange between us. And by strange, I mean it's too quiet.

Since Friday we haven't spoken or texted with each other. It's been weeks since we've gone this long without hearing from each other, and I have no delusions that it's not because of that damn kiss. Neither of us knows how to deal with it.

Only friends. Only friends, dammit.

I can tell myself that as many times as I want, but it doesn't do any good. I still can't help thinking about her, the taste of her mouth. I can't block the images that keep running through my head. Rayne doing ballet in form-fitting leotards and tights. Rayne dancing in her contemporary class wearing an oversized shirt that I wish was one of mine. My hat on her head, a little too big for her. The way she lies on my bed, her long hair spread out around her like a fan. The way she stares at the glowing stars on the ceiling and rocks her legs to the beat of the music. Her lips are always moving; she knows the lyrics to every song by heart. I have no idea why I find that so sexy, but I do.

I can't stop thinking about it all, and my body reacts like it's fifteen instead of twenty-two. I get much too hot and . . . shit. I have to stop thinking about her that way, otherwise we can forget about our friendship. Even though in one way I'd like to do that, the thought of losing her is much harder to bear than that of never kissing her again, never feeling her bare skin under my hands, not falling asleep next to her and waking up with her the next morning. Fuck, I have to get a grip on myself.

We're. Just. Friends.

My phone vibrates, interrupting my thoughts. I pull it out of my pocket so fast that I almost drop my guitar, and Beck, who's standing next to me, jumps in surprise.

"What's wrong?" He gives me an accusing glance, but there's a gleam of amusement in his eyes, as though he knows exactly what's going on.

"Nothing," I murmur and put the guitar on the sofa before it actually falls. My heart is pounding with excitement because I have the completely naive hope that it's Rayne texting me. I'm so screwed.

"Did she text?" Colin asks without looking up from his phone. "Then at least we could get back to work, if you stop mooning over Text Girl."

"Dude, she has a name." Jax punches Colin's shoulder, but he just laughs and shakes his head.

Rolling my eyes, I tap the screen and sigh with relief when I see the Instagram notification. It's strange that we still write to each other there, even though we got each other's numbers ages ago and the messaging on Insta is a total disaster. But neither of us has ever changed to a different app. Maybe we're just holding on to how we started.

I open the app first and then our chat, even though part of me dreads reading what she wrote because it could just as easily be the end.

It's not.

mockingbird:
How's the song going? Are you rehearsing yet?

I stare at the message, blinking, and for a moment I don't know what to say because I wasn't expecting something like this. So normal. As usual.

What did you expect? That she would want to talk about the kiss again?

That would be unlikely. She made her point of view pretty clear. Still, I feel disappointed because somehow I was expecting something more.

"Everything okay, East?"

I can feel Beck's curious gaze on me as I stare motionless at my phone, trying to comprehend how her message can be so damn normal.

"Yeah, everything's fine." I clear my throat and then force myself to reply.

eastcoleman:
No, not really.

I bite my lower lip, waiting to see if she's still online. It only takes a couple of seconds before the message is marked as read.

mockingbird:
Why? Don't you want to go to the studio? It would be totally okay if you don't, just wanted to check.

eastcoleman:
Yes, of course I do. I just wasn't sure if you wanted to.

mockingbird:
Definitely! It was my suggestion.

eastcoleman:
Okay, I wasn't sure. We haven't talked all weekend.

mockingbird:
I know, I'm sorry. I wanted to get in touch, but Zoe and Mae were helping me with extra training, and then we went out. When I got back to the dorm, I was so wiped out I fell asleep right away.

My shoulders tense as I read her last message. I know Rayne well enough to know when she's lying. It's not that she didn't text me because she was too busy. She just didn't know what to say to me. And since I understand that, I lie right back to her. That's how it is now. It sucks.

eastcoleman:
It's not a big deal. I've been out a lot too.

mockingbird:
Okay, good. So it's not weird between us?

I suppress a groan.

"Everything okay?" Beck asks.

"Hmm," I say.

"Great answer." I can practically hear him rolling his eyes, even though I don't look up from my phone. I type an answer and keep lying.

eastcoleman:
No, everything's fine! I promise.

mockingbird:
Okay, so listen up. There's a small studio in the West End. I already

called them. We could go there next weekend and record the song if you're ready by then. Or you can go on your own, whichever you want. I don't have to come with you if you'd rather I didn't. I'll take care of everything, and you can go there on your own.

I don't even think about it before writing back. There's only one acceptable answer anyway.

eastcoleman:
Forget it, you're coming with me. It's our song, remember?

mockingbird:
Of course. But maybe me being there would disturb your creative process.

eastcoleman:
You're nuts.

mockingbird:
Okay, sorry. I'll shut up. I'm coming with you.

eastcoleman:
Thank you!

mockingbird:
Do you think you'll be able to have it ready by next weekend?

eastcoleman:
We'll do our best, Birdy.

mockingbird:

That's what I wanted to hear. And since you're practicing anyway, maybe you have another song or two that you'd like to record. If we're going anyway, we might as well make good use of the time.

"Is it a good sign that he's got a stupid grin on his face?" I look up at the sound of Jax's voice and see my friends staring at me curiously.

"You're too nosy," I say.

"If we're nosy, you should try to fix your screwed up love life somewhere other than right in front of us." Colin gives me a saccharine smile.

"Colin, you're such a jerk," Jax says, but Colin waves it off.

"It's not like you didn't throw the same shit at me when Emma and I were having problems in her first year of college."

"The difference is, you and Emma are a couple. Rayne and Easton are just friends," Beck says and laughs. "Or at least they pretend to be."

"You guys suck," I say, but I can't stop a stab of pain from shooting through my chest at Beck's words. "You don't deserve to go to the studio with Rayne and me next weekend."

I'm confronted with a stunned silence. Beck is the first to find his voice again.

"Are you serious?"

"Yes."

"Then are you finally going to show us that song you wouldn't let us hear?"

"Yes," I repeat, my mouth stretching into a broad smile.

"Fuck, let's do this!" Jax jumps up in excitement. "Maybe this is the chance we've been waiting for."

"Just because we go to the studio and record a song doesn't mean a miracle will happen," Colin cautions.

But Jax isn't ready to be brought back down to earth. Instead, he grabs a pillow and tosses it at Colin's head.

"Don't be so negative. We're going to the studio to record a song. Just be happy!"

Colin rolls his eyes, but he gives us a crooked grin. "Okay, relax, man. I'm excited."

"Be a little happier." Jax musses Colin's hair, laughing.

"Get your paws off me, Jax." Colin stands up. "Are we going to get started already? We don't have much time left."

"Right. Let's do it." Jax gets up too, while Beck remains seated next to me, eyeing me searchingly.

"Aren't you excited?" he asks, quietly enough that the other two can't hear him.

"Sure. Why wouldn't I be?"

"So everything's okay between you and Rayne?" His eyes narrow to slits, and I try to keep a neutral expression on my face.

"Of course."

"You're a lousy liar, East."

I don't dignify that with an answer. *I know.*

"Why don't you just tell her you've got a crush on her?"

"Because it's not that simple," I admit. There's no point in denying my crush anymore. Beck knows me too well, and I should at least be honest with him if I can't be with her.

"Why not?"

I press my lips together. It's not just a crush. What I feel for

Rayne is more than that. It's deeper. Much deeper. It's been that way from the beginning. I have no idea how to move forward when we want different things.

I've spent the whole week trying to lie to myself, trying to convince myself that I can do this. But the truth is, it's not okay. I don't just want to be her friend.

I want to be everything for her.

PART 6

Pre-Chorus

BEFORE

JUNE 11 AT 4:49 PM

mockingbird:
This is the most cliché question ever, but what's your biggest dream, when it comes to music?

eastcoleman:
If you're going to ask such a cliché question, I have to give you a cliché answer in return, is that clear?

mockingbird:
Of course, that's why I'm asking you.

eastcoleman:
Then you already know the answer.

mockingbird:
No, it depends. There are two possibilities: The clichéd honest answer and the clichéd modest one, that it's all about making music and touching people and blah blah blah. The usual stuff. I'm not quite sure which answer suits you.

eastcoleman:
You don't think I'm modest?

mockingbird:
I do, but I also don't think you need to be, so I hope you give me the other answer.

eastcoleman:
Would you be disappointed if I didn't?

mockingbird:
I would be, but I'd try not to show it.

eastcoleman:
That's very generous of you.

mockingbird:
That's just how I am. Now answer the question. Have you ever noticed that we're both incredibly bad at answering questions directly without first beating around the bush for ages?

eastcoleman:
I've noticed. It's part of our charm.

mockingbird:
Sweet of you to find us both charming. Now go on! No more putting it off. I want an answer!

eastcoleman:
Yes, ma'am. Gosh, I didn't know you could be so bossy, Birdy.

mockingbird:
I'm impatient too.

eastcoleman:
I hadn't noticed that before. But okay, I'll answer your question. I wish we could be heard. Everywhere. I wish people knew our songs by heart. I wish our songs could be felt. That's the modest part of the clichéd answer. But I also wish that our music would enable us to see the world. That we would earn enough money so that we wouldn't need multiple part-time jobs and could concentrate completely on the music. I wish we could buy a big house somewhere with our own studio, so we could record our songs anytime we wanted. Do you want to hear the corny part too?

mockingbird:
I'm a little offended you even have to ask.

eastcoleman:
I hope that nothing changes between the guys and me. I hope we'll always be more like brothers than friends, even if by some miracle we become successful and everything else changes. In our hearts, I want us to always remain the fourteen-year-old guys who started a band because they wanted to make music, and for us to still understand each other no matter what, even years from now.

mockingbird:
That's really corny, but beautiful. Very beautiful. I wish the same for you guys. All of it. The honest, the humble, and the corny. Someday all those dreams will come true, I know it.

CHAPTER 28
Rayne

I pace restlessly in Zoe's room with my phone in my hand so I don't miss Easton's text. It's almost nine thirty, and our studio booking starts in thirty-seven minutes. If the guys aren't here to pick me up in the next seven minutes, we'll definitely be late.

"Rayne, relax." Mae sips from her cup with a straw. She's lying on Zoe's bed, totally chill, while I'm a bundle of nerves. Then again, for her, today is a day like any other. For me, it's absolutely not.

"Why are you so nervous?" Zoe casts me a curious glance in the mirror, while her hands are busy in her hair creating a very complicated braided updo. It's gorgeous.

"Because we haven't seen each other all week and I'm pretty sure it's going to be weird today," I say, nibbling on my fingernails.

"You've seen each other every day." Mae raises her eyebrows and tilts her head.

"Yes, during class. But that's different. We don't have a chance to talk there. Before, we always used to spend time at his place. But not this week."

That bothers me. I don't know how we're going to react to each other now. Will it only be a little strange, or fully awkward? Can we hug without it being weird? *Please, God, I hope so.* I need his hugs and closeness. I need *us*. Like we were before the kiss.

"Maybe you should have done that; then it wouldn't be so awkward today."

"Sure, but it could have gotten very complicated, and then today would be worse than it already is."

"It won't be awkward. Everything will be fine," Zoe says, trying to reassure me. "You won't be alone with him. That will definitely help."

"Hopefully," I sigh. If only Easton had just said I didn't need to come, then everything would be a little easier right now. But that probably would have been the beginning of the end, and that's not what I want, either.

"Do you want us to come?" Mae offers. "I'm sure Zoe could move her date with Jase, and if you need moral support, we'd be glad to help, wouldn't we, Zoe?"

"We would, but today I really can't come. It's my dad's birthday, and that means the whole family will be there." She gives me an apologetic look and reaches for her lipstick.

I dismiss her worry and try to ignore the stab in my heart when I realize that I'll never celebrate another birthday with Mom and Dad.

Don't think about it. Just don't start to think about it now.

"No problem at all," I say. My voice sounds a little forced. "I'll be fine. It's not like we've never spent time together before." I put on a smile that Mae obviously doesn't find very convincing.

She looks at me critically. "Are you sure? I can come with you by myself if Zoe can't."

"That's sweet, but no. Besides, you have plans with Tristan, don't you?"

"Yes, but not until tonight. I'd have time until then."

I shake my head. "I'll be fine, thanks." I have to figure this out on my own.

"Okay." She gazes at me a moment longer, then shrugs and gives me a smile that doesn't quite reach her eyes. She can see right through me. "If you change your mind, just text me. I'll come and rescue you."

"I will, but—" I break off as my phone vibrates. My heart skips a beat. It's a text from Easton.

eastcoleman:
We're here. Are you coming down?

mockingbird:
Give me two minutes.

"Ready to go?" Zoe asks. She grabs the cream-colored cardigan lying at the foot of her bed and slips it on.

I take a deep breath and force a smile, even though my stomach is starting to flutter nervously. "Yes. Looks like it."

Mae tosses Easton's hat to me from the bed. I still haven't given it back to him. I've been wearing it every day instead, consistently ignoring the fact that I definitely shouldn't be.

"Let us know how it goes, okay? I'll set up a group chat," she says before I can even nod in response to her question. "I'll call it Ballet Girls. It's a big cliché, but whatever. We can always change it later. Now go." She shoos us out the door, even though she's still holding her cup in one hand and her phone in the other. A second later, my own phone vibrates. I've been added to a group chat.

"I'll text you guys later," I promise, putting on the hat and my winter jacket.

"By the way, East's hat looks really good on you," Zoe says. "Jase said I should tell you that."

I blush. "Thanks," I murmur, and I'm glad I can disappear now, before Mae laughs. "See you later."

"Have fun!" Mae calls after me as I step out into the hallway and close the door, my cheeks burning. Cheerful laughter drifts from the common room. For the past two weeks, most of the seniors have been meeting there on Saturdays to study for their finals. I can't help wondering if I'll be doing the same in three years.

My stomach tightens. I force myself to put the thought aside, because today isn't about me. I hurry down the stairs. It's freezing outside, and the sky is clear. The sun is shining for the first time in weeks, and I can't help but smile as I feel it on my skin.

Easton and the guys are waiting in the van in the parking lot with the passenger door already open. Colin, Jax, and Beck have made themselves comfortable in the back seat, and Easton is behind the wheel. I hesitate briefly before climbing into the front. The guys are watching me, curious and excited. But they look a bit too much like they know something I don't.

"Good morning," I say, making an effort to sound lighthearted and smile cheerfully.

"Good morning, Sunshine!" I see Beck grinning, and I'd like to smile at him, but unfortunately my gaze catches on Easton.

There's a slightly insecure expression in his blue eyes, which is all too familiar because it's the same insecurity I'm feeling, I'm sure of it. He knows as little as I do about where we stand with each other, and it doesn't help that we've been texting regularly again over the last few days. Texting and being in the same room with each other are two completely different things.

He smiles crookedly, and my stupid heart beats out of time. "Hey, Birdy."

It's not fair how my body reacts to the sound of his voice. I get a warm, tingling sensation and the idiotic urge to return his smile.

I clear my throat. "Are you all ready and well-rested?"

"Sure. We went to bed extra early last night, and Willow made us warm milk with honey," Colin says so dryly that I wonder for a moment if he's serious.

"Really?"

"It's true, she did." Jax taps Easton's headrest. "Come on, let's go or we'll be late."

Easton glances at me briefly, his lips part . . . and I want to kiss him. Right here, right now, just like that. It's not right. I don't get it. This isn't what I want. It can't be. Except . . . it's exactly what I want. God, I'm so confused!

I quickly turn and stare out the window. "Let's go."

Easton doesn't say a word. I wish he would say something. Anything. But he's silent. The van's engine roars to life, and we leave the parking lot.

* * *

The Twenty-Seven Hour Studio is in the West End. It's a small studio that's technically fully booked out for the next few months, but I am who I am, and I wanted We Are No Saints to be able to record our song here. It's the studio where Dad recorded his first album twenty years ago, before he and Mom moved to LA.

I didn't really think about whether it was a good idea to choose this studio, of all places. I just did it. I still think it was a good idea, but one part of me wishes right now that I had given it at least a moment's thought. I didn't really think it through, and now here I am, with this hole in my chest that feels way too big. Way too empty, way too dark.

I forgot what it was like, to be in a studio. I've forgotten how familiar it all feels, even though I've never been to this one before. But just like ballet schools all have their similarities, so do recording studios.

This reminds me a bit of Dad's little studio in our villa in LA. It's a cozy room with moss-green walls and scruffy sofas and armchairs. It looks more like a living room than a place to work.

The two recording technicians who are with us today are explaining something to the boys, but I can't listen. There are too many images in my head. Dad in his studio, a guitar in his hand, big headphones on his ears. I see him at the piano, his fingers dancing quickly and confidently over the keys. His voice filling my ears, the room, my heart.

Hearts can break from time to time
Fragile little souls
Getting smaller, seem to hide
The things you used to know

I don't remember if his voice really sounded like how I imagine it, because it's been over six months since I last heard him sing live. Just the thought that I might be remembering it wrong makes everything hurt. My vision blurs, and I pull my phone out of my pocket and lower my head so no one notices. I don't want Easton to see me crying again just because I can't help it. It would be unfair.

Coming here was a mistake. A really stupid mistake. I see myself in Dad's studio at home, sitting in one of the armchairs with my legs tucked under me, reading while he records his songs. Me with my notebook and a pen in my hand, words in my head that need to come out. Thoughts, song lyrics, poems.

Dad coming over to me and reading my lyrics, trying to persuade me to find a melody for them, and me saying no, over and over again. No to the melodies, no to singing, no to my lyrics. No, always no. Now I wish I'd said yes just once.

"Hey, Birdy." Easton's voice is very close. He sounds worried. "Are you okay?"

I shake my head. Lying is useless. He knows me so well that there's not even any point in trying. I don't want to lie to him, anyway. It feels wrong. "No."

"You're thinking about your dad." A statement, not a question.

I nod. "He recorded his first album here," I explain, my voice sounding hoarse.

"I know," he says simply. Of course he knows. Why am I even surprised?

"He should be here with you and the band. He would have loved to be here."

Easton goes silent, knowing that's not the whole truth. He knows that I need my dad here. Today. Always. He strokes my hand, a hesitant, inquiring touch. I shouldn't wrap my hand around his; it's not fair, because I don't know what I want. But I need his closeness. His fingers between mine, and the short, encouraging squeeze that reassures me that he's here.

"You should start," I finally say, letting him go and wiping the tears off my face. "Have fun."

For both of us.

Easton hesitates, then nods. But before he goes to his friends, he turns back again and smiles at me. "I'm so happy that *you're* here, Rayne."

My eyes fill with tears again and my heart aches. But I return his smile anyway.

"I am too."

CHAPTER 29
Easton

Why Won't You Love Me—5 Seconds of Summer

My voice sounds strange to my own ears as we record "Dance with You 'Til Midnight" over and over again. It's not enough to be good. We have to be better. We have to be perfect.

Recording in this studio is different. We're recording live, all at once, to capture the fresh energy of the songs, just like Liam must have done when he recorded here. Usually all the instruments or at least the vocals are tracked separately. But we want to keep it raw and honest, and that means we have to do it in one take. My voice. Us. Our songs. Our energy. We play as if our lives depend on it, and in a way, they do. Our whole damn future depends on it. We play as if we're not in a small studio in the West End of Boston. We play as if our audience isn't just two recording technicians and Rayne.

My heart is pounding to the rhythm of Jax's drums. I'm sweating and my fingers are almost numb, but I hardly notice. I'm caught up in our music and in the words Rayne and I wrote together.

I won't turn back
I won't give up
I'll make it fucking right
Get lost in music
Lost in you
And dance with you 'til midnight

This isn't just a song. These aren't just words that make up a verse, a pre-chorus, and a chorus.

It's us. Rayne and me.

We are this song, and we could be more. We could be anything we want, if she would just give us a chance.

My gaze wanders over to her all by itself. It's been like this all day. I can't stop. I look at her, and she looks at me with that expression in her eyes that's sad and happy and proud and everything in between. Her lips are moving silently along with mine as I sing the chorus one last time. Her gaze burns into mine. She has tears in her eyes again, but she smiles, and I must be a terrible friend because everything inside me is urging me to go to her and put my arms around her. I want to press my mouth against hers, to taste her, to feel her, to lose myself in her.

The instruments fade away, leaving only my voice for the last line, and then silence—a silence that rings on in my ears. I take off my headphones when Phil, one of the recording technicians, gives us a sign.

"That was good," he says, and Miller, his colleague, gives us a thumbs-up. "I'd say it's time for a break."

"Thank God." Jax groans with relief. "I don't think I'll be able to move my arms tomorrow."

"Then you're going to have a problem if we ever go on tour," Colin says.

"No worries, I've got plenty of time to work on my guns before then."

"To do that, you'll have to use them," Beck says with a laugh, putting his guitar aside.

Colin and I do the same, and Rayne comes over with her arms full of water bottles, which she hands out to us. She gives me the last one, and my fingers brush hers, sending an electrifying tingle straight up my arm to my chest.

I can tell she feels it too when she bites her lower lip and her eyes get darker.

It would be so easy to kiss her right now. So damn easy. But it's not what she wants or needs, and I have to accept that, damn it.

"You did great," she says, her voice hoarse, as if she were the one who'd just spent the last few hours singing the same song over and over again.

"Really?" I ask, hearing how insecure I suddenly sound, even though two minutes ago I was convinced we were good. Really good. But this damn self-doubt doesn't care; it just pops up without warning.

"I promise." She reaches for my hand because she knows what I'm thinking, squeezes it briefly, and then lets go. I have to fight the urge to reach for her, to intertwine her fingers with mine, because it feels so wrong not to. "It was even better than I thought it would be," she says. "You were just incredible—" she breaks off, shaking her head. "Just keep it up, okay?"

I nod because I suddenly don't know what to say. I hate that it's so difficult to talk to her now. I have no fucking idea how we're going to get back to when it was easy. There are so many things I want to tell her.

I miss you. I want you more than I've ever wanted anyone. I want to be with you all the time. You're not losing me. Trust me.

I open my mouth to speak, and Rayne looks at me, her eyes gleaming. I swallow, she holds her breath, and I have to say it now, there's no other way. We're not friends. We're more than that. She knows it, and she doesn't need to be afraid of it.

"Rayne . . ." I begin, even though it's the wrong place and time because we're not alone. That doesn't matter now. Nothing matters except her and me. "I think—" I break off when a large hand meets my shoulder.

"Shall we continue?" Jax asks cheerfully. The wrong moment, which could have been the right one, is over now. Jax really has terrible timing.

Rayne is the first to find her voice again. "Yeah, keep going. I need to make a quick phone call. I'll be right back." She rushes out of the room, not taking her hat or jacket, even though the dress she's wearing is much too thin for February. I want to follow her, but I can't move.

Fuck.

"Is everything okay with you two?" Jax asks. There's a deep crease between his brows. "Did I interrupt something?"

I sigh. "Let's just get on with it."

CHAPTER 30

Rayne

I Can't Breathe—Bea Miller

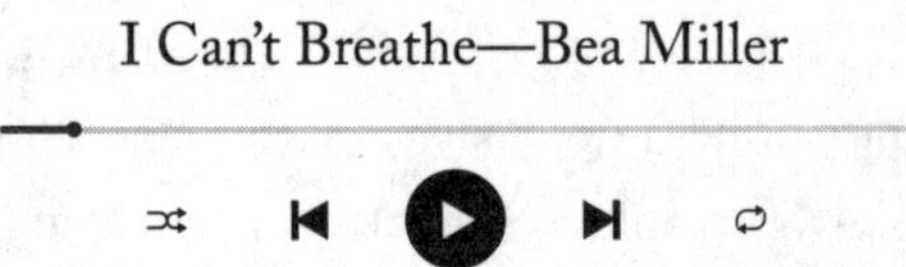

I'm not going outside to make a phone call. I'm going outside because I can't breathe. I don't know what to do or what I want. I need Mom. I need her to tell me what to do about Easton, to help me with the rest of my damn life. But mostly with Easton.

When he looks at me, I can't think anymore. My mind just goes blank, and all I can see are his blue eyes and his lips. I want him to pull me close and kiss me.

God, what's wrong with me? Why am I like this? Why can't I stop thinking about kissing him? He's my best friend. I told him that I don't want more, but I'm still thinking about him all the time. I have to stop, but I can't. Why can't I?

My hands tremble as I scroll through the contacts on my phone. I pause when I come to Mom's name. I never deleted her number, or Dad's. I want to call her so badly it hurts. The pain is still there, every time my heart beats, but now . . . in this moment it feels like it's going to tear me apart from the inside. The black hole in my chest is trying to devour me, and I'm so close to just letting it.

My whole body trembles. I bite my lower lip until I taste blood to suppress the sobs. I don't think about it as I tap on her contact, I just do it. I freeze as I hear her voice. Cheerful. Carefree. Alive.

"Hi, this is Laura. I'm not available right now. Leave me a message and I'll get back to you later."

My heart stands still. One second, two, three. Then it starts beating again, much too fast. I hear a rushing sound in my ears, but it's her voice, it's still there. It was there the whole time; I just never called her. I could have heard her, but I never tried.

There's a beep, and I should hang up.

I must.

But I can't.

"Mom." My voice breaks. It's so wrong, what I'm doing. *Hang up. End the call, damn it.* "Mom, I don't know what to do. You always told me what I should do when I couldn't figure it out. You have to help me. You have to tell me how it feels to be in love, because I have no goddamn clue, okay? I don't know how it goes, or how you're supposed to feel, or if it's normal that I want to kiss my best friend. How does it all work? What should I do, Mom? Am I making a mistake? And if I am, is it when I let him be more than just my best friend, or is it when I don't? You have to tell me! You know these things! You and Dad . . . you were perfect! You have to tell me what to do!"

I gasp for air. My throat is tight. God, I have to stop this. Instead, I start walking, continuing down the narrow alley behind the studio. There's no one else here, but even if there were, I wouldn't care. I've started talking and now I can't stop.

"You should be here, Mom! You and Dad! You should be here

helping me. But you're dead, and I have to manage on my own, and I'm so . . . shit, I'm so angry!" An incredulous laugh escapes me as I suddenly realize that it's true.

I'm sad. I feel lost. But I'm also angry. So incredibly angry.

"Why did you have to go to that stupid party? Why didn't you come home earlier? Or later? Why did you have to decide to leave at exactly that time? Why didn't you drive home the normal way? Why did you take that damn detour? Why, Mom? Why couldn't you just come back home to me? Why—" I stop when there's a beep at the other end.

The call is over.

Just like that.

No, no, no!

I wasn't done. There is so much I have left to say. So much that I have to get off my chest, even though she'll never hear it and will never answer.

A hoarse scream escapes from my throat, frustrated, sad, and destroyed. I cling so hard to my phone that the edges dig deep into my palm. I hardly feel it. All I can feel is this tension inside me, this unbearable pain that's tearing me apart. Every day. Every minute. Every second.

Underneath it all is this burning anger that I've suppressed and refused to acknowledge. Until now.

"Rayne?"

At the sound of Easton's voice behind me, I close my eyes. My heart is pounding against my ribs so hard it hurts.

The fury takes my breath away.

I can't breathe again.

Why won't it stop? Why won't it ever stop?

CHAPTER 31

Easton

Until I Found You (Piano Version)—Stephen Sanchez

I don't know what made me follow her. I told the guys that I needed a moment before starting again, and I went outside to find Rayne.

Maybe it was the expression on her face, or the way her voice shook. Or my damn heart trying to force me to finally say what I need to say, because saying anything else is no longer an option.

"What's wrong?" I ask when she doesn't answer. She has her back to me, and her shoulders are hunched. She's clinging to her phone. I couldn't hear what she was saying or who she was talking to, she was too far away, but I heard the anger in her voice.

"Nothing. Just go," she says, and a part of me wants to do what she asks. I want to give her the space she needs, but I can't because I feel her pain, and it's unbearable.

Instead, I reach instinctively for her hand, without thinking about it. Her skin is ice cold. It's no wonder; I'm freezing my ass off out here. She doesn't resist my touch or shake me off, and I take a breath of relief.

"Rayne, talk to me," I beg her, tugging gently on her hand until she turns around. Her gaze darts restlessly over my face, her gray eyes even brighter than usual.

"It's nothing," she lies, even though it's so obvious that something is wrong.

"Who were you talking to on the phone? Why are you so angry?" I ask. I *have to* ask.

Her mouth opens and closes again. Her eyes glisten, and tears are hanging on her long lashes. It almost kills me, because suddenly I'm very sure I know who she called. Who she talked to without getting an answer. It tears me apart to see her like this. I want so badly to help her, but I don't know how.

"Rayne—" I begin, but she cuts me off.

"I shouldn't be here, okay? Not in this damn city, not at this ballet school. I shouldn't be here *at all*!" She pulls away from me. I want to tell her it's not true, that she's exactly where she belongs. But that wouldn't be the truth. Not really.

"I'm angry because I have no choice but to be here. Because I have nowhere else to go!" she shouts. Her phone hits the wall of the studio with a crack and lands on the ground. Rayne doesn't even flinch or check to see if the screen is cracked. She doesn't care. "I'm angry because my parents are dead. It's unfair! They shouldn't be dead. They didn't deserve it! They didn't do anything wrong. They were good people! They were just in the wrong place at the wrong time. It's not fair!"

Her words break my heart because she's right. It's not fair. This whole fucking life is unfair. I want to take her pain away, but I can't. There's nothing I can do. Absolutely fucking nothing.

"I know, it's—"

"No," she snaps. "You have no idea! I need her. I need my mom. She has to tell me how to do this!" Her voice breaks again, and something about her words scares me. I reach out for her again, but she dodges me this time.

"What do you mean? She has to tell you how to do *what*?"

She shakes her head and presses her lips together.

"Talk to me, Rayne," I say, struggling to get the words out. My pulse is racing, and a knot of helplessness and panic is forming in my stomach.

"I've been talking to you the whole time. I just can't . . ." she shakes her head and takes a step backward. Away from me.

"What can't you do?"

"Why can't I stop thinking about that kiss?" she suddenly says. Her hands are clenched into fists, and her whole body is shaking. I don't know if it's from cold or anger. "Why can't I stop thinking about *you*? It drives me crazy, you know? You're doing this to me, and I don't want it. I don't know what to do with all these damn feelings, Easton!"

Her words hurt.

I don't want it.

"Do you think this is any fun for me, either?" For a moment I'm just as angry as she is. It's a helpless fury, nothing that makes sense, but it's there, and we're both losing control. Too fast, too suddenly. "Do you think I'm any less confused than you are?"

She's silent again, her chin jutting forward defiantly and an angry glare in her eyes. What are we doing? We shouldn't be arguing. I have to stop and be stronger than the anger and frustration, stronger than this damn longing that pulls me to her like a magnet, again and again. But I'm not strong, and I keep talking. I can't stop myself.

"I didn't plan this! None of it. Certainly not the kiss. I didn't know it would be like this when we finally met. I wish I could be the person you need. I wish I could just be your friend!"

"Then be my friend, damn it!" she yells. She moves toward me, too fast for me to react or dodge her, though I wouldn't have done that anyway. She pushes against my chest so hard with both hands that I stumble backward.

"I can't!" I shout back at her.

"Why not?" Her voice rings with the same desperation I hear in my own.

"Because I'm in love with you," I blurt out, hoarse and desperate. She flinches, and I have to stop myself, but it's too late. I can't stop. I can't go back. "I'm in love with you, and I didn't plan it this way. I wanted to be your friend because that's what you need me to be, but I can't, because I can't stop thinking about that kiss, and I want more, okay? I want to be with you all the time, Rayne."

"You want . . . *what*?" She stares at me in disbelief, her big gray eyes going wide.

I take a step toward her. I have to end this now and tell her everything, because she deserves to know the truth, and I deserve to tell her.

I put both hands on either side of her face, needing to touch her. Her soft skin, her lips. Again and again, her lips.

"I want you. I wanted you from the very start. I just didn't dare to let myself think about it because . . . damn it, you're my best friend, but I wanted you even before we ever met. When you were still the girl I wrote endless messages to. I want you because you understand me and I understand you. Because you help bring out the best in me, because you believe in me, and because I can't stop thinking about you. I can't stop thinking about that kiss, and how I—damn it, I want *you*, Rayne! Because I'm in love with you." I stroke her cheek with my thumb. My heart is racing. I've destroyed our friendship, for good. There's no way back, only forward. "What do *you* want?" I ask her.

PART 7

Chorus

CHAPTER 32

Rayne

I'm Yours—Isabel LaRosa

"I want *you*, Rayne! Because I'm in love with you." His voice is a hoarse whisper that makes my heart beat faster and sends shivers down my back.

My skin is glowing with heat, even though it's freezing out here. But I hardly feel the cold. All I can feel is him. His hands on my face, his thumb gently stroking my cheek.

"What do *you* want?" He gazes at me, and his eyes are an infinite blue.

We're standing at the edge of an abyss, and I can't run away anymore. Not now. There's no point. I could lose Easton at any time, any day, regardless of whether we're friends or . . . something more. There are a thousand ways I could lose him. I can't run away from the what-ifs. Easton is here, standing in front of me. He's the one holding me, gazing at me, making my heart beat out of time. He's my best friend. He's the one who makes me feel safe. He's my home. He's the one I want to see every day and talk to about everything.

All at once, everything is so simple.

So I jump.

"I want you," I say, and then my lips find his. His lips on my mouth, his hands on my face, his warm skin against mine. Kissing Easton is like breathing. Once I start, I can't stop.

It's better than anything in the world. Better than the best song. He *is* the best song.

His heart beats beneath my hands; I can feel it. My fingers dig a little deeper into the soft material of his hoodie, and the rhythm of my heartbeat matches his.

He tilts my head back, confidently but infinitely gentle. My lips open of their own accord, his tongue touches mine, and I die a little. A part of me dies a painfully beautiful death.

Maybe it's the last remnant of my fear.

A stifled gasp escapes me as he takes my lower lip gently and firmly between his teeth. I can feel his muscles tense under my hands in reaction to the gasp I made, and I love it. Everything about it.

Kissing him, breathing him in, tasting him.

I've never felt this way before. So desired. So beautiful. I feel it in a strange way that I don't understand, but I'm not going to question it. It's too good for that. Much too good. I stand on tiptoes, wrap my arms around his neck, and bury my fingers in his hair, which is softer than it looks. I feel dizzy and I can't breathe, but this time it's because I'm kissing him. I never want us to stop, because this is everything and more.

All I can hear are soft gasps and heavy breathing. It sounds so much like *us*. I let him go, just for a moment, to slide my hands under his sweater. I need to feel his skin. It's warm, and he gasps as I touch him with my cold hands. But he doesn't pull away. Instead, he comes even closer, his hands in my hair. He tilts my head back again with his tongue in my mouth, hot and hungry, and my body throbs with longing. I don't think I've ever wanted anything as much as this. *More.* I need more. None of this is enough.

Then all at once he pulls away from me, and it feels like he's literally taking my breath away. The world is spinning, and for a few seconds, everything goes blurry. I feel light and heavy at the same time. He seems to feel the same way, because he's breathing heavily as he leans his forehead against mine. I blink up at him. His eyes are closed, but he's smiling. I smile back without even thinking about it.

"Rayne," he whispers, his voice resonating with emotion. I hear it. All of it.

"Easton," I whisper back, praying he understands I heard what he said without words, and that this is me saying it back. His smile widens.

"Did you know that no one but you uses my full name?"

"I like your name."

His lips brush mine, not a kiss, just a feather-light touch. It's a silent promise. Then the touch turns into a kiss again, slower this time, but deeper. No longer so hungry, but still full of longing. His hands slide down my back, cup my bottom, and then he lifts me up. Instinctively, I wrap my legs around his hips. His jeans are cold, I can feel them through my tights, but I wish the fabric would just disappear, because it's too much to have between us. I want to feel him everywhere. His fingers, his tongue, everything.

He takes a few steps until my back touches the brick wall of the studio behind me. A quiet voice in my head tries to remind me that we shouldn't be doing this, not here, not like this. It's too cold. Someone could catch us at any moment. But the voice is too quiet and my pulse is too loud, the throbbing in my body too urgent.

I move my hips, not consciously, but it just happens. It feels right. Easton groans, his hips pressing against mine. Heat and throbbing desire. My heart is beating so fast I think it's going to jump out of my chest.

The sound of someone clearing their throat makes us both freeze.

"I really hate to interrupt, but Phil asked me to let you know that there are surveillance cameras aimed right where you are now, because you're so close to the back door of the studio."

At the sound of Beck's amused voice, Easton groans in frustration and leans his forehead against mine. "Go away," he says without even turning to look at his best friend, while I'm trying to clear the fog in my head and get my heart to slow down to a normal rate.

"I don't know if it's such a good idea to leave you two alone right now. Who knows if you can control yourselves."

"Get lost, Beck," Easton grumbles, still not moving or letting go of me.

"Only if you promise to come right back in so we can keep recording."

"We promise," I reply.

"Thanks, that's enough for me." There's a hint of amusement in Beck's voice, even though I can't see his smile because I haven't moved any more than Easton has. My legs are still wrapped around his hips, and his hands are still on my butt. I hear footsteps and then the sound of a door closing, and Beck is gone.

I look up at Easton. His eyes are half closed, his long lashes making shadows on his cheeks. I have to smile, and I get a warm feeling in my chest. It's a different kind of warmth than just a moment ago when he was kissing me. This is gentler and happier.

A soft laugh escapes me, a giggling sound I've never heard from myself before, and it makes Easton open his eyes. His gaze meets mine, and when he breaks into a grin, I can't help but laugh. His eyes light up and he brushes his nose against mine, a tender touch that makes me feel an ache of longing.

"I don't want to go in," I whisper against his lips, even though we have no choice. The songs won't record themselves. Especially not without a lead singer.

"Me neither."

"But we should."

"Yes," he says with a sigh. "We should."

I slowly unwind my legs from his hips, and Easton carefully lowers me until my feet touch the ground. He reaches for my hand, and our fingers intertwine. "Ready?" he whispers.

I nod. "Let's go inside. After all, you still have a song or two to record."

"I guess I do." He smiles again, and it's the most beautiful smile I've ever seen.

* * *

It's late when we finally drive back to the house. Easton doesn't even ask me if he should bring me back to school or if I want to stay over. He just looks at me and knows the answer.

We spent the whole day in the studio, much longer than

planned, but the guys were too good to just stop after the second song. In the end, they recorded four absolutely brilliant songs that I hope will help them reach the stars.

"Do you know when we'll get the final mixes?" Jax asks, leaning forward between the seats so he's close to my ear. "I wanted to ask Phil before, but I forgot."

"Probably in a few days," I say, not admitting that I promised Phil and Miller I'd give them a little extra for a rush order.

"Does that leave you enough time to create your choreography?" Easton asks, turning the van into the driveway.

My shoulders tense. I haven't thought once all day about using "Dance with You 'Til Midnight" for contemporary dance class. Today was just about the song, and that was a very good feeling.

"What choreography?" Beck asks.

"It's nothing," I say. I try to ignore the uneasy feeling in my stomach because I don't want to think about it right now. Not about contemporary dance, and not about ballet. Not about school or college. That all feels like it's a lifetime away right now. It's been less than a day since I left campus, but something's been different since we got to the studio. Not just between Easton and me. I can't quite figure out what it is.

The engine cuts out with a quiet stutter. I open the door and get out quickly, but Beck isn't so easily put off.

"It doesn't sound like nothing."

"It's really not important. I just have a course where we have to choose a song to choreograph a dance to, and I wanted to use 'Dance with You 'Til Midnight.' That's all."

"You want to dance to one of our songs?" Jax catches up with us and looks at me curiously.

"It's her song too," Easton reminds his friend. He shoves himself between Jax and me and takes my hand. I have to smile in spite of the feeling in my stomach, because he says it so casually, and he intertwines his fingers with mine as if it were the most normal thing in the world.

"Yeah, I know. But that's not what this is about."

"It kind of is," Easton replies.

Jax groans in annoyance. "No, it's about the choreography. Do you have any ideas yet?"

"No, not really." I don't. I just know that it has to be our song. That's it. That's all I've got.

"Let's order something to eat, I'm starving." Colin is already walking up the steps to the front door.

"Me too." Jax picks up his pace but turns back to me as he continues walking backward. "You have to tell me your ideas later."

"But I don't have any," I try to object. But he's already turned around again and disappears into the house after Colin.

"You're committed," Beck says with a grin. "You're one of us now."

It's just a few words, but they're enough to make a lump in my throat. Beck sounded so sincere, like he really meant it. As if all at once, I actually belong.

"Hey." Easton's quiet voice makes me turn. His gaze is curious and a little worried. "Everything okay?"

"Yes, I . . ." I swallow hard. "I just didn't expect that." I stop again, not knowing how to put what I'm feeling into words. But I guess Easton understands what's going on in my head, because the corners of his mouth twitch and he smiles before stopping and pulling me in for a tender kiss. It's different from the kiss we shared earlier in the little alley behind the studio. Different from our first kiss in his room. Much shorter, less hungry, less desperate, but no less intense.

"Beck is right, for once," he says and looks down at me. "You belong here."

You belong with me.

He doesn't say it, but I can see what he's thinking.

"Yes," I murmur, thinking the same thing.

And you belong with me.

I want to say it, but I can't get the words out. I have no idea why.

"Guys, please come inside so Colin can get something to eat." Jax appears in the doorway, drumming his fingers impatiently against the wood, and the moment is gone. "You'll have all night to yourselves."

"You're all so annoying today," Easton says, rolling his eyes. But I think Jax knows as well as I do that he doesn't mean it. Not really, anyway. Maybe just a little. After all, Jax did pick a bad time to show up.

"We're hungry, come on."

"Let's go," I say, smiling. I pull Easton up the stairs and into the house. Colin and Beck are already on the sofa, hunched over a phone, scrolling through some food delivery app.

Easton sinks into one of the big armchairs, wraps an arm around my waist, and pulls me into his lap. It's strange how right it feels. Just a few hours and everything has changed.

"So what's your choreography going to be like?" Jax asks, getting back to the subject that I'd really rather ignore right now.

"It's not anything yet. I still have to figure it out. All I know is it'll be a dance set to your song."

"Our song," Easton corrects me, and I have to smile again.

"Yes."

"Like in a music video?" Jax's eyes light up with excitement, and Beck lets out an incredulous laugh.

"You're not serious."

"What?" I ask. I must have missed something.

"Jax has dumb ideas," Colin says. He's tapping away at his phone. Probably texting his girlfriend. Easton told me about Emma, about their long-distance relationship and how difficult it is for them sometimes.

"I have brilliant ideas."

"You don't." Easton sighs behind me, his breath brushing warmly against my neck. I get goose bumps and snuggle closer to his chest. I can feel his heart beating against my back.

"Can someone fill me in?" I look questioningly from one to the other.

"I just thought . . . since we've already recorded the song and you're working on the choreography . . . maybe we could do something with it."

I blink, and then I understand what he's getting at. "So you're suggesting we shoot a music video?"

He shrugs and grins. "Why not?"

"Maybe because we can't afford it?" Colin points out, while I just sit silently, my gaze jumping between the boys.

My head is suddenly way too full and at the same time terribly empty. A music video. With our song and my choreography? That's completely crazy. But maybe crazy is good.

"Oh, come on, it doesn't have to be that elaborate. Skye is always making videos for TikTok and stuff. They turn out pretty good."

"Skye makes TikToks?" I stare at him in surprise, forgetting for a moment what we're actually talking about, because Skye is the last person I can imagine making videos and posting them on social media. I have no idea why; it's not like I know her well enough to judge whether it suits her or not. But somehow I wouldn't have thought she was the type, and she's never mentioned it. Neither has Jase, Zoe, or Mae.

Then Jax blushes, awkwardly rubbing his nose. "Yes. But the thing is, I wasn't supposed to tell. Skye doesn't like to talk about it, and I don't think anyone knows except me."

"Well, I'd say you failed miserably, dude." Beck pats him on the shoulder.

"I thought there was nothing going on between you two." Colin's eyebrows go up, and Jax makes a face.

"There isn't, I've just known about the videos for a long time. But it doesn't matter now. Just picture it for a second: our song, Rayne's dance . . . It could be really good. Maybe we'll go viral, and then a label will notice us, and then we'll become rich and famous." He beams at us, and suddenly there's a tingle of excitement in my stomach.

"And they lived happily ever after," Colin says sarcastically, leaning back and crossing his legs. "You're kidding, right?"

"No, why should I be?"

"Because it's pretty unlikely."

"But not impossible," Jax argues. "It's definitely worth a try, right? What have we got to lose?"

"Not much, really," Beck admits, looking at Easton and me. "What do you think?"

Easton's arm around my waist tightens. I turn to look at him.

He looks at me, only me, and for a moment it feels like we're totally alone in the room. In the world. He tilts his head, a tiny movement. *It's up to you.*

My pulse races. It really is my decision. "You don't need me for a video. You can do it without me."

"Of course we *could*," Colin says, and I turn around again to face the guys. He smiles a little. "But if we're going to do this, let's do it together. Easton's right, it's your song too."

"Okay, but I don't even know if I can do the choreography. I've never done anything like this before," I protest.

"Neither have we." His smile widens. "All or nothing, Rayne."

My heart skips a beat. This is the first time Colin hasn't called me "Text Girl."

You're one of us now.

I stand up, suddenly unable to sit anymore. My legs are tingling, and so is the rest of my body. My thoughts are racing and I have to move. A song. Choreography. A music video. It's completely crazy. It probably won't even work. In fact, I'm pretty sure it won't.

But what if it does?

It's Dad's voice in my head, warm and encouraging. I stand still and close my eyes, taking a deep breath.

What if it does work, Mockingbird?

I don't think about it anymore, I just open my eyes and make a decision.

BEFORE

JUNE 15 AT 6:43 PM

mockingbird:
Sometimes I don't understand guys.

eastcoleman:
Why? What's going on?

mockingbird:
Prom is in two weeks. Two!!! Today that idiot Damien asked me to go with him. Everyone else asked their dates weeks ago, and now he comes at the last minute and expects me to say yes. He can't be serious!

eastcoleman:
Maybe he didn't have the courage to ask you before.

mockingbird:
Oh, come on. We were going out at the beginning of the year, for a few weeks. He was the one who broke up with me. I really doubt that's the reason.

eastcoleman:
Well, if he broke your heart and now wants to get closer again, it's understandable that it would be difficult for him, isn't it?

mockingbird:

Hey, whose side are you on, anyway?

eastcoleman:

Yours. Always.

mockingbird:

Thanks. But he didn't break my heart. It's not like we were together because I was madly in love with him.

eastcoleman:

Then why were you with him?

mockingbird:

If I tell you, you won't like it.

eastcoleman:

Tell me anyway.

mockingbird:

Hailey was dating Damien's best friend at the time, and I thought we'd start hanging out more if we were both dating guys from the same group. Turned out to be a mistake. Hailey still didn't have time for me, and when we were all out together, she was all over Josh.

eastcoleman:

. . .

mockingbird:
I told you that you wouldn't like it. Are you pissed off?

eastcoleman:
No. But I really can't stand Hailey.

mockingbird:
You don't have to. But please explain to me why Damien is back now.

eastcoleman:
He broke up with you?

mockingbird:
Yes.

eastcoleman:
Why?

mockingbird:
There was another girl, and it probably didn't help that I wasn't interested in going out with him that often. I prefer to stay at home, and he wanted to drag me to parties every weekend. But like I said, it's not like he broke my heart or anything.

eastcoleman:
Okay, to be honest, I have no clue what he wants. He didn't just suddenly realize that he has feelings for you after all, did he?

mockingbird:
His original date probably canceled on him.

eastcoleman:
And do you want to be his new date?

mockingbird:
No way. I don't even want to go to the prom.

eastcoleman:
You can't miss your prom.

mockingbird:
Sure I can.

eastcoleman:
If it's about having a date, I could come.

mockingbird:
You would do that?

eastcoleman:
Yes.

mockingbird:
That's really sweet of you. But no, you can't fly to LA just for my prom.

eastcoleman:
I could.

mockingbird:
That's so nice, but you don't have to. I really don't want to go. I just don't like events like that.

eastcoleman:
Let me know if you change your mind.

mockingbird:
Thanks, Easton.

eastcoleman:
Anytime, Birdy.

CHAPTER 33
Rayne

Midnight Rain—Taylor Swift

It feels almost surreal when Easton and I go upstairs to his room later. The last time I was here, we kissed. Earlier today, we kissed again. Everything is different from last time, and when I walk into his room, I realize just *how* different.

I don't really know how to deal with it.

Easton strokes the back of my hand, and I look up at him and meet his questioning gaze.

"Should I drive you back to school?" He sounds reluctant, as though he doesn't want to be asking this at all.

I shake my head. "No. Unless you want me to go."

"No," he says immediately. "I want you to stay."

I breathe a sigh of relief. "Okay. Me too."

He smiles. "I'll just check in the bathroom to see if I can find a toothbrush for you. You can use Willow's stuff, I'm sure she won't mind." He walks over to a dresser, pulls open a drawer, and hands me one of his T-shirts. "Here. My sweatpants will probably be way too big for you, but you can have a pair if you want."

"No, that's okay," I reply. I want to feel his warm skin against mine.

"I'll be right back. Do you need anything else?" He runs a hand through his hair, looking strangely embarrassed, as if he's just as insecure as I am. That helps the nervous tingling in my stomach ease a little.

I smile. "I've got everything I need."

"Okay." He walks to the door but glances back over his shoulder, and a tingle goes through my whole body.

I nod even though he didn't ask a question, but I can't just stand there and look at him, even though it's what I want to do most. Easton bites his lower lip, and I immediately gaze at his mouth. Those lips . . . He hesitates, then turns away. I can hear him take a deep breath before finally leaving the room.

The lamp next to his bed is the only source of light. I toss the T-shirt he just gave me on the bed and pull my phone out of my small backpack. The display is miraculously intact after I threw it against the wall earlier. Only the case is cracked. I tap the screen and discover half a dozen messages from Zoe and Mae in our group chat, and I realize it's later than I thought. It's almost midnight.

I open our chat; I have to at least let them know that I won't be coming home tonight, otherwise they'll definitely worry. I bet Mae has been knocking on my door every few minutes for hours to see if I sneaked back to school without saying anything. I haven't written all day, even though I promised I would, and my guilty conscience makes me send a quick text back.

MAE:
How's it going?
MAE:
Come on, Rayne, we're curious.
MAE:
Please answer me.
MAE:
Raaaaaaaayne, I'm going to keep bugging you until you write back!
ZOE:
Gosh, Mae, don't be so nosy. She'll get in touch.
MAE:
I can't help it. Rayne not answering must mean something. Right?

RAYNE:

I completely forgot to get back to you, I'm sorry. It went well. I'll tell you everything tomorrow.

It takes less than ten seconds for Mae to reply.

MAE:

Finally. I was starting to worry.

RAYNE:

I'm sorry!

MAE:

No biggie. If you want to tell us everything tomorrow . . . does that mean you're not coming home tonight?

I feel the blood rush to my cheeks, though I have no idea why I'm so embarrassed.

RAYNE:

Yes. Looks like it.

MAE:

OMG! Does that mean what I think it means?

My face gets even hotter, and I pray that Easton doesn't choose this moment to come back. I quickly type a reply.

RAYNE:

I think so. I'll tell you everything tomorrow, I promise.

MAE:

You better!

ZOE:

Good night, sleep well!

MAE:

Or maybe not, heh heh.

I have to laugh. Then I wish them a good night and slip my phone back into my bag at the exact moment that the door opens and Easton comes back into his room.

"I have a toothbrush and a towel for you. Willow's makeup remover and creams are lying around. Just use whatever you need," he says.

I reach for his T-shirt. "Okay, I'll be right back."

The bathroom is one floor down, right next to Willow's room. The guys' voices float up from the living room along with the background noise of the movie they're watching. Closing the door quietly behind me, I step toward the sink.

I pull Easton's hat off my head. My hair is complete chaos, and I grab a brush from the shelf. Once I've managed to smooth it down, I take off my makeup, moisturize my face, and brush my teeth. Then I exchange my dress and tights for Easton's T-shirt. It's much too big for me and reaches all the way to my thighs. It smells like him, and I love it.

I fold my clothes neatly before leaving the bathroom and climbing the stairs to the attic. The steps are cold under my bare feet, but that's not the only reason I'm getting goose bumps. It's mostly because Easton is waiting for me in his room. I'm going to fall asleep with him and wake up with him again, and everything in between.

My heart is beating way too fast as I slip into the room and quietly close the door behind me. Easton is already in bed, wearing a T-shirt, which is kind of a shame and kind of cute at the same time, because I know he's trying to take the pressure off me.

He pulls back the covers, and I climb into bed with him. He pulls me close until my head is resting on his chest and his lips brush my temple. It's warm under the covers, and his body against mine makes me feel calm. It feels familiar and new at the same time, and absolutely right.

As if it were meant to be this way, from the very beginning.

I look at him. There's nothing I'd rather do.

"You don't have to do the music video if you don't want," he says. "Maybe it's a silly idea."

"No, it's not. I want to do it." I swallow. "It feels nice to be a part of it."

"I'm glad you want to be part of it," he whispers. He kisses my forehead again, and I close my eyes for a moment. I haven't felt this safe in months.

"I'm glad Colin doesn't call me Text Girl anymore."

Easton laughs softly, the sound vibrating in his chest. "Me too. He's been doing it long enough. At a certain point, it's not funny anymore."

"Do you think they really want me to be involved?"

"They wouldn't have suggested it otherwise. Not Jax, and definitely not Colin."

"What about Beck? He didn't really say anything about it."

"Yeah, but he likes you. I think he just doesn't want to pressure you. He's a little more empathetic than Colin and Jax."

"You don't say," I reply with a smile. But my smile fades quickly. "I just don't know if I'll be able to do the choreography. Please don't get your hopes up too high. I might be totally useless at it."

"You won't be."

"You don't know that."

"Yes, I do. You know, Willow is a dancer, and even though I don't know as much as either of you, I've learned enough from her to be able to tell if you're good. And you are."

"That doesn't mean—" I start to say, but Easton cuts me off by pressing his lips firmly against mine.

"Don't say it. Seriously. Have a little faith in yourself, Rayne. Please. And if you don't like what comes out in the end, that's okay. We'll just forget about the video. But I'm sure it'll be great. Your song turned out amazing."

"*Our* song."

"Our song," he confirms with a smile.

"It is, isn't it?"

"Yeah." He turns slightly so we're both lying on our sides, my head resting on his arm. He lifts one knee so I can slide my leg between his.

We're so close, but it's a completely different kind of closeness than this afternoon when my legs were wrapped around his hips. This feels more intimate. More real. His skin against mine, warm and soft.

"Have you thought about whether you'd want to write another song?" There's a cautious tone in his voice I don't recognize, but somehow it feels familiar anyway. It sounds so much like him.

"No," I lie. I have. Not recently, but I used to. I told him I wanted to make music back when we were first messaging. He knows that, which is why he's asking. But that was then, and this is now. It's become much more complicated to make music. Even to think about it. "Yes," I admit a second later, because he already knows the truth. He knows me.

He's silent, waiting for me to continue. If I want to. He gives me time.

"I don't know what I want," I finally admit. "Writing that song with you felt . . . right. It felt good. But I'm not sure I can do it again."

"You could try."

"What if I fail?"

"Then so be it. But it wouldn't be the end of the world. At least you'll have tried."

I bite my lower lip. If only it were that easy. But it's not. It never has been. Because I am who I am, and Dad was who he was. I'll never be like him. I open my mouth to say that, but something else comes out instead.

"I called my mom this afternoon. It was stupid. I knew she wouldn't answer, but her number hasn't been disconnected yet, and when the voicemail kicked in, there she was. I got so angry. Why did I get angry?"

"You're allowed to be angry."

"Really?" My eyes fill with tears. "It doesn't feel that way."

"You're allowed to feel everything."

The next breath burns in my chest. It hurts, and part of me wants to stop talking and avoid the pain and sadness, at least for tonight. But I can't avoid it, and I have to let it out. "I miss her. I miss talking to her. I want to tell her and Dad about you."

"I wish you could." He sounds moved by the idea. He blinks, and his eyes are just as wet as mine probably are.

"It's so unfair that I can't tell them anything about you. I wish they could get to know you. I want—" I break off and take a shaky breath. "I spoke to Mom's voicemail. It was terrible. *I* was terrible. And I can't take it back. I talked to her, and I know she'll never hear it, but I said so many awful things." There's a note of shame in my voice.

"I'm sure you didn't."

"I did. I shouted at her." I cover my face with my hand, and Easton's arms tighten around me. "I asked why they didn't take a different way home that night, or choose another time to leave. Why not earlier or later? I told her how angry I was."

Easton is silent for a moment, then takes a deep breath. "I'm sure your mom wouldn't have thought that was awful. I think she would have wanted you to let your feelings out instead of swallowing them. She would have understood, I'm sure of it."

He's right and I know it. I knew the whole time, but until this moment, I wasn't sure if I believed it. Sighing, I nestle more tightly against him.

"She would have liked you. Dad already thought you were great."

He gives me a tiny smile. "I don't know if he would still think that. Most fathers aren't very happy about seeing their daughters with boyfriends."

"Is that what you are?" I ask, surprised by how uncertain I sound. Easton already told me he's in love with me, after all.

He puts one hand on the side of my face and gently strokes my cheek with his thumb. "If that's what you want."

"Yes," I say, my breath catching as his thumb touches my lips. "That's what I want." The words come so easily, as if I should have said them from the very start. I probably should have.

Easton sits up and bends over me, his weight pressing me into the mattress. In a good way. Much too good.

"I don't want to worry anymore," I say. "You're my best friend, Easton. But you're also much more than that, because . . ." I take a shaky breath. "Because I'm in love with you too. I probably have been from the beginning; I just didn't know it. I don't want to be scared of it anymore."

His eyes glow with emotion, and he's so beautiful that my heart can hardly stand it.

"I want to kiss you," he murmurs, his voice deep and husky. I love his voice. It's *everything*. When I hear it, my body is suddenly nothing but heat and urgent wanting.

I put my hands on either side of his face, and instead of answering, I pull him down to me until he kisses me.

Our mouths open at the same time. His tongue is hot, and the world around me blurs until it ceases to exist. It's just him and me. His weight is pressing me into the mattress, but he's still not where I want him to be, where I *need* him to be. I move my hips, and he understands. In one fluid motion he slides his whole body on top of mine. His groin presses against mine, and I spread my legs. I can feel his erection against my center. It's almost more than I can bear.

His mouth wanders from my lips down my jaw, my neck, to the collar of my T-shirt. The shirt has to go. His clothes too. I want to feel his skin beneath my hands, on my lips, against mine. I grab the hem of his T-shirt and push it up. His hips instinctively press into mine before he sits up and quickly pulls the shirt off over his head.

I swallow as I look up at him. He's beautiful. So beautiful. Not as toned as the boys in ballet, but slimmer and more athletic. His muscles aren't as defined, but he's still buff. My gaze wanders over his chest, his stomach, and down to the very visible bulge in his boxers before I look back up at his face. His eyes are dark and full of desire, his lips swollen from our kisses. His hair is all messed up; I did that. I forget exactly when and how, but it doesn't really matter.

I sit up, holding his gaze, and break eye contact only briefly as I take off my shirt. He's holding his breath; I can see him exhale as soon as I let the T-shirt fall.

"Rayne." My name sounds like longing when he says it. I reach out a hand to him. I need him to touch me again; It's almost unbearable when we aren't connected.

"Are you sure?" he asks.

I nod. I don't think I've been this sure of anything in a long time.

He hesitates, his jaw tense, and I know what his next question will be even before he says it. "Have you ever—"

I nod again, more quickly this time. Yes, I've had sex before. It wasn't very good, but it happened.

"Are you really—"

I interrupt him by sliding both hands around his shoulders and pressing my mouth against his.

"Stop talking," I whisper, and he moans in a way that sends jolts of electricity through me, while at the same time making my body tingle with happiness.

He pulls me toward him and the kiss changes, getting deeper and hungrier. Somehow I end up with my back on the mattress again. Easton is next to me, not on top of me, and I move my hips impatiently because this isn't what I want. I want to feel him on me, inside me.

God, I want it so badly.

His hands move agonizingly slowly over my body, my hips, waist, and breasts, and I writhe under his touch. His breath brushes hotly against my skin as he lifts his mouth from mine and his lips travel down my neck, lower and lower until his tongue finds my nipple and he sucks on me. *Oh God.* Heat builds in my lower abdomen, and my muscles contract.

And then his fingers are finally where I want them, stroking me through my underwear, which is now alarmingly wet. I can't breathe . . . I can't . . . breathe . . . in the best way possible as he pushes the thin fabric aside and touches me. A whimper escapes me, a sound I've never heard from myself before, which he inhales as he kisses me again. I feel him quake beneath my hands, just as I do beneath his fingers, because he's found exactly the right spot. Everything is spinning, and it's both too much and not enough.

I cling to him, gasping into his mouth, pressing myself against his fingers, begging him not to stop. He doesn't. He keeps going, and when he slides first one finger and then a second inside me, I completely dissolve. I see stars. I glow, I disintegrate, I die while he continues to caress me, thrusting his fingers inside me. I am nothing but throbbing and longing and wishing for more.

My legs tremble and the muscles in my abdomen contract with desire. *More, more, more.*

I kiss him, tongue, teeth, heat, and wanting. My hips tilt and he lowers himself over me. I press myself against his erection, more throbbing and then burning heat inside me as the orgasm washes over me like a wave.

He swallows my cry, and then we lie there, breathing heavily and trembling all over, his forehead leaning against mine, our lips almost touching.

"That was . . ." I begin, but fall silent because I have no words for what he's done to me.

"Yes," he says. The tip of his nose brushes mine, and I love it so much. I stretch until our mouths meet again because I can't get enough of him. Of this. Of us. I want more, need more. More of him inside me, on top of me, everything about him and everything about me—everything about us.

I put a hand on his shoulder and push him back. His eyes flicker, and then a smile flits across his face as I nudge him down until he's the one on the bottom. I stand up because I'm still wearing my underpants. Easton's gaze follows my every move, watching me as I slip off the last bit of fabric that was covering me and stand completely naked in front of him. He swallows.

"Fuck," he murmurs, and I have to smile because he sounds so admiring. I've never felt so beautiful.

"Do you have—" I don't even have to finish the question. He's already nodding and stands up and goes over to one of the dressers. He opens a drawer and returns with a little plastic package in his hand. He hesitates for a second and then pulls down his boxers.

I gaze at him, letting my eyes glide over his body just like he did with mine, and it feels so completely right.

"Come here," he whispers, and we move toward each other. His hands caress the back of my neck, his fingers in my hair. I stroke his back and move lower, sliding to the front. Easton groans as I wrap my hand around him. I smile at him and take the condom from his hand.

CHAPTER 34
Easton

Friends—Chase Atlantic

Rayne's eyes are dark with desire as she slips the condom onto me. She meets my gaze, and I drown in her eyes. I can't think. My blood is boiling and I've never been this hot before. All I can feel is her hand on my cock, her touch firm and confident.

I moan as she slides her hand down. Then she smiles, and I almost lose control. I almost lost it once already when she started making those soft noises and pressing herself against my hand. Now she stands on tiptoes and wraps both arms around the back of my neck, leaning into me.

Her naked body against mine is almost too much. Everything about her is so perfect, in her own way. My breath comes in heavy gasps, and I lean my forehead against hers, fighting for self-control, our mouths almost touching.

"Kiss me," she whispers, a plea in her voice.

So I kiss her, deep and hot. I'm so hard now that it hurts. I forget that I wanted to be careful, to take my time, because I want it to be right for her. I can't think anymore, and she's the reason why. Rayne in my arms, her taste in my mouth, her skin against mine.

I lift her up and she wraps her long, slender legs around me, legs that have been driving me crazy for weeks. Everything about her drives me crazy. There's a rushing sound in my ears and my cock twitches and begs for more. With her in my arms, I walk back to the bed. I find my way without looking, let her sink onto the mattress, and then sit up so I can look at her.

Her purple hair spreads out like a fan around her head, and she looks up at me. My mouth goes dry. She's so beautiful.

"Easton," she says. I love hearing my name coming out of her mouth. I love her voice, especially the fact that it sounds a little deeper than usual, a little huskier. Rayne reaches for me and pulls me down, spreads her legs and wraps them around my body. I feel her heat against me, and I think I'm going to die.

"Please," she begs. I give in and reach between us. She's so wet. She's my downfall, and I don't mind at all.

I enter her carefully and pause, giving her time to get used to me. She moves first, her pelvis lifting slowly. I follow her movement until we find another rhythm, hard and fast. We lose control and—fuck, nothing has ever felt this good.

I'm losing it, and I don't give a damn. Her hips thrust forward, and mine meet hers. A familiar pressure builds inside of me, but too fast, too soon. This isn't supposed to happen yet. But I can't stop myself, and she gives me no choice, moving faster, her legs holding me where she wants me.

"Fuck, Rayne, I can't! I have to slow down—" I break off as she shakes her head.

"No, not slower. Keep going, please!"

She kisses me, and I want to do what she's asking, I really do, but I can't, so I brace myself with one hand on the mattress to give me enough space to slide the other hand between us.

"Easton." She moans my name and starts to say something else, but before she can, another moan escapes her lips as I find the right spot. We gasp at the same time as she arches her back, lifting her pelvis a little higher. We push ourselves toward each other and I thrust into her, letting my fingers circle.

She comes before me, just by a few seconds, with a cry that pushes me over the edge. Her muscles tighten around me and I. Can't. Take. Any. More.

I come, and I didn't know it could feel so damn good to lose a part of myself.

* * *

Rayne's head is on my chest. We're still awake, and her fingers wander over my skin, a feather-light touch. Her eyes are closed, and there's a smile playing around her lips.

"You're in love with me," she murmurs, and now I have to smile too.

"Yes."

"I'm in love with you too." Her voice is suddenly soft and sleepy.

"Yes," I repeat. I feel warm, but a different kind of warm than before. She falls asleep, nestled against me, naked skin against naked skin. Her breathing becomes slow and heavy, as does her body. She sighs softly and I close my eyes. It's crazy, but I never want to do anything else but fall asleep and wake up again next to her.

CHAPTER 35
Rayne

Head in the Clouds—Hayd

"Well look who's back," Zoe says, greeting me with an amused smile as I enter the ballet studio on Monday morning, shortly before class starts. I'm running late, and Zoe and Mae are already stretching. I drop my bag on the floor with a thud.

"Good morning." My breath comes a little too quickly because I've been running across campus.

I quickly take hairpins out of my bag and start doing my hair. Everyone else is already here and ready to go, and class starts in just a few minutes. I should have been here fifteen minutes ago too so I could warm up properly. But Easton and I couldn't get out of bed, and by the time we finally got going, it was so late I only had time to rush to my room and change before hurrying over here.

"You broke your promise again," Mae says with a pout, but I know her well enough that I can tell she doesn't really mean it. She's not mad at me, even if she's pretending to be.

I give her an apologetic smile. "I know, I'm sorry."

"You said you'd tell us everything yesterday, but instead you didn't even come home. Admit it, you don't want to tell us anything." She sighs theatrically, which makes Zoe laugh.

"Yes, I do," I insist. "I'm sorry." It's not even a lie; I feel a bit guilty, but I haven't had time to text them to let them know what happened. I couldn't have gone to the dorm yesterday, either. I mean, I guess I could have, but I really didn't want to. It was much too nice to spend the day in bed with Easton.

"That's okay," she says with a mischievous smile. "You were busy."

The way she says it makes me blush immediately. "Yes," I murmur, unable to stop myself from smiling as I think of Easton. His hands in my hair and on my body. His mouth exploring every inch of me.

"You're blushing," Zoe observes. Not helpful.

I sigh and put my hands over my face before I can look at my friends again.

"Does that mean you've figured out how you feel when you're with him?" Zoe smiles at me, her eyes glinting.

"Yes." I lower my gaze, my cheeks burning.

Mae squeals excitedly. "I knew it! God, you have to tell us everything!"

"I will, this time I really will." I join them at the barre and finally start my warm-up. Every minute counts.

"Did everything go well with the song?" Zoe asks, leaning far over her outstretched leg.

I nod. "Really well, actually. The guys recorded four songs, and they all turned out great."

"What are they going to do with them now?"

I don't get a chance to answer Zoe as Mr. Conrad enters the studio just then, followed closely by Easton.

It's been less than half an hour since we said goodbye after he walked me to my room, but it still feels like an eternity. It's silly. He's wearing a dark-blue hoodie that makes his eyes look even bluer, his hair falling messily over his forehead, and I want to go over and kiss him. Again and again and again.

He smiles when he sees me, and I am infinitely in love.

"Hi," he mouths, and I read his lips.

"Hi," I whisper back. There are butterflies in my stomach. Mae and Zoe are watching us, giggling softly.

"God, you two are so adorable," Mae says. I can hear the smile in her voice, and I can't help but agree.

I turn to my friends again when Easton sits down at the piano. I can't stare at him the entire time, even though I'd really like to. God, what's happening to me?

"Good morning, everyone. Let's start right away. I have a lot of plans for you this week," Mr. Conrad says. Any other day, this would be the moment the happy butterflies in my stomach transform into a bundle of nerves, but not today.

Today I couldn't care less that even after almost two months of extra practice with Zoe and Mae on the weekends, I'm still hopelessly behind, and that's not likely to change anytime soon.

I don't care because Easton is here, glancing at me in the mirror from time to time, making me feel much too warm while his fingers glide confidently across the piano keys. I don't know if it's because I'm not really into it today, not as determined or focused as usual, but somehow everything seems a little easier.

When we move from the barre to the center to work on our jetés,

I find I can jump a little higher and keep my legs a little straighter. My muscles are burning, but it's the first time that I've been able to keep up with the tempo—and with everyone else—as we switch legs in the air to land with a different foot forward each time.

I feel strangely weightless, and it's crazy how easy everything is all of a sudden. I feel so light. I'm probably just imagining it because I'm surrounded by a pink cloud of total infatuation, but even that doesn't really matter to me right now.

"Much better, Rayne. Try to pay a little more attention to your hands, but otherwise very good," Mr. Conrad says, praising me.

A beaming smile spreads across my face, even though I'm breathing heavily. My stamina has improved, but not enough to get through an hour with Mr. Conrad without any problems. Especially when we're practicing jetés. Maybe it's only in my mind that things are easier.

"To finish up, let's work on your grand jetés," Mr. Conrad continues, and Mae lets out a barely audible, tortured groan next to me. She hates grand jetés, where we have to leap with our legs stretched into a split. I can't blame her. I would hate them too, any other day. But today . . . well, not so much.

We're divided into groups because there isn't enough space for us all to leap at the same time. I'm together with Zoe, Jessica, and Kelly, and when I leap, legs stretched wide, higher than I've ever leapt before, it feels a little like I'm flying.

* * *

The day goes by quickly, with pointe class passing just as fast as the first lesson with Mr. Conrad. When Zoe and I finally enter the contemporary dance classroom, Melanie is already waiting for us, even though we're early. She greets us with a brief nod and a warm smile.

"Did you have a nice weekend?" she asks, sounding genuinely interested.

We both nod at the same time, and Zoe starts laughing as I blush again.

Melanie raises her eyebrows. "Did I say something wrong?"

"No," I reply hastily. "We had a great weekend."

"Very good. I hope you got some rest. Breaks are important."

I want the ground to swallow me up when Zoe starts giggling uncontrollably.

"Rayne must be totally rested," she says, and I nudge her warningly in the side.

Melanie looks confused for a moment, then smiles again. "Glad to hear it."

Her gaze shifts to someone behind us, and she greets Lia and Katie, who are just entering the room. I'm not sure if Zoe has also seen Jase's sister, but she hooks her arm through mine and pulls me to the other end of the studio without even looking in Lia's direction. I still don't know what the problem is between Jase and Lia, but it's pretty obvious that it's not something that can be easily resolved. Even Zoe, who is usually nice to everyone, ignores her consistently.

"I thought Mae was the only one making fun of me," I protest, pretending not to have noticed anything. Whatever is going on, it's none of my business.

"I'm not making fun of you, honestly." Zoe blinks innocently at me, and I roll my eyes, grinning.

"Of course you're not."

"No, I really think it's beautiful how clearly in love you are." She hugs me briefly before letting go and smoothly lowering herself to the floor. I sit down next to her a little less gracefully.

"I think it's pretty crazy," I admit. "I didn't think it would feel like this." I can't quite find the right words to express what I'm feeling, but Zoe gives me a knowing smile. She understands what I mean anyway.

"Yes, I know." Her voice sounds soft. She turns her head, and when I follow her gaze, I see Jase and Skye entering the room. Skye is gesturing wildly with her hands as she talks to him. There's a deep crease between Jase's eyebrows.

"Everything okay?" Zoe asks as the two of them collapse onto the floor next to us. Jase leans over and kisses her. When they pull apart, they gaze at each other for a moment in a way that makes me feel like I've interrupted an intimate moment.

"Skye has secrets," Jase finally explains.

"Don't act like I'm the only one." Snorting, Skye removes the hairpins from her dark curls until they fall in long, tousled locks down her back.

"I didn't say it bothered me," Jase argues, grinning at her. "I'm not mad or anything. I just wanted to know why you're bringing this up now after not saying a word about it for months."

"Can someone explain this to me?" Zoe looks from one to the other, confused.

But Skye's gaze is fixed on me, and suddenly I know what's going on.

"How quickly did Jax betray me?"

"Uh . . ." I say, unsure how to respond.

She sighs and waves her hand dismissively. "Never mind. Jax and the guys want to shoot a video for the song they recorded over the weekend, and they asked if I could help because I've made a few TikToks. No one knew about them except Jax. But I should have known he couldn't keep his mouth shut, and now somehow it's common knowledge."

"You make TikToks?" Zoe asks incredulously.

"That's exactly how I reacted," Jase says, reaching for Zoe's hand and intertwining his fingers with hers.

"Which is exactly why none of you know about it." Skye gives us a saccharine smile. "Well, too late now. It doesn't matter anymore."

"I still don't quite understand what this is all about," Zoe says.

Skye nods at me. "You explain it. You're more involved in this than I am."

"It's not really a big deal," I begin, then briefly summarize the idea the boys have been talking about over the last couple days.

"Sounds like a big deal," Zoe says when I've finished.

"It's really not." I realize I'm trying to downplay the whole thing. "It's just—" I break off when Melanie claps her hands in the middle of the room, and all conversation stops abruptly. We stand up and join the others.

"Now that we're all here, let's get started," Melanie says. "How's your choreography coming along?"

No one says anything. No one moves.

An amused smile flits across her face. "Has anyone started yet?"

Five of us hesitantly raise our hands, including Skye and Lia. Next to me, Jase makes a dismissive sound, but when I look at him, he has a neutral expression on his face.

"Okay, I suggest we do this a little differently than originally planned. I assume by this point you've all at least decided on a song and whether you want to work alone, in pairs, or in a group."

This time, everyone nods, although I suspect there are still a few who haven't even gotten that far.

"Wonderful, then let's get started. Find your partners, if you have any, and then find a place to sit. I'll see if I can organize a second room for us so it doesn't get too crowded in here. I'll be right back." Melanie leaves the room without waiting for a response. She probably wouldn't have gotten one anyway.

"Have you started yet?" I ask, and Zoe and Jase both shake their heads.

"Not really. We have an idea, but nothing concrete yet," Jase replies.

"A duet is much more difficult than a solo," says Skye, tucking a strand of hair behind her ear.

"How far have you gotten?" Zoe asks, and Skye actually blushes a little.

"Almost done." Her answer sounds almost like a question. She shrugs. "But I actually enjoy choreography. I need it for my videos."

Melanie returns before any of us can reply. She leads half the class into an empty room at the end of the hallway. Skye, Zoe, Jase, and I stay behind with the other half.

I see Jase's shoulders slump a little in relief as his sister leaves the room.

"I'll start with you guys," Melanie says as she reenters the room, pointing at the four of us. "Are you a group?"

We shake our heads simultaneously. Skye and I step back.

"We're working alone," Skye says.

"Then let's get started. Please find a spot and begin." She

turns back to everyone. "I just drilled this into the other group: Remember, it's not about perfection. It's about your emotions and the music. Use that. Don't just focus on the rhythm, but also on the lyrics. Get into it. *Feel* it. If you have trouble with the beginning of the song, start somewhere else. You don't have to develop the choreography from start to finish. You can begin at the end if that helps," Melanie says, then turns to the first group.

I walk over to the window and stand there indecisively for a moment before closing my eyes, taking a deep breath, and blocking out everything around me. When I think about the fact that I'm not alone, I feel like I'm being watched, and that makes me sure I'll mess it up.

Emotions and music. That's what it's all about. That's all that matters.

Blinking little lights
Seems like a night sky right at my feet
I've been here a while
Wondering if once again we could meet

Easton's voice in my head. Soft and deep. The noises around me, the quiet conversations of those working in groups, fade into the background. I relax my shoulders, recall the movements Melanie has been teaching us over the past few weeks. Less control, more grounding.

I open my eyes, find myself in the mirror, and take the first step.

CHAPTER 36
Rayne

Fuck It, I Love You—Lana Del Rey

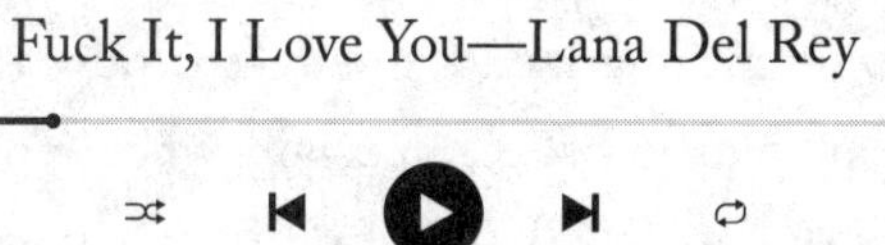

It's already dark by the time I walk across campus to the practice building for the second time that day. Bright light spills out of the tall windows, but I can't see anyone from down here.

Most people have finished training for the day, and I'd normally be the last one to go back in the evening for more, but today I'm too restless. I have been ever since I started thinking seriously about the choreography for "Dance with You 'Til Midnight."

The practice building is quiet; apart from my footsteps, I can't hear a sound. Until I reach the second floor. Soft piano music drifts into the stairwell, and I don't know why, but instead of continuing up to the third floor as planned, I walk down the second-floor hallway. I just follow the music until I spot a blond girl in the second studio on the left.

I'm not all that surprised when I recognize Lia. She's dancing, and she's beautiful.

Her movements are fluid and graceful. It looks so easy. But I know how incredibly exhausting what she's doing is. I know how much her feet must hurt in those pointe shoes. I know how tense every muscle in her body is.

But you can't see the effort, and I guess that's what happens when you combine true talent and a dream you're willing to cross every boundary for. Her short tutu flutters as she spins. She's perfect. A half step, then she gathers momentum and spins again. And again. And again.

I count along, mesmerized. Fouetté en tournant, one of the most spectacular spins in ballet, especially when repeated as many times as Lia is doing now. Fourteen, fifteen, sixteen. She keeps going. In *Swan Lake*, this spin is repeated thirty-two times. There are only a few dancers who can perform it perfectly so many times in a row without a break.

Lia is perfect. More than perfect; she's breathtaking. I stare at her and can't move, even though I shouldn't be here at all, let alone watching her.

But when someone like Lia is dancing, you can't just look away.

The expression on her face is soft, and a smile plays around her full lips, even though I know she must be concentrating intensely. But smiling is drilled into dancers just like any other exercise.

She manages twenty-five turns before losing her balance. Cursing, she catches herself and leans on her thighs with both hands. Her chest rises and falls as she breathes quickly. Only now can you see the effort she's making. A deep crease forms between her eyebrows. She looks dissatisfied.

With a frustrated sigh, she straightens up and stretches her legs. I try to sneak away as inconspicuously as possible, because there's nothing worse than being caught secretly watching someone, but I'm a little too slow.

Lia turns toward the corridor, her gaze darting from her bag, which is lying next to the door, to me. When she spots me, the disappointment on her face disappears instantly. She puts on a friendly smile like a mask. A very pretty mask that I almost would have believed was real if I hadn't just seen her without it. Something tells me she doesn't take it off very often.

"Hey," she says, and I raise my hand awkwardly.

"Sorry, I didn't mean to disturb you."

"You didn't." She waves it off, but something in her eyes makes me think she's not telling the truth. Even though I don't know her and we haven't spoken before, it's absolutely clear.

"I just wanted to . . ." I start, gesturing vaguely toward one of the other studios. "You're so good," I say instead, in a stupid attempt to save the situation with small talk. It's instantly clear I've said the wrong thing.

"Thanks." Her smile slips almost imperceptibly, her eyes flicker, and suddenly I see something of myself in her. It's absurd, because Lia is more graceful and talented than anyone else I've seen at this school. She's even better than Zoe, and Zoe is damn good. But the insecurity in Lia's green eyes is familiar. She doesn't think she's good enough.

An awkward silence takes over. I shift uneasily from one foot to the other and force a smile. "I'm going to leave now. I actually wanted to work on the choreography for contemporary . . ."

Lia nods. "Good luck." Then she turns back to the mirror, and I hurry away.

The studios on the third floor are all deserted. I choose the last one on the right, throw my bag in the corner, and pull my hoodie over my head. Wearing only a T-shirt, leggings, and socks, I start my warm-up exercises, but my thoughts are still with Lia and the look in her eyes. I wonder if it should make me feel better that she's just as insecure as I am, even though she's obviously so much better than most of the other dancers at this school. Maybe it should reassure me that I'm not alone in feeling that way, but it doesn't. It just makes me sad that Lia seems to feel the same way despite her talent.

"Hey, Birdy." Easton's voice snaps me out of my thoughts. I can't help but smile when I see him in the doorway, both hands buried in the pockets of his sweatpants, wearing the hat I've worn every day for the past few weeks.

I get up happily and walk over to him. "Hey."

He pulls me toward him as if he's done it a thousand times before and kisses me in a way that takes my breath away.

When we pull apart, my face is already glowing with heat again. Smiling, he brushes a strand of hair from my forehead.

"Hey," he whispers again, an octave lower than before, and my brain shuts down. There's nothing but fog in my head, and the heat moves down from my cheeks, settling in my chest, my stomach, my lower abdomen, until it starts throbbing urgently between my legs.

He caresses my chin, playing with my hair, and I can't think anymore when he's doing that. But I have to be able to think, because there's a reason he's here now. And even though I can think of one pretty good reason that has a lot to do with his mouth, his hands, and the rest of his body, that's not what we're here to do.

I force myself to take a step back so my mind can start working again. Easton's blue eyes light up knowingly, shining with amusement.

"How was your day?" I ask, clearing my throat because my voice sounds so hoarse.

"Unspectacular." He shrugs. "The record store was busy."

"Sounds like a good thing."

"Good for the store, bad for me and the songs I was hoping to have time to work on if there hadn't been so many people." He smiles. "How was your day?"

"Good, I think. I was working on choreography for our song. I started, at least. I don't have much yet. But that's why I wanted you to come. I thought you could play the song, and I'll show you what I have so far. I had everything in my head at lunchtime, but it's different when I actually hear the music."

"That's the only reason you wanted me to come?" he asks, raising an eyebrow. He smiles, and I feel way too hot again.

"That's the only reason," I confirm, trying in vain not to let him see what he's doing to me.

He sighs with disappointment, but I don't buy it for a second. "That's sad."

"I know. Very sad." I nod seriously and move backward toward the grand piano by the mirror. My pulse is racing. This isn't why we're here, but somehow it is.

"Incredibly sad." Easton follows me until I finally bump into the piano with my butt and can no longer avoid him. Not that I want to.

He leans over me, supporting himself with both hands on the lid behind me. I'm trapped between his arms, but I've never felt safer. I feel his warmth and forget how to think and breathe again. I inhale his familiar scent and it's almost too much for me. I'm overwhelmed by his closeness, by the way he smells and the way he presses me against the piano until I feel like I'm falling backward.

But I can't fall. The instrument is behind me and he's in front of me, making sure I stay standing.

His lips brush against my mouth, and I moan. My eyelids flutter shut. I can't resist him.

"Don't forget to breathe, Birdy," he says, and I can feel his grin. Then he kisses me. Not like before. This isn't a kiss of greeting. It's a *being-completely-alone-in-a-ballet-studio-and-way-too-in-love* kiss.

My mouth opens, and then I breathe. I breathe him in. I feel his tongue on mine and the heat in my abdomen. The throbbing between my legs comes back, more urgent than before. It drives me crazy in a good way.

Easton groans as I press my hips against him, and now he's the one not breathing, which makes me happy.

"Don't forget to breathe, Easton," I whisper into his mouth, just like he did to me, except this time I'm the one kissing him. Deeply and hungrily, because I can't do it any other way.

I can feel his erection and I'm relieved that he's only wearing sweatpants rather than the jeans he had on this morning. I can feel everything through the soft fabric. His hands wander under my T-shirt, and I sigh as he caresses my bare skin, from my hip bones up my stomach to my breasts. I'm wearing a thin bustier, but that doesn't stop him, and God, I'm so glad it doesn't.

I didn't know it could be so exciting to kiss someone in a place where you're not supposed to kiss. After all, this is a school, and someone could catch us at any moment. But it's late, and no one is up here at this hour. Our studio is at the back of the building. The window looks out onto the administration building, which is also empty this late at night.

We're completely alone, but if I'm being honest, the thrill that someone might come and ruin everything is also what makes this so damn hot.

Easton's mouth wanders from my lips to my neck, and I have to bite my lower lip to suppress the moan that tries to escape as his tongue glides over my skin. He hears it anyway. His pupils are dilated with desire and his lips are a little swollen. Because of me.

Easton slides both hands under my bottom and lifts me up. He sets me down on the piano. The wood is cool, and I can feel it through the fabric of my leggings. My skin, on the other hand, is burning.

My feet rest on the lid that protects the keys. I spread my legs just wide enough for him to slide between them. I need him closer. Once again, his mouth finds mine. He leans over me, and I lift my hips toward him, a bittersweet pressure building inside.

Easton pulls away from me, his gaze burning into mine. His fingers close around the waistband of my leggings, a silent question in his eyes.

"Do you want this, Birdy?" he whispers hoarsely, because he wants to do it right. Yes, I do. Way too much. His voice sends hot shivers down my spine, and at that moment, I realize his voice was the first thing I fell in love with.

That voice, like silk on sandpaper. That's what I thought the first time I heard it. I remember it so clearly.

"Yes," I whisper. My mouth is dry, my heart is beating too fast. I know we shouldn't be doing this right now, not here, but God, I don't care. Nothing matters except this unbearable longing inside me. I need him to do something about it, because otherwise I'm going to die.

I lift my hips again, and this time he pulls my leggings and panties off in one fluid motion. The fabric lands on the floor with a soft rustle. My T-shirt—one that I stole from him last night—slides up my hips as Easton pushes me firmly onto the grand piano. Now I notice how cold the wood actually is. I swallow. My whole body is throbbing, nothing but burning heat. I'm on fire.

Easton pushes up my shirt and bustier, exposing my breasts. He brushes his lips over my nipples, his tongue teasing me, and I moan with longing, a wordless plea. He gives me more, moving his mouth down my stomach, lower and lower. I gasp for air when I feel his tongue right where I need it.

My head falls back and I sink onto the piano until I'm lying in front of him, legs spread, completely exposed. Nothing has ever felt as good as his head between my legs, his tongue on me.

I moan as he slides a finger inside me, slowly, teasingly, driving me crazy. His tongue moves in the same rhythm, and I'm dying. Gasping, I writhe beneath his touch, the room blurring around me. My fingers find his hair, tugging as he dives into me. He's the only thing I can feel, licking, moving his finger inside me, harder, deeper, faster.

My hips thrust forward and he places a hand on my lower abdomen, pressing gently but firmly, and I don't know why, but the pressure causes a wave of glistening heat to shoot through my body. My muscles cramp around his fingers and I moan, forgetting who I am, where I am, and why we're here.

Easton straightens up as my body comes to rest again. It feels heavy and light at the same time and doesn't seem to belong to me anymore, because it no longer obeys me. I blink up at him, his mouth glistening. I'd like to sit up, but unfortunately my muscles aren't cooperating. Easton pulls me up and kisses me. I can taste myself on his tongue.

"That's why you shouldn't come here," I murmur.

I can feel him smile. "But I like coming here."

He kisses me again. He can come here anytime he wants.

CHAPTER 37
Easton

She Looks So Perfect—5 Seconds of Summer

"So what was the plan for tonight again?" I look up at Rayne. Now I'm sitting on the piano bench, and she's standing a few steps away from me, running her fingers through her long, messy hair and trying to tame it. It's the first time I've seen her in a dance studio with all the rings on her fingers, and I have no idea why, but with them she somehow seems more . . . complete. More like herself.

She gives me a look of amusement. "The plan *was* that you help me with the choreography by playing the song."

"I can still do that."

"You'll have to." She smiles, and I love it.

"I know. By the way, Jax uploaded a few videos of us to TikTok with the songs we recorded before I met you. They're not as good as the ones from last weekend, of course, but—"

"All your songs are good," she says, glaring at me reproachfully.

"Okay, okay. Sorry. Anyway, it seems to be going pretty well. At least there are a few people who want more from us."

"Of course they do. How could they not? You guys are great." She nods confidently, as if she hadn't expected anything else. She probably didn't.

"He also took a few videos from our day in the studio and posted them as Instagram stories. I have no idea when he had time to make them, but right now it really looks like something could happen."

"It will, because you're good. So much happens on social media these days that I'm really not surprised." She shrugs.

"Maybe dreams come true after all." I have to swallow the lump in my throat, otherwise I won't be able to get the words out. I still don't really believe it, no matter how good we might actually be. There are a thousand others who are just as good.

Her gaze softens. "I'm sure they do."

"Yeah, but it probably would have been a good idea to deal with all the marketing stuff first."

Rayne makes a face. "Stop being so negative! You're just getting started, and it's going to be fine. Besides, so much of this stuff is so unpredictable that it's impossible to say whether it would have made any difference. What matters is what comes next. And to make that work, we should really get started now."

"Yeah, just a minute." I reach out to her because I need to touch her. I'm addicted to feeling her skin against mine. But Rayne laughs and takes a couple of steps backward.

"Oh no. Your hands have to stay where they are." She points to the piano. "Otherwise we won't get anything done today."

"Okay." With a sigh, I give in and turn around on the bench so I can lift the lid. It's hard to ignore the fact that a few moments ago, Rayne was sitting right there in front of me, her feet propped up and my head between her legs. The memory of her scent and taste makes me much too warm. And all the blood in my body goes south again. I'm glad I'm not wearing jeans, otherwise they would be getting uncomfortable.

"Ready?"

I look up and catch her eye in the mirror. She raises her eyebrows in a question. I want to say no because I'd really like to disappear into her room with her and take off her clothes again. Actually, the T-shirt belongs to me, but it looks much better on her, even though it's way too big for her. Maybe that's exactly what makes it so hot.

Get a grip on yourself.

I clear my throat and nod. "Ready."

"Let's go." She smiles, her eyes sparkling as if she knows very well that I'm not ready at all.

I take a deep breath and put my hands on the keys, even though "Dance with You 'Til Midnight" isn't actually a piano song. But it will be okay to work on the choreography like this. In the mirror, I watch Rayne close her eyes and take a breath. When I start singing, she takes the first step.

My fingers find the right keys all by themselves. I know the melody by heart; it's become second nature, just like the lyrics. That's pretty useful right now, because I wouldn't be able to do this if I had to concentrate.

I can only look at Rayne, my eyes following her every movement. It's clear that she feels the song the same way I do. She dances, I sing, and it's perfect. Not in a controlled, truly perfect way but her own kind of perfect.

Her steps are sure and light, her hair flying as she spins. Slow steps, fast ones, turns and leaps. I have no idea how she does it, but I can't look away. I watch Rayne dance every day in ballet, and I saw her in that one contemporary class, but somehow this is different. Better.

Because it's our song, and because every one of her movements fits with our words. Because the dance is powerful and strong, but also sad and fearful. I didn't know it was possible to see emotions, but when she dances, I can.

Forgot to breathe
Forgot to see
Forgot my fucking name

I really do forget everything when I'm watching her, but the words don't disappear because she embodies them. I only come back to reality when she pauses and turns to look at me. It takes a few seconds for me to notice and stop playing. The last notes ring out, and then the piano falls silent.

"What do you think?" she asks. There's a kind of uncertainty in her voice that I know all too well. "Of course I'm not finished with it, it can't be done so fast. That was just what came to my mind first. Melanie helped me a little with the moves during class, but I'm not quite sure if everything fits yet. Maybe it would be better not to do the video, or maybe I just shouldn't dance, and you and the guys do the video alone. Of course no one will be interested in seeing me dance, and—"

"Stop." I interrupt her, and her mouth snaps shut. "That was . . . I can't even explain how that made me feel, Rayne." I stand up and go to her, taking her hands and wrapping my fingers around hers.

"You're going to dance in this video. Unless you really don't want to. But you should, because you're part of this song. Okay?"

Her gray eyes shine as she looks up at me. "Okay." Then she smiles. "I was wondering if we should do some of the dancing together."

I have to laugh. "I can't dance."

"Neither can I," she argues.

"You just saw yourself in the mirror, didn't you? At least a little bit?"

She shrugs. "Yes, but—"

"No buts." I put my hands on either side of her face. Her skin is warm and soft. "You can do this. Why do you always doubt yourself so much?"

Her long black lashes cast shadows on her cheeks as she lowers her eyes. "Because I'm not as good as my mom," she whispers, so softly that I can barely understand her. "I came here because I want to be like her. But I just can't do it."

"That's not true."

"Yes, it is. But today, for a moment I thought I might be able to get there after all. Everything was going really well in class, and then . . ." she swallows and exhales with a sigh. "Then I started working on this choreography and it was . . . a lot of fun."

My brow creases. I don't like the way she makes it sound. "Why are you saying that like it's a problem?"

"Because none of the others enjoy it. Everyone else wants to do ballet, and contemporary dance is just a course that they have to take because it was assigned to them. And I'm . . ." she trails off and bites her lower lip insecurely.

"You're you," I say firmly. "You don't have to be like your mom or anyone else at this school. You don't have to be anything. You are who you are, and you're perfect just like that. You're talented and beautiful and . . . Damn it, Rayne, can you please try to see yourself the way I see you?"

She doesn't say anything for a moment, just looks at me. Then she smiles. It's small and seems a little sad, but it's still a smile.

"I'll try." She stands on tiptoes and kisses me lightly, and I get goose bumps. "Dance with me," she whispers against my lips. "Just once. I want to know what it feels like."

I rest my forehead against hers. "If you want to dance with me, I'll dance with you until you don't want to anymore."

"That will never happen," she says, and in that moment, we both truly believe it.

PART 8

Bridge

CHAPTER 38

Easton

Hopes & Dreams—Caskets

"East!" I look up at the sound of Beck's excited voice. My best friend storms into the record store, closely followed by Colin and Jax. All three of them have the same feverish expression on their faces, and my pulse races to dizzying heights. I've never seen my friends like this before, with their eyes wide and their faces pale.

"What's going on?" I ask, sirens going off inside my head.

"You're on your phone every damn day for months, and the one time we need you, you don't even look at it?" Colin complains. But there's a teasing undertone in his voice I recognize, and I'm sure he doesn't mean what he's saying. He's way too excited, but there's no panic involved. My shoulders relax a little. If something bad had happened, Colin wouldn't be acting so normal right now. Basically, his complaining is probably a good sign.

"Sorry, I was busy." I point to the boxes of records that arrived a few hours ago, which I've been sorting ever since. It was surprisingly busy here this afternoon, so I didn't get as much done as I would have liked, and I really didn't have time to check my phone.

"I can see that." Jax grins at me, a wordless apology for Colin's grumbling.

"Everything okay?"

"More than okay!" Beck grabs me by the shoulders and shakes me, a beaming smile on his face. "Phil sent us the songs."

"Already?" I look from one to the other in disbelief. Colin and Jax nod in unison. It's only been five days since we recorded. I didn't expect the mixes to be ready until next week at the earliest.

Our songs are finished!

"Phil emailed us about an hour ago." Beck finally lets go of me.

"Have you listened to them yet?" My voice sounds so strange I have to clear my throat, but that doesn't change the fact that I suddenly have a lump there.

Our songs are really done. So done that we can listen to them.

"What, without you?" Colin gives me a disapproving glance that makes me grin. "Like we would."

"Why do you think you have so many unread messages and unanswered calls on your phone?" Jax winks as he takes off his hat and runs a hand through his spiky hair.

"I'm sorry," I apologize, but Beck just waves it off.

"We're here now. Rudy's speakers are better than ours at home anyway. Is he here?"

"No, just Evie." I glance over my shoulder to the café. Three tables are occupied, so Evie is standing in front of the espresso machine making coffee instead of scrolling through TikTok or checking Insta like she usually does.

"So we can play the songs here?"

I roll my eyes. "We'd be able to if Rudy were here too," I reply. He would be the last person to stop us.

"True." Beck puts his phone in my hand. "I already downloaded the songs."

As I walk away, I type in his passcode. He's had the same one for years because he can't remember anything else. We all know it. Beck always says we're his backup in case he ever forgets it.

I connect his phone to the speakers with an aux cable; Rudy is so old school that nothing here works with Bluetooth. I scroll through the download folder, and adrenaline rushes through my body as I find the tracks. My hands are shaking. This is really happening. We recorded our songs in the studio, and now we can listen to them.

I want to press play, but I can't. Rayne isn't here. And she should be.

"East, what are you waiting for?" Colin asks impatiently.

"Rayne." I look at my friends. "We can't do this without her. If it weren't for her, we wouldn't be standing here right now, about to listen to our songs."

Jax groans. "Are you serious? I mean, I get what you're saying, but come on, East. We're dying for this!"

"I know, but . . ." I stop, unable to press play, even though I *know* that's what Rayne would want. She knows how important this is to us, and how long and hard we've worked for this moment. But I want to be here when she hears our songs for the first time, especially "Dance with You 'Til Midnight."

"Then call her and tell her to come over," Beck suggests.

"I can't." I glance at the clock hanging above the cash register. "She's still in class."

"We could listen to the songs now, and when Rayne comes later we could just pretend we haven't heard them yet," Colin suggests.

"Because we're all such amazingly good liars, right?" I say. "I can't do that. I can't lie to her and I don't want to. And I know she wouldn't mind if we listened without her. If I called her now, she'd probably ask me what I'm waiting for, but . . ."

"Yeah, then what are you waiting for?" Beck asks.

I grimace. I can't make up my mind. I want to hear our songs now. But I also want the first time I hear them to be with Rayne. Especially *our* song.

I take a deep breath. "Okay, I think I have a plan." An excited tingling spreads through me. We recorded four songs, one of which belongs to both her and me. The one we wrote together that night on the beach.

"Does your plan include us?" Beck gives me a knowing grin; he probably figured out what I was up to even before I thought of it myself.

"Not this time." I shake my head and press play.

This is truly our moment. It's for Colin, Jax, Beck, and me. Four guys who played together for the first time years ago in a music room at school. Four guys who have fought and made up over the past few years, who live for music and have never stopped dreaming. One of our dreams has come true.

"Meet Me at 3 AM" starts with Jax's drums and Beck's guitar. Then Colin joins in, and finally me. My voice is rough and deep. It sounds different coming out of the speakers, a little strange. I get goose bumps as I listen; it's totally crazy. We're all silent. No one says a word, no one moves. We just listen and can't believe it's us.

We can't believe we recorded this song, and it turned out so good. But it did. Damn good.

"Fuck," Beck murmurs reverently as the last note fades away. I think he's speaking for all of us. "Was that really us?"

"Yes." A stunned laugh escapes me.

CHAPTER 39
Rayne

Someone, Somewhere (Acoustic Version)—Asking Alexandria

"Rayne! Where are you going?" The reproachful tone in Mae's voice makes me pause in the middle of the hallway. I slowly turn around.

"Uh, nowhere?" I say. It sounds too much like a question as I quickly try to slip my bag behind me so she doesn't notice it. I should have known this wouldn't work.

"Rayne," she says warningly, just like my mom used to when she'd come into my room in the middle of the night and catch me watching one music video after another on YouTube.

The memory hits me completely out of the blue. My heart tightens. But this time it hurts just a tiny bit less. Realizing that hurts even more.

"You're going back to the practice building already?" Mae puts her hands on her hips, distracting me from the emotion building up inside me.

"Yes," I admit meekly. There's no point in lying; she'll see right through me anyway. "I wanted to go over my choreography again."

"You've been doing that nonstop since Monday. You need to take a break sometime."

"I know, but I had an idea earlier, and I think . . ." I go silent as she shakes her head and giggles. "What is it?"

"Nothing. I'm glad you're having so much fun. But you have to take care of yourself, okay? If you overdo it and get hurt, you won't be able to do what you want."

"I'll be careful."

"Please do. Otherwise, everything Skye is planning for your music video will be a waste, and she's really putting her heart into it. I don't know how she finds the time."

"That's a very good question."

Over the past few days, Skye has sent the guys and me countless short clips of what she thinks our music video could look like. Well, sort of, because my choreography will be different, of course. But she was more concerned with the camera angles, the lighting, a thousand other details that none of us would have even thought about.

"Well, as long as she's enjoying it," Mae says with a shrug.

"That's the most important thing. I'm going now. See you later, okay?"

"Want some company?"

"Thanks, but I really need to go through it alone." I give her an apologetic smile.

"All right." She laughs. "See you later. Or tomorrow. Don't stay up too late."

"I won't," I promise, then turn and run down the stairs.

Mae is right, I've probably been working a little too hard on the choreography over the last few days, but once I get started, it's almost impossible to stop. Every time I go through the steps again, I notice something I want to change. Sometimes a step, a turn, or an arm movement isn't quite right yet—not the way I want it to be.

I still want to keep working on it, even though Easton said my choreography was good and I could tell he meant it. But maybe that's exactly why it needs to be a little better. I'm not quite sure. Either way, I can't stop.

The air is clear and smells a little like spring as I leave the dorm and walk across campus. It's still cold, but not as freezing as it was a few days ago. Most of the dorm rooms have their lights on, and I can hear bright, cheerful laughter somewhere. I've almost reached the practice building when my phone vibrates in my jacket pocket.

I know before I even take it out that it's Easton.

"What are you doing?" he asks when I answer. He sounds so excited that my heart skips a beat.

"I'm just about to go over the choreography again. Why? Is everything okay?"

"Yeah, it's fine," he says quickly. "I'm in the parking lot. I want to show you something. If you want to see, that is."

"No." I roll my eyes, even though he can't see me. "Of course I don't."

"You don't even know what it is."

"Are you trying to talk me out of it?" I ask, my steps quickening of their own accord. I've already turned and am walking in the opposite direction from the practice building, away from the dorms. "It's a little late for that. I'll be right there." I walk through the gate and spot Easton's van. The headlights cast bright beams of light onto the asphalt.

"I don't want to pressure you." I can hear the smile in his voice.

"That's so dumb I won't dignify it with an answer." I reach the van and open the passenger door.

Easton hangs up and grins at me. He looks so good that I can't breathe for a moment. Something is different today and I can't quite put a finger on it, but he's positively glowing, and that makes me happy.

"You answered at least," he says as I climb into the car.

This time I don't get a chance to reply, but that's his fault because he pulls me in for a kiss. If I weren't already struggling to breathe, I would be now.

"Should I ignore you next time?" I ask as we pull away from each other, breathless.

"Please don't. I like your voice." His eyes light up, and I really am hopelessly in love.

"Thanks." I can't fight the smile spreading across my face. "What do you want to show me?"

"I'll tell you in a minute." The engine roars to life, and Easton turns the van out of the parking lot.

"You're mean." I say with a pout. "First you lure me into your van, and now you kidnap me?"

"Do you want to get out?" He glances at me, and I shake my head.

"Of course not. I'm far too curious."

"I was hoping you'd say that."

"Will you at least tell me where we're going?"

Now he's the one shaking his head. "It's a surprise."

* * *

We drive to the beach. Easton tries to distract me the whole way there, asking me how my day was. He asks whether I've started studying for exams yet, and is clearly going to great lengths to keep me from figuring out what he's up to. But I notice, because the route is somehow familiar, even though this is only the second time we've driven to the beach together. And because I know Easton.

He parks the car in the same spot as last time. It's dark, just like it was before. Except everything is different. The sky is clear, clear enough to see the stars. It definitely won't start snowing tonight. It still smells a bit like spring, especially here, because the sea always smells like summer. That doesn't actually make sense, but it does to me.

Easton takes my hand as we get out and walk down to the water. The sand gives way under our feet, and it's quiet apart from the sound of the waves crashing.

"Phil sent us the songs today," Easton says, breaking the silence between us.

I stop abruptly. "What?" I stare at him in disbelief. "Wow, already?"

"Yes."

"You're only telling me this now?"

He shrugs, but he seems pretty pleased with himself. "Otherwise you would have wanted me to play them for you in the car."

"Uh, yeah! It's a little rude that you didn't." I nudge him in the side.

"I know, but it's so much nicer here." He points to the sea in front of us. The waves are higher this time, and I can't tell if the tide is coming in or going out. "After all, this is where we wrote the song." He rubs his nose and suddenly looks so embarrassed that I have to laugh.

"I guess that makes sense, even if it is a little cheesy."

"Good cheesy or stupid cheesy?"

I wrap both arms around his neck and beam at him. "Good cheesy. Actually, it's extremely sweet."

"That's just how I am."

"You are." I brush a strand of hair from his forehead. "But please tell me you've listened to the songs already."

"I have. The guys came to the store. They were too impatient."

"Understandable. I would have been too."

"I wanted you to be there too, but I think if I'd made them wait, Colin and Jax would have killed me. And besides . . ."

"You wanted to be a little romantic," I tease him, stretching and kissing him on the tip of his nose.

"That too."

"Are you happy with them?" My stomach starts to flutter with excitement. The songs are finished. They're finished, and they have to be good. *Please.*

"Yes." The single word comes out of Easton's mouth as a sigh of relief. "They're absolutely amazing. They don't sound like us at all. Well, they do, but the recordings turned out so well, the whole thing is pretty surreal."

"The songs are good. *You guys* are good. And that's why every single song sounds like you." I kiss him again. I can't help it.

"Do you really not mind that we already listened? I wanted to wait for you and I figured you wouldn't mind, but—"

He stops when I put my hand over his mouth. "Easton, this is your thing, not mine. You guys wrote and recorded these songs. You're the band."

He breathes a sigh of relief, and I realize that he was probably a little unsure. "Okay."

"It's really okay," I reassure him.

He pulls his headphones out of his pocket, opens the case, and hands them to me. "Ready?"

I put the buds into my ears and nod. "Go."

For a couple of seconds there's complete silence, then he pulls his phone out of his pocket, and the first notes of our song begin to play. Soft but somehow stormy. Between Easton's voice, our words, and the guys' instruments, the song is everything, everything I could have imagined.

The lyrics feel familiar, but somehow new. Even though it's not the first time I've heard Easton sing our song, this is different. It does something to me. I can only look at him while I hear his voice in my ears. His words and mine, our thoughts. Darkness and fear, hope, courage, and everything in between. This song is as much *us* as it can be.

I won't turn back
I won't give up
I'll make it fucking right
Get lost in music
Lost in you
And dance with you 'til midnight

Tears well up in my eyes and I can't hold them back. My head hurts because I suddenly remember that Dad will never hear this song.

He would have loved it, I know that. He would have loved that I wrote it with Easton.

I know you can do it, little Bird. Believe in yourself. You were born to make music.

I'd blocked out the memory of him saying that, the morning before the accident. A few hours before he left with Mom to go to that party. I sat in my room, countless pieces of paper and dozens of pens scattered around me on the floor, trying to take what was going on in my head and put it down on paper. I was frustrated and angry at myself, convinced that I would never, ever be able to write a song that was really good.

And now here I am, and I've done it. With Easton. This song is truly everything, and that's exactly what I want. I want to put my thoughts and feelings down on paper, shape them into words and verses that come together to create something whole.

It's exactly what I've always wanted. I just forgot along the way, or I didn't let myself remember. I suppressed my desire to write. But now I can't do that anymore. Easton reaches out to me, gently wiping the tears off my cheeks. He knows what's going on inside my head, even without me saying it. The song fades away, and I give the earbuds back to Easton.

"It's so, so beautiful," I say, my voice choked. "Honestly, I didn't think it would be this good. I mean, I did, but this is—"

"Everything," he says, finishing my sentence. Yes, he definitely knows what's going on in my head.

"I wish my dad could hear it."

"Me too. He'd be so proud of you."

"Yes." I try to swallow the lump in my throat and fail. I sigh. "He would have been."

Easton pulls me close, his lips brushing my temple. We stand there for a while, his arms wrapped around me, my face buried in his jacket. Then I lift my head.

"When we shoot the music video . . ." I begin. I'm captivated by his gaze, and for a moment I think I see the stars reflected in his eyes, but that's impossible. I want to believe it, though, because somewhere up there is the star that Mom and Dad gave me. That makes me feel a little like they're still here, as long as I can see it.

"What?" Easton whispers softly, his breath brushing against my skin.

"Will you dance with me? It's *our* song, right? Then let it be our dance. Please."

I need him to say yes because he has to know that it's all or nothing. Dancing with him on Monday felt so right. Besides, it was fun, and maybe that's exactly how it should be. Maybe that's all dancing needs to be for me. Something I do because it brings me joy. Not necessarily something I want to spend every day of my life doing.

Could it be that simple?

I have no idea, but I don't have to decide right now.

Easton smiles and nods, and for the first time in months, for the first time since that night that changed everything, I believe that someday I might be totally happy again.

And that being happy would be okay.

CHAPTER 40
Rayne

Save Tonight—Tom Speight, Lydia Clowes

"Oh my God, I'm so excited! Are you guys excited too?" Mae grabs my hand and almost crushes my fingers. She's squeezing so hard I can hardly feel them.

"No, not at all. I'm totally chill about all of this," I say, rolling my eyes. Zoe and Jase start laughing.

"Sure, that's why you can't stop running back and forth to check if the guys need help and if Skye is happy with how we've set everything up," says Jase.

Embarrassed, I start to brush a strand of hair behind my ear, but Zoe stops me. "Hands off, you'll ruin the curls."

"Sorry," I sigh. "It's just . . . Was this a stupid idea? Maybe I shouldn't have agreed to do this."

"No," they say simultaneously.

"It was a great idea!" This time, Mae squeezes my hand more gently. "Really. The video is going to be absolutely amazing, I'm sure of it."

"Me too," Zoe agrees. "You've been working so hard on the choreography these past few weeks. There's no way it isn't good."

I swallow. It *has* to be good. If it isn't, I'm going to cry. Zoe's right, I spent every free moment over the last few weeks working on this dance. I had to give up on a few parts once I added Easton dancing with me, and cut some other sections I just didn't like anymore. I practiced the dance so many times that I even started dreaming about it. But now every step is perfect, and it feels good, because I know what I'm doing it for. This video.

That's why we're all here today: Easton and the guys, Jase, Mae, Zoe, and Skye. We're in a dilapidated old factory in Southie, with broken windows letting in the freezing cold air and steel beams that probably used to divide the hall into separate areas. Zoe, Jase, and Mae have spent the last few hours decorating every beam with dozens of strings of fairy lights. If everything goes as planned, the lights will look like stars.

Skye knows the owner of the building, an old friend of her aunt's, who lets her use it for her own videos. That's why there's electricity, even though the hall has probably been empty for years. Skye hasn't said much about who her aunt's friend is and why she chose this place, but we quickly realized how familiar she is with it.

The guys are setting up Jax's drum kit in the back, and Skye is shooing them around until she finds the perfect spot.

"Okay, that's good." Her voice echoes loudly, and Jax groans with relief and collapses onto his stool. She gives him an amused glance before turning to Easton and me. "I'd say we're ready to go. It's your turn now. We'll shoot the dancing first, and then we'll film you playing the song."

"All right." My stomach tightens nervously, but then Easton puts a hand on my shoulder. He smiles. "Ready?"

I nod and take off my coat, handing it to Mae, whose eyes are shining with excitement. "Have fun," she says.

"You can do it." Zoe gives me a quick hug. "You're going to be great!"

I just nod and pray she's right. The air is cold on my warm skin. The dress I'm wearing is much too thin for this time of year. It's black with a tight-fitting top and long sleeves, and a short full skirt that swings around my thighs when I spin.

Easton holds out his hand to me, and his fingers close around mine. "Ready," I reply.

He smiles again and pulls me away from my friends, into the center of the hall. Skye explains how she wants to film each sequence, and I become more restless and nervous with every passing minute, afraid that I won't be able to do it. But I can do this. I must.

Then I feel Easton's hand on my waist, and all at once I feel completely calm.

"Everything will be fine," he whispers, as if he can sense my unease. I feel his breath on my cheek, and my skin begins to tingle. I lean against him for just a moment, needing his closeness and warmth, the certainty that he's here with me.

"Okay," I whisper back.

He lets me go and we get into position.

The music starts somewhere nearby, too quiet for the video, but that doesn't matter. Skye will add the soundtrack later, and then it will be perfect.

I take the first step, then the second one. My body relaxes. My muscles are supple and flexible; I already warmed up.

I dance, and I'm the girl I'm meant to be. The girl Easton dances with until midnight. Everything inside me feels lighter. I spin, and he's right there where he's supposed to be. I put my hand in his and his grip is warm and firm. We spin together. A smile spreads across my face all by itself. I forget who I am and what I've lost. I only exist in the moment; I'm the girl from the song. I look up and meet the gaze of those blue eyes.

He smiles, and I love him.

One more spin, my hand in his and butterflies in my stomach. We look at each other, and everything is so simple. Dancing, with him, here and now. It's all about the music and the emotions we want to share with whoever is watching us. I move away and Easton grabs my hand, pulling me back toward him in a spin. My hand comes to rest on his chest, and I can feel his heart beating fast and hard. I look up at him again, meeting his blue eyes, and his gaze flickers to my mouth.

He's breathing heavily, just like me, and suddenly I feel so warm. We're caught up in our own frenzy. Seconds turn into minutes and then hours; I don't know how long it's been. We go through the steps, every move, over and over again, with short breaks when Skye wants to change the camera angle or if a spin wasn't quite how I wanted it.

"That was great," Skye says at last. "One more time, and then we'll move on to the band, okay?"

Easton and I just nod; we're breathing too hard to talk.

"Let's go. Positions!" She smiles at us and disappears behind the camera again.

I look at Easton and I'm tempted to change the choreography, even though I shouldn't. But I can't help myself. There's something in his eyes that makes my whole body tingle. My skin is glowing and I feel incredibly warm. It's just him and me. My heart is racing, joy rushing through me. I smile as I go into the last spin.

I move away from him and he pulls me back, my hand on his chest. I feel his heartbeat beneath my fingers, and my smile widens. Then it fades when I look up and meet his glowing gaze. It's only for a few seconds, but those seconds stretch into infinity. Our very own infinity, captured in a brief moment. That moment holds everything.

We move closer. It just happens, completely instinctively. He hesitates just a fraction of a second, because this isn't part of the plan, but it doesn't matter. I don't care, and neither does he. He lowers his mouth to mine. Our lips meet gently and firmly, and it's so, so warm. My eyelids flutter shut and my body lets go. All I can feel are his lips on mine, but it's not enough. His hands are on my back, roaming over my dress, but I want to feel them on my skin. Heat floods me, and my heart stumbles.

We only break apart when we hear our friends laughing. "That was a really nice ending," Skye says with a smile.

"Thanks," I mumble, embarrassed, my cheeks glowing red as I look back at her. Easton's face is glowing just like mine, but that doesn't stop him from pulling me toward him and kissing me again. Longer. Deeper.

"You were amazing," he whispers against my lips, his fingers wandering over my back, giving me goose bumps. Not because I'm cold, though.

"You too." I smile. I think I could get used to dancing with him.

"Okay guys, we don't have all day." Skye cuts Easton off before he can kiss me again. "You can get changed, Rayne. Guys, it's your turn."

Easton lets go of me with a sigh, and it's clear how much he hates doing it. I feel the same, and to be honest, part of me would love to get out of here and do something completely different. But we have a job to do, and we're not done yet. I walk over to Mae, who hands me my coat. As I slip into the long sleeves, I can feel the cold of the room again.

"Here," Zoe says, pulling a hat over my head. "Now you can ruin your curls all you want."

"Thanks." Shivering, I wrap my arms around myself. "Have you seen my boots anywhere?"

"Yes, just a sec." Jase disappears briefly and returns a moment later with my warm fur-lined winter boots. I take off the dance slippers I've been wearing for the last few hours and sigh with relief when I can't feel the cold floor under my feet anymore.

"That was so great." Zoe grabs my hand and Mae puts her arm around my shoulders. They both beam at me. "Really. It was so, so beautiful."

"You two were so cute! And pretty hot, actually." Mae laughs and pretends to fan herself with one hand. I promptly blush a little more. "Honestly, we could really feel the chemistry between you. I think I died a little when you kissed."

"Oh God, please don't exaggerate," I beg her, but I also have to laugh when I see Jase staring at us blankly, obviously having no idea what Mae is talking about. I, on the other hand, know exactly what she means.

"I'm not exaggerating. It really was beautiful!"

Skye saves me from having to answer. "Quiet down in the cheap seats, we want to get on with it!"

All at once we go quiet, and she nods with satisfaction and signals to the band. We Are No Saints starts playing, Easton's voice fills the empty hall, and everything is absolutely perfect.

CHAPTER 41
Easton

Better Days—One Republic

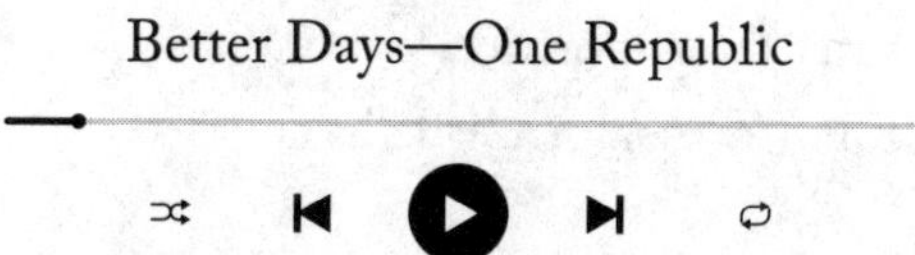

Stunned, we sit huddled together on the sofa, which is much too small for all of us, staring at Skye's iPad. Rayne is on my lap, her fingers digging into my hand. Jase is crouched on the armrest with Zoe leaning back between his legs. The guys sit next to me on the sofa, and Mae and Skye are standing by the coffee table. Skye looks nervous; it's the first time I've ever seen her this way. The living room is silent.

"Can someone please say something?" Skye laughs, but even that sounds anxious.

"This is just . . ." Jax starts, but breaks off because his voice fails him. Mine isn't working either; I can't get a sound out.

"Wow," Colin says, finishing Jax's sentence for him.

"Insane," Beck adds.

We're all still staring at the little screen, which has gone black now. Just a few seconds ago, we were watching ourselves on it. Us. In a music video.

It's a music video that was semiprofessionally shot by a dance student in an empty warehouse, with a band that has never done anything like this before. Except you can't tell any of that from the video. Not at all. Whatever Skye did, she exceeded every expectation.

"How did you do that?" Rayne turns a little on my lap to look at Skye, who actually blushes.

She shrugs awkwardly. "It's not rocket science," she says dismissively. "It's all a matter of practice."

"It's incredible," Zoe says, a little in awe.

"Really?"

"Really," I say with a nod, finally finding my voice again, even if it still sounds a little strange. "It's really, really good."

She exhales, and only now, as her shoulders relax a little, can I see how tense she actually was. "Okay. Good. Thank you. Oh my God." A relieved laugh escapes her. "I'm so glad you don't hate it."

"As if we ever could! How could anyone ever hate this? It's amazing!" Jax stands up and reaches out his hand to her. Only at the last second does he seem to remember that whatever was going on between them no longer exists, and he pivots to running his fingers through his hair as he clears his throat. "Seriously. It's totally mind blowing."

She gives him a small smile. "Thanks." Then she turns back to the rest of us. "I edited a few shorts for you guys to use on TikTok and Insta. The full video is probably better for YouTube. I'll send you everything later, but I wanted to see if you liked it before I show you the rest."

"You did more?" I stare at her in disbelief.

"Yeah, well, I was in the flow, and we had so many good

sequences that I couldn't use them all for the long video. Besides, you'll need to spam social media with teasers anyway, so everyone wants to see the video and hear the song."

"You don't happen to want to be our marketing manager?" Beck's question sounds like he's joking, but I'm pretty sure he's serious.

Skye shakes her head. "No way. I've got enough to do. But I'd be happy to keep editing your videos."

Beck gets up and hugs her. "Thanks! You're the best."

"Oh, stop. I enjoy doing it," she says, letting go of Beck and giving him an awkward pat on the shoulder. "I'll send you the ones I've already finished, and we can upload the first one right away. It's best to make your song into a TikTok sound so everyone can use it. And then hopefully you'll be famous."

Colin, Jax, Beck, and I exchange glances, and for a moment, it's just us and the absurd hope that this could actually work. That we could really do it. That our dreams could come true.

"Then let's get started." Skye's voice rings with enthusiasm; I think she's almost as excited as we are. Understandably. She put an infinite amount of effort into this video. She wants it to be worth it. I don't know how we'll ever be able to thank her.

* * *

Hours pass, and we post the first videos on TikTok and Instagram. Skye has edited dozens of shorts, some with the same sequences, always with the first chorus of our song in the background. The first video does well, the next two don't, but we have enough views to keep going and post more clips. Two or three a day.

Days pass, and people comment wanting to hear the whole song. They want more. More from Rayne and me. It's crazy. We post the video on YouTube, and our friends share it, then lots of other people do the same. Thousands. More than we ever thought possible. Comments and DMs flood our account.

A week goes by. We post the short where Rayne and I kiss, and everyone goes crazy. It's totally wild. They don't know us, aside from what they see in the video, but suddenly there are thousands of comments from people who want to know if we're really together; they say if we're not, we definitely should be.

"Dance with You 'Til Midnight" hits like a bombshell. It's surreal. It can't be possible. But it is. It's true. It's our reality, and our life.

PART 9

Breakdown

NOW

Rayne Bellamy Reclaims Her Life Months After Her Parents' Tragic Death

Boston—Nine months after the death of her parents, rock star Liam Bellamy and former ballet dancer Laura Bellamy, Rayne Bellamy has made her first public appearance in the music video for "Dance with You 'Til Midnight" by We Are No Saints, an up-and-coming pop-rock band from Boston.

Rayne Bellamy has been out of the spotlight over the past few months while coping with her parents' death. The fact that she is now appearing on screen as a dancer gives hope that she has come to terms with her loss.

Liam and Laura Bellamy died last June as a result of a tragic car accident.

Rayne Bellamy Dances Her Way Back into Life

Los Angeles—No one could have expected this: Nine months after losing her parents (as we reported **here**), Rayne Bellamy is following in the footsteps of her mother, Laura Bellamy, who was a dancer herself before Rayne was born.

In recent months, there has been much speculation about what has become of the rock star's daughter who left Los Angeles after the death of her parents—the memories must have been too painful. Many expected her to follow in the footsteps of her musician father sooner or later. She certainly has musical talent, as her former classmates have told us. You can see for yourself **here**, in footage we've obtained showing Rayne at a school performance in eighth grade. But it seems rather than her father's footsteps, she's chosen to go with her mother's ballet slippers.

We Are No Saints—From the Living Room to the Spotlight

Boston—Until a few weeks ago, hardly anyone knew of We Are No Saints, a band from Boston that performed their songs mainly in their living room rather than on the world's biggest stages. Now the band has released their first music video and enlisted some prominent support: rock star daughter Rayne Bellamy, who appears in the video as a dancer.

According to rumors, the relationship between front man Easton Coleman and Rayne Bellamy is not purely professional.

Let's hope that Coleman isn't just using Liam Bellamy's daughter to finally find his way into the limelight. After everything she's been through in the last year, she certainly deserves better.

Rayne Bellamy & Easton Coleman—What's Going on Between the Rock Star's Daughter and the Musician?

Los Angeles—Most people will have already seen the music video for "Dance with You 'Til Midnight" by We Are No Saints, but if not, you can find the uncut video **here**.

The chemistry between Bellamy and Coleman is almost

palpable as they dance. It's no surprise that countless fans on social media are speculating that they're a couple.

But what's really going on between them? Is this a real relationship, or just hype to promote the song? If it is a marketing strategy, it seems to be working. The music video has almost eleven million views on YouTube, and the band's videos have been going viral on TikTok for days. A kiss scene between Bellamy and Coleman in particular has inspired countless edits on the social media app. It remains exciting, and we continue to ask ourselves: What's going on between the rock star's daughter and the musician?

Insider Claims That Easton Coleman Is Using Rayne Bellamy

Boston—For days, thousands of fans have been wondering what's going on with the relationship between Rayne Bellamy and Easton Coleman, the front man of We Are No Saints, a band from Boston that has experienced a meteoric rise in the past two weeks. Bellamy is said to be one of the reasons behind their success. There's no denying that the band owes its rise to fame primarily to the rock star's daughter and her appearance in the music video for their first single, "Dance with You 'Til Midnight."

According to an insider, Coleman has been working hard over the past few months to build a relationship with Bellamy after the two met in Boston. Admittedly, it's a strange coincidence that the band, which was previously unknown, is suddenly everywhere. Only the two of them know how much truth there is to the rumors. However, we hope that Coleman does not live up to the band's name, as Bellamy has been through enough in recent months.

CHAPTER 42
Easton

IDFC—blackbear

I feel sick as I read one article after another. There are too many, and I know I need to stop, but I can't bring myself to put my phone down and leave it alone.

Using Liam Bellamy's daughter . . . marketing strategy . . . insider . . . spotlight . . . relationship . . . no denying that the band owes its rise to fame primarily to the rock star's daughter.

My mind is racing, my head is too full, my heart is beating too fast.

I should be happy that the video was so well received, and people want more from us. They want our music. Instead, everything feels wrong because of these damn articles. I've been reading them for what feels like ten hours without being able to stop myself. I'm obsessed in the unhealthiest way, and part of me knows that it's all absolute bullshit.

There are no insiders, and our relationship isn't some crappy marketing strategy. It's just Rayne and me. We're successful because our song is good.

Unfortunately, there's also a small part of me that sees it differently. I'm afraid the people who write these articles are right, because the doubts in my head are too loud. What if some of what they're saying is true? Before Rayne came to Boston, before we met, things weren't working out with the music. Not the way they should have. We gave it our all, but it was never enough.

And then we wrote this one song that changed everything, and we did it together.

"Stop feeding yourself that crap." Beck appears behind me so unexpectedly that I'm startled. I didn't even hear him come home. He was still at work last I checked, while Colin was on the phone with Emma in his room and Jax was upstairs busy taking care of our social media accounts. He took charge without being asked, and I'm grateful because I probably wouldn't be able to handle all the toxic crap on TikTok and Instagram. Not even if the positive feedback outweighs the negative at the moment.

"I can't," I reply. I shout in protest as he takes my phone away.

"You have to!" His eyes narrow to slits. "You know that none of what those idiots write is true, right?"

"Yes," I reply, but even I can hear that I don't sound convinced.

"East . . ." he says warningly, because he knows exactly what's going through my head, and I groan in annoyance.

"I know it's bullshit, okay? Rationally speaking."

"Well, then please try to look at it rationally." He smiles warningly, and I would really like to do what he asks, but unfortunately, it's not that easy.

"Do you think we could have done it without Rayne?" The

question bursts out of me before I can stop myself, and I hate myself for even asking it.

Sighing, Beck plops down next to me on the sofa. "Does it matter?"

I want to say no, but that would be a lie.

"It's just . . . Never mind. It's stupid." I let my head fall back and press my palms against my eyes.

"East, come on. Spit it out."

"I feel like the biggest asshole ever."

"You're not."

"You're just saying that because you're my best friend."

"And because I know you. Come on. Tell me."

"Remember when I had that fight with Rayne? When I freaked out after we wrote the song?"

He nods, of course he remembers. It wasn't that long ago, after all.

"I felt like a failure because I couldn't do it without her. And now I feel the same way, only worse, because things are going really well now, and maybe those stupid bastards are right," I blurt out.

"Which part of the crap in those articles are you referring to? Just so I know what I have to talk you out of." Beck nudges me in the side, and I grimace.

"What if it's true? What if I just used her?" I ask quietly.

Beck doesn't answer. He stays silent until I have to look at him, and then he returns my gaze incredulously.

"Do you want me to punch you now or later?" he asks, trying to sound friendly, and I roll my eyes.

"I'm serious."

"Yeah, me too. East . . . Jeez. You know that's not true."

"Isn't it?"

"You tell me." He changes his tactic. I should have seen it coming; after all, I know him as well as he knows me. "Did you use her?"

My heart skips a beat. Everything in me resists Beck's question. And with that, I guess I have my answer. But I'm not ready to admit it. My mind isn't cooperating. The doubts are too loud and I wish I could just turn them off. But it's not that easy.

"Not consciously." It's a small concession I'm willing to make.

"Not even subconsciously." His voice has taken on a gentle undertone that I haven't heard from him in a long time.

"But what if she thinks I was?" I can't look him in the eyes, staring at my hands instead as my shoulders tense painfully.

"You don't really believe that, do you?"

I slowly shake my head. No, not really. But in another way, I somehow do. Why is everything so damn complicated? Why the hell am I like this?

"You would never take advantage of anyone. Especially not Rayne. This thing between the two of you started long before you even knew who she was."

My fingers close around the bracelet on my wrist. He's right. I *know* that. But knowing something and feeling it are two completely different things.

"I hate my mind," I mumble.

"Don't say that. Your mind is great. You do some pretty good things with it. Writing songs, for example. Damn good songs. None of us can write like you, East."

"I'm better with Rayne."

"What's wrong with that?" he asks, and I guess that's the million-dollar question.

"Nothing," I admit with a sigh. "The thing is . . . I want to write with her. I want to write a thousand songs with her. Because everything is better with her. And easier. So why can't I get the idea out of my head that I have to do it alone?"

"I'd love to tell you that there's a logical explanation for that, and I'm sure there is. If I'd studied psychology, I might be able to tell you. But I didn't, and I can't. Just give yourself some time, okay? And talk to Rayne about it. I think that might help."

I roll my eyes and smile lamely. "Talking helps? Really?"

He laughs. "I've heard rumors." He stands up and slaps me on the shoulder. "Now go talk to her. She knows all about drama with the press. I'm sure she can talk you out of this mess even better than I can."

"Hmm, you've done a pretty good job already."

"I'm good at this. Now I'm going to go see if Jax needs any help. He's taking this too hard, but at least he's not as emotionally involved as you are." He's almost at the door when I stop him again.

"Hey, Beck?"

He glances back at me questioningly over his shoulder.

"Thanks."

"That's what best friends are for."

I nod. Yes, that's true. But my doubts haven't really gone away yet.

CHAPTER 43

Rayne

"This is so crazy." Mae scrolls through one video after another, a look of awe on her face. Glancing at her phone, I see another edit of the music video replaying the kiss in slow motion, and I fall back onto my bed with a groan.

"Mae, stop watching that."

"But the fan edits are really great. Do you know how many people have already used the song as their audio? Thousands. Seriously, it's crazy."

"I know."

"Why aren't you happy?"

"I am," I say. "It's just . . . I didn't think it through properly before."

Mae gives me an uncomprehending glance. "What do you mean?"

I sigh. "I wanted the video to do well. I just didn't think that people would read so much into it about Easton and me. It feels . . ."

I stop, shaking my head. "I can't really explain it right now. It's just strange."

"Okay." Mae puts down her phone and looks at me apologetically. "If it's strange for you, I'll stop watching the videos of you two."

"Thank you." I reach for her hand and give it a short squeeze.

We're hanging out in my room after dinner. Zoe and Jase are at the theater tonight seeing *The Sleeping Beauty*. Jase got tickets, since it's Zoe's favorite ballet, which is why Mae and I are here by ourselves. I'm happy for the distraction, because I've already spent half the day waiting to hear from Easton.

We saw each other in class like we always do, but we didn't have time to talk properly. It's been a hectic day. So I wrote to him later asking if we could get together. But he hasn't answered yet, and something about that makes my stomach tighten uncomfortably.

"What happens next?" Mae asks after a while, when only Gracie Abrams' soft voice is filling the silence in my room. Mae has her chin resting on her hands, her green eyes sparkling with curiosity.

"What do you mean?"

"You know. With the band."

"I don't know. I think they'll keep going until some label says they want them. Or they'll try it without a label, if that doesn't happen."

Her gaze becomes more intense. "What about you? What do *you* want to do?"

I freeze. "Nothing?" It comes out sounding too much like a question.

Mae's finely arched eyebrows rise skeptically. "Come on, Rayne. You can tell me."

My mouth opens, but I can't get a sound out. I don't know what to say.

Mae looks at me expectantly, and I'm saved by a gentle knock on my door. I get off the bed to open it and suddenly find myself face-to-face with Easton.

My heart leaps. We saw each other this morning, but right now it feels like weeks have passed, not just a few hours.

"Hey," I say, a little surprised. "What are you doing here?"

"Sorry, I know I didn't tell you I was coming, but . . . can we talk?" he asks, smiling uncertainly. The uneasy feeling in my stomach is back. He seems tired. There are dark circles under his eyes, his hair is even messier than usual, and he looks a little pale.

"Sure, come in." I step aside and then remember I'm not alone.

"I guess that's my cue to leave." Mae gets off my bed and winks at us.

"Oh, sorry, I didn't mean to chase you away. I can come back tomorrow."

"Nonsense," Mae says. "I see Rayne every day. I can survive without her for one evening. Especially if you two have things to talk about." She gives him a quick hug, and a moment later the door closes behind her.

Easton and I are alone, but something is different. I can't quite put my finger on it, but it makes me uncomfortable.

"Are you all right?" I reach out a hand, my fingertips brushing his, and breathe a sigh of relief when he immediately slips his fingers between mine.

"I am now." He sounds relieved and I have to smile.

"Are you sure?"

"Yes. I think so. Today has worn me out." He gently pulls me close and caresses my face.

"Why, what happened?" My fingers slip under his sweater; I need to feel his skin.

He hesitates briefly and bites his lower lip.

I wait and gently stroke his bare skin.

"Have you been reading those articles? About . . . us?"

I tense up. "No."

I don't even need to ask to know he has.

"Why not?" he asks quietly.

"Because I know none of what they're saying is true. None of it."

"What if it is?" He sounds so insecure that it breaks my heart a little.

"What did you read?" I ask, even though I don't really want to know. But I have to, because whatever it was, it's bothering him.

"A few things about you and your parents." I shiver, but don't get a chance to ask him more before he quickly moves on. It's probably better that way. "Also some things about us. They say our music video is only popular because you're in it. And that I'm using you."

"But you know none of that is true, right?"

Easton is silent, the kind of silence that means he wants to agree but isn't entirely convinced. I stroke the back of his neck, nestling against him and breathing his familiar scent.

"When I was little, I didn't know my dad was famous. Mom always took me to his concerts, and I'd wear these huge headphones, but I never realized that all the people there were there because of my dad. How could any kid understand that?" As I remember how Mom showed me pictures of us, me in her arms with huge headphones on, my eyes fill with tears. But I also have to smile. It's a beautiful memory. "It took me years to realize who he was. My parents always tried to keep me out of the public eye as much as possible. Even though we lived in LA, we were just outside the city. Even as a child, I preferred being at home to anywhere else."

Easton's hands move from my face to my hair. He's still silent, waiting for me to continue. Which I do. But I'm not really sure what I'm trying to tell him.

"Eventually, of course, I got curious. Google is a gateway to hell when you're in the public eye. I read so many things about my parents that at some point I didn't know if I really knew them anymore. Which is absurd, because of course I knew my parents. Much better than those fake journalists who'll write anything to generate clicks. It took me a long time to realize that it wasn't good for me to read what was on the internet. Not just about my parents, but about myself too. It started when I hit puberty. So much crap was being written that it was hard to bear. So I made a clean break and stopped reading all of it. It was really difficult at first, but eventually I got used to not Googling certain things. What I'm trying to say is that none of what you've read is true. They have no idea. The music video is popular because it's great. The song is great, and sure, we were a little lucky. Maybe the timing was just right, who knows? It doesn't matter, the important thing is that it's working." I stand on tiptoes and wrap both arms around his neck, looking him straight in the eyes to make sure he not only hears me but also understands me. "The idea that you're supposedly using me is the biggest load of crap I've ever heard."

His blue eyes flicker. "So you don't believe it's true?"

"Not for a second. I know you, Easton."

He leans his forehead against mine, his breath brushing my skin as he sighs. "I hate that I worry about stuff like this. And I hate that I feel bad because sometimes I think I should be able to do this without you. But I don't want to do it without you. Does that make sense? It doesn't, does it?"

"Yes, it does." I stroke his lips with my thumb. "It makes a lot of sense to me. I think thoughts like that are normal when you work in a creative field. But Easton, you can do anything, with or without me. You write amazing songs, I know that."

"You too," he whispers. I don't know why, but I'd rather pretend I didn't hear him.

"Please don't read those articles anymore," I say quietly, snuggling a little closer to him.

"Okay."

"Promise?"

"I promise."

"I love you." The words come out of my mouth before I even think about saying them. It just happens. Maybe that's how it's supposed to be. Maybe you're meant to say those words without even thinking about it. When you just feel it. And I feel it very strongly right now.

"I love you too." Easton's voice sends shivers down my back. He smiles, and then he kisses me. It's a gentle kiss. Just because he wants to kiss me. Because we're in love with each other. *So in love.*

Tears fill my eyes because right now, at this moment, I'm so damn happy. I can hardly comprehend it, but somehow I am. It doesn't matter what gossip magazines write about us. There's only one truth. Maybe I'm crying a little because Mom and Dad will never know that I've found someone I can love. Someone I want to love.

Easton looks down at me when he tastes the salt on our lips. His gaze is dark, clouded and worried.

"Don't cry," he whispers.

I shake my head. "I'm sorry," I murmur, wiping the tears off my cheeks and swallowing the lump in my throat.

"What's wrong?" He holds my face in both hands, his gaze gentle.

"Nothing," I reply, shrugging. "I'm just . . . happy."

"That's why you're crying?"

"Yes."

"Then they're happy tears?" A small smile tugs at the corners of his mouth, a little uncertain and very much like himself.

I nod and blink away the last tears. "Yes, because you make me happy."

His eyes light up, and when he kisses me this time, it's different. Slower, deeper. *More.* A kiss that makes us both forget why he came here and what we were talking about. A kiss that makes me forget everything.

I open my mouth when I feel his tongue, arching my back so my body presses closer to his. I let my hands wander under his sweater again, and he immediately gets goose bumps. I smile against his lips, tugging at the sweater that desperately needs to come off so his skin can touch mine. I want to feel his heat. I want to feel *him.*

"Rayne, do you know what you're doing to me?" he murmurs hoarsely, without taking his mouth off me. His breath caresses my chin and my eyes open. My gaze meets his and his eyes are darker than before, almost black. Dark with desire.

My body reacts instinctively to the excitement in his eyes and the way he's touching me. Now he's the one stroking my lips, and my breath catches for a second. Then I lick his fingertip, and he gasps.

"The same thing you're doing to me," I say. I press my chest and hips against him. He's hard already. One kiss, one touch, and he's hard.

Easton groans as I rub against his erection, the sound sending waves of heat through my entire body. I grab the hem of his sweater; we have to get rid of all our clothes. Right now.

I pull off his sweater while he kicks off his shoes.

I've seen him with his shirt off a lot over the last few weeks, but I still haven't gotten enough of the sight. I can't help staring at him now.

Next he takes off his pants and stands in front of me in his boxers. I want him so much.

"Take your clothes off," he whispers, his hands clenching as if he has to stop himself from doing it for me.

He wants me to undress, and even though I've done it many times in the last few weeks, even though he's often watched me do it, this feels different. This time I'm not undressing *in front* of him, I'm undressing *for* him.

I nod toward the bed. "Sit down." He does what I want, and I do what he wants.

I'm wearing my usual clothes, leggings and a hoodie. It's one of his, a fact I'm sure he's well aware of, judging by the way his gaze wanders over the fabric as I wrap my hands around the hem and then change my mind because I'm not wearing a bra, not even a bustier. Instead, I slide the leggings off first, slowly, with little pauses that make his breath catch.

My movements are smooth and supple. I never thought that dance training would pay off in the bedroom, but turns out it does.

"Rayne." He says my name like a plea.

I lift my head, blink innocently at him, and finally push the leggings aside.

"Are you trying to kill me?" He moves his hips restlessly, his hands still clenched. He wants to touch me, I can see it in his eyes.

"Not today," I say softly, and pull the hoodie over my head in one fluid motion.

His gaze wanders over my naked body, my breasts. It feels like he's touching me, even though I'm standing a few steps away from him. His gaze wanders lower, to the wine-colored panties I'm wearing, and just the way he looks at me makes the muscles in my abdomen contract.

"Come here." He reaches out to me, and again I do as he asks. I walk over to him, my skin, my lips, and everything else tingling. I need him to kiss me and touch me. I can't take it anymore.

I take a condom out of my bedside table drawer before placing my hand in his, letting him push me onto the bed.

Then he's on top of me, his gaze darting from my eyes to my mouth. He kisses me, and I forget how to think, how to breathe, and who I am. He kisses me, and every muscle in my body tenses. I need more.

I clutch his arms and his breathing quickens. *More, please more.*

I don't know if I say it out loud or if he just senses what I want, but now his lips wander over my neck, finding the sensitive spot just behind my ear, and a sigh escapes me. I move beneath him, it's pure instinct. My mind isn't working, I can't think anymore.

But thinking isn't important right now, feeling is, and that's what I'm doing. I stroke his shoulders, his chest, and his back, feeling his muscles tense under my fingertips. I love that. But it's not enough, because even though he's leaning over me, he's not really on top of me. He's supporting himself on the mattress with his elbows, but I want to feel his weight on me. I want him on top of me, inside me—everywhere.

"Easton," I say, just his name, because I really can't think anymore. He smiles against my skin as his mouth moves farther down my neck to my breasts. "Come here." Now I'm the one asking him, but I can't help it. I'm on fire, and it's his fault.

I reach for the condom and the plastic rustles softly as I tear open the packet. I pull down his boxers, he pulls down my panties, then he straightens up enough so that I can slip the condom over him. He watches me as I do it, twitching in my hand, and that makes me way too hot.

When I pull him toward me this time, he sinks heavily onto me and kisses me, his tongue in my mouth. I breathe him in, and the throbbing between my legs takes me over. He has to do something about it.

Easton reaches between us. He's exactly where I want him, and I hold my breath as he enters me. We move at the same time, slowly and carefully. I lift my hips and he thrusts into me, and then nothing is slow or careful anymore.

Short kisses, sharp gasps, his lips on my neck. I pull him closer, my hands trembling. I'm shaking. I need him deeper, a little harder, a little more. Easton groans, and the sound shoots straight to my core. He slides both hands under my butt, lifts me up a little, and suddenly the angle is different, and everything changes. Heat in my stomach, a burning pull and tingling that spreads throughout my entire body.

I've never come like this before, not without his fingers or his tongue, but the moment he thrusts into me again, he pushes me over the edge. I have to bite my lower lip to suppress a scream. He kisses me, but it's more than kissing; it's more like breathing. A shiver runs through his body, and then he goes completely still inside me and on top of me.

My muscles relax. Suddenly I'm tired, so tired, but it's the best kind of exhaustion you can imagine.

I don't know how long we lie there, entwined, on top of each other and inside each other. Eventually, Easton pulls away from me after a short but intense kiss and gets up to throw away the condom. He's back almost immediately, pulling me to his chest. I feel his heartbeat against my back and nestle against him with a soft, contented sigh, skin to skin, and once again his mouth finds my neck.

"I love you, Birdy," he whispers, and I want to hear him say it forever.

I don't know why, but at that moment, it feels a little like goodbye. It's not. It can't be. But for a split second, it feels that way. Then the moment is gone, and I fall asleep without another thought.

CHAPTER 44
Rayne

Exile—Taylor Swift, Bon Iver

Today is not a good day. It's Thursday morning, and I can tell something is off as soon as I start my warm-up exercises. I don't know what's wrong; I can't put my finger on it, but I don't feel good. There's a strange feeling in my stomach, a kind of restlessness.

I slept badly, maybe because Easton wasn't lying next to me for the first time this week. I spent the last few nights with him, but yesterday the guys were out and I was so exhausted from class that I climbed into bed right after dinner, picked a series on Netflix, and fell right to sleep. I woke up in the middle of the night feeling a bit off. I put my laptop on the nightstand, drank a glass of water, and fell back to sleep quickly, only to find myself in the middle of very confusing dreams.

I guess it's possible that the strange feeling in my stomach is just because I'm tired and overworked. In the weeks before we shot the music video, I spent so much time on choreography that I neglected a lot of other things. For example, the exercises that are supposed to prepare me for pointe dancing. I finally need to exchange my slippers for pointe shoes and at least get close to what the others are achieving. Not to mention the theory lessons. I should really be studying for the upcoming exams, but I haven't been able to get myself to do it, and the fact that Zoe and Mae finished their notes ages ago isn't really helping to motivate me. With everything else that's happening, I'm falling behind again.

"Rayne?" A slender hand touches my shoulder. I turn to see Zoe's concerned gaze. "Are you okay?"

"Huh? Yeah. Sorry. Everything's fine."

"Are you sure?" A deep furrow forms between her eyebrows. "Jase said that Easton has been reading too many articles about you guys online. Have you been looking at them too?"

"No, not at all." I shake my head decisively and let go of the barre for a moment. "If you read too much of that stuff, you might as well go straight to therapy."

"You have a point there. I haven't read many, but I can imagine how much crap is being written."

"You get used to it eventually." Unfortunately.

"So you're not worried about it? Sorry, I don't mean to be nosy, but you really look like you're not doing well, and I'm a little worried about you."

"That's sweet of you, but I'm fine. Really," I add with more emphasis than I feel.

She doesn't seem convinced, probably because I'm not either. But how can I explain to her what's going on when I don't understand it myself?

"I just slept badly."

An understanding smile crosses her face. I'm not sure if she buys my excuse, but at least she lets it go. "I understand. I think it was a full moon last night," she says, as if that explains everything. "I didn't sleep very well either."

"Yeah, it was probably the moon."

Zoe still looks worried as we continue with our warm-up exercises, but she doesn't say anything else, and I'm grateful for the silence and the fact that Mae is on the other side of the room talking to Kelly about something. She wouldn't have let it go as easily as Zoe did.

My head feels like it's wrapped in cotton as I stretch, forcing my muscles to work. Unfortunately, my body isn't really cooperating. I'm stiff, and I hope it's just because I'm overtired and have been pushing myself too hard over the last few weeks. I should take a break, I know. But I don't have time for breaks, I still need to improve.

But why do you need to improve?

The voice in my head is quiet but very familiar. It sounds like my mom. *Why are you doing this, Rayne? Why do you always feel like you have to be better?*

Blinking, I shake my head, trying to block out the voice, but I can't. It's there, and it won't go away.

Why are you torturing yourself so much?

I close my eyes, suddenly wanting to cry. I realize I don't know the answer myself. Not really, anyway. Maybe I just can't admit the truth to myself. Like I said, today is not a good day.

"Good morning." Mr. Conrad's voice makes me look up. In his usual good mood, he enters the hall and directs us to our seats while Easton, who enters the room behind him, sits down at the piano. He smiles at me, and I feel an urge to smile too, but it isn't genuine and he can tell.

His eyes flicker, his mouth silently forming the same question Zoe asked me earlier. *Are you okay?*

I want to nod, but I can't, and suddenly Mom's voice is in my head again. I realize that there are always going to be days like this. Bad days when I miss her and Dad a little more than usual. Days when I'm exhausted and a little lost.

I think that's okay. I don't like it, but it's okay. I know the pain will never go away. I have to learn to live with it, and some days are a little easier than others. Today just isn't one of those days.

* * *

"Hey, Birdy." Easton comes up to me after class and pulls me close, even though neither of us really has time before we have to get to our next classes. I let myself lean on his chest anyway and immediately feel a little better as I smell his familiar scent.

"What's wrong?" he asks gently as I bury my face in his chest.

I shrug without saying a word. He strokes my back with one hand and gently lifts my chin with the other, looking searchingly at me.

"Hm?"

"I just want to sleep," I murmur. That's at least half of the truth.

He studies me intently, looking directly into my eyes, and I think he really understands what's going on inside me.

"Is there anything I can do?" His thumb strokes the corner of my mouth, and I almost smile.

"No. Tomorrow everything will be better."

"I'm sure," he says, sounding so convinced that I almost believe him.

Sighing, I turn away from him. "I have to go now."

"Will I see you later?"

"Sure. I'll come by tonight." I stand on tiptoes and kiss him lightly on the lips.

"Okay."

I start to walk away, but he pulls me back to him and kisses me, a little more intensely, a little more like we're alone and the studio isn't gradually filling up with the next class.

But we can't pretend we don't have places to be anymore. Sighing, Easton lets me go. I grab my bag and head for the door. But I barely make it there when Easton calls me back.

"Rayne, wait! Shit, what's happening?" His voice sounds different than it did a second ago, a mixture of excitement, panic, and disbelief in it. I whirl around, and there he is, phone in hand, staring at the screen. He's pale as a ghost.

I take a few quick steps back to him, and for a split second I forget that today is not a good day, that I feel strange, and that everything is off. Easton looks like he's seen a ghost. "What's going on?"

A stunned laugh escapes his lips, and he holds out his phone to me. My eyes fly over the display. I read the message. Once, twice, three times.

"It's real, isn't it?" he asks, his voice trembling. "I'm not just imagining it?"

"No, you're not just imagining it," I say, a chill running down my spine as I read the email from Redrock Music Group for the fourth time. "They want you. They want you to come to LA for an interview."

CHAPTER 45
Easton

Bad Liar—Imagine Dragons

When I get home later, I can't remember how the rest of the day went. All I know is that we got the email from Redrock. The hours that followed are just a blur. I somehow managed to get through the two classes I had left that day, but I really don't know how. I canceled my shift at the record store, even though I felt incredibly guilty about it, but I had no other choice. I would have loved to skip my classes at the New England School of Ballet too, but since I was already there, I couldn't really do that, even though I was so excited I could have died. Every minute my fingers weren't on the piano keys, I was texting the guys.

Beck, Jax, and Colin are sitting in the living room when I enter the house. Their voices sound loud and excited; they're talking so fast that I can barely understand what they're saying.

"Hey," I greet them, and all three fall silent at once. But the next moment, they leap up and we fall into each other's arms because our biggest dream is coming true.

"We did it!"

"LA, here we come!"

"Fuck!"

"Oh God, can you believe it?"

"Dude, this is crazy!"

"I have to call Emma! Just think, if we move to LA, then . . . we could finally see each other more often again."

We're all talking at once and it's almost impossible to understand a word, but we all know what the others are talking about.

"Did you guys answer yet?" I ask at some point.

"We waited for you," Colin replies solemnly. I've never seen him grin as broadly as he does right now.

"Let's get started, then." Jax rubs his hands together, throws himself onto the sofa, and opens the laptop on the coffee table. "I think the answer is obvious, right?"

"No, we'll write back and tell them we're not interested and would rather stay in Boston." Laughing, Beck steps behind him and messes up his hair. It's usually cropped short, but it's gotten longer over the winter.

"Good idea," says Jax with a grin, typing a short email to Redrock Music. Then we sit silently, staring at our inbox and waiting for a reply.

My heart is beating so fast I can feel it in every cell of my body. There's a rushing sound in my ears. Redrock wants us. *Redrock.* Holy shit. This is one of the biggest music labels in the country. One of the best. They want us to come to Los Angeles and play more of our songs for them. They want to get to know us. They want *us.*

"Hey, they answered already! They want us to fly over this weekend if we can make it!" Jax's voice is trembling with excitement.

“This weekend?” Beck asks incredulously.

“Tomorrow.” Jax nods vigorously. “They’ll send us plane tickets right away if we agree.”

“What the hell?” Colin laughs in disbelief.

“Apparently they’re trying to sign us quickly.” Jax leans back, stretching his arms above his head. “Oh my God, this is so cool! We’re flying to LA!”

“Tomorrow,” I repeat, and suddenly it all seems to be happening way too fast. It’s absurd. This email is everything we ever wanted, everything we’ve worked for. For years. It’s not too fast. But it still feels that way.

I think of Rayne, and I feel cold.

CHAPTER 46
Rayne

I Know It Won't Work—Gracie Abrams

The problem with wanting something more than anything else is that sometimes you lose sight of how much you have to sacrifice to get it. We were so focused on the band finally finding a label that we didn't think about what it might mean for Easton and me. It's kind of ironic that we're probably going to end up swapping cities.

First I was in LA, and he was in Boston. Soon I'll be in Boston and he'll be in LA.

I never gave a second thought to the fact that our time together in Boston might be limited. Now I wish I had. There's a sharp pain in my chest as I stand in front of Easton's house, staring indecisively at the door. I've been standing here for quite a while because I don't dare to knock. If I go in, decisions will probably have to be made, and I don't know if I'll be able to do that. I'm afraid I won't.

"Hi." I hear Willow's voice behind me, and I can tell she's smiling.

I turn around and force a smile. "Hi."

I haven't seen Willow in weeks. She's been traveling a lot and is hardly ever home. The fact that we're meeting on the porch right now, just like the first time, feels somehow significant. It's like we've come full circle. Except I'm not so sure if that's a good thing.

"Won't the guys let you in?"

I shake my head, a tiny white lie, because there's no way I can tell her I'm just too scared.

"Good thing I have a key." She steps past me and opens the front door. I want to follow her inside, but it's incredibly difficult because my throat suddenly feels tight.

"Rayne, are you coming?" Willow gives me a questioning look from the hallway.

"Yes." I straighten my shoulders and enter the house.

Everything is the same as always, but only on the surface, because today everything is different. The atmosphere in the house is more tense than usual, more excited. It's no wonder.

I'd like to say that I'm one hundred percent happy for Easton and the band, and I mostly am. Really. But there's also this fear that ties my stomach in knots because I know what's coming. What *has to* come. That's why it would be a lie to say something else. I'm happy because their dream is coming true, but I'm only ninety-eight percent happy. The other two percent is pure reluctance, and that makes me a terrible friend.

I take my time removing my coat and boots before going into the living room. I can hear Willow squeal with excitement; Easton must have just told her the good news. I want to turn around and run away so we don't have to have this conversation. But that would be unfair and cowardly.

So I pad into the living room in my socks, where Willow is holding Easton in a vice-like embrace, repeatedly telling him how incredibly proud of him she is.

"Hey, Sunshine." Beck spots me first. His eyes are shining, and he's literally vibrating with excitement.

"Hey." I walk over to him and hug him first, then the others, tightly and a little too long, telling them how happy I am for them, how great this all is, and that they deserve this offer more than anyone else in the world. Then I come to Easton, and the lump in my throat suddenly feels so big that I can't get a sound out. For the second time today, I just want to cry.

Without a word, he pulls me toward him. I guess he can sense what's going on inside me, or maybe he feels what I'm hoping for but at the same time don't want to hope for.

"We're going upstairs for a minute," he says to his friends, then grabs my hand and pulls me out of the living room. The stairs creak under our feet, and I fight back the tears burning in my eyes. I'm terrible. I should just be happy, and I want to be, because he really deserves it. He deserves *everything*.

As soon as he closes his bedroom door behind us, I burst into tears. Salty streams run down my cheeks.

"Hey, please don't cry," he says, sounding as if he's about to cry himself. Which somehow makes everything worse.

"I'm sorry." Sniffing, I wipe the tears from my cheeks, but it's pointless because more immediately follow.

"You don't have to be sorry." He reaches for me, his hands stroking my back soothingly.

"Yes, I do. I'm terrible. I'm happy for you, I really am. I'm so proud of you! You've worked so hard for this. And that's incredibly great!" I sob into his chest, clearly not finding it great at all.

"You're not terrible!" He sounds a little helpless, and I immediately feel even worse.

"Yes, I am!" I break free from his embrace and step back a little because his touch only makes everything worse, because it reminds me that soon this might not be possible anymore. My head is a mess. I know I have to think clearly, calm down, but I can't. I'm breathing too fast, my heart is racing, and I can't stop crying. "I'm standing here with you, crying, instead of celebrating with the band. I'm terrible and selfish and . . . God, I hate this. Why am I like this?"

"You're not terrible," he repeats firmly.

I just shake my head.

"You're not selfish either."

"Yes, I am! Your dream is finally coming true, and all I can think about is that soon you'll be in LA and I'll be stuck here in Boston, and that thought alone hurts like hell!" My voice gets louder with every word, and I lose control, even though the last thing I want is to argue with Easton. But I'm feeling too much and I need to get it all out, otherwise I'll go crazy.

"Do you think I feel any different? Do you think I haven't thought about that?" he snaps, suddenly just as angry as I am. Although it's more despair than anger. Or a mixture of both.

"No, but—"

"They might not even take us," he says, interrupting me. "Maybe we'll fly to LA, get to know the people, and in the end it turns out they don't want us after all. Maybe it's not the right fit."

"That's silly. It'll work out! They'd be stupid not to take you, and you know it."

"I don't know. But maybe—"

"Oh no, don't you dare! Don't say that!" I shout.

His chin juts forward defiantly and he glares at me. "You don't even know what I was going to say."

"Of course I do. You were going to say that it might not be right for you, that this whole label thing might not be worth it."

Easton is silent, and that's answer enough.

"Don't do it," I beg him. "Don't try to convince yourself not to take it. Not for me. You want this. *You all* want this. It's all you've *ever* wanted. Don't ruin it because of me."

"If it were just about me—"

"It's not just about you. It's about you and your best friends, your brothers, damn it. And even if it were just about you . . . You've been fighting for this for so long. For ages. This is your biggest dream, Easton."

"But it's about you too, Rayne! It's about *us*. What if they sign us? What if we move to LA? What will happen to us then?"

"I don't know, okay?" I yell at him, even though he hasn't done anything wrong, and I hate myself for being like this. I want to stop, but I can't. Suddenly it's back, that horrible fear of losing him. Maybe it was there all along, somewhere beneath the surface where I couldn't really see it, where I could deny that it existed. Now I can't deny it anymore.

He's going to leave and I'll be alone all over again. Different this time, but in a weird way, the same. I'll be alone, and when I think about it, I can't breathe; everything hurts. My palms are getting clammy, my forehead is throbbing painfully, my vision blurs, and it takes a second before I can see properly again. None of this is fair, especially not the words that come out of my mouth next. I want to stop them, stop myself, but I don't know how. I'm losing control, and I'm ruining everything. Because fear is consuming me. Quickly and without mercy.

"Maybe it's fate. Maybe we were only meant to be together for a limited time, maybe . . ."

"Don't start with that bullshit," he whispers.

I grimace because it was just a stupid attempt at an excuse anyway. But I had to at least try, right? Easton takes a deep breath and reaches for my hand. Part of me wants to pull away, but my body fights against the urge. My fingers intertwine with his of their own accord, and everything inside me suddenly calms down.

"You and me, we're real, Rayne. We're real. I love you. And whatever happens in LA this weekend, we'll work it out, okay? We'll find a way."

My lower lip trembles as I look at him and nod. I have to nod, there's no other option. He has to be right.

"We wrote to each other for months without seeing each other. And somehow it worked, and now . . ." He pauses and the expression on his face changes. He has an idea, I can see it. "You could come with us," he blurts out. "If we really move to LA, you could just come with us."

His eyes light up with hope, and I want to say yes.

God, I want to say yes so badly that it tears me apart inside. But I didn't leave LA for nothing. I didn't come to Boston for nothing.

One tiny little word, three letters, but I can't bring myself to say it.

CHAPTER 47
Easton

Blossom—Dermot Kennedy

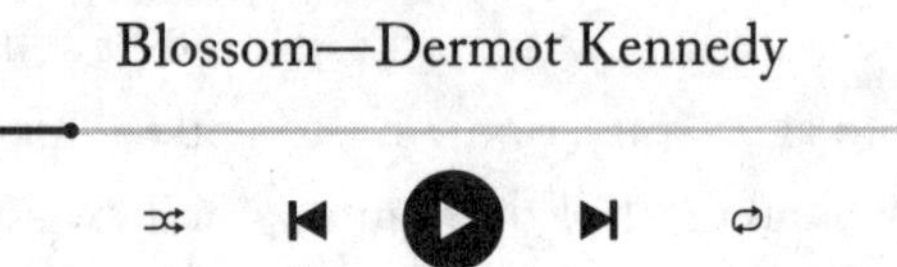

The air is gentle and warm when we land in LA, the sky clear and bright blue. The sun is shining and it's a beautiful spring day. Everything is perfect.

We're picked up at the airport by a driver Redrock sent. He's waiting for us with a sign in his hand that says We Are No Saints. Jax starts laughing when he sees it and punches Colin on the shoulder. George, the driver, leads us outside to a black SUV that will take us to the Redrock offices. Beck sits in the front, while the rest of us climb into the back. Squeezed between Colin and Jax, I stare out the window as we drive from the airport toward the city. My friends talk around me, but I don't really listen because I'm not fully there. My thoughts are still with Rayne.

Rayne, and the question she didn't answer. It wasn't fair to ask that of her in the first place, I know. It's selfish, and I shouldn't have just blurted it out like that. It's not a decision you can make on the spur of the moment. She's built a new life for herself in Boston, made friends, found a home.

In LA, she would be confronted with too many painful memories. But the thought that my future might be here on the West Coast while hers is on the other side of the continent is just unbearable. I had to ask her, even though there's no guarantee yet that we'll get a record deal, or even if we'll move here. I had to ask her because I can't imagine not living in the same city as her, not being able to see her every day.

You and me, we're real, Rayne. We're real.

Unfortunately, that doesn't change the fact that I shouldn't have taken her by surprise the way I did. I flinch when Jax nudges me.

"Are you zoned out or what? We're here." He grins at me, and I force a smile.

I know I should be happier. Our dream is coming true, and I should be enjoying it. I should be enjoying every single second.

"Sorry, I was just thinking about something."

"Then it's time to get back to reality. We're in LA, dude!" His grin widens even more; he's too excited to notice what's going on inside my head, and I'm glad he doesn't. He wouldn't understand.

"Let's roll!" Colin calls impatiently. He and Beck got out of the car a while ago and are already waiting for us at the entrance.

"Come on." Jax climbs out of the car, and I follow him with a suppressed sigh, forcing myself not to think of Rayne. Right now, it's time to focus on the guys and our shared dream. Our dream, which is now within reach.

The Redrock Building is a tall skyscraper made entirely of glass, sunlight reflecting brightly off the facades. Palm trees stand at regular intervals along the sidewalk, making it look almost surreal.

"Everyone ready?" Colin asks before we enter the building.

"So ready." Beck puts his arm around my shoulder and pushes me into the building.

The lobby is bright and decorated with palm trees in pots, significantly smaller than the ones outside. In front of the large windows facing the street are comfortable-looking armchairs gathered around low tables that look like tree trunks.

We sign in at the reception desk, and a few minutes later a tall woman with short black hair steps out of the elevator and greets us with a friendly smile. She introduces herself as Constance Roberts, a talent scout for Redrock.

"Nice to meet you. Did you have a good trip?" she asks. We nod simultaneously. "Excited?"

"Maybe too excited," Beck says honestly.

"I get it. But don't worry, we don't bite, and we're really glad you were able to come at such short notice." She points toward the elevator and presses number fourteen after the doors close behind us with a soft ping.

On the way up, Constance talks about the hotel we'll be staying at and tells us she has a few things planned for the day if we're not too tired after the meeting.

"I can imagine you didn't get much sleep," she says with a wink. She's right. We really didn't sleep much, mainly because of how early our flight this morning was. It was still dark when we set off for the airport.

"Not at all, actually." Jax grins cheerfully.

"I hope tonight will be different." The elevator doors slide open and we step out. "This way."

We follow Constance into a large conference room where

another, much shorter woman with red, curly hair is already waiting for us at a round table.

"This is my colleague, Amy."

"Nice to meet you." Amy shakes our hands one by one, then asks if we want anything to drink and if we're hungry. She seems nice; her smile is warm, and her brown eyes are clear and appraising.

All four of us shake our heads. We're too nervous to eat anything.

"Let's get started, then," Constance says after we all sit down around the table. "I don't think it should come as a surprise that we found out about you from your music video. We were extremely impressed. Did you put it all together yourselves?"

I nod. "A friend of ours filmed the video and handled all the editing. She knows more about it than we do."

"Does she do that professionally?" Curiosity flashes in Constance's eyes.

"No, she's studying dance," Jax explains.

Amy and Constance exchange a quick glance that I can't interpret. "It's really wonderful. You should be proud that you've done so well together," says Constance.

"Yes, but we think your songs could be even bigger than the video. We looked at your social media profiles and the music you've uploaded so far," Amy adds. "There's a lot of good stuff there. Some of it could be developed further, and we think you have a lot of potential. Especially considering your current hype on social media. It would be a shame not to take advantage of it."

"That's why we'd like to work with you on an album. We can rework some of your existing songs, but I think we'll need a few new ones as well. Who writes your lyrics?"

"Mainly Beck and me," I say.

"So you wrote 'Dance with You 'Til Midnight' together?"

I shake my head. "I wrote that song with Rayne Bellamy."

"Ah, the dancer from your video." Amy and Constance look at each other again. I'm glad she's referring to Rayne as the dancer and not as Liam Bellamy's daughter.

"Do you write songs together often?" Constance asks.

My heart skips a beat. "That's the only one so far."

Her eyes narrow slightly as she studies me. "I think you should change that. You have amazing chemistry together. Not just when you dance. 'Dance with You 'Til Midnight' is an exceptionally good song. The other ones aren't bad either, not at all, otherwise we wouldn't be sitting here today, but that song is something special. We heard it and immediately felt something. You tell a story that feels real, and that's exactly what we're looking for."

For a moment, I can't breathe and my palms are sweating. I wait for the voice in my head and the doubts that are always there, but there's nothing. The voice is silent, and for the first time, I believe that what Rayne, Beck, and everyone else said to me is true. I don't have to try to create something great on my own. It's okay to do it with someone else. With her.

Because together we're real, and together we can bring out the best in each other.

"We want to work with you either way, but if Rayne continues to write songs with you, that would be a big plus. I'm just saying it like it is, because there's no getting around it: She's a well-known name. Having her on your side could really help. Besides, it looks like a lot of people think you're great together." Constance smiles, and I feel my cheeks flush.

"Oh really?" I mumble embarrassedly, hoping she won't answer.

Over the last few days, Jax has shown me too many comments from complete strangers who, for whatever reason, hope that Rayne and I are not only a couple in the video, but also in real life.

"Looks like it." Amy's eyes sparkle with amusement.

I look at my friends because this isn't a decision I can make on my own. Rayne has to make her own decisions, obviously. But this is also about the band, and if Redrock wants Rayne to be part of it, that's completely different from me just asking her to come to LA. It's about our band, our future, and our friendship. Our music.

"She's part of it," Beck says with a grin, and my shoulders slump in relief.

"We can't let Rayne turn into Text Girl again," Colin says, which Amy and Constance acknowledge with confused frowns.

"East will talk to her," Jax says.

Yeah, I guess I will.

"Great. Let's get down to facts and figures." Constance stands up and takes a stack of paper from the shelf next to the door. She divides it into four parts and hands one to each of us. "This is what we can offer you."

CHAPTER 48

Rayne

How Do I Say Goodbye—Dean Lewis

What am I doing here? What the hell am I doing here?

I shift my weight from one foot to the other as I stare up at Grandma's house, just like I stared at Easton's house the other day. I have no idea what I'm doing or why I'm here. It's been months since I've been here, and since I last saw my grandmother. She hasn't been in touch and neither have I, and I think that pretty much says it all. We have no relationship and we're not family. It makes no sense for me to be standing here because she can't help me make the decision I need to make. I need to decide whether to stay in Boston or to go to LA with Easton, that's what it's coming down to. One or the other.

Except my grandmother isn't the kind of person who can help me with this. She doesn't know me. She has no idea who I am or what I should do.

We did it! They want us! We're supposed to move to LA as soon as possible so we can start recording an album. And they want you too. They want us to write songs together.

Easton's voice has been echoing in my ears for hours and I can't think of anything else. He left a message on my voicemail while I was still in class. I should have called him back the second I heard the message, but I didn't. I hate myself for it. He deserves an answer, one full of pure joy. But instead of joy, all I feel is a growing knot of fear in my stomach because I don't know what to do.

Stay or go. I have to make up my mind. It's not just a casual "you could come with me" anymore. It's no longer just a possibility that the band will get signed; it's a reality. They've made it, and they want me to join them to write songs with Easton. Part of me wants to say yes to everything so badly that it hurts. And the other part . . . doesn't know anything anymore. With a soft sigh, I turn around to go back to school but stop immediately when I see Grandma walking toward me.

"Rayne," she says, a little surprised, but still with the same cool and distant tone she always uses.

"Hi, Grandma." I raise my hand awkwardly and wave to her, then immediately wish I hadn't.

"What are you doing here?"

"I was just in the neighborhood and thought—" I stop when Grandma's neatly plucked eyebrows go up. Well, if I were her, I wouldn't believe a single word I said, either.

"Would you like to come in?" She points to the house.

I hesitate for a second and then nod, following her up the stairs to the door. Nothing has changed here in the months since I moved out; everything is exactly as it was before. There's even a bouquet of flowers on the dining table that looks identical to the one she had at the beginning of the year.

Grandma's house still feels strange to me, even though I lived with her for six months. When she tells me to sit down at the dining table, I realize that I've always felt like a guest here, not like this was my new home. Not like the New England School of Ballet felt from the very beginning, including the dorm, my room there, and the people I live with.

Grandma disappears into the kitchen and returns a few minutes later with a tray holding a teapot and two cups.

"So why are you really here?" she asks after sitting down across from me, gracefully lifting the dainty cup. I haven't touched mine yet.

I open my mouth. I want to tell her, but something else comes out instead. "Why didn't you ever reach out to me? You said you would that day we saw each other on campus. But you never did. Why not? Don't you care about me?"

She doesn't bat an eyelash. Instead, she sighs heavily. "Rayne," she says, setting the teacup down with a delicate clatter. "I do care about you. I just don't know you."

"But you could have gotten to know me. After all, I was right here."

"Yes, you were here, hiding in your room all day. You weren't interested in getting to know me."

For a minute her words leave me speechless. "I was trying not to lose my mind," I manage to say, my stomach clenching. This is all going in the wrong direction. "I'd just lost my parents. I didn't know how to—"

"And I lost my daughter," she replies, a very familiar pain flashing in her gray eyes.

"I know," I reply quietly. "But—"

"No, you don't know," she says. "Losing your only child is . . ." she stops and shakes her head. Her shoulders are tense, her back as straight as a board. "It's even worse when you realize you already lost that child much earlier."

My eyes burn, and suddenly I wish I hadn't come here. But I'm here now, and I can't just leave.

"You mean when Mom went to LA with Dad?" I ask.

She nods. "I was against it. But your mother always had a mind of her own. She threw away everything we had built up over the years: her career, her life. She gave it all up for your father."

"And for me." The words come out as a whisper. Mom was already pregnant when she dropped out of college and went to California with Dad.

"Yes. Laura had a great career ahead of her. She was the best dancer in Boston. You should have seen her."

"I did see her," I reply, my voice trembling. "Every day. She kept dancing." She was beautiful, and above all, she was happy.

"But she never made it on stage, even though she had so much talent." Grandma sighs again. "Be that as it may, your mother made many decisions I didn't agree with."

"Is that why you stopped talking to each other?"

She avoids my gaze. "I'm afraid it's not that simple."

"Why not?"

"Rayne." Another sigh. "It was all so long ago. We were both far too stubborn. We made mistakes, and eventually so much time had passed that they couldn't be undone."

"Do you wish they could be?"

"It doesn't matter anymore."

"Yes, it does. I'm still here," I say, even though I don't know why. There's complete chaos in my head. I didn't come here because of Mom. Or maybe I did.

"You remind me a lot of Laura, do you know that?" Grandma says, as if she hadn't heard a word I said. She smiles faintly. "You look so much like her. Other than the purple hair, you look exactly like her when she was your age."

I don't answer because I don't know what to say. It's not true. I don't look like Mom. My eyes are the only thing I got from her.

"I do care about you, Rayne," she continues. "I'm just afraid I'm not able to give you what you need."

I bite my lip to keep from crying. It's stupid. What did I expect? That I would show up here and we would just magically become a family? No.

"I think I should go now." I stand up, feeling sick. My legs feel like they're about to collapse beneath me.

"Yes, that sounds like a good idea." Grandma gets up too. I can't believe that's her reaction. But if I'm honest, I wasn't expecting it to go any other way. Neither of us made an effort. We're strangers, and it looks like we're going to stay that way.

"I'm thinking about leaving school and going back to LA," I blurt out when I reach the door. I don't know why I say it, or what I expect to gain from it. I don't know if I expect approval or rejection. Or that by some miracle her reaction will help me to decide if this is really what I want.

Grandma just smiles a little. "I told you, you're just like your mother," she says and then closes the door. That's all. Then I'm alone.

I should feel something—anything. But instead, I just feel empty. All I know is that I want to go home. I want to talk to Mom and Dad because they would know what I should do. They would know what I want to do, even if I don't know it myself. They would know, and I have no idea.

* * *

I stare at my phone, knowing I should call Easton. He's still waiting for me to respond to his message. I haven't done it yet because I don't know what to say.

You could come with me.

I get out of bed and reach for my headphones. I have to get out of here. I can't think. Laughter drifts out of the common room as I leave my room. It's Friday, and Zoe mentioned earlier that a few people were planning a movie night. She asked if I wanted to come along to take my mind off things and stop thinking about Easton all the time. It was a kind offer, but a movie isn't enough for that.

I leave the cheerful voices behind me, walk down the stairs, and leave the dorm. There's a lot going on tonight on campus. The lights are still on in the practice building, but for once, I don't want to go there.

The door to the administration building is unlocked, so someone must still be here, but when I enter the lobby, there's no one around.

My steps slow, my heart beating faster with every second. It's pounding so hard against my ribs that it almost hurts. I haven't been here since my first day of school. My gaze automatically falls on the photos hanging on the walls. In all the time I've been here, I haven't come back to look for Mom's picture. Maybe I was afraid I wouldn't find it and what that would mean.

I probably shouldn't attach so much meaning to a picture. But there are a lot of things I shouldn't do. Slowly, I walk past the portraits, looking at the dancers in their poses, and finally find Mom on the right-hand side. It's the second-to-last photograph.

She's young and beautiful. She's wearing a black leotard with a black practice skirt, her hair pulled back into a strict bun. The pose looks simple, her back arched slightly backward and her head tilted upward, her arms outstretched. She's standing on the tips of her toes on one foot, the other leg bent. It looks simple, but it's special. No complicated leap, no extravagant costume. Just my mom.

Tears fill my eyes as I look at her, and my heart aches. She was so beautiful.

"Hey, Mom," I say quietly, sinking to the floor and putting on my headphones. A moment later, I hear Dad's soft voice in my ear for the first time in months. I take a breath, my whole body trembling.

He sounds so much like home. I cry because I can't help it. Everything hurts. Why does missing someone have to hurt so much?

"Hey, Dad," I manage to say, choking back a sob. I wipe the tears off my cheeks. "I don't know what to do."

No one answers. Of course they don't. Dad keeps singing. I'm listening to "Mockingbird" because it's the only song that makes sense right now. The song that started it all.

"Is it crazy that I'm talking to you guys here? Probably, right? Talking to yourself is a little crazy." I pull my knees up and wrap my arms around them. "How do you know what choice to make?

How am I supposed to know what to do? Whether to stay or go with him? How is that supposed to work?"

The song fades and starts again.

"I wrote a song, Dad," I say. The memory of that night on the beach, Easton and me in the van, pen and notebook in hand, fills me with a painful longing. "I wrote a song with Easton, and he asked me to go to LA with him. The guys got an offer, and he asked me to come. And I want to. I really do, but I don't know if I can. I mean, it's crazy, right? What would I do in LA? Easton and I have only been together for a few weeks. Leaving with him now is totally crazy. I mean, who does that? You would have killed me if I'd made a decision like that just for a guy."

For a moment I almost believe he's going to answer, just for a split second, because I need it so badly. But of course he doesn't.

"But I want to go with him, Dad. I want to go with him because he's my best friend, and because what we have is . . . real." I suppress a laugh.

You and I are real, Rayne.

"If he goes and I stay, it just won't work. But how can I leave here now? I came because of Mom. I wanted to be like her because she wanted that so much, you know? She was always a little sad that I loved music more than ballet. I know she didn't really mind, though. She just wanted us to have something together, and I wanted that too. I still want that. God, I miss her so much." A tortured sob breaks out of me, and I cover my face with my hands, even though there's no one there to see my tears. "I'm afraid I'll disappoint her if I go back, you know?"

Hearts can break from time to time. Fragile little souls, Dad continues singing, and I can't breathe anymore. Everything hurts. Easton should be here; I need him to hold me and tell me it's okay. It's okay to break down, to not want to decide, to be afraid.

I want him to tell me what Dad would tell me. Because Dad would say that no matter what I choose, I wouldn't disappoint Mom. The most important thing to her was that I was happy. And that's why I should do exactly what makes me happy.

Ballet doesn't make me happy. It never did, and I think deep down I knew that all along. Every day in every lesson, I fought so hard to achieve something that just wasn't right for me. I knew it then, but I pushed it away because I had no idea what else to do, where to go, what to dream of.

But my dream was actually there the whole time. I just didn't dare to let it in. It was already there before Mom and Dad died, back when I was just texting Easton. He asked me what I wanted to do, and my answer was simple.

"Do you think I can do it, Dad? Can I write songs?"

You can do anything, little bird.

He said that so many times, every time I doubted myself.

"I want this. I think I really want this. Everything else here is nice, but it doesn't feel right. It feels like a part of me is missing. And I don't think I'll find it here," I say. Suddenly it's easy to make a decision, with Mom's picture in front of me and Dad's voice in my ear.

Spread your wings, untie your chains
Let your voice be heard
We'll be dancing in the rain
My lovely mockingbird

I have to be brave and fly.

CHAPTER 49

Easton

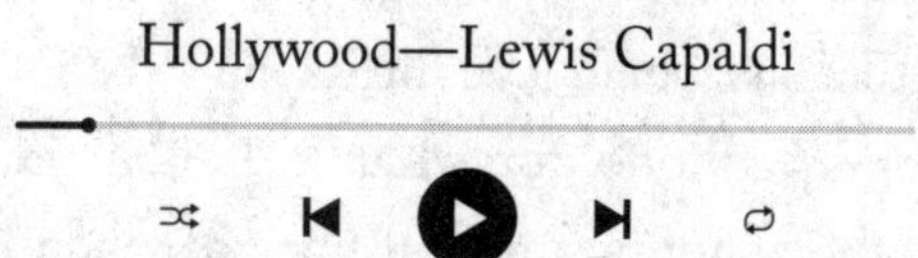

Rayne isn't answering her phone, even though I've been trying to reach her for hours. My texts aren't going through either, and she hasn't responded to the message I left on her voicemail. I'm trying not to freak out, but it's damn hard.

It's so hard that eventually I text Jase and ask him if Rayne is okay. His reply comes quickly, but it only calms me down a little.

JASE:

Don't worry, she's out with Zoe and Mae. Zoe said it was a girls' night out as a distraction.

A distraction from what? Has she made up her mind and it's over, or she hasn't made up her mind and doesn't know if she'll be able to? My thoughts are racing. I need her to get in touch before I lose it.

But she doesn't call, and I can't sleep. My friends and I are lying in our beds in the suite Redrock booked for us. I can hear Jax snoring softly. We got back to the hotel late after spending the whole day with Constance and Amy, celebrating.

They have big plans for us: an album, more social media marketing, TV appearances, interviews. They want us to tour as soon as the album is finished. We're supposed to move to LA as soon as possible so we can start working on our songs. Constance said several times that she would love for Rayne to be involved.

I reach for my phone, for what feels like the thousandth time in the last few hours, and bolt upright when I finally see a reply.

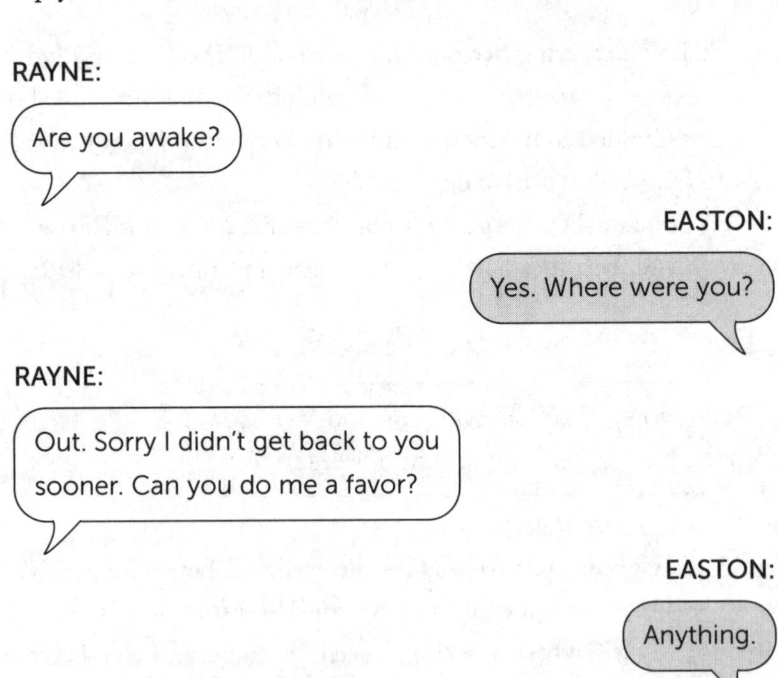

RAYNE:

Can you drive to Santa Monica Beach and take a video of the sunrise for me?

I stare at her last message in disbelief, a tingling sensation spreading through me as a foolish, foolish hope starts to blossom.

EASTON:

Give me half an hour.

RAYNE:

Sunrise is in 23 minutes. Hurry!

I get out of bed and dress quickly, sneaking out of the suite quietly so I don't wake my friends.

* * *

Even though it's so early, Santa Monica Beach is already busy, mostly with surfers trying to catch the first waves of the day. It's strange to see so many people on the beach so early.

The sky is just getting light as I take off my shoes and feel the cool sand under my bare feet. The salty air fills my lungs. I think back to the two nights I spent with Rayne by the sea, how she said she always feels at home here.

Here it is again, that foolish hope I just can't let go of. My heart beats excitedly as I jog along the beach looking for Rayne. She has to be here. There's no way she asked me to come here just to take a video of the sunrise.

She's here, I'm sure of it.

But she's the one who finds me.

"You're not taking a video," I hear her say.

I whirl around, and there she is, right in front of me. Here. There are dark shadows under her eyes, she looks tired, but she's smiling, and she's beautiful. So beautiful.

"You're here," I say, taking a step toward her, reaching out my hand. I need to touch her to make sure she's real.

Her fingers lock with mine, and I know it's true.

"Yes," she says. "I'm here."

CHAPTER 50

Rayne

Lucky Again—Louis Tomlinson

Eight hours earlier

"I can't believe you're actually doing this," Mae says, rushing alongside me toward the security checkpoint. I don't have any luggage, and I've already checked in online, so I don't need to go to baggage check. It's probably closed now anyway. I'm late.

There are people everywhere, and we have to pick our way through the crowd.

"We'll miss you." Zoe grabs my hand as we walk. The two of them insisted on taking me to the airport after I told them what I was doing. They're real friends.

"I'll miss you too." All at once I have a lump in my throat. I stop so abruptly that Mae keeps walking for a couple of steps before she realizes that Zoe and I are no longer with her. I hold out my arms to her, and we hug.

"You'd better come back and visit us all the time." She sounds choked up, and when she lets go of me, there are tears glistening in her eyes. Mine immediately fill with tears too.

"You can visit me too, as often as you want."

"You can count on it! You won't get rid of us so easily," Mae says.

"Definitely not," Zoe agrees, her brown eyes about to overflow.

"I hope so. I'm so glad I found you—"

"Stop! Don't do that." Mae shakes her head frantically. "If you get sentimental now, I'll start crying and then you'll have to comfort me, and we're already late. You have to catch your flight!"

"I know, but—"

"No buts," Zoe says. "You'll be back anyway. There's no time for a proper goodbye. You have to tell Easton that you want to make music with him."

"Yes, it'll be great. I'm already looking forward to listening to every song you write! Now go." Mae grabs my free hand and tows me along. We reach the security checkpoint, and now it's time to say goodbye, at least for now.

"See you Monday," I say. Easton and the guys are flying back on Sunday anyway; the plane tickets have been booked for a while. Besides, I still have to talk to Mr. Pearson. The thought of actually leaving the New England School of Ballet makes my heart ache. At the same time, I feel excited because now I know it's the right thing to do.

I'm not a dancer, not the way I should be if I want to continue attending this school. My passion is for the songs in my head that I need to write. The songs I want to write with Easton.

We hug one last time, and then I leave my friends and head for Los Angeles. To Easton. There are things I need to say to him.

* * *

I don't sleep at all during the flight. Instead, I listen over and over to the songs the guys recorded in the studio. After listening to Easton for hours, I finally arrive in LA.

Home.

I drive to the beach and wait for him. When I see him, I have to smile, and I'm immediately glad I came. He walks around without taking his phone out of his pocket. He guessed that I was coming. He knows me.

But he doesn't see me at first. Not until I'm right behind him, the sand beneath my feet, the sound of the waves beside us.

"You're not taking a video," I say, amused.

Easton stops dead when he hears my voice, then slowly turns toward me. His eyes light up, he smiles, and now I know for sure that I made the right decision. My heart hurts a little less when he smiles at me like that.

The pain won't go away, I know that. It will always be there. I will always miss Mom and Dad. It will always hurt to think about how much of my life they'll miss. Too much. It's not fair, but I can't change it. All I can do is keep going and remember the good things. Mom's smile and Dad's music. How she danced and he sat on the patio with us and wrote dozens of songs.

They'll always be with me.

"You're here," Easton says, his voice hoarse. He takes a step toward me, reaches out his hand, and I put my hand in his. Our fingers intertwine.

"Yes," I say. "I'm here."

"Why?" He pulls me toward him, resting his forehead against mine. His breath brushes my skin, and I close my eyes.

"Because this is where I belong. I want to come home," I say, and I know he knows what I mean.

He's my home.

He always has been. Ever since I first heard him sing "Mockingbird." Ever since I first wrote to him, and he wrote back to me.

PART 10

Outro

EPILOGUE

Rayne

"Ready?" Easton asks, giving me an encouraging smile. We're standing in the driveway of my parents' villa. I haven't been here since last summer, but it's still my home. I nod, but I can't speak as I cling to his hand. No, I'm not ready, not even a little. We've been living downtown for the last five weeks, in a hotel directly across from the studio where We Are No Saints recorded their first album.

It turned out great. Easton and I spent every night writing songs. We were obsessed, and it was a dream that none of us wanted to wake up from. My head was so full I could have written a thousand songs. It was like a wall came down in my mind, and finally all the words that had been waiting so long for me to write them came pouring out.

We hardly slept and I don't know how we survived. The adrenaline probably helped. Every time we finished a new song, the guys would go into the studio the next day to record it. In the end, we ended up with far too many songs for one album. Not all of them fit into the story we wanted to tell, so we had to make some cuts, but we still love every single one.

Now the album is finished, and it's time to take a little break before the guys go on their first tour.

Time to come home.

My heart is beating way too fast as we walk to the front door. The yard still looks exactly the same, except Dad's car isn't in the driveway. It's in the garage, even though he never parked it there.

I take a deep breath and put the key in the front door. It swings open, and we step inside. I can feel tears coming. Everything is the same as always and yet completely different.

The furniture is still in its place: the sofa, the dining table and chairs, Dad's grand piano. Mom's bookshelves. Everything else is gone. The jackets that always hung on the coatrack, Mom's handbags, the shoes. It's all gone, of course. Grandma paid people to clear out the house when I moved to Boston. Mom and Dad's things are stored in a storage facility in town. Grandma wanted to donate them, but I refused. Eventually, I'll figure out what to do with all the boxes, but not right now.

"It's nice here," Easton says as we walk into the living room. We step up to the large window that looks directly out at the sea.

"Yes." I sigh softly and feel calmer as I look outside.

"Are you okay?"

"Yes," I say, smiling. "I'm really fine."

"And it's really okay if we all live here?" he asks, a little uncertain.

"I wouldn't have offered if it wasn't. It'll be nice for the house to be full again. Besides, you guys belong together. I can't just let you move in here without them."

"You could." He pulls me close, grinning. "But Beck can cook."

"Right. And we can't cook at all, so we need him. Plus, we're closer to the airport and have more of a straight shot to the highways from here, so it'll be easier for Colin to see Emma more often." I wrap both arms around his waist and look up at him. "I'm so glad you're all going to live here."

His answer is a kiss, tender and gentle. "Are you glad to be here too?" he asks.

"Yes," I say, and I mean it. "It was the right decision."

I chose music over ballet. It was a dream I didn't allow myself to dream for far too long.

But now I'm here, and the dream has come true. And I'm not alone, because Mom and Dad are always with me. Easton and the guys are with me. And I also have Zoe and Mae. We may live in different cities now, but I know they'll always be there for me. They're all the family I never expected to have but found at exactly the right moment.

Easton

We're playing our first gig in Boston at the Lighthouse. We all agreed this was where it had to happen. It's where it all started. "Dance with You 'Til Midnight" was officially released seven weeks ago, and everything that's happened since then feels like a fever dream. We made it into the Billboard Top Ten, something we never expected. Our album is out, the tour has been announced, and every single concert is sold out. We're playing clubs like the Lighthouse, not huge arenas, but we don't need that yet. We're just getting started, after all.

"I think I'm going to throw up." Jax is backstage, clutching his stomach. He's gone pale.

"Then do it now and not when we're on stage," Colin says, but he sounds about as nervous as Jax. We're all bundles of nerves.

"Have you seen how many people are out there?" Beck pushes back his hair nervously.

"Tons," I say, even though I didn't look. But I can hear a lot of voices coming from the main room of the club.

"Where are Emma and Rayne?" Colin asks, looking around.

I nod toward the stage. "They're in the front row, with Jase, Zoe, and Mae, so they can have the best view."

Colin is about to say something, but then Amy walks toward us. She'll be accompanying us on the tour.

"Are you guys okay?" she asks. We nod, but Jax immediately turns a little paler. "Let's go then, it's showtime! Have fun." She ushers us onto the stage, and then it begins. It's the beginning of everything.

The Lighthouse is completely full. I don't know if I've ever seen so many people here before. I step up to the microphone, my heart pounding wildly in my chest, beads of sweat running down my back already. It's the excitement, not just the heat of the stage lights.

"Hello, Boston! We're happy to be home! Are you ready?" I shout.

They're ready. The screams that echo back at us are so loud they almost hurt my ears. At the same time, adrenaline rushes through my veins.

I find Rayne in the front row before I start the first song. I need to see her because I'm doing this for her, and because this song is where it all began. "Mockingbird."

She's standing between Zoe and Mae, holding their hands. Her smile hits me right in the heart, but I also see her eyes glisten suspiciously as I sing the first line.

You were always chasing heights
Beautiful and brave
Dancing fearless through the nights
Knowing you were safe

Her lips move along with mine, along with everyone else's. Everyone here knows the lyrics, and I think everyone knows why we're starting the tour with this song. I gaze at her while I sing, only her. Her eyes burn into mine, and for a moment we're completely alone.

No one else, only us. And we are real, you and me. We have been from the very start.

AFTERWORD

I can't believe you're already holding *Stay Here* in your hands and that we're slowly working our way through this series. We're taking very small steps, because fortunately the stories of Lia & Phoenix and Skye & Gabriel are still waiting for us.

Like Zoe (and everyone else), Rayne has her own problems with ballet. I thought a lot about how I wanted to express this, and I could have added external pressure from the teachers and other students to the pressure she put on herself, because that would be realistic. After all, the performing arts are far too often associated with stress.

However, in the end I deliberately decided against putting external pressure on Rayne because I wanted to create a place with the New England School of Ballet where my characters, but also you, the readers, can feel comfortable, a place that really feels like a second home, and I hope that this is what you wanted too—even if reality might look different sometimes. But let's be honest: We want to escape reality a little when we read, don't we?

Either way, I look forward to seeing you again soon, when Lia gets to tell her story in *Shine Bright* and we return to the New England School of Ballet for the third semester.

ACKNOWLEDGMENTS

We owe it all to two very special people that you were able to read Rayne and Easton's story in its final form. Without them, this would have been a completely different book, and that would have been a pity.

So thank you, Katharina and Steffi, for everything. For every email, message, and phone call. Thank you for putting so much time and energy into this book; I really don't know what I would have done without you. I say that every time, but this time it matters even more than usual.

Thank you, Steffi Bubley and the wonderful LYX publishing team for allowing me to write these books and for making them so beautiful. Many thanks to the team at LYX Audio for the very best audiobooks. Many thanks to the marketing team.

Thank you, Andrea Berlauer, for simply everything you do!

You too, Kathrin! Thank you for everything you do for my books.

Vivi, I'll keep it short this time, but in capital letters: THANK YOU!

Sarah, thank you for kicking me in the butt again; our writing sessions saved me!

Maike, thank you a thousand times for the songs you wrote for me. They are absolutely stunning, and I wish there was a band out there that could bring them to life.

Becca, Elena, Charlie, and Lui: Thank you for proofreading, for your special messages, and for your endless voice messages. Thank you for your enthusiasm and love; your feedback has made me infinitely happy and helped to silence my self-doubt.

Mom, Christina, and Jan: Thank you for always believing in me, for always supporting me, and for being so enthusiastic about my dream.

Benedikt, thank you for spending this best year ever with me and making it even better.

And last but not least, I would like to thank all the booksellers, bloggers, and readers. Your enthusiasm for *Hold Me* has exceeded everything I could have hoped for. I am so incredibly grateful for every review, every picture, every message—for everything you've done for me.

ABOUT THE AUTHOR

Anna Savas was born in 1993 and cannot imagine a life without books. Ever since her childhood, writing has been like breathing to her, and she always carries a notebook with her just in case a new idea decides to visit her. Anna loves to hear from her readers on Instagram (@annasavass).

CONTENT WARNING

(and spoiler warning!)

This book contains potentially triggering content.
This includes

Death
Loss of loved ones
Car accident
Grief